Praise for Protected

"This anticipated sequel sizzles with equal parts thriller, suspense and romance. A spine tingling story I could not put down." ~C.K.Bryant, author of *BOUND*

"From bullies to terrorists, Christy faces challenge after challenge in this stunning sequel that raises the stakes, both for her safety, and her love-life. A fantastic addition to a series that is sure to catch the hearts of readers." ~Heather McCorkle, author of the Channeler series

"A suspenseful, romantic, and intriguing novel. Protected is a riveting novel that I couldn't put down until the very last word."~Miriam Barton, author of *Meatless Meals for the Meat Eater*

"I loved *Watched,* and the sequel, *Protected*, didn't disappoint. Christy not only has to learn how to survive, she has to learn a lot about herself, and what she's capable of in the process. Touching. Funny. It was a fast-paced thrill ride, full of surprises at every turn." ~Jenny Moore, reviewer

Protected

Ashley
your choices
create you!

Protected

Cindy M. Hogan

Also by Cindy M. Hogan

Watched: Murder was just the Beginning

Watched series: Book 1

Visit the author at
cindymhogan.blogspot.com

O'neal Publishing

Layton, UT.

March 2012

Cover design © by Josh Winward

Picture © by Lisa Pennington

Edited by Charity West

Library of Congress Number
2012932337

ISBN-13:9780985131807
Printed in the United States of America

For Bill, my sweet husband, who never stops giving of himself

Chapter One

Over the last three weeks, I'd moved like a ninja through the halls of Helena High—invisible, stealthy—going from class to class, taking the least traveled paths. At least that's what I'd convinced myself. It took the horrible, sing-song voice of Katie Lee for me to realize I was no ninja master. More like a giant target with a bull's-eye painted on my forehead.

"Christy Hadden. Oh, Christy Hadden."

My heart froze. Katie Lee had bullied me since the first day of my sophomore year, nine long months ago.

"Hey, look," she had said that first day. "It's that homeless girl we saw eating out of the garbage at the mall last week." The three girls with her had laughed liked hyenas.

There was a hint of truth in what she'd said. They had seen me, but I hadn't been scrounging for food. I'd accidentally dropped my retainer in the trash can with the garbage from my meal only a few seconds before they'd walked up. My parents would have killed me if I didn't get it out. "Money doesn't grow on trees," they would have said. Since then, I'd only worn it at night.

I heard steps getting closer, and wished I could make my feet run. But, I couldn't. Like a statue, I stood; I couldn't even breathe. Why did I let her have this effect on me? I thought my experience with terrorists in DC had made me stronger than this.

The bell rang and the off-the-beaten-path-hallway in front of me was nearly deserted. I was late. One more thing to add to the suckiness of the moment. Katie Lee bumped me hard into the wall, her face only inches from mine.

"You've been hard to find lately," she said, sneering. "Where've you been?"

I just stared. My mouth refused to move.

"Speak!" she growled, her round face knotted with mean delight.

"Arf! Arf!" came from behind me. I didn't have to look to know it was Katie Lee's sidekicks. They always barked at me whenever they saw me.

"Let's go for a walk." Katie Lee grabbed my arm, turning me around and leading me back to the bathroom I had just passed. A bathroom no one ever went into because it always smelled like a sewer. Her cronies stood as sentinels in the doorway and I bumped into one of them.

"Down boy, down," she said, her tiny, pug nose lifted toward the ceiling.

"You silly," the other said. "Can't you see it's a girl?"

They laughed maniacally while stepping further into the bathroom. Katie Lee dragged me inside, pushing me up against a wall near the back corner of the room. All three stood between me and the exit.

"You know, Christy, English final papers are due Monday." She paced in front of me. "We would've given you more notice, but, it's like, we haven't been able to find you. We figured you would be thinking of us and know we needed to get the papers in. So, where are they?"

All three held out their hands.

My jaw dropped. What? They'd never asked me to do their work before. Only kids in my old junior high had tried that. These girls had always just teased and taunted me until now. Taunting that often led to bruising me in some way or humiliating me beyond hope, but what could I do?

"Oh. Did you eat them?" Katie Lee asked, looking at my gaping mouth, her sharp, cruel face sneering.

I closed my mouth. She moved in.

I will not scream. I will not give her the satisfaction.

"Open wide!" She wrenched my mouth open and looked inside. I felt my lips crack. Immediately, my mind raced to the time she kicked me so hard in the shin I could hardly walk for two days. All I'd done was smile at her the second week of school, hoping to win her over.

"Nope," she said, letting go and taking a step back. "Well, we need 'em Sunday night. Have 'em ready for us. Oh, and we don't want any of that AP crap you do. We only want "B" papers. Can't have 'em thinking we didn't do the work. Got it?"

I just continued to stare, wishing my hand would jump up and clock her square in the jaw. Did they really think I would write their papers? I couldn't write a "B" paper even if I wanted to. Nothing came out of me except "A" work.

"Got it, Hadden?" She came at me again.

"Got it," I croaked, not wanting her to get any closer but knowing I'd never write those papers. Why hadn't I told the principal the first time they'd harassed me? There were only five days left of school anyway. What could they do to me? Uh, maybe make my life more than miserable for two more long years. I had to overcome this, but how?

I stayed rigid against the wall until they disappeared around the corner. I sighed, let my shoulders slump, and slid down the wall to the floor, my thighs coming up tight against my chest as I sat. I wrapped my arms around my legs and pulled my chin to my chest, resting my forehead on my knees.

Determined not to feel sorry for myself, I thought of the letters I'd received from Jeremy, my real-life FBI Special Agent. Paralyzed from a bullet that was meant for me, he'd never once felt sorry for himself that I knew of and neither should I.

I pushed the screaming "poor me" thoughts to the back of my mind and searched for good memories. It didn't take much effort to find some: Alex's touch, Rick's kiss, and Marybeth's friendship. Those two weeks in DC had been the scariest, hardest, and most painful of my life and yet they had also been the most wonderful. Too bad I couldn't forget the bad that had happened there and only hold onto the good. Instead, I remembered it all with nightmare clarity—with the bad always finding its way into my thoughts, no matter how hard I tried to block it.

I'd been back home almost a month, and Iceman still haunted my dreams at night, turning me into a paranoid schizophrenic during the day. I would be minding my own business, when I would see several robed, Middle Eastern men walking my direction, who, at second glance were really only normal, everyday Montanans. Knives turned into large, curved swords, but only for a second. When things fell on the ground, they became heads seeping blood.

On my last day in DC, Jeremy told me everything was all over. I just wished I could have seen Marybeth. I wanted to know what had happened to her. I would have called her if my parents would have let me. They said it cost too much and I should just email. I didn't have her email. I wished I could talk to her about everything that had happened. Jeremy's last letter even told me the terrorist leader would soon be put to death for his crimes. Amazing how quickly people can be brought to justice behind the secret, closed doors of government. So why was my mind so unwilling to forget? I couldn't rid it of the worry that some of the bad guys must have gotten away.

Unfortunately, the amazing memories of Rick and Alex had a painful edge to them, too. After three weeks, neither Alex nor Rick had called. Alex hadn't promised to, I guess, but he had said I was *his*. Why hadn't he called if I was his? Rick, on the other hand, had told me he would call, and yet, he hadn't. I couldn't believe Rick, the most dependable, caring guy in the world, hadn't at least tried to keep in touch.

The crazy thing was, I would rather think of those two weeks in DC, with all their horror and gore, than focus on reality. Sure, I didn't have Marybeth, the best roommate anyone could have had in DC, anymore to make me somehow look way better than ever before, but I did my best to let everyone see how I'd changed. None of it seemed to matter. I remained Christy Hadden—the smart social outcast.

The bell rang.

Crap. I had sat there the whole period. Mrs. Adams would kill me. I heard masses of people walk by the bathroom. My tailbone screamed as I stood. Sitting on a tiled floor, with all your weight on your tailbone for almost an hour and a half, was not a good thing. I limped to the sink, rubbing my behind. I looked at my face and washed my hands. I had to find a way to stand up to those girls.

The loud sounds of crowds moving through the halls disappeared. I took a deep breath and made my way to the front doors of the high school. Unfortunately, a large group of the most popular and mean kids sat on the steps outside, working on a large banner for the last school stomp of the year. Their laughter carried through the open doors, and pangs of jealousy whipped through me.

DC had shown me what it was like to have friends. Coming home and being alone again tore at my heart.

I stopped and watched them until Janae, a pretty cheerleader, looked up the long set of stairs to the street and said, "Who's that? He's hot! No, he's mega-hot!" Even I had to follow her gaze, up the almost-thousand steps to the street, where a black, shiny convertible BMW served as a leaning post for a smoking hot guy wearing trendy jeans, a t-shirt, and sunglasses.

My heart pounded.

It couldn't be.

He lifted those glasses and seemed to stare right at me, shifting and then standing up straight.

"Is he looking at me?"Janae asked.

"Maybe he's looking at me," a beautiful redhead said.

"Or me," said another callous classmate.

They all stood up. I froze.

Not a word for almost a month and there he stood at my high school in all his perfection? Almost immediately, my mind started playing tricks on me. The mean mind, with the mean voice.

"It's not him," it said.

I resisted the urge to run to him.

"Don't make a fool of yourself. It's someone else. No one would come for you," the voice continued.

He leaned forward, squinting, and then a grin spread across his face.

There was no doubting it now. My crazy head couldn't make it less true. It *was* the most beautiful boy in the world. Alex McGinnis. Our eyes locked as he sprinted down the stairs. I still couldn't move. My body simply refused to accept that he was here. My insides buzzed so fast I thought I might burst.

Janae, now only feet from him, said something to Alex I couldn't hear. He walked right past her, without a glance, and pulled me into his arms.

The silence was thick around us. I could feel the stares of all the girls as I focused on him. "Mmm" was all I heard from Alex as he lifted me into the air and spun me around, every fabulous feeling from DC flooding back, the horrors of earlier receding. I giggled, then drew in his spicy scent, while saying, "I can't believe you're here. What are you doing here?" When my feet hit the ground, our eyes locked once again and our hands found each other's.

"Isn't it obvious? I came here for you," he whispered in my ear.

I thought I might burst. He was what I needed. Then the unthinkable happened. He kissed me. It wasn't just a little kiss, either. It was one that makes you feel like you could die today and it wouldn't matter. When he finally released me, he said, "At last."

He took a step back, looked me over, holding our hands out to our sides and said, "You look amazing!"

My smile couldn't have been any bigger. Goosebumps spotted my arms. He looked around at everyone gawking at us, opened his mouth like he was going to say something to them, then turned to me instead. "Should we go?"

"Yeah." Nothing else came to my mind. It was like it had stopped working. The girls next to us gasped.

I could hear, but couldn't understand the whispers of the girls below us as we walked up the almost never ending stairs back to the car.

"They rent this kind of car here?" I asked as we stepped onto the sidewalk next to the convertible.

"Of course. You can get anything for the right price."

He opened the door for me. After sitting, I looked down at the mean girls on the steps of the school, forcing myself not to watch Alex walk around to the driver's side of the car. Not only were all eyes still on us, but now, the jaws of those snotty girls had dropped. I tried to suppress the chuckle of satisfaction that escaped my mouth as Alex's door shut and he started the car. He took a deep breath, leaned in and kissed me, soft and gentle. "I've been waiting to do that for almost a month," he whispered and kissed me again.

My mind raced as my heart thudded. He pulled away from the curb. He had no idea how those seemingly innocent kisses could, and probably would, change my life forever. Two things were sure to happen.

Number one. I would finally be accepted. No one could be kissed by a guy as perfect as Alex and not fit in with the popular kids. I had hoped just because of the changes I felt after what happened in DC, I could slip into a different social status, but that was just a crazy dream. I was just beginning to accept I would always be seen as the plain-honest-straight-"A"-teacher's-pet-who never broke a single rule, for the rest of my high school career until the Kiss.

Kiss that, Katie Lee.

However, I couldn't forget the second thing that was sure to happen because I was seen kissing a boy one week before my sixteenth birthday. I would be killed. Pure and simple. When word reached my parents that I had kissed a boy, and it would, (the dangers of living in a small town)—I would no longer be allowed to live. Of that, I was certain. My parents had a strict no-dating-before-you're-sixteen policy and no doubt kissing someone on the steps of the school was a million times worse.

"Where to?" Alex asked as we came to a light.

Where to? Right. Where to? We couldn't go to my house. My parents would flip that I had ridden in a car with a boy unsupervised. It wouldn't be smart to go anywhere I could run into anyone I knew or that my family knew. Where could we go? Holter Lake popped into my head. We had gone there last week for a family outing and it had been quiet and almost deserted—the perfect place to hide out and catch up with Alex. This could be my only opportunity to alone with him "Uhh, the lake, I guess."

"The lake, huh?" he said. "We should stop and pick some things up then."

"Like what?" I asked.

"Uh, food and other stuff." A big grin stretched across his face. "Where's the nearest store?"

I directed him to a shopping center not far from where we were, and he bought a couple blankets and a flashlight. I borrowed his phone to call my house to say I wouldn't be coming home until late. My mom didn't even ask what I was doing. I'm sure she was certain I wouldn't be doing anything wrong. She even told me to have fun. The perks of being the "good girl." I pushed the guilt I'd started to feel away. She should have asked me what I was going to do, right?

Alex drove us to a deli and got a bunch of food. The more I thought about going to the lake, the more excited I got. To have Alex here with me was a dream come true.

What was I doing? I had been so caught up in the brilliant moment of having Alex come for me, that I forgot that in DC I had decided to let him go and had chosen Rick. Alex wasn't the best guy for me, after all. I didn't do good things while I was with him. I looked at him singing along with the blaring music, driving casually, and holding my hand as the wind blew in my hair. I swallowed hard. The reality was that Alex was here. He had chosen *me*. Rick obviously hadn't. Did that make it alright to be with Alex now? Why hadn't Rick called? I glanced at Alex, wishing I had the courage to bring it up, but I didn't want to ruin a minute of the time we had together.

I'd never really thought he'd come for me. Could I have been wrong about him? Maybe this was a sign that I should've chosen Alex, that he was the better of the two guys for me. Goosebumps covered my arms as I thought about being with Alex. I wanted to see where things would go. Maybe it would be different, away from DC, and he *would* bring the best out in me. It was only one week until I was legal—in my parent's eyes at least—and we could date for real.

My heart pounded hard on my ribs. I had to give Alex another chance. I took a deep breath and looked at him again. He must've felt my eyes on him, because he turned to me and smiled. This had to be the right decision. He was perfect, after all.

Chapter Two

We drove past Lake Helena and went deeper into the hills to Holter Lake. The water looked black and the hills surrounding it made it feel secluded. We pulled into the day-use parking lot and climbed out of the car. Without a ripple on the lake, we easily saw the bottom, and not a soul was around to spoil the peace. We explored the edge of the lake and climbed around some of the steeper banks being sure to steer clear of the water. We didn't want to freeze our butts off. May was still pretty cold in Montana.

We found a grassy spot that jutted into the lake and spread a blanket out to picnic on. With our knees only inches apart, and only a few awkward, quiet moments that always ended with Alex telling one funny thing or another, we ate. Our time together had been limited to DC, so we picked it all apart, recounting story after story, deftly avoiding the subjects of terrorists and Rick.

Alex said, "Remember when we couldn't find Eugene in the spy museum, only to find him thirty minutes later talking to a computer specialist and looking at a giant archaic computer? And how he talked about how cool it all was that whole night?"

We laughed and laughed. Each story made my gut ache a little bit more.

"Remember when someone gave me the most beautiful dress ever and took me to a gala?" I said, still a bit amazed that Alex had done that.

He smiled. "Only the best for you."

"I felt like Cinderella."

"Exactly what I wanted."

"Speaking of that night, why don't you finish telling me what you were saying to me? You know, right before—"

He jumped in before I could finish. "I don't know what you're talking about." He grinned like a kid who thought he'd just gotten away with something.

"You do, too," I said, giving him a gentle punch in the arm.

He looked at his lap for a few moments and then his eyes found mine. He had that look, the look that I'd seen on so many guys' and girls' faces when they really liked someone. My heart thumped hard.

"I just wanted you to know that I chose you and I wanted you to choose me." It was getting dark and I couldn't be sure, but I thought I saw some pink in his cheeks. He was going out on a limb.

"I had chosen you," I said. "I thought that was pretty obvious."

"Not when you went dancing with another guy on our night."

My face burned and I felt a strange awkwardness come over me thinking about dancing with Rick that night.

"I've already explained that."

"I know. I just got a little jealous is all."

"Jealous, huh? Then what's been going on the last month? You don't call. You don't write. Nothing. And then, out of the blue, you show up at my high school. Are you crazy? What if I'd forgotten about you—"

"Hold on," he interrupted. "I tried to call you. First off, when the FBI sent us home without you, Rick, and Summer, I realized that I didn't have your phone number. Could that be because you didn't have a cell in DC so I didn't have it programmed into my phone? Who doesn't have a cell these days anyway?" He grinned and playfully pushed my legs.

"Tell my parents that, would you?" I said.

"When I got to Turkey—"

"You went to Turkey?"

"Yes. Don't change the subject. I'm redeeming myself here." He smiled and raised his eyebrows.

I snickered, wondering how he was going to get himself out of this one.

"So, anyway, when I got to Turkey, I tried everything to get your number. Did you know your family doesn't seem to exist?"

"Very funny."

"No, really. No search I tried on the internet showed any Haddens in Montana. None. No call gave me any information on you or your family. Weird, huh? So, I called Marybeth thinking if anyone had your home phone number, she would. But she didn't. So, out of desperation, I called Mrs. J. Only after promising her my first million would she give me your number."

"You're so dramatic." I giggled, my heart doing flip-flops. I could hardly contain my disbelief.

"Then, I called your number and called your number, but you were never home."

"What?" I said. "You never called. Give it up. I've been home—"

"Did, too. Some kid answered *every* time. 'Not here,' he'd say and hang up."

"Really?" I asked. "Did you have the right number?"

He rattled off my number.

A tiny tremor slipped through my gut. He knew my number. "Hmm." After a few seconds it dawned on me. "Uh, was it a little boy who answered?"

"I don't know, but it sounded like a little baby," he said. "I figured it was your way of telling me to get lost."

"No way…Henry? My three year old brother? How has he gotten away with answering the phone? I had no idea. I've been home almost every day since I got back. Why was he telling you I wasn't home?" My face squished up in confusion.

"Beats me. I started to get paranoid, thinking you didn't want to see me anymore. Maybe my nightmare had really happened and you had chosen Rick." He looked sheepish.

My mind went crazy. He had no idea how perfect he was. Could Rick have been trying to contact me, too? Should I really be with Alex if Rick had been trying to get a hold of me, too? I would have to answer the phone from now on and find a way to call Rick. Since we didn't have long distance, I'd have to use a pay phone. Come to think of it, I didn't even know where one was. Alex had gone to so much trouble to find me. Wow! "I thought *you'd* forgotten me." *He had worked harder than Rick.*

"Never. Besides, I love the chase."

That's what Rick had said about Alex when he'd warned me to stay away from him. My heart skipped a beat. Could I really trust Alex? What was I doing?

"Man, when I saw you come out of the school and I thought I saw you see me, and you just stood there…I felt like the biggest fool to think you would have wanted me to come. But there was something about the way you looked at me that made me go down those zillion steps, sweating a bit more with each one. I couldn't wait to have you in my arms."

"Me neither." The butterflies in my stomach were frantic now. How could he worry about me wanting him? That had never been the problem. "I couldn't believe it was you."

"I've been worried sick about you since the FBI dragged us away from the gala in DC. No one would give me straight answers. Eugene, Josh, Kira, and I were taken to some safe-house until Marybeth came. She was in bad shape. The terrorists had broken her leg and shaved her head—and I mean all of it. Her face was pretty bruised up, too. I was surprised she didn't go totally crazy."

His words sent a razor to my heart. "Are you freaking kidding me?" I couldn't believe what he was telling me and almost stood up, I was so angry. "I should have found a way to call her. I had no idea they'd hurt her. It should have been me they hurt."

"I can't believe you still think you are responsible. You warned us and we didn't listen. We're all responsible."

"No. I made Marybeth watch what happened. I didn't give her a choice."

He stared at me for a second, looking thoughtful, then went on. "When we got to the airport and you guys didn't meet us, I really started to worry. All they would tell us is that you were safe. It was driving me nuts. Then, no one had your number. What happened to you guys?"

"Well, the short of it is, Summer, Rick, and I were taken to a safe-house, too. Then, the terrorists tried to capture us. They shot Jeremy, my FBI agent, and almost caught me. I was pretty banged up, and they kept me in the hospital for a few days so that my face could heal."

He reached out and rubbed his fingers over my face, examining every inch.

An amazing chill swept over me.

"I don't see anything."

He was a good liar. I knew I had scars.

"I'm so glad you're safe," Alex said. "Seriously, though, don't you think it's crazy that there's no information on the web about your family? None. Zero. Zilch. There's info on everyone and everything, except your family. Why?"

I had looked myself up on the internet before going to DC and there had been a lot on the web about me. All academic, of course. There had also been a ton on my dad. "Don't know.

Maybe it has something to do with the person looking." I chuckled and started sliding away from him. "I mean, I've looked and found myself."

"Ha, ha," he said, lunging at me.

I scurried away from him, jumped up and ran behind a tree. Before I could get around it, Alex met me on the other side, laughing breathlessly. He wrapped his arms around me and rubbed his nose against mine. "You think you're so smart," he whispered.

My breath caught, feeling his nose brush mine. I couldn't think.

We stood there in the silence for a long time, just holding each other, our foreheads together. Despite the fact that my insides were burning up, I shivered.

He pulled away from me. "You cold?"

"I guess so."

We walked back to our picnic site, and Alex grabbed all our garbage and threw it away. I sat on the blanket and watched him get the second blanket from the car. "This should help," he said, wrapping me up.

"You're not cold?" I asked.

"Not yet," he said. "Seriously, what do you think?"

"There's actually a lot of info on there about me."

"Did you look on the same web I did…and recently, I mean?" His face was totally serious, so I didn't laugh.

"I'm pretty sure—"

"Well, let's just look." He pulled out his phone and punched some buttons, handing it to me. Despite being amazed he had service, I input my name in the search bar and pushed go. No matches found.

"See what I mean?" he said.

I tried again. Still, no matches found. I tried my whole family. Nothing.

"That's weird." I tried to work out how it could be possible that I was there one day and not the next. I thought if something was published on the web, it stayed forever.

"It's like you've been erased or something," he said. "If you've looked yourself up and you were there, and now you aren't...." He spoke softly, like he had something to think through.

In a flash, DC came to mind. Acid filled my stomach. "Do you think the FBI did it so no one could find me? I mean, they disguised me and gave me a new name to get through the airport. Maybe the bad guys are still out there. I guess they just don't know where I am."

"Yeah, or I suspect you wouldn't be here."

My breath caught. "I hadn't thought of that."

He raised his eyebrows. "Hmm. Let's look up someone else from the trip. Say, Marybeth, and see if she's still there."

No matches found. I moved on to Summer. Rick. Josh. Eugene. Alex. Everyone in our little group back in DC. I shivered as my mind processed how everyone's name came up with the same empty result.

"Whoa!" Alex said, putting his arms around me, holding me tight. "We've all been erased. It's not just you."

"Why would they 'erase' us if we weren't in danger? The FBI said we weren't in danger anymore." I whispered. "That freaks me out. Maybe it really isn't over."

"It freaks me out, too," he said. "But, I guess no one will be able to find us because we've been erased." He chuckled.

"You found me." My whole body felt cold. I wanted to talk to Jeremy, the FBI agent who had watched out for me in DC. If Alex could find me, others could. No wonder I couldn't get rid of the feeling I wasn't safe. I must not be.

We sat in contemplative silence until the sun started to slide behind the hills, and then we lay back on the blanket to get a better view of the sunset. It felt soft, cushioned by the grass beneath it, the perfect spot to watch the sun disappear. The romantic glow of the moon reflecting off the lake mesmerized me. Alex squished up next to me, tugging on the blanket.

"Getting cold?" I asked.

"Just a bit." He grinned.

I pulled the blanket out from under me and put it on top of us. His arm, warm and smooth against mine, made me forget all about DC, the FBI, and being erased. We laid there, staring up at the stars, afraid to break the spell that had been cast over us.

After what seemed a long time, he turned over on his side, propped himself up on one arm and kissed me. He wrapped his leg around mine and stroked my face with gentle fingers. I loved kissing him. I never wanted this moment to end. The kisses became harder, more urgent. My insides were in a total tingle. I lost myself in the feeling until a voice rang out in my head.

Get vertical!

Get vertical? Did I just hear my church youth group leader's voice in my head? I refused to listen. Alex's leg pulled in on mine and another decadent power took hold of my body. Horizontal earned a lot more points in my book than vertical, and I wanted to tell the voice to go away. Instead, I rolled away, gasped and then blurted, "We can't," still fighting the amazing feelings that had taken over my body. I wanted nothing more than to kiss him again.

"We just were," Alex said, his lips pressed together.

"It's not smart. We can't." I stood up. The reasons for choosing Rick over Alex rushed back to me. Alex wasn't safe here. It wasn't like we were in our hotel in DC and I could leave him and go to my room. I had nowhere to go. I wrapped my arms around my waist, knowing Rick would never tempt me like this.

Alex was sitting now, his arms around one of his knees. "What are you afraid of?"

"Lots of stuff."

"No, now. Why are you afraid to come back down here with me? I won't hurt you. Don't you trust me?"

My mind searched for an answer. Did I trust him? I thought I did. But why did I always do stuff with him that I normally wouldn't do? Why couldn't I be strong around him? Then, I realized, I didn't trust *myself.* The thought was terrible. Why couldn't I trust myself? We'd only been kissing. But what I felt inside was taking over, and I didn't seem to be able to control my thoughts and actions. They had quickly started to control me. I surprised myself when I whispered, "It's me I don't trust." My head hung because I didn't know whether I should be proud of coming to know this about myself or not. "I need to be in control, and I wasn't just now." A burning heat lit up my stomach like a gas grill.

"In order to enjoy some of the best things in life, you have to surrender yourself."

"Where this leads…I can't go there." Did he live his life like that all the time? Going only after the things that felt exciting?

"What? You don't intend to ever kiss me again? You don't intend to be my girlfriend? You don't intend to feel amazing? What are you saying exactly?"

My face burned. Did he just call me his girlfriend? "I just don't trust myself."

"No. I want you to say it. Come on…You don't *intend* to have sex with me. Isn't that it?" His voice softened as he continued, but a sly smile slithered across his lips. "Look, kissing isn't sex."

"But it leads to it," I said, feeling my face turn a deeper shade of red.

"True. But you can stop."

"Don't you see? That's why I got up. This was as far as I could go and be safe."

"Look at you—all out of breath. Come down here where you belong. I know I can stop. I'm in control."

I didn't move. I just looked at my feet.

"Get down here so we can finish what we started." He held out his hand to me.

Instead of going to him, I took a step back, clasping my hands behind my back. Feeling the tree behind me somehow gave me strength and I leaned against it. "I'm safer up here."

"You can trust me not to let things go too far," he smiled, reaching out with both his hands now.

I wanted to go to him, but knew I couldn't. He would probably think it was a mistake to come all the way to Helena for me, a goody-goody, if I didn't, but I couldn't. I shook my head, trying to push further into the tree.

"I'm staying vertical," I whispered, looking away from him. "You can join me if you want." I could almost hear my church youth leaders cheering me on. I kept my eyes on my shoes, thinking it wouldn't hurt as much when he walked away from me. Even through my fear of his reaction, I was surprised that I felt a deep, warm satisfaction in my gut. He chuckled, and I heard him stand.

I looked up just as a forest ranger arrived.

"Day passes end in twenty minutes," the ranger said, shining his flashlight from me to Alex and back again. Saved by a ranger. How funny was that? I exhaled in a loud gush, trying to stop the giggle I felt coming on. It diffused my nervous tension and I was so glad he hadn't come any earlier and caught us kissing.

I knelt to gather the blankets. When I stood, holding two corners in my hands, Alex pulled the opposite corners of the blanket up. We worked in silence. He handed me his side of the blanket and then wrapped his arms around me, pinning my arms in front of me, his face only inches from mine, his breath sweet and warm.

"You should trust me, ya know," he whispered. "I would never hurt you."

I believed him. At least I knew he didn't *want* to hurt me. An edgy peace settled over me.

"Okay," I said. "But we're still staying vertical." Even though I said it with determination, I faltered when he kissed me so softly.

You should trust me. His words echoed in my mind. The gentle press of his lips sealed his promise to me. My heart thudded hard on my ribs. I liked him so much it made me want to cry. Why did he have to be so amazing?

When he pulled away and looked at me, all I could do was repeat, "Vertical."

He threw his hands in the air and laughed out loud. "You're so funny. Frustrating, but funny."

Holding the blankets in one arm and me in the other, he walked me to the car.

I wondered how long it would take for him to forget the funny and only find me frustrating.

Chapter Three

Once his luxurious car hummed to life, Alex looked down at the clock. It was only nine.

"Man, this park closes early. Let's hit a party." He pushed a button and the leather top of the car covered us, giving shelter from the chilly wind that had kicked up.

"A party?" I said, shivering. Why did he want to go to a party of all things?

"Yeah," he said. "While I waited for you at the school, wondering if you'd gone out another door—'cause it took you so long—I heard a lot of people talking about parties. It's Friday, ya know. It's party time. Let's go party." He sang the last line *let's go party*, and backed out of our parking space, turning onto the main road to town.

I took in a deep breath, the smell of leather somehow making me a bit nauseated. Maybe it had to do with the dread of Alex discovering the real me.

My insides knotted. What would he think of me if he knew—really knew—what a dork I was? I still felt cold, despite the warm air blowing on me, and I hunched over, sliding my hands back and forth over my thighs for warmth.

"It'll be fun, and from the reaction of the girls on the steps of your school, I think it'll be eventful." He chuckled.

My face felt hot.

"Uhh…" Why would he suggest we go to a party when he seemed to already know it would cause problems? He must not really understand what a complete social outcast I was or he wouldn't suggest it. My nausea grew more intense. I knew at that moment that it definitely wasn't the leather making me feel sick—it was the idea of going to a party.

"You're in high school, you know. Parties are everywhere."

Afraid I might truly get sick in his immaculate car, I decided it was time to clue him in on the awful truth. I guessed he already sort of knew anyway—or why would he have mentioned the snotty girls on the steps of the school?

I fought to maintain my nerve by twisting my hands together and taking a deep breath. "There may be parties, but none that I would've been invited to." I felt like crying now, but I held it in.

"You don't have to be invited to parties like these," Alex said. "You just show up. The more the merrier."

"No," I insisted. "When I told you back in DC that I was a social outcast, I meant it. I wasn't exaggerating. If I showed up at a party—"

"What? The world would stop? You think you're that important?"

I felt my face burn. All the nervousness I'd felt rushed out of me in twisted anger. "You think I'm not accepted because I'm some sort of a snob? That I think I'm better than they are? You live in the popular world, so you couldn't understand." Hot tears burned my eyes.

He pulled the car over to the side of the road and stopped. "Hold on. I thought the kids at your school treated you badly because you're so darn smart. And smart kids can't help but make people feel inferior. I was teasing you."

I was close to hyperventilating when he grabbed my hands, prying one away from the other and rubbing it.

His touch caused my tears to gush. I couldn't hold them back. The last month had been more than horrible and all the disappointment and sadness of it flooded my whole being. Not to mention, I was mortified he had to witness it. I bent over, trying to hide somehow.

Alex moved in closer, enveloping me in his arms, shushing me and telling me it would be okay. A new inner warmth consumed me. After several minutes, I gained my composure and sat upright, feeling a bit foolish.

He touched my face, turning it so I looked at him while he used his thumbs to brush away my tears. "Honestly, Christy. I didn't mean to make you cry."

Looking into his deep brown eyes somehow gave me courage to respond. "You really thought that I believed I was better than everyone else, didn't you?"

He paused, which wasn't good, and I sighed and shook my head.

"Wait. Hear me out." His sheepish look told me he knew he'd been caught. "Give me a chance to explain."

I looked away.

"When you told me you were a social outcast, I thought, *no way*. I couldn't imagine why anyone wouldn't want to be around you. I figured you were exaggerating or something. The only reason I could come up with was that you must make everyone look stupid all the time and it makes them mad.

"You're the smartest person I know. I mean, listening to you debate in DC made me feel completely dumb. And while normally that would have sent me running, I couldn't get over how attracted I was to you. I also couldn't imagine why anyone would want to hurt you. I'm sorry if I didn't have the whole picture, but you never clued me into *why* you thought you were a social outcast."

My heart hammered. Was it really just a misunderstanding? I turned to look him in the eye. Butterflies filled my stomach. Did I dare tell him everything? What would he think of me if I did? He had been willing to accept me while thinking I was an intellectual snob. Would he still accept me as a total nerd?

"I'm sorry," I said, feeling my hands shake slightly. "It's just since I've been back from DC everything has been wrong. Well, not wrong, really, just not how I hoped it would be."

I took a deep breath and felt comfortable again. My hands stopped shaking. He would be the first person I'd ever told the whole truth. I had come close with Rick. Could I trust Alex with the information and my fragile heart? Something in his eyes made me think I could.

"I went to DC in hopes of somehow magically transforming myself into someone people would like," I said. "I know it sounds stupid to think I could change my life in two weeks, but I was desperate." I breathed in hard.

"You see, about nine months ago, I discovered there was more to life than information and adults. As crazy as it was, I'd never realized I was so alone until then. I'd started to notice how people treated me—and it was terrible. I'd been in my own world, not realizing I'd been the brunt of jokes and mistreated my whole life. Suddenly, though, I wanted friends. I tried all kinds of things to let everyone know I really wasn't weird and could be a good friend, but the bullying and teasing only got worse.

"Then, on the trip, miracle of miracles, I made friends…and guys were even interested in me. It was more than I could've hoped for. It made me think when I got home, it would really be different. I thought people would see the new me and want to be my friend. I was totally wrong, though. Instead of getting friends, I was tormented when I got home."

"You're kidding, right?"

"You've seen the movies where popular kids in high school torture certain kids. I'm one of those certain kids."

"I guess it's something I never had to deal with, since I never went to high school. I'm really sorry."

He looked sincere. He even looked a bit embarrassed. Did I see some regret, too? He had to be wondering why everyone treated me so badly. He must. I would. I thought he was so lucky to have been tutored his whole life. "That's just it, Alex. *You* would never have experienced it. It would never have happened to you."

"What are you talking about?" He looked a bit miffed now.

"You, you…you're perfect," I stammered. "You would've been at the top of the food chain at any school you attended." He looked shocked. "Have you seen yourself? The good-looking people are always the ones at the top—"

He cut me off short. "In that case, it must also be true for girls…and you would have to be at the top with me."

I huffed. "Funny, funny."

"It takes time for people's opinions to change. Give it some time. They'll come around."

"Hmphf," I said. "You mean I won't be pond sucking scum much longer?"

"One of the parties tonight will change all that," he said, with a glint in his eye.

I thought about our kiss in front of the popular girls at school and also about telling Alex that I already had a good start because of that kiss, but for some reason, I didn't. I really didn't want to go to a party, especially after the bathroom incident at school, so I came up with another excuse.

"Invited or not, my parents won't allow it."

"You've got to be kidding me. Your parents have forbidden you to go to any parties?"

"Not exactly," I admitted.

"Then we're going." He put the car in gear and pulled back onto the road. The car was so smooth, I could barely tell we were moving.

"You just won't give up, will you?" I asked, exasperated. My heart fluttered at the thought. I rubbed my hands over the soft leather seat.

"Nope. I won't. So, tell me about some of the things these guys have done to you."

I didn't want to. The helplessness I felt while my classmates taunted me entered my heart. Alex grabbed my leg and squeezed. It tickled, and I laughed.

"Spill it. It'll be therapeutic. Think of me as your shrink." He made his best *shrink* face and I chuckled, my insides tingling. He had the craziest effect on me.

It turned out to be easy to tell Alex some of the most horrible moments of the last nine months—laughing while doing it.

Once we reached town, Alex drove up and down a bunch of streets, looking at houses. Was he still looking for a party—even after what I had told him?

"Look for lots of cars parked outside houses and listen for music and—"

"Have you heard a word I've said?" I asked.

"Every one, and that's why we're for sure going to a party tonight."

"Even if the world does stop turning?"

"Yep…Even if it turns you into pond sucking scum."

I couldn't believe I could laugh about it. A lot of the sting of the torture was gone. He'd been right. Talking about all the bad stuff had somehow set it free. Set me free. But, I didn't know what to feel. I was freaking out inside. I was nervous, scared, and excited all at once.

The little voice inside my head spoke again.

Go home.

I didn't listen.

"You know, I have a confession," Alex said.

"Really?"

"I love pond scum."

I felt my face burn. Did that mean what I thought it meant?

I looked at the clock. Nine fifty-five. I felt the clock ticking. "Alex, you have to promise me you'll get me home by eleven, okay?"

"Eleven? Your curfew is eleven?"

"Not exactly," I spilled. "It's just when my sisters' curfews have been. I'm sure mine would be the same. I need to honor that."

"What did your parents say when you called?"

I wanted to tell him that I never stayed out. I didn't have a curfew because there was no need and no one missed me when I was gone anyway. In fact, no one seemed to notice me when I was home. I just never did anything that would make me stand out among my six brothers and sisters. They always had things going on. Things to be taken care of. I took care of everything myself. Basically, my parents trusted me, because I'd never given them reason not to. But I knew he'd take advantage of my words, so I said, "My mom told me to have a good time."

"See. She wants you to enjoy yourself. I'm not taking you home at eleven for a "would be" curfew. If your parents haven't specifically given you one, then you don't have one."

"Well, technically, I shouldn't need one. You see, I'm only *fifteen* and am not allowed to *date* yet." I felt my temper rising.

"Oh, is that what this is?" he teased.

My anger dissipated.

"No way," Alex said. "This is so far from a date that no one, and I mean, no one, could misconstrue it as one. I'm just a friend from out of town who you ran into."

It was silly, because I knew he was teasing. It was a date. But I couldn't call it that out loud. "What if my parents check my room, and I'm not there?"

"Have they ever?" He raised his eyebrows.

He had a point. "They've never had the need."

"I know you have a thing about honesty. So, if they do ask you about tonight, tell them the truth. You ran into a friend from DC, and you showed him some of the town. It's the truth."

Not the *whole truth*, the little voice in my head reminded me.

"It's time you party. You need to stop letting other people dictate how you feel about yourself. You *are* going to a party and showing everyone you won't let them rule over you anymore."

Out of excuses, I found myself letting Alex drive around neighborhoods, looking for a party, half hoping he'd find one. After all, he was right. I should face this. After going up and down about ten streets in the mansion district of Helena, streets and streets of enormous, old homes—a byproduct of the gold boom—Alex stopped the car behind a long row of cars parked along the street. He pointed to a house three doors down. Small groups of kids were hanging out on the front lawn. It was Amy's house. Of course he would find a party thrown by the friend of my arch enemy. Katie Lee would have a field day with this. My chest strained. My breath caught, and I was sure I couldn't go in. I felt frozen. All the bravery I'd mustered disappeared.

Alex grabbed my hand and as if he could read my mind, said, "You're not alone anymore. I'm with you."

I struggled between wanting to believe him and knowing what I knew. This was Amy's house. They'd never let me in.

My hand held his in a vice-grip. He tried to pull it away and get out of the car, but I held tight.

"Come on. We'll only go in for half an hour. You need to own it, though. Be proud of who you are. People like them smell fear and use it to their advantage."

If Katie Lee and her cronies were in that house—and most likely they would be, I'd have to muster some pride. I couldn't let his hand go.

He rubbed my hand with his thumb. “Let’s go in.”

“You don’t know whose house this is.”

“I don’t care whose house it is. They’ll let you in.”

“They’ll never let me in. I’m scared.” There. I’d said it out loud.

“I know. But, don’t be. You’re not going to let them bully you anymore. You only have one week of school left anyway and then you’re out of here.”

“Where do you think I’m going?

“College.”

“Are you crazy?” I said. “I’m only fifteen.” I squinted at him.

“A week or so away from sixteen, and besides, I overheard Mrs. J. talking to some of those political guys at the debate in DC. She said you’d already taken the college entrance exams and had perfect scores on them. She said your parents are keeping you here—that they wouldn’t let you go to college early. But, you’ve got to go.”

“I can’t.”

“Yes, you can.” His eyes were intense on me. “You have perfect scores on the tests and straight ‘A’s’ in all your classes. All you need is to get a few teacher recommendations and to write a few essays. Then you’ll have a full ride to any school you choose.” He paused, smiling at me. “You are going to college! We can go together.”

“I can’t.”

“You can. Face it. You need to be in college, not hanging around here in this little town. You’re meant for bigger things. Besides, you won’t be alone. I’ll be with you.”

I almost believed him. I wanted to believe him. “Yeah, until you move on to another girl.” Did I say that out loud? My whole body tensed.

“Why would I do that?”

“Isn’t that what always happens?”

"There's no one I want to be with but you. So, let's do it. You want east or west coast? I've already applied to both, of course. I've already heard back from some of them, but I might not make it into the high caliber kind of school you should attend.."

"Ha. Ha," I said. "You're just as smart as I am—you probably know more than I do—with all your travels and being tutored."

"Let's not go there," he said. "You're getting out of this place. You're moving on. Only one week of school left and two weeks to get your applications in for late admission."

Somewhere during our conversation, my hand had relaxed and he took advantage of it. He pulled away, opened his door, and bounded to my side of the car. The front window had fogged over and when he opened the door, cool air rushed in. He reached for my hand. When I grabbed his, I held it without climbing out of the car and said, "Look, I don't want to make a scene or anything. Let's just go in, let people see us, walk right through and come back out. All right?"

He rolled his eyes.

"All right?"

"Okay. Okay. Okay." With that, he pulled me up and out of the car.

Chapter Four

As we walked up the sidewalk, it felt strange to see spring flowers lining it. Loveliness didn't belong here. What was I doing? A dark, horrible feeling fell over me. I should've gone home. Why didn't I insist we go home?

Alex opened the large, heavy wooden door, and we walked right into the devil's lair. Music blared, and a wave of hot, stuffy air assaulted us. Alex shut the door. All peace left me. We stood in an entryway with a huge, shiny chandelier above us. Intricate walnut woodwork surrounded us. My heart pounded hard. The light coming from the entryway straight ahead told us to ignore the two darkened doorways to either side of us. We took a few steps forward, looking into the crowded room. The dim lighting cast eerie shadows as at least fifty teens danced and moved about to the beating music. I took a very big breath and looked up at Alex.

"Okay," I said, having to shout to have him hear me. "I came. I saw. Let's go now." I tried to turn back, but Alex didn't allow it.

"Not yet," he said, smiling. "We need to conquer."

His grip tightened on my hand as he led me forward about ten steps. The ceilings went up forever, magnifying the spaciousness of the room. Beautiful, dark, shiny wood covered the floor except in areas that had couches and chairs, where thick, plush rugs covered the wood. Kids draped themselves over the furniture, laughing and talking. The center of the large room served as a dance floor for scantily dressed girls and the drunk boys who clung to them. All the most beautiful people of my high school looked far less than beautiful in their current state.

Alex pulled me in a few more steps, completely exposing us to the crowd. Several people looked our way as he pulled me toward the bar acting like we belonged, and a scurry of movement followed. I couldn't act cool or brave at the moment, and I didn't have to wonder what was going on. Many of them blatantly pointed at us and talked animatedly to their closest neighbors. They all had one thing in common, the shocked look on their faces. In less than a minute, it seemed every set of eyes looked at us and all movement in the room stopped. Stares stung my body. Then, the crowd on the dance floor parted, allowing none other than Amy to walk through. A few kids who enjoyed tormenting me followed closely behind. Time seemed to freeze as they moved toward us. Even the music stopped. So much for not making a scene.

I yanked on Alex's hand, hoping for a quick retreat, but he didn't even sway in the direction I pulled. He kept leading me toward the booze. He was too strong to resist. I noticed that many of the stares were drunk, glassy-eyed ones. Creepy.

I bent slightly, wishing to disappear.

Blue eyes flashing, Amy asked, "What do you think you're doing?" Those eyes bored into me, and the kids that had been following her lined up, creating a human wall between us and the rest of the party.

"Hey guys!" Alex said, louder than I thought he should, "We saw you were having a party and couldn't pass it up."

"She," Amy said, pointing at me, "can't stay." Her eyes left me and landed on Alex. I noticed the slight slur in her words now. "You, on the other hand, please do." She walked forward a wobbly step, raising one eyebrow.

"Too bad," Alex said. "She's with me. I was hoping to tell Taylor Swift all about your awesome party tomorrow night after her concert in Chicago—but if she can't stay," he leaned into me, "then…whatever." He turned and pulled me back toward the front door.

Was he really going to see Taylor Swift? I pressed close to Alex.

"Wait," Amy said, somehow already right behind us, grabbing Alex's arm. "Do you really know Taylor?"

"Uh, yeah," he said, still walking toward the door. "We grew up together."

Then I knew it was just a lie.

She pulled on his arm again and said, "Do you think you could introduce me to her or maybe get me a backstage pass or something?" Her alcohol laden breath assailed me as she moved around us, standing between us and the door. I scrunched up my nose. "I mean, I have tickets for the concert in New York and it would be so cool to actually meet her." Even though Amy's eyes were a bit glazed, they were on fire at the prospect of meeting Taylor. I couldn't believe how she groveled.

"I might be able to work something out," Alex said. "But, you know, she plans way in advance, and I can't guarantee anything." He had a glint in his eye. He loved this.

"Oh, I know," Amy said. "I know. I know. But if there was even the smallest chance…" Her lips pouted like a girl used to getting her own way.

"I'll see what I can do." Alex said, taking a step forward around Amy, grabbing the door handle.

"You're not going are you?" Amy asked, putting her hand on Alex's.

"I thought you said Christy couldn't stay."

My heart stopped.

Stay? Please, no. Dread filled me at knowing Alex would get his way.

"Oh, no," Amy stammered, her eyes darting between Alex and me. "I was just kidding. Stay. Really."

"All right then." He let his hand fall from the door handle, and Amy let go of it as he turned around, pulling me along, walking back into the party.

"Where's the music?" Amy yelled. "This is the best party in Helena, after all."

Immediately, the music started back up. Amy turned and gave Alex the fakest, most brown-nosiest smile in the world. How long would we have to stay?

As a few bodies started flailing around again, Alex pulled me to the left, toward the bar. He let go of me—I thought I would shrivel up and die—and grabbed two plastic cups with foamy amber liquid inside and handed me one. Beer. Not again. I took it, too shocked to do anything else.

Alex acted like he belonged and chugged his beer down in one gulp and grabbed another. All eyes were on him. Alex had cast a spell on the party. He owned it now. If he had told Amy everyone should leave except us, she would have followed his orders—without question. She sat on the arm of a chair, staring at Alex. He chugged his second beer and then pulled me into the dancing crowd. We passed a small end table and I set my cup down.

What was he doing? Feeling eyes boring into me, I just wanted to leave. Alex pulled me close and whispered, "It wasn't that bad, was it?"

"Yes, it was."

"Look around. No one's even staring anymore. Well, almost no one."

I saw Amy staring, and then right behind her stood Katie Lee, her eyes drilling holes through me, but I felt a shift in myself. I thought about what Alex had done for me. He had made 99% of the kids at the party forget who I was. I wanted to be able to do that for myself.

"I kind of liked it when everyone was staring," Alex joked.

"Very funny," I said, looking up at him. "What about Monday? You won't be here Monday." My insecurities reared their ugly heads.

"Just don't go to school." Before I had a chance to say anything, he leaned down and kissed me.

I wanted to push him away—he tasted awful—but at the same time, I wanted everyone to see him kiss me—see that someone wanted me. I wanted to play the game they always played and this was my chance. I could do it all with Alex by my side. I waited for a natural break in the kiss and then laid my head on his chest, his scent lulling me into the spell he had cast on the party. I really considered not going to school on Monday, until an incredibly fast, loud, obnoxious song rang out and broke the spell. I pulled Alex back to the front door and out onto the stoop. The cool air settled crisply over me. No one lingered in the yard anymore. We were alone.

"What were you thinking?" I tried to look mad, but failed miserably. I could see the alcohol was taking effect on him by the way he moved a bit more slowly than before, less sure. I tried to ignore it.

"Thinking?"

"First of all, what will happen to me when Amy doesn't get her backstage passes to see Taylor? Secondly, a kiss like that will be all over the school by Monday." I blushed.

"First of all," he said, grinning from ear to ear, "I'll call Amy and let her know I tried my hardest but there weren't any passes left. But, after the tour, Taylor would give her a call. Secondly, a kiss is exactly what you needed."

My heart jumped. He was right.

"Really, this is a small town and when my parents find out…" I started, trying to be official.

"All the better. Then they'll see that they can't keep you here, that it's your choice to go to college or not."

"If I'm in a grave, I won't have a choice—and I can't believe you're on the college thing again." Despite my tingles, my hands sweated. I really would get killed. My parents would definitely start paying attention to me anyway.

"Look. You don't want to stay here and go to high school with those kids again and sit in classes that you could teach. It would be a waste of your time."

"But, I do care about what my parents think. Even if they don't seem to notice me most of the time, they are my parents. Maybe they see something in me that makes them think I should wait to go to college. Maybe I can't see myself clearly enough to make that decision."

He grabbed my shoulders, leaned down and said, "*I* see you clearly. It's time for you to move on."

My heart raced at the thought of really going to college and leaving this town for good.

"I don't know if I can," I insisted, unwilling to believe it could be a reality.

"Didn't you get goose bumps when we went to Georgetown University?"

For a split second, I was back in Georgetown, kissing Rick for the first time under the spray of a fountain. I shook my head.

"Come on," he coaxed. "Admit it."

I pushed the memory of Rick aside, feeling a bit guilty, but then said, "I did add Georgetown to my list." I tried to hide my smile.

"You have a list!" Alex said. "I knew it."

"Well, I haven't really researched it thoroughly yet."

"You haven't, huh?" Disbelief shadowed his face.

"I have done a little, just not enough."

"Thought so. Who's on the top of your list?" Alex persisted.

"Probably Harvard. Maybe Stanford." I paused for a minute. "Their scholarship ratios are about the same. I'm just not sure if I want to go out east to school. I'm not sure if I'd fit in."

"Tomorrow, we're filling out applications for all the schools on your list. Unless a school isn't on *my* list, that is. You want to go back in?" he asked, smiling at me and gesturing for us to go back to the party.

"Ha, ha." Even though I felt like I could go back in, I had this desire to be alone with Alex.

He led me to the car with a noticeable bounce in his step.

Millions of stars and a full moon lit our path. Even the flowers looked appropriate now, closed and asleep. I refused to let him drive even though the car wouldn't be insured if I got in an accident. I would be extra careful. My heart started to pound when I saw the clock. Ten to eleven. I was going to get home past my siblings' curfew. It would take at least twenty minutes to get to my house. I tried to tell myself it would be okay.

We recounted our party entrance play by play and laughed and laughed.

"The Taylor Swift thing was an awesome idea, but it was my chugging the two beers that sealed the deal for us," he said.

"Why do you drink?" I blurted, wishing instead I'd asked how he knew Amy liked Swift.

"What do you mean?"

"Why did you grab those beers at the party, and why did you drink at that club in DC?" Why was I asking him this? Things were going so well. Why couldn't I let sleeping dogs lie? This was not the time to get on my soap box.

"Uh," he said, looking at me a bit cock-eyed. "It makes me feel good. Why else? Everyone drinks. Even you drank in DC."

My face flushed, followed by a good thirty seconds of silence.

"Everyone doesn't drink." I felt a twitch in the corner of my eye.

"You drank right along with everyone else," he insisted.

I scrubbed my sweaty hands on my pants. "Actually, you know that plant that hung out behind me?"

"Yeah."

"It felt woozy by night's end." I clasped my hands together and looked at him out the corner of my eye.

"But I saw you drink it." His eyes squinted and he nodded his head in short, clipped movements.

"You thought you saw me drink it. My lips were closed."

"Are you kidding me? Why didn't you just ask for something else?"

"Are *you* kidding me?" I said, with a slight mocking tone. "If I'd have asked for water or soda, I would have been laughed out of town. Your friends would never have accepted me."

"That's not true."

"Really? Come on. Honesty here."

His eyes fixed on the road like he wasn't even paying attention, but then he snapped out of it and looked at me. "Well, I guess it depends on your reasons for not drinking. Why don't you drink?"

"Nothing good comes of it. You have no control over yourself. People act stupid when they drink and besides, it's bad for you. I just don't believe in it."

"Tell me how you really feel," he said, chuckling.

"I just didn't want you to think I was backward."

"I already knew you were backward. Big deal."

"Thanks a lot." I punched his arm hard.

"No problem. Why do you worry about what other people think? Do what's best for you. Shoot, if I could've gone to college at sixteen, I would have."

"Back to the college thing again?"

"Yep." He waggled his eyebrows at me.

He reached over and turned up the music, grinning at him and truly considering the possibility of going to college while he sang along to the music.

When we were a few houses away from mine, I stopped the car.

"The GPS says your house is still down the street a bit," he said.

"It is, but we're stopping here."

"Ashamed to be seen with me?" he asked, a strange look on his face.

"The timing's not right, that's all. It's past eleven and you're a boy. You haven't forgotten that already, have you?" I grinned and reached for the door.

"Let me at least open the door for you." He jumped out and ran around to my door, opened it in a flash and held out his hand to me.

I took it without hesitation, smiling all the while. Once he shut the door behind me, he drew me into a hug.

"What? You didn't want your parents to see this awesome hug? Or maybe it was this you didn't want them to see." He kissed me, soft and long. I leaned back on the car, willing the moment never to end. My shaky legs seemed unable to hold me up anymore. I breathed hard and felt my temperature rise. When he finally pulled back, I had a hard time opening my eyes and standing up straight. I walked away like I'd drunk that beer Alex had handed me.

"Steady, Nellie," Alex said, letting my fingers slide away from his. I looked back. He stood still, watching me. "You know, it's eleven-fifteen. Are you going to have a heart-attack?"

"I don't think so," I said, running now and turning my body around in a circle as I passed my neighbor's house, coming up on my driveway. "At least not from how late it is." I started toward the house, waving goodbye and spinning in circles as I went.

As I turned, at the beginning of my driveway, I noticed a car, one that I didn't recognize, parked just down the street from my house. It looked out of place, somehow. I stopped turning, starting to walk across my driveway and stared at the car.

We lived in a pretty small, stagnant neighborhood. Only two new families had moved here in the last two years. I knew everyone *and* the cars they drove. Heck, I even knew what their relatives and friends drove. I kept walking, wondering if it belonged to someone visiting my next door neighbor. They never had visitors, though, and I mean never. They were crotchety old people who sat on their porch and yelled at kids all day long.

My eyes flicked back to the out-of-place car. It couldn't be our neighbors across the street, either. They were old, and the only visitors they ever had were their son and his family once a year, in the summer. It was late. It shouldn't be there. I couldn't take my eyes off it as I walked, more quickly now, up the walkway toward my door. I thought I saw a shadow move inside the car and froze, halfway there. I stared hard, afraid to turn away. No more shadows. Had it been my imagination? I turned, ready to run back to Alex, but just as I did, I could see his taillights turn the corner off my street. That's when I realized I should have driven him home. I never should have let him drive. I was so worried about getting home on time, I hadn't thought about him getting home. I couldn't do anything about it now.

I turned back, eyeing the unfamiliar car, trying to ignore the chill that crept into my bones. Without looking away, shivery and weak, I hurried up the rest of the sidewalk to my porch. After opening the door, I looked back at the strange car once again. The window on the passenger side rolled up. Or did it?

My breath caught and I slipped inside, shutting the door behind me. I leaned my back against it until I mustered the courage to look again. I don't know how long I stared out of that skinny piece of glass that ran up the right side of the door. But at last, my eyes strained and looking away, I locked and chained the door—something I had never done before in my entire life.

Chapter Five

The silence in the house spooked me. It was weird to have it so quiet on a Friday night, but then again, it was past curfew. I ran on tip-toe down the hall and stairs, into my room, and flung myself onto my bed. Did that car have anything to do with me? Was I being watched? Had they found me or was I just crazy?

I sighed, pushed my face into my pillow, then stood and looked out the window. I knew all I would see would be the inside of my window-well, but I couldn't help myself. I wanted to check out that unfamiliar car one more time without going upstairs. The silver window well stared back at me. I checked my window. Locked. But how easy was it to break glass? What if the person in the car was a bad guy who'd gotten away from the FBI? What if I was a sitting duck? What if…

I shook my head, hoping to get rid of my paranoid thoughts. "You are *not* afraid, Christy," I said out loud. "You will not allow them to make you live in fear. No one is there. You are brave." I punctuated my sentence with a fist in the air.

I took a deep breath, trying to believe the words I'd spoken.

Despite my best efforts, I couldn't turn off my mind. I replayed what had happened with Alex after school and at the party over and over again. I couldn't stop. I rolled off the bed and thought about turning out the light. Maybe then I could sleep. The back of my foot hit something hard as I stood, and I reached down to see what it was.

My college box.

I pulled it out with some effort, sat on the edge of the bed and then set it on my lap, looking around the room as if someone could be hiding around the corner wanting to catch me doing something wrong. A guilty pleasure of mine, I loved to imagine being at college and what it would be like. Knowing my parents didn't approve, I hid it from them.

Last year, my ninth grade counselor had had it out with my parents, telling them they were hurting me by keeping me here in Helena. He told them I needed to stretch my wings and that they would be surprised at the heights I would attain. My parents told him that he would be surprised at the depths he would attain if he persisted in filling my head with nonsense. "She's too young to go to college," my parents had said. "She needs to be with kids her own age." They would not have their daughter mature before it was necessary. I needed to be a kid, apparently. Sometimes I just didn't understand my parents, but I would obey them, nonetheless.

They had learned they didn't need to pay much attention to me to have me perform scholastically. So, they never discussed school with me, except when I showed them my report cards. They always patted me on the head. Literally. Then they would say, "We can always count on you to be the top of your class. And look, all honors. You're such a good girl. We never worry about you." And they didn't. It was like I was a ghost, non-existent most of the time. They did, however, pay attention when they wanted to use me as an example for my six brothers and sisters.

My siblings' glares could've sliced through me each time my parents said, "Why can't you be like Christy? She does her work without being asked, and she does it well." "Why can't you be honest like Christy?" "Why do you have to always complain?" "You don't hear Christy complaining." "Be like

Christy, she's such a good girl." "She never does anything wrong."

Why didn't my brothers and sisters just do the things my parents asked them to do? I didn't get it. Their lives would be so much simpler, and I would have avoided some sound taunting when my parents weren't home. My older sister Janet and my older brother Luke were the worst. Occasionally, I would have to lock myself in the bathroom to escape their wrath. They wanted me to stop being so good. I just couldn't. It had always been so natural for me to do the right thing. Had that changed?

I looked at the heavy box on my lap and shoved it onto the bed. After opening it, I went through it, pulling out the eight brochures from my favorite colleges. I scanned them, wide awake, hoping to take my mind off the scary car. It was time to research my favorites so I could have more time with Alex when he came tomorrow. Twelve o'clock. I'd have to be quiet. I tip-toed up the stairs and into the family room. Matt, one of my younger brothers, was watching TV with the sound turned way down. He held his finger to his lips and said "Shhh!" I smiled, assuring him I was no threat and sat at the computer. It felt good to have someone near.

Two hours later, I had printed a ton of new information and my eyes burned. I walked back down to bed and slid the now much heavier box back underneath it and climbed in. It only took me a moment to fall asleep.

My mom startled me awake when she pressed her hand to my forehead.

"Oh, sorry," she said. "It's six-fifteen and you're not in the garden. Did you forget that we needed to plant the corn today?"

I turned and looked at the clock. Six-sixteen.

"You okay, sweetheart?" she asked. "Are you sick?"

"No," I garbled out. "I just must've been tired."

“I guess so.” She stood up straight. “This is the first time you’ve ever been late. You had us worried.”

“I’m okay, Mom.” I said. “I’ll be right out.” Funny how they only notice me when I don’t show up.

“Okay.” She walked out of my room.

With a lot of effort, I climbed out of bed. Going to sleep at two o’clock hadn’t been the smartest thing to do on Friday at the Hadden house. Saturday was work day. Six o’clock sharp we were expected to be in the garden in spring and summer months. Four hours of sleep hadn’t been enough.

When I reached the top of the stairs, I remembered the scary car from last night and hurried to the door. I slid the chain off and then reached to unlock the door handle. It was already unlocked. Weird. A shiver went down my spine as I slowly opened the door to peek out. No out-of-place car. Was that good or bad? My stomach churned. Why was the door unlocked but the chain was still on? You can’t go out the door with the chain on. Did someone unlock the door from the outside, but then found the chain on the door prevented them from coming in?

I re-locked the door and put the chain back on before going out the back door to work in the garden. I made quick work of planting my rows of corn. After eating breakfast, I did my daily chores, showered and went back to bed.

I woke this time to knocking on my door. “Christy. Someone’s at the door for you.”

It was my little sister, Susan. “Who is it?” Just as I asked, I remembered and flew out of bed.

“I don’ know,” she said. “But it’s a boooyyy!”

“Tell him I’ll be up in a minute,” I said.

“Kay,” she said as I opened my door and ran down the hallway to the bathroom.

After getting ready in the bathroom in record speed, I ran upstairs. There stood Alex in all his beautiful glory. He smiled, leaning on the doorframe. He wore a perfectly starched button-up shirt, khaki pants and dress shoes. I'd only seen him out of jeans and a T-shirt once. At the gala in DC. And he'd worn a tux. Why was he dressed like this? In contrast to his serious, business like attire, his eyes were open wide, as if he couldn't get enough of life.

"Oh my gosh, Alex," I said, walking toward him, my heart a speeding race car. I clutched my hands together "I can't believe Susan left you at the door like that." It took all my effort not to be a shaky mess. He was here. Alex was here at my house. What would my parents think?

"It's no big deal," he said. "What took you so long? Were you solving the world's problems?"

"Very funny." I grabbed hold of the open door and was about to ask him why he was dressed the way he was when I heard footsteps behind me.

"Oh. Hello," my mom said and walked straight past me, drying her hands on a dish cloth and then extending one for Alex to take. Susan followed behind her.

I rolled my eyes and stepped back. "Mom, this is Alex. Alex, this is my mom."

"Well I'll be," she said, staring wide-eyed, shaking Alex's hand, "So, you know our Christy?" That was always the first question they threw out at new boys.

"I sure do, ma'am," Alex said.

The ma'am was too much. I had to pretend to cough to disguise my laugh.

"Well come on in," she said. "Surely Christy doesn't intend to leave you standing in the doorway all day."

"Of course not, Mom," I said. "Susan left him here." I glared at her. After Alex walked in, I couldn't help but glance outside to see if the strange car had reappeared. The only different car was Alex's convertible. I locked the door after I shut it.

"Great," I said under my breath. Alex poked me in the side. A huge grin wrapped around his face. We walked down the hall and turned right to go into the living room, while my mom went straight into the kitchen while saying,

"I'll get your father, Christy. We'll have a nice chat with Alex."

I poked Alex back, and we chuckled. Alex sat in a chair and I sat on the sofa, kitty-corner to him. We both leaned over, our elbows on our knees, and whispered.

"Here it comes."

"What?" Alex asked.

"The inquisition."

"What inquisition?"

"The one you are about to experience. Every guy my sisters ever brought here had to face the inquisition."

"I can't wait," Alex said, chuckling. "Don't worry. I've got my best meet the parents attire on. They'll love me."

He could be so manipulative. "Be careful," I said. "They see through…"

I heard footsteps coming closer and sat up. Alex followed suit. My mom bustled around Alex's chair and sat on the sofa with me, staring at Alex. My dad, on the other hand, walked to the side of the sofa my mom was on and stood next to it.

This didn't look good.

After a few seconds of awkward silence, mom said, "Well, Alex." Her voice was calm and somehow slower than normal. "How is it exactly that you know Christy?"

"Well, we met in DC."

"Oh," she continued. "You went on the political trip, too, did you?"

"Sure did," Alex said.

"And you live here in Helena?"

"No, ma'am," he said, laughing quietly. "My parents are here for work, and where they go, I go. They'd rather I be tutored than separated from them in some boarding school. Family is really important to them."

I could see the relief wash over both my mom and dad. The wrinkles between my mom's eyes softened and my dad's shoulders relaxed. My dad even had my mom move over closer to me so that he could sit.

"Your parents have business here?" Dad asked.

"Yes, sir," Alex said. "They work for the government."

"Montanan?"

"Oh, no, the U.S. government."

Was he lying? Come to think of it, I didn't know what his parents did. If they didn't work for the government, then he was a better liar than I'd ever thought.

"That sounds interesting," Dad said. The funny thing was that he looked interested.

"Sometimes," Alex answered. "But, it gets old going to all these different places, not knowing anyone."

"Your parents travel a lot then?"

"Yep, and I can't tell you how nice it will be to have eight new friends spread over the U.S. That makes eight cities where I don't have to be alone while my parents work."

"I can imagine," Mom said, her voice dripping with sympathy. She'd bought it, hook, line and sinker.

"Hey," Dad said. "We're about to have lunch. Would you like to join us?"

Even my dad had bought it. Wow. Alex was good.

"Yes," my mom joined in. "Why don't you join us?"

"Well," he said, "while that sounds great, I was kinda hoping Christy could show me the town. I could try some local fare and see the sights. We fly out early tomorrow, so I don't have a lot of time." He looked my parents straight on, his eyes submissive somehow.

My mom and dad looked at each other for a few long seconds. I wondered if they could communicate with their eyes or something. I knew they wouldn't allow it. My mom gave a slight nod, and then my dad spoke. Here it comes, the big *no*.

"We usually don't allow our girls to be alone with boys until they're sixteen…" Dad paused, looking Alex over, "but, maybe in this case, since you're here for such a short time, we'll allow Christy to show you Helena."

My mouth dropped.

Alex looked at me as if this was new information to him and then looked back at my parents. "Oh, I don't want to go against any rules you have. We could just stay here. Christy told all of us in DC what a wonderful cook you are, Mrs. Hadden, and…"

"It'll be okay," Mom chimed in."We don't want the only thing you see in Helena to be our family. We trust Christy. She has her head on straight."

Guilt swept over me, as I thought about how many times I'd disobeyed them in the last month—and even last night.

"Are you sure?" Alex asked.

I couldn't believe it. He was so good. I was dumbfounded. How in the heck had he done it?

"Yes, you go and have a good time."

"Okay," he said. "My car is out front. Oh, shoot. I didn't think to ask Christy if she even wanted to show me around." He looked at me smiling.

"Oh," I said, trying to get my senses back. "Yeah. It would be fun."

We all got up and walked out of the living room and down the hall to the front door. As I unlocked it, my dad said, "Now, listen here, Alex." He gave Alex the stern eye. "I expect you to treat her like a lady. She's precious cargo."

I don't know how Alex kept a straight face. "I most certainly will. I'm glad to see your family is as important to you as mine is to me."

"I do need her to call me every few hours," my dad said, "to let me know where you are and what you're doing."

"That'll be no problem, sir," Alex said. "I have a cell right here she can use."

Sir? This cracked me up.

"Great," my dad said. "Now use it often, Christy."

"I will, Dad," I said. "Every few hours."

"Be back for dinner," he said. "You hear?"

"I hear you, Dad."

"Okay, then. Have fun," Mom said, as we walked down the steps to the sidewalk and to his car.

Alex opened the door and as I sat, I let out the breath I didn't know I'd been holding.

Unbelievable. Totally unbelievable.

I watched Alex walk around the front of the car, wave to my parents, who were still standing on the porch watching us, and then climb into the car. I shook my head. He chuckled as he started the car, and we drove away.

"I don't know how you did that," I said.

"Look," Alex said. "Parents are reasonable creatures, and you just have to make them think what you are doing is reasonable, too. It's as easy as that."

"How did you come up with such good lies?" I asked. "You had them eating out of your hand." While in awe of his ability, it also made me nervous that he was so good at it.

"I mix as much of the truth in with what I'm saying as I can. That way, what I say has the ring of truth."

"So, how many times have you mixed the truth in what you say to me?"

"For you, Christy, there is only truth." He said this with gusto, like he was trying out for a part in a play. I didn't know if I wanted to dig deeper, so I let it go. I was afraid of what I might hear.

"I thought we were going to apply to colleges today."

"You can do that tomorrow when I'm not here. Where should we go for lunch?"

Trying to ignore the sudden squeeze I felt in my stomach about him leaving tomorrow, and all the research I'd done last night, I forced myself to say, "Feel like pizza?"

"Sure."

"Great. There's this place near my school everybody likes."

"Show me the way."

After I told him where it was in relation to the school, he turned the music up, and we flew down the road to the pizzeria. At the first light he pulled off his button up shirt. I took a deep breath and looked away, feeling my cheeks heat up. Then he slipped on a tight-fitting dark T-shirt that accentuated every hard curve of his chest and arms.

The sun felt good, beating down on us as we waited for the light to turn green. Alex was singing along to the songs blaring on the radio, not caring what anyone thought. It made me smile, and I wish I knew the words to the songs he sang.

Once inside the pizzeria, Alex glanced at the menu and ordered in the "To Go" area. I gave him a look that said, *we're going somewhere?*

He turned to me. "We don't want to eat in here when it's such an awesome day outside. Besides, I saw a cool place yesterday when I was waiting for you to get out of school that I want to explore." He grabbed my arm and led me to a bench to wait for the pizza. I leaned on his arm. He slouched a little and leaned his head on mine.

"Do your parents really work for the government?" I asked.

"Yes," he said.

"Really?"

"Yes."

"Hmm." I couldn't help but think about what he had said earlier, about telling as much truth as possible to give things the ring of truth. I realized I couldn't tell if he was lying or not. That wasn't good. He was staring at me intently, so, I said, "There is just so much about you I don't know."

He smiled his mischievous smile and he grabbed my hand and held it until the pizza arrived, my heart thundering along the whole time. He asked for plates and napkins and we walked out to the car.

As I waited for Alex to get in, I noticed a car that looked just like the one that had been parked near my house last night. It pulled back out of its stall and drove away. Strange. Was that the same car or was it only one that looked like it? Was it even the same color? It had been too dark last night to be sure. I took note of the Montana license plate, so I would know if it was the same car if I ever saw it again: 2C 5467.

Alex climbed in, set the pizza on the back seat, planted a kiss on my mouth and pulled onto the main road. My drumming heart made me forget all about the car.

"Now, your rival school is this way, right?" he asked, grinning and pointing. The smell of pizza made my stomach growl. I couldn't wait to eat.

"Yep," I said, "You want to eat at my rival school?"

"Maybe. You're gonna have to wait to see."

"Well, okay, but it better be good."

Alex turned up the music again, and we drove the short distance to Capital High. He pulled into the parking lot and then drove over to the cemetery that was just behind the school. He pulled the car right up to the black, sturdy fence and said, "Come on," and opened his door and hopped out. He reached in back to grab the food and rushed to open my door.

I could see the allure of this cemetery. The wrought iron arched entryway led us to hundreds of large, cool, old grave stones. "You know," I said, half serious, half giggling, "we're not supposed to use the graveyard as a picnic site."

"Really?" he said, "Where's the sign that forbids it?"

"Does there have to be a sign to tell you what you should and shouldn't do?"

"Maybe." He grinned. I followed him around the fence, to the entrance. Since it was still May, it was a bit cool in the shade, so I was glad he found a nice sunny patch of grass to sit on.

"Why are you here, Alex?" It was out of my mouth before I had time to stop it.

"I'm here for lunch." He laughed, grabbing for the pizza box.

"No, really." Some foreign bravery took over and I asked again, "Why are you here?"

There was a long pause that caused every organ in my body to threaten failure.

"I don't know exactly. There's just something about you that I can't seem to resist. I'm drawn to you. But, no, it's more than that. When I'm with you, I want to be a better person. You make me something greater than I am on my own. I've never experienced that before and I like how it feels."

"Why is it then," I asked, trying to hide how uncomfortable I felt with his blatant honesty, "that whenever I'm with you I'm always doing stuff I shouldn't and you try to change me?"

"You know," he said, opening the pizza box, "there's a whole other world out there, and I want you to see it, experience it, and be a part of it, if only once. I want you to see me."

My heart pounded, but in a bad way. It was a painful thudding.

"What you don't understand is that I've had a taste of it, and it was miserable. Well, most of it anyway. You can't have forgotten about DC already?"

"Of course not. But, as you so aptly put it, DC isn't the real world, either."

"A lot of what we've seen makes me want to stay away from that other world you're talking about. After what we've seen, we should be more wary, more scared." My mind raced, thinking once again about the terrorists. "Why wasn't anything about what happened in DC on the news anyway? It's been over four weeks and the story still hasn't broken. There's something wrong about that. Don't you feel it?" My hands were sweating, and I had an icy feeling in my bones.

Alex grabbed my hands in his and scooted closer. "Whoa. Slow down. Take a deep breath." He spoke softly. "You're safe. I don't feel anything but glad that I'm here with you. Maybe what you're feeling is how much I love being with you." He moved in, letting go of my hands and hugging me tight. "I not only want to show you my world, I want to experience yours. I'm here, aren't I?"

I took a few deep breaths, trying to calm myself. This should be one of the happiest moments of my life. I was with Alex and we'd been having so much fun. But something was making me on edge. Was it the car that was parked near my house last night? Was it the same car as the one at the pizzeria? I wished I would have thought to look at the license plate when it had been parked in front of my house. I couldn't help but worry.

Alex let go of me. "I want to know what makes you you." He paused and we looked at each other for several seconds before he said, "Let's eat." He opened the pizza box, took a big slice.

I reached for a slice too, but wasn't ready to give up on our conversation about the bad guys. "I just thought I would've seen it on the news. I mean, how could they get rid of a senator's aide without anyone knowing about it?"

"You've got to let it go. It's gonna eat you up."

"I know. I try to forget, but I can't. It doesn't seem like I should forget."

"Well, maybe a deal was made that prevented any media coverage. They're probably working on a cover story right now.

Think about it. It wouldn't make the U.S. look very good if it got out. It's probably a diplomatic decision."

"That makes sense, I guess," I said. I still felt uneasy.

The pizza was great and so was Alex's company. It helped me put the worry aside. Cars were pulling into the parking lot next to the cemetery, for a soccer game on the field across the street. We talked about high school soccer and how Alex had always wanted to play soccer for a high school. Of course, he'd never had the opportunity since he was home-schooled.

"I always wanted to play on the school basketball or volleyball team," I said, "but haven't ever been interested in soccer. I've always been too chicken to try out and have ended up just playing for my church's youth league."

"And I bet you're the star of the show," he said, laughing.

"What? You doubt me?" I gave him a friendly slug.

"Yes, I do. As you have taught me, I simply must tell the truth."

"Well, contrary to your belief, I hold my own." I laughed, too.

"I'll have to test that one of these days."

The pizza was gone and so was our sunny spot. It had moved, and the new leaves on the trees shaded us, so we got up and walked around to look at the gravestones.

"This place could be spooky. It looks like a lot of these are miner's graves." Most of the graves had something written on them about a mine or had a depiction of the person being a miner.

"Yep," I said. "Helena was a miners' boomtown. Unfortunately, the boom ended. If Helena hadn't been chosen to be the capitol of Montana, it would be a ghost town today."

"Maybe ghosts are in the graveyard right now," Alex said, laughing.

"I think I see one right over there," I said, starting to run in the opposite direction I was pointing, "and he has a pick in his hand! He must not take lightly to people picnicking in his place of rest."

"Don't worry," Alex teased. "I'll save you."

We pretended like we were being chased by ghosts and zigzagged our way out from one headstone to the next until we ran, laughing, back out the arch to the parking lot, which was now half full from the cars coming to the soccer game across the street.

It felt good to be in the sun again and I was almost sorry to climb into the car.

"What's next?" he asked, as we pulled out of the parking lot.

"Uh, there's always hiking."

"Sounds good," he said, "Where to?"

I thought of the national park first, but then, worried it would be way crowded, suggested we drive up the highway a bit to find a less populated trail.

We pulled into one of many open spots and excited to have the trail to ourselves, I jumped out of the car. Alex opened his door and stood up, giving me a look. He hated it when I didn't wait for him to open the door for me.

"Sorry! I haven't been on this trail in years, and I can't wait to show you the amazing view. In this weather we should be able to see forever once we get to the top."

"I'll forgive you this time, but watch out." He reached down next to his seat, and I heard the trunk pop open. He walked behind the car and grabbed the blankets we had used last night. "It'll probably be a little cooler on the trail, without the sun. I wish I'd have thought to bring jackets."

"All I need is you," I said.

We started up the trail. Alex cradled the blankets in one arm and with his other hand, held mine. We hiked for only about half an hour when I needed the blanket. We stopped, and he wrapped it around me, grabbing me into a hug. He was so warm. His spicy scent drew me in further. I didn't want him to ever let me go. My body screamed for him. His fingers moved softly, slowly down my back. His breath felt warm on my skin. Who cared about the view? My heart pounded, and I wanted to kiss him so badly that I looked up at him almost begging him to do it. I wanted it to be soft and amazing, like Rick's kiss. But Rick had deserted me. I shouldn't be thinking about him. I didn't think my heart could beat any faster, but it did when Alex leaned down to kiss me. His lips grazed mine, and I had to use all my strength not to press my lips harder against his. Why was he so tempting? He kissed my cheek and then my nose and finally my forehead. I held my breath and closed my eyes. Lifting my chin, waiting for the real kiss, I heard footfalls. Someone was there. Alex heard it too and pulled away just a bit.

Chapter Six

My blood froze. Somewhere, deep in my soul, without even looking, I knew it was Iceman.

Alex turned around in slow motion to look at the man who had spoken, which gave me a clear view of the man.

He pointed his gun directly at us. "You will come quietly and orderly back down the path to the parking lot," Iceman said.

Alex looked at Iceman's gun and then back to his face. I could tell Alex was sizing him up—creating a plan for our escape. Iceman must have noticed it; he waved the gun from side to side and said, "Do you really think I would come alone?" His voice was harsh and not how I'd imagined it at all.

With those words, large, black machine guns, carried by four men in camouflage, appeared from the trees. Alex's face fell, and my frozen heart dropped. Iceman turned his head to the side, his eyes piercing, and waved his gun down the path. Iceman turned his head to the side, and waved his gun down the path. We had no choice but to do as he directed. I heard some of the men in camouflage fall in behind us.

It wasn't far to the parking lot. I reached out and grabbed Alex's hand as we walked onto the asphalt. He squeezed hard, reassuring me. It made me want to cry.

They herded us over to a large, white van, opened the sliding door and shoved us in. I hit my shin on the footboard and flinched. There were no benches in the back. I watched two men crawl out from under Alex's rental car and head for the van, laughing. Weird. What were they doing under there? Several men jumped in, pushing us against the far side of the van. My head hit the metal wall with a loud thud, but I didn't feel any pain. The door shut with a clang, and the men hollered out as the van drove away.

I found myself staring at the men, wondering how they'd escaped the FBI's ever-watchful eye. One of them noticed me staring at him and said something to his comrades in their harsh-sounding language. Then they all looked at us. I pushed myself harder into the van wall and reached for Alex, wishing for a place to hide. They laughed. One of them came over to us, a maniacal smile on his face and a rope dangling from his hand. He grabbed Alex first, pushing his face into the carpeted floor. The camo-clad kidnapper wrenched Alex's hands behind his back and tied them together. Grabbing Alex by the shoulders, he then slung him back against the van wall. Alex gasped.

"Alex!" I cried, tears filling my eyes.

A hand slapped my face so hard it stung. "Silence."

"Don't hurt her!" Alex yelled.

The hand made a fist and hit Alex in the face with a sickening thud. I inhaled sharply, watching Alex's head slump forward. My insides burned with hate and fear. They bound Alex's feet and gagged him. I wanted to touch the already bright red spot on his cheek, but someone pushed my face onto the floor, like they had Alex's. My skin burned as it scraped along the van carpet. The ropes sawed at my wrists. I fought off a scream and pursed my lips. They pushed me against the van wall next to Alex, then tied my feet together and gagged me. The cloth cut into the corners of my mouth. I tasted blood.

I saw the clock at the front of the van. Four o'clock. *Wake-up, Alex. Wake-up,* I kept thinking between my frantic prayers. The noise of the laughing and talking made my ears ring. A few slept, while others smoked cigarettes. It was hard not to cough.

I slid as close to Alex as I could without bringing too much attention to myself. He felt warm. Tears streamed down my face as I curled my body further into his.

I must have fallen asleep—loud laughing and talking woke me as the van screeched to a stop.

"Isn't that right, sweetie?" One of them said with a heavy Middle Eastern accent. "Yes, very valuable. At least for a few more hours." Riotous laughter broke out as the men in the back slid the side door open. Alex was awake now, but he was still propped against the van wall. I sucked back tears and my body shook against his. One of the camo-men grabbed my feet and pulled me to the door, my arms burning on the carpet. I saw the clock again. Seven. Three hours from the trailhead. The man lifted me over his shoulder. Trees loomed over us, blocking any view of the sky. It wasn't light, but it wasn't dark, either. The blood rushing to my head made me scared I might pass out.

My captor carried me up a few wooden steps. He crossed a large porch and entered a building, my head banging into his back. The building looked like a rustic cabin. He took me through one large room, where I could see down a narrow hall and into a small, empty room. I overheard someone in the large room say, "…into town. A few hours ago." He flung me onto the wooden floor of the empty room, my back and head hitting hard, despite my attempt at keeping my chin pressed against my chest. Black flashed before my eyes, and I must have lost consciousness for at least a few moments. When my eyes opened, the man was gone. My back and arms screamed and yet a wave of relief rushed over me. I was alive.

Seconds later, a very large man in camo dragged Alex into the room, his legs scraping along the bare wooden floors, and dropped him next to me with a thud. The men left us alone, closing the door behind them.

I scooted next to Alex, grateful to be near him again and thankful to have not been left alone.

A small window gave the room its only light—though the moon behind the clouds did not give much. The room smelled old and musty. I gagged.

I grabbed Alex on the leg just as seven men walked into the room, arms loaded with electronic equipment, cameras wires, and chairs. One man hoisted me by the arm and slammed me onto a chair he'd hauled along with him. Another clutched several large pieces of poster board. I caught a glimpse of my name on one of them before he propped it against the wall.

Two men fumbled with some of the electronic equipment. The other men in the room gathered around and they began to argue. Not being able to understand the words seemed to make it even worse for me. My body trembled as I watched them violently shake the equipment.

All of a sudden, they gathered everything up and shoved me to the floor. They took the chair and all they'd brought and stormed out of the room, leaving me completely confused. I could hear their shouts continue as they walked down the hall. I wished I could understand Arabic.

I had landed on my side, my hip burning and the splinters in my hand stinging, but I slid right next to Alex anyway. I pushed into his body, needing his warmth. Alex mumbled something through his gag. We pressed our bodies as close together as we could. I didn't want to move, but my arm ached. I shifted. He shook his head at me, not wanting me to move either. For a bizarre moment, I thought he was going to kiss me, but he bypassed my lips and hooked his teeth over the gag tied around my head and tugged on it, trying to loosen it. I felt my lips crack as he tugged.

I couldn't stay on my side any longer. My left arm needed a break from having all my weight on it, so I rolled onto my back and bound hands. Alex rolled over onto his knees in one swift motion. It took me several attempts to accomplish the same thing. Alex scooted over to the wall by the door and sat against the wall. I did as he had, failing to get into sitting position three times before finally making it. We pushed together, like we'd been in the van, and I tried to control my shaking body, overwhelmed. Why hadn't they killed us when they found us on the trail? Why bring us here? I heard loud voices and laughter from the other room.

I'd been taught my whole life not to fear death. I believed my grandparents and relatives would all be waiting for me, arms open wide, ready to receive me. If Alex died, would he be there waiting for me? Would the things I'd done in my life exclude me from the life I knew awaited good people? Did I know certain things I did were wrong and yet did them anyway? I knew about the mercy of God and had felt it, but could justice be satisfied in my case—or would justice claim me? I found myself snuggling deeper into Alex, hoping everything would work out all right. We would find out soon enough.

My shoulders ached. I wiggled my wrists, trying to free my hands. Alex wiggled, too. He leaned against the wall with his shoulders and slid his bound hands under his rear-end to the front. The same move took me forever and left me breathless once I succeeded. I tried to pull my gag away, but it was too tight—and having my hands tied together didn't help. Frustrated, I faced Alex. He had already gotten his gag loose. So, I helped him. Using a finger, I pulled and jiggled the loose end of his gag until it came free. He flexed his lips and then kissed my cheek.

"I love you," he said, grinning from ear to ear.

My heart lept. Did he say he loved me? Did I hear him right? If he did say what I thought he'd said, he couldn't be serious. He must just be glad that he'd been freed—right?

"Can you undo my wrists?" he asked, still grinning. "Then I can free you."

I nodded.

I tugged and pushed at the tight knots, feeling the need to cry in frustration that my tired fingers wouldn't do as I wanted. The darkness made matters worse. I kept jerking and pulling. until the ropes on his wrists came loose.

"Ahhh," he said. I could hear him rubbing his sore wrists. "Give me those precious hands."

He didn't have to ask me twice. My fingers needed a rest. He picked and prodded the knots on my wrists for a while and then said, "What am I doing? Let me get that nasty gag off first." He had it undone in no time. I didn't have a chance to move my lips before his were on mine. It was a weird sensation to have our dry lips move over each others', but I didn't care. Tingles overtook me and my heart raced like a hummingbird. I forced myself away. We couldn't forget the danger.

Next, we tackled each others' feet. The cold in the room helped keep me alert. As I finally finished undoing the last of the rope on Alex's legs, I let out a long sigh. My fingers ached. I flexed them over and over, trying to keep them limber. I noticed the room had started to lighten—just a hint. I could see outlines and shadows now. He continued to work on undoing the ropes binding my legs.

"It's almost morning, Alex," I whispered, my throat tight.

"We've got to hurry," he said.

"Let me have a go at it," I said. "My fingers are rested now." They were, but they still ached. Maybe by using them I would prevent them from stiffening up.

"Okay," he said, standing up and going to the window. The room lightened even more.

Being able to see made it easier to free myself. My legs hurt when I stood, but I joined Alex at the window anyway. He counted something under his breath.

"What are you doing?"

He put up a hand to caution me to silence.

I waited, looking out the window to see if I could see what he was counting. A man came into view. He walked slowly, surveying the woods, the sky and the cabin. It was still dark, but we could barely see his outline as he went by.

"You know, he's very consistent," Alex whispered. "I've watched him walk back and forth five times now. It takes him between four minutes and fifteen seconds and four minutes and thirty seconds to walk his route each time. I don't know if it's enough time for us to escape, but we have to try before it gets any lighter. There are a few bushes along the house. Let's get the window open and see how long it takes for you to climb out. There doesn't seem to be anyone else around. The other terrorists must be asleep somewhere in the cabin."

As soon as the man walked out of view, Alex pushed the window open. It stopped about three-fourths of the way up. He pushed and pushed, but it wouldn't budge. We didn't dare hit anything against the window, fearing it would get someone's attention. He tapped it lightly with his palm, but it was a no-go. The watchman came back into view and we ducked, hoping he wouldn't notice the partially open window. We counted the minimum seconds for him to disappear and looked out. He was gone. Alex lifted me up, and I slid out, scraping my exposed arms on the weathered wood. With a thud I fell onto the ground. I froze.

When no one came running, I counted to 180 seconds and moved behind a bush that pushed up against the cabin. I watched Alex try to wedge his way out. He got as far as his waist, and couldn't go any further. He mouthed, "Help." I stood up and pulled on him. He wouldn't budge. According to my count, the guard would return in about ten seconds. I motioned for him to go back in and I jumped behind the bush again, leaning my back against the cabin wall. Alex slid back in just in time.

The guard now smoked a cigarette as he walked. Once I hit the maximum count for him to be gone, I dared look up. Alex hung halfway out the window again. I stood and pushed up on the window as hard as I could. Alex wriggled and wriggled and fell out the window like a butterfly emerging from its cocoon. Even with his black eye, scraped face, and cut lips, his face was beautiful. I quickly moved to the second bush and lay on the ground while Alex stayed behind the first bush, still as a cat hiding from a roaming dog.

I had lost count, but Alex obviously hadn't. He popped his head up and motioned for me to follow him. Crouching, we ran in the opposite direction the guard had gone. The yard was empty, so we sprinted, full-out toward the woods. Twenty yards from the cabin, we reached thick brush, but we didn't stop to hide in it. We ran straight though it, scratching every inch of visible skin. We didn't care. We had to make it as far away as we could. We had no way of knowing which direction we were running, we just ran. It was still dark under the cover of the tall trees, but light peeked down on us when we hit spaces with less dense cover. The underbrush cut into our shins, and we stumbled often, but we managed. Alex held back branches for me and I did the same for him, huffing and puffing. We had done it. They had no idea we'd left.

Chapter Seven

The cold air made it hard to breathe. At least we could see now that it was dawn. We came to a clearing, and some deer looked our way and then took off. We ran forever. My lungs couldn't keep up with my legs.

"Alex." I huffed. "I need to catch my breath."

"All right," he said and stopped immediately, then pulled me into a hug, rubbing my arms and back. Like a furnace, he warmed me. We sat on a fallen tree, looking into another meadow. We didn't sit for long. It was too cold and we were too scared. Alex pulled me up, and we walked until we came to a river.

We were dying of thirst. Our hands froze in the ice-cold water, but we dunked them anyway.

"We should follow the river downstream," I said. "Rivers always lead to towns, right?"

"I think so," he said. "Let's go."

We hurried hand in hand, stepping onto stones, dragging our feet through the water to hide our tracks, following the river down the mountain. I began shivering violently, so we moved away from the cold river, keeping it within hearing distance, and walking almost parallel to it. We ran every now and then in an attempt to stay warm. We felt secure in our escape. We'd be long gone before they even knew we were missing.

We couldn't help but talk all about the abduction and theorize about what they had been planning to do with all that electronic equipment.

"The only logical reason to tape us would be to use it to get a ransom, but what could they want?" I asked.

"Money?" he asked.

"Why would the government give them money for us?"

"They wouldn't, but maybe they don't want money. Maybe they want access to something. Who knows?"

We even plotted ways to tell the person getting the video where we were so they could save us. We ruled out talking in code, because we figured one of us would be reading the poster board I'd seen.

"Can we talk in Morse code somehow?" he asked.

"No. I think we'd do better with sign language."

"Do you know sign language?"

"I've played around with it before," I said, though really I'd studied it extensively and the signs I'd learned were seared into my brain. I do, after all, have a photographic memory.

We tried using signs as we walked and talked. It was too difficult, but when we just used the letters to spell, we could do it incognito most of the time. I taught him a bit of Morse code, and we tried to use it by blinking or crossing a hand across our chests or nervously tapping a finger into a shoulder. I knew it because I'd studied it in history class when I was bored, and if I ever saw something, I never forgot it. We practiced and practiced spelling out the letters for terrorists, woods, river, Montana, times and directions over and over on our legs, as we moved our arms through the air, and as we touched other parts of our bodies, like we were gesturing as we talked.

"I never would be able to talk and do either Morse code or sign language at the same time very well. If either of us were to get away with it, it would be you, Christy."

"Good thing neither of us will have to do it. It probably wouldn't work anyway." I gave him a pressed smile.

Every now and then we thought we heard someone, but it was only a scurrying chipmunk, an owl, or another deer. A quiet stillness lulled me into thinking all was well—that we had escaped and were therefore safe. We had truly given them the slip.

After what seemed hours of walking, with the air warming up, we came upon a little town. We hurried into the first business we saw, a gas station called Trenton's, to use the phone. I swung the door open and immediately wished I hadn't.

There, at the register, buying a Coke, was one of the men from the cabin, no longer in his camo. After a split second of hesitation on both our parts, he grinned like he was expecting me, took a few steps away from the register, and pulled a radio to his lips. He said something in Arabic.

I slammed the door shut, running into Alex, who had lagged behind outside.

"Run!" I yelled grabbing his arm and pulling him back into the woods. Once we hit the river, we ran alongside it, hoping to reach a bigger town soon. We saw a large bridge and quickened our pace. We only needed one car to stop for us. We scrambled up the bank and onto the road. I stood up, only to find myself looking at Iceman. The largest of the bad guys stood right behind him.

Iceman grabbed me, and the other guy grabbed Alex. They dragged us, our feet stirring up rocks and dust, to the van that stood only feet from us on the side of the road.

Inside were two others. I was sure one was the guard from outside the cabin we'd snuck past; he had a swollen lip and a black eye to match the one Alex wore. Probably payment for letting us escape. He snarled at us, hit me across the face and bound me tight. My cheek throbbed as the van pulled onto the road.

The largest of the men beat Alex until he no longer moved, and then tied him up again, too. I felt like throwing up. The clock read noon.

"Try that again," Iceman said in a deep, cutting voice, "and you're dead."

We traveled in silence. No one in the van spoke. Once the van stopped, I made a note of the time. Three o'clock. We had run a long way to that store.

They dragged me like a rag doll, my legs bouncing up the steps as he pulled me along. They whipped Alex's head and body into anything and everything in the path or near it. They tied us up really tight this time. I could feel the rope cutting the skin on my wrists and ankles. Every move I made seemed to make the cuts deeper.

"Maybe," Iceman said, "the pain you feel now will motivate you to stay put."

I wanted to gouge his eyes out. They left, laughing, the shrillness of it raking against my ears. At least they hadn't gagged us this time.

"Alex," I said, trying to twist my body to see him. "Alex. Talk to me."

"Uhhh," he moaned.

He was at the opposite end of the room in a corner. I tried to inch my way toward him, but the ropes cut with increasing zeal with each movement, and I had to lie still.

The horror, fear, and pain overwhelmed me, and I sobbed. A long time passed and I was exhausted before I heard footfalls coming to our door.

When it opened, all seven bad guys came in, bringing the chair, video equipment and posters. They set the chair in the middle of the room. One man grabbed me by the arm and stood me up. I cried out in pain. He cut the ropes that bound my hands and legs. I had rings of fresh blood on all four of them. Despite the revulsion I felt, I swallowed hard, trying to get moisture back into my mouth. He pulled me over to the chair and had me sit.

Alex tried to stand, and one of the five men kicked him in the mouth, laughing. I cringed, biting my tongue. At least he stayed conscious this time; he found the courage to wink at me. I gave him a meager smile, wishing I could hold him.

Were they going to torture me on film now? My heart pounded, and my hands shook.

Iceman spoke, "Listen. He's going to hold up cards for you to read. You will read them, exactly as they are written." He pointed to a man holding large pieces of poster board, standing behind the one holding the camera.

Ransom. It was all about a ransom.

I crossed my arms, trying to be defiant, only to regret it as the pain of my wrists seared through me. Iceman hit me hard across the face, knocking me to the ground, the chair clattering beside me. My eyes stung from his hand, my head throbbed from the floor.

The rant began. "You will read them. Because of you, your government took our beloved Abdul Azeez away from us, and we will get him back, no matter what it takes."

My mind flew back to the moment I pointed out his brother's picture at FBI headquarters.

He said something in his language to one of the other men, who held a laptop, while another picked up the chair and shoved me with a vengeance back onto it. The man with the laptop held the computer in front of me.

I closed and opened my eyes, squinting, hoping to hold a headache at bay.

"I thought it might come to this," Iceman said. His evil voice chilled me. "No worries. I am prepared. You see, I know you will help me, and how do I know? Just take a look at the screen, here. What you see will ensure me your cooperation—You think you can take my brother from me and get away without any pain, any consequences? No. You will feel the pain I have felt losing a brother, but it will be worse for you. Your whole family is mine if you do not help me get my brother back. Seven silly American lives in exchange for his…no, it should be more. He is worth more."

"You see," Iceman said, pointing to the computer screen, that is Aamil, and if you look closely, you will see he is in a car in front of your house."

I shrugged, trying to appear calm, but I recognized the car as the one that I had seen at my house and at the pizzeria. The license plate showed up clear as day.

"Oh, what is this?" Iceman continued. "He is walking up your steps. Hmmm."

I felt my eyes widen with each step.

"Who would be home at your house right now?"

My pulse sped up and I had to hold my breath.

"How many of your brothers and sisters will he have the pleasure of meeting?"

Sudden dread washed over me. They wouldn't dare.

"Let's watch him. . . Oh, look. He is almost at your door. His hand is on the knob."

"Okay! Okay!" I yelled. "I'll do it!" Tears streamed down my face. Tears of rage.

"I thought so," Iceman said. "Let's get on with it."

Alex and I would be dispensable if I made the video. Would they hurt my family even if I complied?

Iceman stood behind the man holding the poster board. The camera man said, "Begin now."

"Wait! Wait!" I yelled. "Promise me he won't hurt my family." I had to try.

They just laughed.

"Begin," the camera man said again.

What else could I do? The practicing Alex and I had done in the forest with sign language flitted across my mind. I read the words on the poster board nice and slow, my body shaking, I exaggerated the fear and nervousness I already felt, enough to sign the letters in between shakes and clenches of my bloodied hands. I did it slowly, my fingers signing the words I hoped the camera would see and the FBI would read.

"I am Christy Hadden. I am a U.S. citizen and I will be put to death along with Alex McGinnis," the cameraman panned over to Alex, huddled in the corner of the room, and then back to me, "unless you release Adbul Azeez to his followers. He must be taken to the farmer's market in Dupont Circle and released within twenty-four hours, or we will die a slow, painful death." I added, "Please hurry. We don't have a lot of time."

The men laughed and hooted, repeating my last words. They tied me to the chair this time, but still didn't gag me. As they left, Iceman said, "It's been a pleasure. Allah smiles on us this day. My brother will be returned to me." And he shut the door.

"Alex," I whispered. "Alex."

"Hmm?" he said.

"I have to tell you something. Can you get over to me?" I knew it would be a sacrifice for him because the rope was sure to cut into his skin each time he moved.

"Maybe."

"I know it'll hurt, it's just really important."

I tried to hop my chair in his direction as he slid, very slowly across the floor toward me. When he reached me, I whispered, "We're going to be rescued."

"We are?" he said, grunting from the pain, disbelief in his voice. "Those jerks have what they wanted. Now we're disposable."

"No. Really," I whispered. "I did what we talked about in the woods. I signed with my hands while they were filming me. I did it really slowly. I signed the name of that gas station we found, Montana, near Helena and then signed the time it took to drive here and up river. I barely had time to sign it all. I had to add a few words to give me time to sign the message. I'm sure the FBI will pick up on it. They'll come."

"Hopefully before these creeps decide to dispose of us." Alex said. It hurt to see him give up. Where had his wink gone? We couldn't give up. We had to hang on to hope. My stomach growled. Eating seemed a luxury at the moment. I couldn't think as clearly anymore. I could feel the sharp edge of my thoughts jumble. Were we truly expendable now, like Alex thought? The idea hacked away at my optimism. Alex laid his head on my feet and I fought to stay alert enough to tell him stories of hiking, biking, and gardening to get his mind off our situation until I heard even breathing. I was so uncomfortable sitting on the hard chair that I thought there was no way I could sleep, but I did.

Someone touched my hand, and I startled awake. "Hhhh?" Within a second I heard, "Shhh." Whoever it was, his big, rough man hands were cutting mine free. Having a knife next to my skin terrified me. In the pitch black, not knowing for sure who sawed at the ropes binding me, fear gripped me. My heart raced. I hoped it was the FBI, but couldn't be sure. It was so dark, if my hand had been an inch from my face, I wouldn't have been able to see it. In a matter of seconds, though, I was free and didn't care who had managed it.

I reached down for Alex, but he wasn't there. I wanted to ask for him, but the person who freed me pulled me away from my chair. It was a man. My wrists and ankles burned as I felt my wounds re-open. He took me to the window and lifted me up with ease. The window, fully open now, allowed me to easily climb out. I slid along the house to allow space for my rescuer to climb out, too. He had to be FBI. They must've been able to read my signs. But, where was Alex?

Once the man was out, he grabbed my hand and pulled me away from the house, into the woods. I couldn't see the guard anywhere, but it was hard to make anything out. I guessed clouds hid the moon and stars tonight. Had my rescuers captured the guard? Where was Alex? Tentative and afraid of running into something, I shuffled my feet, falling now and again. My rescuer pulled all the harder. While I could barely make out shapes, this man ran, albeit silently, with me stumbling behind. How did he know where to go? Could he somehow see?

He stopped and I gasped for breath. I heard the click of what sounded like a car door opening. Hard, muscled arms threw me into a large truck of some sort, but the overhead lights hadn't come on when the door opened, so I couldn't see anything. My senses told me someone else was there. Possibly more than one someone. The door clicked shut behind me, and after two more clicks, the truck moved. The inky blackness was freaking me out and before I could try to see who was in the car with me, we bumped and jostled violently. Out of necessity, I grabbed hold of the seat in front of me as we high-tailed it out of there. I peered hard into the darkness and made out the outlines of things. Someone sat behind the driver. Was that Alex on the bench next to me? After a good twenty minutes, with my head thrumming, we burst out of the dense coverage of trees and some light filled the car. Scattered clouds hovered above us, but it was obvious dawn was about to arrive.

He was there. Alex spotted me at the same moment, and he slid next to me in a flash. I trembled inside as he pulled me to him and whispered, "You were right. They came for us. I was wrong to lose faith." As smooth as silk, he kissed me while lifting my legs and setting them sideways over his lap. He then grabbed me around the waist and put me on his lap.

I felt relief go through me and put my arms around his neck, kissing him hard. I didn't care who saw, my relief of seeing him alive and out of that horrible cabin overriding any sense of decorum as we bounced along the forest floor.

He kissed my cheek and up to my ear, sending tingles down my spine, and whispered, "I can't ever lose you, Christy—ever."

I couldn't remember how to breathe. With the rush of emotion pulsing through me, any discomfort I had felt from my wounds seemed to disappear. He kissed me more urgently, his hands caressing my back. I rubbed his neck, enjoying the firm softness of his skin.

"DC and Washington are safe and clear. It's a go," a woman's voice from the front seat said. Alex froze, then pulled me to him, holding me in a tight hug and whispered, "Listen. I want to listen."

"Ten-four," a man's voice from the front seat said, "It's a go. We're clear."

"Alex," I said into his shoulder, my voice muffled by his shirt. It was starting to get hard to breathe, his grip was so tight. "Alex."

"Sorry, Christy." Alex slid me back into my seat and gave a head nod toward the two masked people in the front seat.

"Who are you guys?" Alex asked.

"All you need to know is that we are with the FBI," the man in the passenger seat said.

I let out a big breath of air.

The truck took one last bounce that almost threw me into the ceiling. We landed on a smooth, paved road and then sped away. I buckled up, watching the speedometer needle climb. Alex did the same.

I stared at the two masked people in the front seats and then back to Alex, whose eyes wouldn't leave them.

"Can you at least tell us where we're going?" Alex asked.

"Not yet."

After a short time, the man said, "At the fumigator." And we pulled off the highway and down a narrow dirt road. We bounced through potholes and ruts coming to a stop in front of a large white van, not unlike the one we were debugged in after the gala in DC.

"Hop out you two," the man said. "We need to check you for bugs. We know you have at least one, Christy."

"A bug? I have a bug?" I asked, but everyone was already out of the car and didn't hear me. I hopped out and climbed into the white van. Alex had just asked the woman a question.

"We were lucky," the woman said to Alex. "Christy happened to have a bug in the hem of her pants. I guess from your stint in DC. It saved us a ton of time locating you."

Once again, a man ran a large wand over our bodies and then told us to go in the back of the van and change. I expected the locator to buzz wildly when it came across a bug in my pant leg. But it never did. I felt the hem of the pants, wondering if I could feel the bug. Nothing. Then I realized I hadn't even taken these pants to DC. I found them on my bed when I arrived home. One of my sisters' cast offs. It couldn't have had a bug. Had they lied? How did they find us if it didn't have anything to do with a bug?

We left the van supposedly free of bugs and in plain gray sweats. The bands on the wrists and ankles of the sweats tore at the sores the ropes had left and I had to roll them up, exposing the gashes. An odd ache started in my gut and spread to my chest.

"We've got some ointment for that," the woman said, looking at the bloody, raw sores.

"Great," I said, climbing back into the truck with Alex.

As I climbed in, I couldn't help but notice some bloody wet wipes and gloves strewn over the front seat. The masked man was cleaning more blood away from some type of metal tool that looked a lot like a small garden hand rake. I pushed back against the back rest, my face scrunched up in horror. The missing guard? I didn't dare ask, but motioned for Alex to look at what I'd seen. The man seemed to have noticed and said.

"Don't worry. We just had to take care of a little nuisance." He handed a tube of ointment back to me.

"Is that blood?" Alex asked.

"The less you know, the better," the man said.

I winced as I spread the gooey stuff all over my wrists and ankles. Then I went to work on Alex's sores. I was surprised when he rubbed some on the rug burns on my face. My insides tickled feeling his gentle touch. I returned the favor.

The silence was thick and heavy as we pulled away and drove back to the highway. The sun had come up completely, but I felt blind.

"Now that we're bug free, can we know where we're going?" Alex asked.

"To a safe-house nearby to get you two cleaned up."

"Why don't you take off your masks?"

"We work in counter-terrorism and are often undercover. In the unlikely event you two get captured. We can't have you blowing our cover."

Alex nodded. "Fair enough. It's just a bit creepy is all."

They both chuckled.

"Do you know what's happening with my family?" I asked.

"Sorry, no."

"Can you tell us about these terrorists? I thought they were all captured or dead." Alex said.

"There are some agents at the safe-house who will fill you in when we get there."

A half hour passed before we once again pulled off onto a narrow dirt road. Branches dug into the sides of the truck with a horrible scratching sound as we drove, and ruts jarred our bodies as we went over them. As a rustic gray cabin came into view, one of the two garage doors opened. The porch sagged dangerously and the roof needed some tlc. Vines grew over much of the house, making it look even more abandoned and decrepit.

Nonetheless, we pulled in, the door closing behind us. I looked at Alex and his eyes also showed surprise at the size of the garage. Two other cars were parked inside, all clean and perfect, as if someone was just about to drive away in them.

"Let's go," the woman said, opening her door and climbing out. She grabbed a bag and something else that resembled ski goggles as the man grabbed all the wet-wipes and his own black bag. He slid out of the truck and up the stairs to the house door. After punching in a code on an alarm pad, they went inside. I followed, Alex close behind.

We entered a modern kitchen. The outside of this place was obviously just a façade. The man dropped his goggles onto the table and I reached for them, curious to see if they were night vision goggles.

As if the man read my mind, he said, "Night vision goggles."

I looked closely at them, lifting them for Alex to see. "Cool," he said. Then, I set them down when a man and a woman, without masks, came into the room. The woman's thick, dark hair hung in waves below her shoulders. The man's deeply tanned, rugged complexion nearly made me gasp. He scratched his cocoa colored hair beneath his ears, then turned his blue eyes straight at Alex.

Alex's hands pressed into my waist and he whispered, "Mom? Dad?"

I looked back at Alex. His eyes were fixed on the two new people, and his hands left my sides as he moved forward into their waiting arms. I looked behind them, waiting for my parents to walk in. They didn't, so I focused on Alex and these people he called his parents. He had hugged his mom and was now hugging his dad. Now I knew why Alex was so beautiful. He was a perfect blend of both of them.

"How?" He rasped, pulling away from their embrace.

"Well, it's a long story—" his mom said, brushing her fingers over the scrapes on his face.

"You know how we told you we're government analysts?" His dad said.

"Yeah, of course."

"Well, we do work for the government, but not as analysts."

He let this sink in. I couldn't see Alex's face, but I could only imagine how it looked.

"Huh?"

"We," his mom interrupted, "work for the FBI."

"What? Are you some kind of spies or something?" He chuckled, taking a small step back and glancing at me, his face mocking.

Trying to give him support, my lips curved.

"Not exactly," his dad said. "We are part of a black-ops division of the FBI."

Moments passed in utter silence. Alex's head hung, I'm sure he was considering this little revelation. My mouth hung open. When Alex finally lifted his head, he said, "You guys are black-ops agents?"

They nodded their heads.

"So, you've been lying to me my whole life?"

They stared at him. I saw a smile tug at the corners of his mouth. He was playing with them.

"Well…"

"I guess you could say that," his dad said. "But it was for your own good."

"My own good?" He couldn't keep the charade any longer and a smile spread over his lips even though he kept attacking. "In what world is it good to lie to your own son?"

His dad narrowed his eyes and cocked his head to the side and then smiled. "In our world." His dad grabbed his son into another hug.

"That's even cooler than spies. So cool," Alex said, pulling away from his dad.

His mom's eyes were wide, unbelieving, and she didn't speak or move.

"It's true," his dad said, with a small cough. "We just didn't expect you to take it so well."

"This so makes up for my crappy childhood."

"Crappy childhood?" his mom questioned. "We gave you everything."

"Except a real home somewhere, friends, public school—"

I couldn't help thinking about how hard it must have been for Alex his whole life having to live everywhere and nowhere.

"Okay, okay," his mom said.

"Why didn't you come get us, then?"

"We wanted to, sweetie," his mom cooed. "But the director thought we were too close to the situation. Your dad had to call in all sorts of favors for us to be here now."

Alex didn't seem to be listening. "Why didn't I know you were agents?"

"We're very good at what we do, Alex," his dad said, his chest seeming to puff up.

I thought about Alex and how easy it was for him to deceive others. He had learned well, even if he didn't realize his parents had set the example. A nervous twitch developed in my left eye.

"You've been lying to me my whole life. I should be mad, but it's so totally awesome that you're black ops." A grin grew on Alex's face and the mischievous look I loved appeared.

His parents smiled.

"But if you're FBI agents, why didn't you come to our rescue in DC and put an end to all this back then?" Confusion scored Alex's face.

"We were in Turkey, honey, on assignment," his mom said. "Remember, you came there after the trip?"

"Yeah, but—"

"We didn't even know about all of this until you told us about it when you arrived in Turkey."

"I don't get it, though. My agent, Nick, in DC, said I had nothing to worry about. It was over."

"They thought it was. But, then they found out who exactly you'd been dealing with. Everyone thought Ahmed, or Iceman as you know him, was some foot soldier for the Mahkan terrorist cell. They only discovered who he really was after interrogating men from the safe-house in DC several weeks after you went home. Ahmed is Azeez's brother."

He paused and Alex said, "So?"

"Ahmed is the brother and heir apparent of the biggest, most influential terrorist cell in the Middle East. And he's crazy mad. In his eyes, you guys are the reason his brother's locked up. He wants you kids dead. He especially wants Christy dead. In the world of terrorism, it only takes one person to create a whole new war. Yes, he wants revenge, but he also has a small problem. He has to prove himself as leader. He won't let his brother's dynasty come to an end.

That's why he concocted the plan to find you and use you as ransom to save his brother. Now that his attempt has failed, other factions will perk up their ears to see if they have a chance to take over what's left of Azeez's followers and power. To prove some of these other terrorists are the better choice as leader, they just might come after you, finishing what Ahmed couldn't."

"I don't get it. I'm just one stupid girl who saw something she shouldn't have," I whispered.

"Terrorists are their own breed," his mom chimed in. "It might be easier to think of them as a pack of wolves. Each wolf submits to the leader—presumably, the best wolf. Most do this willingly, but there are some wolves that crave power and are waiting for the leader to make a mistake so they can take over.

"Also, if you look at the bigger picture, each different pack has their own territory and neighboring packs watch for the opportunity to take it over. They want more territory, more places to hunt, more power. It's instinct for the wolves and instinct for the terrorists—always vying for more territory, more power. The second a weakness is found, you better bet they're going after the power that suddenly seems up for grabs. You, Christy, symbolize that power to them. The craving for power is all consuming."

"It's ridiculous!" Alex said, grabbing my hand.

"True," his mom said. "The real question is, do these other terrorist groups have something to gain by taking you out? Definitely. In the eyes of the pack, it shows their strength. They'd have accomplished what Ahmed couldn't. Of course, there's also all those who don't care about *you* so much, per se, but they do care about sticking it to the U.S. They will know the only way you survived was with help. The ability to stick their middle finger up to our government—to show that they're better than the U.S. and that they have the upper hand—is irresistible to some terrorist groups."

"You are one lucky girl," his dad said, his mouth twisted in an ironic sneer. "You came up against the right terrorist group. Otherwise, the government wouldn't be as invested, wouldn't be throwing so much at this."

"What about my family?" I said. A hot rock seemed to wedge itself into my throat. "They said they would hurt my family."

"Your family will be taken care of," his dad said. "The FBI is there in the background. And once you're dead, or they think you are dead, they will leave your family alone.

"It was crazy the way the chatter over the airways picked up a few days ago. We figure that's about the time they kidnapped you two, Christy. Then, there was silence over the airwaves and the video file from the cabin arrived at FBI headquarters."

"We were afraid we were already too late since we had the tape," his mom said, a bitter tone to her voice. "We didn't know why they'd keep you around after they'd made it. We thought you might be expendable at that point. And yet, here you are. Your luck hasn't run out yet."

"I had to make the video," I blurted. "They were at my house. They were going to hurt my family."

"It's okay, Christy," Alex said, pulling me against him. "You did what you had to do. My parents aren't blaming you for this."

His parents stood there without a sound.

I wrung my hands. He was wrong. I had been judged and found guilty by his parents. I could almost feel the noose tightening around my neck.

"Right, Mom?" Alex asked, desperation in his voice. He put his arm around me and pulled me close.

"We all have to make hard decisions in life," his mom said, a sharp edge to her voice. "Sometimes, though, we have to think of others before we make rash decisions."

"What are you saying?" Alex asked. "That Christy should have let that psycho hurt her family, to save us? Are you crazy? After they tortured her family, they would have killed us anyway."

"That's not what your mom meant," his dad said, looking at his wife and placing his hand on her shoulder. "She's just glad you're safe."

I knew what she meant. His dad couldn't change her meaning no matter how hard he tried. She thought it was okay for me to suffer, just not her son. And maybe she was right. I wish I hadn't dragged him into this. Sure, he said it wasn't my fault, but I'm the one that looked into the ballroom in DC and saw the murder in the first place. I was the first domino to fall.

"Look, Mom," Alex said, pulling me even closer. "I chose to look through that vent, too. Christy told me not to. I didn't listen. It's my fault I'm involved, not hers." He knew what she meant, too. Alex's face was ashen and his jaw slack. Only a few seconds had passed and yet it seemed like an eternity before someone spoke.

"We hate to break up this nice family reunion, but you need to get moving, John." So, his dad's name was John. The man and woman who'd saved us from the terrorists walked through the kitchen. "The cabin is clear." I stared at them as they punched in a code to the garage door and left. The loud sound of the truck driving away pulled me back to reality.

"They are right," his mom said, her expression troubled, worry fixing a deep crease between her eyes. "We must get the two of you to safety. Alex, you come with me," his mom said, leading him into the living room area. "We have a long day ahead of us." She turned after putting her arm around Alex's waist and cast a nasty look back at me.

"Christy," John said. "Go into the living room and through the door on the far right. Get showered and cleaned up. You'll find everything you need in the bathroom. Make it quick. We've got a schedule to keep." I sat there, looking around the small space, considering this unbelievable turn of events. "Did you hear me?" his dad said, raising his eyebrows at me.

I stood and walked to the bathroom. I couldn't believe how incredible this little development was. His parents were stunning and cool, but they seemed to have a serious problem with me.

Chapter Eight

The room held only a bed, a nightstand, a lamp and a dresser. Two doors stood opposite the bed. One was to the closet and the other, the bathroom.

The bathroom was small, too, but a bag on the tiny counter did have everything I needed, and a set of folded clothes sat on the closed toilet lid. The mirror revealed the damage the kidnappers had inflicted on my face. A large purple bruise showed itself on my left cheek, and my right was red and raw from sliding on the kidnappers' wooden floor. I didn't have a plastic surgeon here to stitch me up like in DC. Would I be scarred for life? Lovely.

I jumped in the shower, the soft spray soothing my tender skin. I was careful not to let my face move directly into the stream of water, but washed every bit of filth off of me. The water was a deep brown as it went down the drain. I didn't want to get out once the water ran clear, but when I heard a knock on the bathroom door and "Get out," I figured I better. I carefully washed my face using the sink, each wipe of the washcloth caused my eye to throb even more. I dressed and brushed my hair at lightning speed, not wanting anyone to have to wait on me again. I couldn't find a hairdryer, or make-up to hide my scratches and bruises, so I walked back into the kitchen to ask about them.

A bit of panic welled up inside me, thinking I'd taken too long and they had left me. The empty room seemed an omen of sorts. Then, I noticed paper goods on the table. We were going to eat. There were four place settings. My stomach rumbled at the thought. Maybe they left to get food.

Loud whispers I couldn't understand came from behind a door on the other side of the kitchen. Curious, I walked toward the voices, the wooden floorboards squeaking as I went.

"I can't do it," his mom said. "I won't take her." and then stopped, like she knew I was there. I paused just in time to watch the door I was headed toward open, allowing Alex and his parents to walk out. The pinched, we-just-got-caught looks on their faces sent a dagger through my heart.

"All clean?" his mom said with a false note of caring, her lips curving in an unnatural smile.

"Yeah," I said, brushing a hand through my wet hair, pretending I didn't notice. "Thanks." I felt like an intruder, completely out of place, and I looked at my feet.

Alex pushed past his parents, his shoes loud on the floor, and wrapped his arms around me.

I felt that familiar zing go though me.

"You okay?" he asked. His warmth heated my chilled body.

I sighed. "I think so." I forgot about the make-up and the hair-dryer and wondered what it was his mom *wouldn't do*. What they didn't want me to hear.

"Good. Let's eat," Alex said, leading me over to the table and pulling a chair out for me. "I'm starving." He pushed me closer to the table after I sat and walked away. I craned my neck to look behind me, to see what he was doing. He stood in front of his parents, shaking his head and gesturing wildly with his hands. His dad saw me staring and, before I could look away, he opened his eyes wide to Alex and said, "Yeah, I'm not a fan of the cabin either. Let's eat." He pushed around Alex to fill a water jug.

The clanking, sliding sounds of them rummaging in the cupboards and refrigerator muffled some exchange of words they were having. I didn't dare look back again. I clasped my hands together on my lap and felt sweat glue them together. If only I could hear what they were saying.

Minutes later, a feast sat before me: meats, breads, cheeses, fruits and vegetables. The platters had obviously been prepared by a deli. I spread out the paper napkins that were near me and his dad brought the pitcher of water. After everyone sat, a terrible moment of silence followed and his mom stared at me with obvious resentment.

I felt my eyes widen and then dropped my head, closing my eyes. She really did hate me for putting her son in danger. My stomach burned and I wondered if I could eat.

"You better eat up," John said. "It'll be a while before you get another chance." Alex nudged me. I looked up at him. A nervous smile played across his lips, which didn't help settle my stomach at all. Should I say something and get it over with? It was silly for me to feel so horrible without knowing why.

I finally cleared my throat and said, "Okay," and reached for some bread. My heart still thrummed, though, and I couldn't make myself eat. As the moments sped up I felt sweat bead along my forehead and my heart hammered. When I thought it would jump out and land on the table, I knew I had to say something.

"Just tell me, please." I spoke quietly, to my plate, but my words cut easily through the silence. The breath I didn't know I was holding rushed out in a gush of relief. I wanted desperately to look up, but couldn't muster the courage. I felt some movement, shifting in seats, but no words came and the seconds dragged on. Whatever they were keeping from me, it must really be bad.

Alex took my now sweaty hand firmly in his as his dad spoke.

"Your life is about to change dramatically." John's soft, soothing voice coaxed my head up. "After we eat, we'll be separating, and Alex doesn't like that idea."

"Dad, it's not the best plan," Alex said. "Think about it. Having the two of you protect the two of us gives us double the protection. You said yourself that you're great agents. Prove it. Keep us safe—together."

"I'm sorry, son," his dad said, "It simply doesn't work that way. Splitting up gives the two of you the best chance of survival. Two separate targets are harder to hit than one. It's just a fact."

"Your dad's right, Alex," his mom said, a bit abruptly. "Over and over we see this fact proven in our line of work."

A shadow passed over his dad's face, disappearing in a flash. Behind their words lay the truth. I am the target. Away from me, Alex is safe.

"But the two of you can make it work, right?" Alex's voice pleaded.

"No, we can't. We have to stick to the plan. A plan that, by the way, has a pretty rigid time schedule." His dad looked at his watch. "We need to be moving in twenty minutes."

I didn't want to talk, to bring any more attention to me, but I had to know more. "We are splitting up, then?" I felt stupid hearing my voice crack.

"Yes," John said. "I," he drew out the "I" sound and looked at his wife, giving her a nod before continuing, "will be taking you to your new home and Sue will be taking Alex."

Apparently, that was what the argument earlier had been about and John had just agreed to watch after me. Relief filled me to be with John. If I had to be with one of them, I'd rather be with him. He had been much kinder to me than Sue. Questions swirled through my mind. Questions I didn't want to ask with Sue around. The idea that they could eat like nothing was wrong irritated me. How could they eat at a time like this?

My stomach was too upset from the unknown. It seemed hours were passing when only minutes had, sometimes only seconds.

"Okay, you two. It's time to say your goodbyes," John said.

His parents started to clear the table and Alex pushed his chair back, the legs making an awful scraping sound as he did. He brought me into the room I'd been in earlier and shut the door behind him. I half expected his parents to storm the door and sit as sentinel, but they didn't.

We walked to the bed and sat, the bed lumpy beneath us. The sad look in his eyes appeared to come from some deep anguish in his soul. What did he know that I didn't?

"What?" I asked. "What is it?"

He put his fingers to my lips, silencing me, and then pulled me tight to him, our bodies melting together. His lips followed the curve of my neck. A sweet shiver stole through my body. I clung to him, rubbing my sore cheek gently against his jaw. When my lips found his, strong arms closed around me with even greater force. I felt safe and secure. I couldn't imagine ever letting go and I definitely couldn't imagine why he was so sad. We were safe. We sat, hugging each other, our heads leaning on each other's shoulders for what seemed a long time.

"Alex. Christy. It's time." His dad's voice broke the spell that had been cast between us. I couldn't let go. Every nerve of my body snapped alert, and a furious blush rose to my face. I wouldn't let him go. We held tighter still, neither of us willing to say goodbye. Even though I knew I put Alex in danger, I didn't want to let him go, even for a little while. I needed him.

"This is no joke," his dad continued as he stepped into the room. "Our window of opportunity is closing. Get moving, now." The force in his voice and his presence pressed down on me like a massive weight. Alex's grip loosened and he sighed, ever so slightly. His hands brushed through my hair and his fingers gently rubbed my cheek. His head fell to my shoulder and he murmured into my collarbone. "I don't know what I'll do without you, but we'll be together soon. Don't worry. I'll wait for you."

A quick panic pooled in my stomach. His look said he didn't think we'd be together again. That's what he knew that I didn't. The kisses that followed were frantic and close. His mom took Alex's hands in hers and pulled him away, while John placed his hands on my shoulders, holding me in place. It felt like they had taken out my insides and thrown them on the floor. Alex, held by his mom near the door, mouthed the words that lit my heart on fire, filling me with a strange hope.

"I love you."

His mom dragged him around the corner, and then he actually yelled it. I wanted to yell it back, but the words stuck in my throat and came out as a croaked whisper, only his dad hearing the words. My heart seemed to explode as I heard the door from the kitchen to the garage slam shut. Alex and his mom would soon be gone. How long would it be until we could be together again? Would his parents even allow us to be together again? I shuddered and tried to stand up when I heard the garage door rise, but John held me firm to the bed.

"Wait!" I called out, "Wait!" I clawed at John's fingers, trying to pry them away from my shoulders. It was no use. He was too strong. His grip too firm. Tears flowed freely now as I heard the car drive away. Would I ever see him again? My stomach felt hollow and my heart ached.

"It'll be okay," John said.

But I knew it wouldn't.

His hands stopped pressing my shoulders down, and he grabbed me under my arms and lifted me to my feet. I didn't know if I could stand. I felt weak, unstable. I leaned on John and he adjusted his hold, wrapping his arm around me and carrying me along.

Once in the kitchen, he dropped his bag and lifted me into his arms, effortlessly carrying me to the car and setting me in the front passenger seat. I folded into myself, barely aware of my surroundings, sobbing out of control. The car jerked into motion and I fell into a world of nothingness.

I was jarred awake by the sound of a car door slamming and mine opening up as stale air wafted in. We were in a different garage. Again, two other cars were parked next to ours, just like the cabin we had left. For a silly, naïve moment, a flicker of hope burned in me. Was Alex here? I jumped out of the car.

"Alex," I called, racing past his dad to the door that I hoped led to him. It didn't budge. It was locked. John was there in a flash, holding me, saying, "He's not here. He's not here." I felt the warmth in his voice. What was with this guy? Was he comforting me now? My shoulders slumped as he pushed a code into the keypad allowing us access to the house. Even though I knew he was right, I burst through the door and searched all around with my eyes, hoping Alex would materialize. He didn't. I groaned, sat in a kitchen chair and threw my head onto my arms, eyes burning.

"You've got to get hold of yourself or this will never work," John said, plopping himself onto the chair opposite me. "Look, if you want to see Alex again, you need to survive. In order to survive, you've got to pull it together."

His words sunk deep inside me. I knew he was right and sighed deeply, trying to release all the sadness and find a smile. But, I felt wrung out, like a wet rag. My eyes stung with a thousand tears.

"That's the way," he assured me. "Now, I need you to listen to me."

I didn't move.

"Can you please look at me?" he asked.

I raised one side of my head, my now frizzy, curly hair sliding back, revealing one eye.

"I'm going to make you disappear so the bad guys can't find you," he said.

"What are you talking about?" My prayers for a new me flitted across the stage of my mind. Was this the only way to recreate myself?

"We need to erase you."

"Why don't you just let 'em have me? It'd be over. This is too crazy. I can't stand the fact that I've put so many peoples' lives in danger." It hurt like crazy to think I'd never be with Alex again. I thought I'd rather disappear completely.

"You think it would stop them? Not even. You may feel like a huge part in their plans, but in reality, you're a tiny inconvenience—a little piece in the puzzle. It's no longer just about land and renewable resources. It's about getting even and gaining power to put the next devious plan into action. But as it stands, you, your DC group, and your families are all in jeopardy, so you will have to die." There was an unsettling glint in his eye. "But, before we kill you off, we need you to call your parents."

"Now you're going to kill me?" I flinched and wanted to run. I felt a slight headache coming on. A crying headache. I sat up and breathed deeply, trying to get rid of it before it took hold.

"Erased. Dead. It's the same thing. I need you to tell your parents you got lost on a hike and are on your way back, or that you were going to run away with Alex and changed your mind, or whatever your parents will believe. They need to think you're on your way back home. This will help keep them safe."

I stared at him, knowing my parents would see right through either of those excuses.

"Do you understand?"

"Yes, but how is that going to help? Besides, I am a terrible liar. They'll never believe it."

"First of all," he said, "your parents need to hear from you. You've been gone for three days and they're sick out of their minds. Second, we need to give credence to your death. If you're dead, there's no reason to go after your family."

My heart froze. To my death? Was he really going to kill me? Instinctively, I leaned away from him. He must have seen my shock, and said, "Not your real death, your fake death," he said, a sly smile crossing his lips.

"What do you mean?" My heart slowed a bit.

"Christy, I thought you were intelligent. Do I really have to connect all the dots for you?"

"If you can't tell," I said, "I'm a bit out of sorts. My head is killing me and I've just lost the best thing in my life. So, if you wouldn't mind, please, connect the dots."

He stared hard at me, like he was making a serious decision about me. "You are not going home. All you know about yourself is about to change. You're about to enter the wonderful world of witness protection and live a completely different life somewhere else. The U.S. Marshalls didn't think it would be a good idea to move your whole family, so we collaborated and came up with a way to make it appear as if you've died. Besides, putting one person into witness protection is tricky enough, not to mention a family of nine. They would have been in constant danger anyway. If we kill you off, there's no reason for the terrorists to hurt your family or to even search for you. Instead, we'll create a new you and you'll go to college, where you belong."

"What?" I said, horror gripping me, as I thought of my family believing I was dead, I'd never be able to go home again. "I need my family. They need to know the truth."

"I will act as your family from now on."

"You can't be my family."

"I will have to be."

Tension crushed me during a long pause. I didn't have a choice. This was how I could keep everyone safe. I swallowed hard. "How are you going to do it? Kill me off, I mean."

"A car accident."

"But you need a body, witnesses and stuff."

"Yep. We'll have bodies, witnesses, everything. We'll have complete control of the scene, of course, and there will be no question whether you are dead or not."

"But won't they suspect something? A car accident, really?"

"It will be an explosion, actually. And the beauty of it is that they set the bombs. They won't suspect a thing."

"What?"

"They loaded that cute little sports car Alex rented with a couple of nice little bombs."

A memory of men crawling out from under that car and climbing into the terrorists' van popped in my mind.

"It's set to explode about twenty minutes after someone starts it. They'll just think you got dropped off at the car and—" His watched beeped. "Okay. It's time for the phone call. Tell them you hitched a ride to Alex's rental car and will be there in about twenty minutes." He dialed my house number and handed me the phone. "Don't forget to tell them you love them. This will be the last time you talk to them—ever."

I took the phone automatically, but I was frantic. "Why are you surprising me with this? I need time to think." But I didn't have time. Before I had a chance to come up with a good lie, I heard my mom's voice on the other line. I panicked and broke down crying. She had picked up on the first ring, obviously anxious to hear from me. I couldn't imagine what she'd been through. John waved his hands in a forward circling motion, urging me to get on with it. My mom called out on the other end, "Christy, Christy, is that you?" After a few moments of silence, I heard her say, "I think it's Christy. Get your dad. Christy?"

"It's me, Mom." I tried hard to compose myself, walking back and forth in the small kitchen of the cabin.

She gasped. "Oh, Christy. We've been so worried."

"I know, Mom. I'm okay." I sucked in a deep breath and let my head hang back as I looked at the ceiling.

"What happened? Where have you been?"

"Alex and I went hiking and…and…we …" I couldn't lie. It didn't seem right. "We were kidnapped, mom. It was awful."

"Kidnapped? What do you mean, kidnapped? Where are you? Who took you? Why'd they…"

I heard several phones pick up and it became noisy. "They came out of the woods, grabbed us, tied us up, and took us to a cabin about three hours from the trail. They stuck us in a room, but we escaped. Alex was amazing, Mom. I never would've made it without him." My sobs prevented me from going on.

"Ahh! No!" She was sobbing, too. "What did they do to you? Are you hurt?"

"Cuts…bruises."

"Where are you? We'll come and get you."

"No, Mom. We hitched a ride to Alex's car." I sucked in hard from crying.

"What if the kidnappers had picked you up again?"

"They didn't." I took a quick breath and a violent shiver rumbled through me, remembering our first escape attempt and being recaptured.

"You stay right where you are," my dad said. "We'll get you."

"Dad. I'll be home sooner if Alex just keeps driving. Okay?"

"Okay."

"Sorry we didn't call sooner. They took Alex's cell and we had to find a phone booth. I miss you, Mom and Dad."

"We miss you, too, sweetie." I could hear crying and shouts of joy in the background. My heart burned with satisfaction thinking of it.

"Mom. Dad. Listen, I have to tell you something. When something like this happens it makes you think about what's really important in life, and I want you to know that I love you two and the whole family."

I heard my mom take a sharp intake of air. "We know sweetie, and we love you, too."

"We're about twenty minutes away."

"Okay, and you be careful," my mom said.

I covered my mouth with my hand, holding in a shriek.

"Get home to us in one piece," my dad said.

"We will," I cleared my throat to hide the catch in my voice.

I hung up.

Chapter Nine

I heard John talking loudly on the phone and wondered if there was a problem with my dorm at the college I was supposed to be attending. With all the stress he'd been under the past four days getting us to Tallahassee, Florida in one piece, he'd never lost his cool, and now he was practically yelling at whoever it was on the phone. John stared out a window, holding his cell to his ear and running one hand roughly through his hair. " …not a part of the deal. A child can't always have his way…safer in college…no, a family is not important…What if I refuse? ...Sure…three very long months."

So intent on understanding what he talked about, I had moved into the room without realizing it. He turned from the window and noticed me. The sharpness in his eyes cut to my soul and I took a quick step back into my room.

"Just a minute," he said to the person on the phone and walked down the hall and into his room, not taking his eyes off me until he closed the door behind him. I could still hear his voice rise here and there, but couldn't make out more than a few words. I sat down to eat. Room service had provided us with a hot breakfast today: bacon, eggs, toast, and grits. I ate without reservation.

When John left his room, the door slammed shut behind him. My instincts told me not to peek, but I couldn't help myself. I had to know what could possibly be so colossal to make him yell and slam doors.

When our eyes met, he quickly turned away, fists at his sides. I didn't dare stare any longer, so I turned back to my eggs, picking at the yolks. My heart raced and acid burned my stomach. I wondered if the bacon and eggs would stay down. Minutes ticked by, my anxiety growing by the second. After what seemed a lifetime, footsteps pounded towards me from the hall. I took a deep breath and closed my eyes, trying to be calm. Despite that, I still jumped when he spoke.

His voice was even, with no anger evident. "Things have changed a bit."

I knew it. There was a problem with the university. I froze, afraid to move, like moving would make the situation more real or worse. He walked past me and around the table, taking the seat opposite me. His face was composed with a hint of kindness. Who was he now? How could he go from total anger to kindness in a few short minutes?

"I just got off the phone with my wife, Sue," he continued.

The breath I'd been holding rushed out with the relief I felt, and I couldn't help but ask, "Aren't they coming?" My heart felt like it would jump out of my chest.

"No." He paused.

"But I thought—"

"I know what you thought, and we intended you to think it, even though we never specifically said you'd be meeting up again."

"I don't understand."

"It was easier to keep you calm thinking there was a chance Alex would be meeting up with us."

He did *not* just say that. "It's so nice to be manipulated," I said, my fear turning to anger.

"Manipulation is often necessary to get a desired outcome. But you know all about that, don't you? Debate is all about manipulation. I also assume some manipulation was what you used to get my son so enamored with you. Manipulation is as common as sneezing."

He was right—except for the Alex part. I just didn't like to be the one being manipulated. A few seconds of silence followed.

"Like I said, our plans have changed a bit. I need you to promise me something."

That got my attention and I looked right in his eyes.

"I need you to promise me that you will stay away from Alex."

I wouldn't ever agree to giving up Alex. He was the only thing left from my past.

"I'm not gonna—"

"Hold on. Don't say you're not gonna just yet."

"But—"

"Let me finish so you can make an educated decision." His eyebrows scrunched together.

I breathed hard and wanted to leave, but I had to hear him out.

"Alex is worried about you." At the mention of his name, my heart hammered. "Obviously, the U.S. Marshall's plan was to drop you off at the university, but my wife is insisting I do what Alex is begging me to do instead. She even got permission for us to be on family leave for ninety days to accomplish it."

I stared at him. The parts of the phone call I'd heard started to unravel.

"Alex is, like I said, worried about you. He doesn't want me to leave you without giving you more skills to survive."

"What? Where is he? Can I at least talk to him?"

"Would you let me finish?" He ignored my question and went on. "If I'm going to give up three months of my life to you, away from my wife, my son and my work, to protect you and teach you, then you've got to give me something in return." His unreadable face showed no emotion.

I would not agree.

"Look at this from my point of view," he said. "You're the target for who knows how many factions vying for power in the Middle East, including the big one. Their reasons for fixating on you is nuts, but it is what it is. You have become a symbol of power—Azeez's lost power, and Ahmed's hope for power. Not only does this Ahmed want to reclaim his brother's power, he wants revenge. Because of that, anyone near you is also in danger. It's hard enough keeping Alex safe working as FBI agents. I did not spend the last eighteen years keeping him safe only to let you put him in extreme danger every moment of the rest of his life." Emotion betrayed him. His eyes glistened in the light. The real John talked to me now.

I couldn't speak. What could I say? He was right. Alex's association with me had put him in danger. How could I justify being with him? I couldn't.

"So, the choice is yours. You can allow me to create a new identity for you, Michele, and teach you how to stay completely safe for the rest of your life, or you can choose to refuse my offer and go home."

Home? I could go home?

"Well, in that case, I choose to go home."

He shook his head and sighed.

"You've got to be smarter than that. Think this through! How long do you think it will be before the terrorists discover you are alive? How long do you think it will take them to go after you and your family? We went to great lengths to ensure their safety, but you have the power to change all that, don't you? Do you want your whole family to die?"

He pulled out his phone, punched a few buttons. "Oh, you don't have to make the decision this second. It looks like the next flight to Helena leaves in about two hours. That means you have about forty-five minutes to decide. The power is in your hands. And just to make sure there is no confusion, you have two choices. Number one, you agree to stay away from Alex, even if he finds you, and Florida will be your home. I will then provide you with a new life in the next ninety days and place you in witness protection with a family after that. The U.S. Marshalls will take over everything from then on.

"Number two, I put you on a flight back to Colorado and on to Helena. I will disappear from your life and you will go home putting not only yourself, but your whole family and community, for that matter, in danger. If by some luck of the draw, the terrorists don't capture and kill you right away, you'll try to contact Alex—as a consequence, you'll put him in danger. At that point, it won't be the terrorists you need to fear, it will be me." His intense look told me I should believe him and I did.

Realizing there might be a problem with his plan, I said, "Wait, what will Alex say when he finds out I'm dead and that you did it? How will you explain that one?" I smirked triumphantly, thinking I'd found a hole in his plans.

"Oh , that's easy," he said, the words slid off his tongue like a snake. "I'll just tell him you missed home. Couldn't hack it and ran away. By the time I caught up to you, you were gone. You just had too big of a lead. He won't even suspect me. That, I can guarantee." The grin on his face made me feel small, very small and stupid to think he wouldn't have thought it through.

"Choose wisely," he said, slithering into his room.

The echo of the prayer I gave before going to Washington, DC flitted across my mind once more, the one where I'd begged so desperately to become a new person. This couldn't be the answer to my prayers. It hurt too much. Was this God's hand or simply a natural consequence of my actions? There were no easy answers. The tick of the clock on the wall behind me brought a desperate thought to my mind. I *could* run. I could run right now. He would never find me. Years from now, I could search for Alex and all the danger would have passed. Alex and I could be together. I looked at the door to John's room and then to the hotel door. Who was I kidding? He'd find me before I exited the building. It was almost like he could read my mind.

I couldn't let Alex go, though. I'd just gotten him back. He'd said he loved me. I'd never been loved by a boy before. Did I love him too? My breaking heart convinced me I did. The most terrible part was that John had been right. I couldn't go home without exposing myself and everyone else to danger—including Alex. I couldn't do that, it would be the epitome of selfishness. I simply couldn't justify disagreeing with John's conditions. This whole thing was a lot bigger than just me. Tears puddled on the table and burned my eyes. I moved to the couch and curled into a ball, praying once again for comfort and hope.

Warmth spread through my body and my heart thumped in that heavy way in the center of my chest that seemed to accompany my earnest prayers. I wasn't alone after all. The pain of making the decision I didn't want to make lingered, but hope softened it.

I waited, wondering who I would become, trying to bury the memories that made up my previous life until I felt a hand rest on my shoulder.

I sat up.

"Your decision?" John asked.

"I'll stay," I said, amazed at how quickly forty-five minutes had passed.

"And you agree *never* to seek out Alex or to respond to him in a positive way should he seek you out?" He emphasized the word, *never*.

"Yes." My voice seemed to flicker out before completing the "s" sound and a fresh tear dropped from my chin.

"A wise decision. The only real one you could've made. I know it hur—"

"Don't! Just don't! You've taken away my life, so until your life is taken from you, don't you dare say you know it hurts." I swatted at his chest, until my hands balled into fists, wanting to hurt him.

John pulled me close, wrapping his arms tightly around me, until I couldn't hit him any longer.

"Shhh. Shhh," he whispered in my ear, until I stopped struggling and gave in to the sobs that I could no longer hold back. A deep ache spread through my body as I realized the horror of my situation. Somehow I had to learn to trust my life to the very man who had threatened to take it—the same man who had tortured but now consoled me. I finally pulled myself together and pulled away from John.

Fear mixed with anger as I thought about having to work with this pompous man.

"Life is difficult enough without adding the complications you have to yours. I *am* sorry about that, but it's time to move on. From this moment on, you are Michele. You will forget everything about who you were: your family, friends, Alex and DC. Christy is officially erased," John said, his words scraping against my ears.

He sat me on the couch and pulled a chair in front of me. "I have created the ideal life for you, Michele." He said it like it was no big deal. "All the details aren't fleshed out, yet, but I have the basic outline." He grinned, and I could tell this was exciting to him. "You'll have to wait until tomorrow when I'm done with your complete profile to fill you in, but we can get started now, with you watching what's on ESPN." He clicked the TV on and flipped to ESPN.

ESPN? Was he kidding? A basketball game was on.

"Watch this game. Pay attention to what the announcers have to say. Watch and learn." He hopped up and walked to his room, a spring in his step. I stared blankly at the TV screen, my thoughts riveted on the very thing I was supposed to be forgetting, my old life and Alex.

I was vaguely aware of John going into his room to talk on the phone and sitting at the table, tap tap tapping on his computer, but I couldn't focus on anything he was doing. I felt like I was in a fog. Lunch came and went. I wasn't interested. I knew basketball games were being played on the TV, but somehow nothing seeped into my brain. I might as well have been staring at a blank wall.

John brought me dinner, clearing away my uneaten lunch from the coffee table and setting roast beef, vegetables, and a roll in their place. "I suggest you eat your dinner. Tomorrow will be very physically challenging and you'll need the energy this food will give you."

What? Did he want me to be an athlete? Was he crazy?

I looked at the food. Even though it smelled delicious, I had to force myself to eat some of it. It tasted like cardboard. The TV now showed a bunch of ex-sportsmen discussing various baseball players, their strengths and weaknesses. Ultra-boring.

The next thing I knew, John woke me. "Why don't you go to your room? You'll be much more comfortable in there."

What did he know about comfort?

I stood up and started to fall to the side. I must've been sleeping really hard. I shifted my feet to regain my balance just as John reached out to steady me. With a hand on my arm, he guided me into my room. The bed felt wonderful. My head sunk into the pillow and I was out. Unfortunately, I kept waking up hour after hour having the same silly, yet, seemingly real, nightmare. I was in an ocean or a huge lake, and Alex swam out to me, grabbed me and kissed me. After the kiss, he mouthed he loved me just as a shark with John's face came and took him away

Chapter Ten

I was actually happy to see five a.m. on the clock and put an end to the crazy repeating dream. John had already loaded a new, white Jeep with our luggage. Without allowing me the time to take a shower, leaving me totally disheveled, we drove out of the hotel parking lot.

We picked up breakfast on the way to what John called, "Our new home for nine short weeks." We headed west on the freeway. Two hours and two motivational CD's later, my neck sore from bobbing off to sleep and jerking back awake, we turned onto a narrow road that looked like it would head up to a cabin. Sure enough, we pulled up in front of the biggest "cabin" I'd ever seen. Logs the size of Redwoods made up the exterior and a thousand windows winked down at us. At least it didn't give me a gloomy feeling.

We walked up the stone steps, the clunking sound of our shoes echoing as we entered the huge foyer. I tilted my head, marveling at the vaulted ceiling. The foyer opened up into a large gathering area with a piano, tables, chairs, sofas and fireplaces. I could see a kitchen off to the left as John led me through the gathering area and into a hall to the right of the room. He stopped and entered the third door and I followed him into the room.

"Your room," he said, swinging his left arm out to usher me in. I walked in and my jaw dropped to the floor.

Bigger than my kitchen and living room back home combined and elegantly furnished, I couldn't help but contrast this bedroom with mine in Helena. It made me wonder about the safety of my family. I turned to ask John, but he'd already gone and the door was shut. How did he do that? The king-sized four-poster bed was draped with sheer, silky fabric that felt soft between my fingers. It should have dominated the room, but instead it fit gracefully with the rest of the furnishings. There were four large windows and a set of French doors led out to a wooden deck that stretched out into the forest. I pulled on the door handle to let in fresh air, but it was locked—an official reminder that this was not my home and I was not really free.

I made my way to the bathroom. It was almost as big as the bedroom with a spa tub, glass enclosed shower, and enormous walk-in closet for two. I ran my fingers along the hundreds of varying sizes of outfits and gently touched the shoes that filled a whole wall. I sat on the cushioned bench in the middle of the room and looked at myself in the full-length mirror on the wall opposite me. I looked tired. I felt tired. I wanted a nap. I made my way to the bed, but as I pulled the curtain aside, I found some workout clothes and a note that read,

Put these on and meet me in the kitchen.

I sighed and got dressed. A new pair of Nike cross-trainers sat on the floor by the bed. I pulled on the socks that were stuffed inside them and slid the shoes on. They fit perfectly. I lifted my legs up and down, trying them out, like a soldier marching to war. Everything was a perfect fit. John was amazing-scary.

After a few deep breaths, I headed for the kitchen. It was the ultimate in modern. Everything sparkled and shined. Two glasses of water sat on the marble countertop and John motioned for me to grab one. I drank it all in two gulps.

"It's more hydrating to sip water," he said. "Lesson number one."

Lesson number one? I guessed school was in session.

I stared at the empty glass in my hand as he reached out, grabbed it and filled it once more. Giving him a nasty look, I sipped the water with exaggerated primness. He ignored the attitude.

"I still don't have *all* the details of your new life completely put together," John said, "but by tomorrow, it should be solidified. We'll start training today, however. Let's go."

"Wait. So who am I going to be? At least give me a basic outline."

"Like I said, I still don't have all the details worked out. You'll have to wait." He led me out of the kitchen to the left and down a long flight of stairs. We walked through a room with pool tables, foosball tables, ping-pong and other things that I didn't recognize. We went through some tall glass doors into a fully-equipped workout room.

I followed him to the treadmills. He punched some buttons on mine and commanded me to get on. It started out slow enough but gradually increased in speed until the display read ten minutes—our time was up. I was huffing by then, sweat dripping down my back. I was ordered off the treadmill, but not for a break. We rolled out some mats and lay on the ground to do what seemed like a thousand sit-ups, push-ups, and other exercises I'd never seen before. I was tired. We stretched and headed upstairs and out the front doors. I could feel the humidity immediately stick to my skin and I felt heavy. John started to run and said, "follow me".

I took off after him, but it was obvious before even reaching the end of the long drive that I would never catch him. I couldn't even see him. Jerk. It was just like him to leave me. I slowed down to a jog and then started to walk, trying to catch my breath.

"What are you doing?" whispered someone in my ear.

I jumped and almost fell down turning to see whose voice I'd heard. My already deep breaths took on a ragged quality from being startled. It was John. Somehow he'd gotten behind me.

"What are you doing?" I huffed.

"I thought we were going for a run, but I guess it's turned into practice for me. Practice in stealth."

"Ha, Ha. Look, I'm not a runner. I can't keep up with you."

"You've got to push yourself. Go beyond what you believe you can do."

"That's the thing," I said, "I already have." I sat on the ground and sighed.

"Hmpfh," he snorted. "It's not good enough. We'll walk today, but briskly…Now get up, or are you too weak?"

"Now get up," I mocked, standing up. He'd hit a sore spot.

I tried to catch him the whole way. I knew I'd never beat him, but I didn't want him to think he'd broken me. One day I would best him. Every now and then he'd break out into a run and yell back at me to push it. By the time we made it back to the house I was exhausted. I had to clutch the handrails to even get up the entryway steps.

John was looking in the fridge and getting out food when I made it to the kitchen. Only then did I realize how hungry I was. After stretching with John again, I ate until my stomach ached. He gave me two DVDs and told me to watch them. I was excited until I found out they were about the history of football and basketball. At the end of the second one, my eyes drooping, I felt tightness in my muscles.

I spied John at a table looking at a computer screen, so I headed for my room.

"Ah, Michele, right on time," he called after me. Did he have a connection to my brain, or what?

I turned and sighed, noting the ache in my muscles. "What?"

"Any questions?"

"No," I answered. "And look, if you are planning to turn me into some sports star, you can forget it."

"Sports star—no, but athlete, yes."

"You can't be serious."

He smiled at me.

"You do realize you are creating the opposite of what I am. Don't you think it will be a bit obvious?"

"Not opposite. Your body was made for this. You've just never tried it."

I wanted to ask what had given him that idea, but he'd turned the corner and had gone down the stairs. I followed him, each step sent a stab of pain to my muscles. My thighs screamed. We crossed through the game room again and then went into a different door next to the workout room.

This room was obviously a room made to dance in. The wooden floor gleamed and the mirror and bar stretched forever down one wall. A thin man with sharp features and bright tight clothes stood with one leg stretched out on the bar and with his body bent and one arm reaching for the opposite foot that supported him. I guess he heard our footsteps, as he came back up and brought his legs down from the bar to the floor. I had to concentrate not to laugh. With complete grace, he floated over to meet us. "I am Antonio," he said with a flourish, bowing low to the ground. Out of sheer awkward stupidity, I curtsied.

For the next two hours, Antonio pulled and stretched my body in directions I didn't know it would go. I don't know how many times he tisk tisked or shook his head at me. So, I wasn't a dancer. It wasn't news to me. His voice called after me as I left the room with John, who'd come to get me, "Practice. Practice." Was he crazy? I was too tired to practice.

John sent me to my room to shower and change for dinner. As I entered my room, I was met by a beautiful red silky dress, hanging from my bed post. It was the gala all over again. I shuddered. I stood, staring right through the dress and re-living the night that I found out my roommate had been kidnapped by the bad guys. The last few days in DC flew across my memory with lightning speed, but the pain was still sharp. I don't know how long I stood there, but I came out of my stupor when John banged on the door and said, "You ready?"

"Uh... just a minute," I called.

I ran to the shower, stripped, and took a minute express shower. At least I would smell better. I pulled my hair into a quick bun and pulled some strands down and blow dried them. I grabbed my make-up purse and laid it on my bed, then I put the dress on. Unable to ignore the tiny spaghetti straps, the low cut exposing cleavage, I shuffled through the rows of clothes for a cover-up and found one. Sure it was a size too big, but it covered me. Around my neck, I latched the beautiful necklace he'd left for me and slid my feet into the heels that waited for me on the floor. I took a peek into the swivel mirror tucked away in a corner and walked to the door, glancing at the clock on the nightstand as I grabbed my make-up bag. I had gotten ready in fifteen minutes. Whew.

After rapping lightly on the door, John stepped into the room. When his eyes lit on me, his eyebrows raised and a scowl contorted his face.

I looked in the mirror again, wondering what had caused him to scowl.

"What do you have on?"

"The dress you left me."

"Not the dress...that, that thing you put on over it."

"Oh," I said, running my fingers over the front of the shrug. "I felt uncomfortable in this dress and found this to cover up some of my skin—"

"Hello! We're in Florida. It's June first. Take it off, it looks ridiculous."

"No," I said, stomping one foot. "I refuse to be half naked. I want to be comfortable. Get me a dress that covers me and I'll wear it. Until then—"

"Take it off," he said through clenched teeth, his body leaning slightly forward.

"No." I leaned forward, too. "I want—"

At that moment he came at me with a crazy look in his eye. He pushed the shrug off my shoulders, leaving it in a heap on the floor.

"Forget who you were!" he yelled. "You are Michele and Michele wears clothes like this. Christy does not exist."

My face burned with more than anger. The way he'd pushed that shrug off left me feeling vulnerable. I fought the tears that threatened to fill my eyes.

"Now, let's go," he said, taking a step back to allow me to pass.

I bent down and grabbed the shrug, and then the make-up bag, giving him the evil eye, and stomped past him. I refused to give up this part of me. I would wear the shrug in the restaurant. He wouldn't be able to stop me once we were in public. I did not have to dress immodestly to be Michele. I'd prove it to him.

The jeep stayed in the garage this time. We took a Mercedes instead. It reminded me of the car Alex had used to pick me up at school that day, but this was even more luxurious. I used the passenger side mirror to put on my make-up, ignoring John's rolling eyes. One of Haydn's masterful classical pieces played in the background.

The restaurant was fancy. A soulful jazz piece rumbled from outside the door and to the left. John told the maître d' we were the Mattinglys. It would have been nice of him to tell me who we were going to be before going in.

"Right this way," the maître d'said, as he walked in front of us and brought us to a table. The low lighting made me feel sleepy. He pulled the chair out for me and then helped John slide his chair in, too. Immediately, a waiter came carrying wine and offering it to us.

"Yes, I'll take half a glass," John said. "What would you like Michele?"

So, I was Michele Mattingly. Interesting. "Water, please." I smiled brightly at the waiter and he nodded as he left the table.

"Well done," John said.

"What should I call you while we're here?" I asked, half mocking.

"You can call me John," he said, not skipping a beat.

I nodded.

"I will be instructing you on proper etiquette for varying circumstances over the next month. We are starting with formal dining, if you hadn't already figured that out. Now, it is important that you sit up straight and tall throughout dinner. You do not want to appear stiff, but your shoulders need to be back and your head up, hands folded nicely in your lap."

The evening digressed from there. He made me hold the fork a particular way, cut a particular way, chew a particular way and even talk in a particular way. It was tiresome—silly even. I wondered if he was being extra hard on me for putting the shrug back on after we sat at the table. At least the prime rib and potatoes were delicious.

Ready to relax when we got home, I slipped my shoes off and bounded to my room. I stopped short when I saw a leotard and funny scrunchy shoes on my bed. I turned around and found John in my doorway.

"I told you today would be physically challenging," he said, chuckling as he closed my door. I ran after him, jerking the door open and yelling, "You do it! Climb in that leotard and go for it."

His eyes turned dark and I backed up. "Enough!" he barked. "You're upset. I get it. But, here's the thing, if you want to survive, you will do what I say. Remember, Alex wanted this for you. While I'm donating my time to this cause for his sake, the others who will be helping you are not. It has taken a lot of coordination to make this work. Don't make me report to Alex that you're refusing his help."

I gulped. Alex. My heart ached at the thought. I would play nice. For Alex.

We drove about twenty minutes to a large gym. The floors were padded and springy and several trampolines stood around. John scanned the room and then walked over to what looked like an office. Before he reached it, a short, stocky man emerged and met him. John's back was to me, but as he talked to the stocky man, he turned and pointed to me. I gave a half smile. They shook hands and walked up to me.

"So, Michele, you need some tumbling skills, huh?" the stocky man said.

I nodded, but under my breath I said, "Someone thinks so."

"Well, I'm Chip. I'll be your coach for the next couple of months. I don't expect you to be perfect, but I will demand your all. Can you give me everything you've got?"

I looked at John. A mischievous smile spread across his face.

"Of course," I said, more out of spite than belief.

"Great," Chip said, "Then let's get warmed up. Take ten laps around the gym and then do ten sit-ups and push-ups." I gave a quiet sigh, and prayed I wouldn't faint from the pain.

This was going to be a long night. Yet again, two hours later, John showed up and carted me away while my coach shook his head.

"Look Michele," Chip had said. "I took it easy on you today. You're obviously not up to par."

"I appreciate it, I really do. I'm just a bit tired. I'll…"

"In order to get you where you need to be in the time frame we have, you're going to need to be on top of your game. We can't have many days like this one."

"We won't," I said. "I promise."

On the way home, I blocked out the CD John had put on and thought about being about five and marveling at all the athletes on TV during the Olympics. I had decided then and there I would be an Olympian. My dream was short lived, however, when my parents talked to me about the cost. With six children to raise, there was no way my parents could afford to have an Olympian.

I thought ruefully about my disappointment back then and how really I should have counted myself lucky. Tumbling is a lot harder and scarier than it looks.

At home, John gave me an apple with peanut butter and milk and I slid off to shower. It was ten-thirty and I was exhausted, so I climbed into bed, sinking into the mattress. On my nightstand, stood a stack of books, ten high, all about sports. A note was taped to the top one. "Read me," it said. I grabbed the one on the top, but before I'd even read the first page, I was out.

Chapter Eleven

"Buzzz."

Was it morning already? It couldn't be. I peeked at the alarm clock as I reached to punch it off. Five a.m.

I closed my eyes and was once again fast asleep until another buzz startled me awake. Lifting my arm to turn it off again sent sharp pains in each and every muscle. I cried out. "Ahh." Was I too asleep the first time I reached for it to notice the agony? I let my arm fall to the bed at the half way point. The buzzing was driving me crazy, so I tried to slide my whole body closer to the clock to make it easier. My body revolted, my muscles seizing. The pain was more intense than I'd ever experienced. I felt crippled, the buzz of the clock only making it worse. Using every ounce of will I had and screaming out in pain, I sat up and tried to punch it off. It clattered to the floor, but stopped. I sat, trembling, on the edge of the bed, looking at the shoes sitting on the floor and wondering how I would reach them in my condition. I heard a knock at the door. I didn't respond.

"Michele," John called through the door. "You up? We've got to get going."

Get going? I wasn't going anywhere. I thought for a fleeting moment that if I didn't answer, maybe he would go away. I sat in silence, staring at the door, thinking terrible thoughts about the man on the other side. I could barely move because of him.

I thought about lying back down, but knew it would hurt like the devil, so I stayed seated. If I didn't move, I didn't hurt.

I watched the knob on the door turn and John called out again, "Christy?" Seconds later he was in the room staring at me.

"Why didn't you answer me?" he asked, accusation muddling his words.

"Honestly?"

"Of course."

"I thought maybe you'd go away if I didn't answer."

"Sorry, you're stuck with me. At least for the next couple months, anyway."

I snorted and immediately regretted it when I felt pain shoot through my shrugging shoulders.

"Now, hurry up. Our schedule is just as full today as it was yesterday."

"It's not going to happen," I said, "I can't even move."

"A little sore?" he said, eyebrows raising.

"Just a little." I felt my temperature rising.

"The only way to make it better is to work out. So, get moving."

"Look! You worked me too hard!" I screamed, trying to hold my body still while screaming at the top of my lungs.

"No, you look. It's the price you need to pay." His lips formed a thin line as he bared his teeth.

"I can barely move. How do you expect me—"

"To work the acid out of your muscles you've got to work through it. I know what I'm doing," he said, through clenched teeth, as he moved toward me.

"Do you?" It had escaped my lips before I could even think it.

His eyes turned to darts.

"Listen up and listen well. I'm only here because I made my wife a promise. I will give you all the tools to be successful in your new life. I've set it all up for you. Only you can choose to take advantage of it. I couldn't care less if you succeed. In fact, to have you gone would give me one less thing I need to worry about. To see you fail would not hurt me. I've done my part." The only thing that betrayed his calm voice was the tightening and retightening of his jaw as he talked.

The silence bit down hard on me. I couldn't think of anything smart to say. He had me.

"So, I'm going downstairs to warm up and stretch, with or without you," he said in a quiet, firm voice. With that, he turned and left the room, letting the door close behind him.

Without anything to say, I screamed after him. I hated him. I'd never felt a fury like I did at that moment. I hated that I had no choice. I was a rat in a lab and would be conditioned to do as he wanted whether I liked it or not.

I looked at the workout shoes on the floor, blinking away angry, frustrated tears and wondering how I would ever get them on. Then I looked at the dresser, which might as well have been a mile away, and sighed deeply, trying to muster the courage to slide off the bed.

Just as I started to move, my door opened. A woman with severely short, fashionable black hair, olive skin and big brown eyes walked in carrying several bags in each hand. Seeing me, she stopped short, said, "Oh, sorry," and started to back up out of the room.

"No," I said, "Don't go. It's okay." Why I said it, I don't know. It just came out as if she were my friend and I wanted to hang out.

She stopped and said, "I just saw John go downstairs and assumed you were with him. I was wrong, obviously."

We stared at each other for a full minute without speaking. The funny thing was, it didn't feel weird or awkward. It felt somehow as if she were right where she should be.

She broke the silence. "You must be wondering who I am."

I nodded.

"I'm Marian, John's coordinator."

"His coordinator?" I asked, my curiosity growing.

"Yeah. You know, I coordinate everything for him…and you: clothes, shoes, food, activities."

"Wait. You're the one who got me all my clothes and stuff?"

"Uh huh."

"Huh. And I had John pegged for some wunderkind or something—able to do more than anyone else in the same amount of time…and do it right. It was creepy." A strange relief washed over me.

"Well, some might say he is, but as far as clothes and food and stuff goes, while you're here, I'm in charge of that."

"Did you tuck me in last night, too?"

"Yes."

"Whew!"

She laughed, put the bags down on the floor and said, "I'll leave while you get ready. I know how John gets when he has to wait."

"No, wait," I said, grasping at straws. "Uh, could you, I mean, I know you're not my servant or anything, but could you possibly get me some workout clothes from the dresser?" I looked over longingly.

She wrinkled her eyes, but then said, "Sure." She walked over and pulled out a top, shorts and socks and then laid them on the bed next to me.

"Thanks!" I said, "You don't know how much I appreciate it."

She started toward the door and I reached for the clothes, gasping with pain. She stopped and looked at me.

"Yesterday was too much for you, wasn't it?"

"Let's just say my body doesn't like the attention it had yesterday."

"I wondered about that. Leave it to John to push you past your limits."

"Hmpf."

She walked over and picked up my shoes, setting them on the bed and grabbing my socks. She then knelt down and pulled them onto my feet. I couldn't let my pride get in the way of getting dressed.

I'm sure she saved me a ton of pain and I was thankful, but it still felt like someone was scraping knives along my muscles. Marian even helped me down from the bed. She was wonderful. She worked with John on a daily basis and she hadn't turned nasty like him. I would be like her and not let his nastiness rub off on me. I wouldn't give him that power. I left her in my room and had to face the long road to the stairs. How would I get down them?

The first step down felt as though knives were jabbing, mercilessly into my muscles. I had to cry out with each step. At the sixth step, John appeared at the bottom and started up. He looked at his watch and said, "Time to water up and then run," as he passed me. I wanted to rip his head off but knew it was impossible. With much regret, I turned and headed up. Again I yelled out with each step, fire licking my muscles. I pushed harder. I couldn't let him get the better of me. It was bad enough that he could undoubtedly hear every scream and moan that came from my mouth, but to give in—no way.

I made it to the kitchen in what seemed good time, but John was standing there, his empty glass in the sink, waiting. My water sat on the counter and I picked it up, using every ounce of self control I had left to stifle a gasp. I drank slowly as he talked to me.

"I came by your room to brief you on your new life last night, but you were asleep. So, I recorded it for you on this iPod. You can listen to it while we run or walk or drag or whatever it is you are going to do today." He tilted his head to the side, narrowed his eyes, and gave a mocking snort as he set the iPod and earphones in front of me on the counter. "Oh, and I'll leave a trail for you to follow. Keep your eyes and brain alert and maybe you'll see it."

He headed out the front door. "And maybe you'll see it," I said, repeating his nasty tone. I wanted the trail to be as fresh as possible for some silly reason—as if it would make it easier to follow. He already admitted he wanted me to fail. I was sure the trail wouldn't be easy to follow or find, so I chugged the last of the water, put the earphones in, slipped the iPod in my sports bra, and pushed play as I started off toward the front door, cringing with each step.

John's voice filled my head. I grimaced. Great. I'd never be rid of him.

"Welcome to your new life, Michele. You are a seventeen-year-old senior at Niceville High. You were born in California on January 5th. You are an only child of very career-oriented parents. They are both CEO's of their respective companies and are constantly away on business. You were raised by a nanny, Ms. Katy. You are an average student and an average cheerleader."

My mind ground to a halt after the last two statements. Average? Cheerleader? Was he insane? I'd been harassed my whole life by average, underachieving cheerleaders. The fact that I'd only realized it a few shorts months ago added salt to my wounds, and now I was supposed to become one of them? Not a chance. My superior intellect was the only thing that was mine and I wasn't about to give it up.

I don't know how long I walked without hearing a word on the iPod, but then I stepped in a hole, jarring myself awake with pain. John's irritating voice droned on and I took the earphones out, letting them dangle halfway down my chest. My mind went to work on my next challenge: how to debate John about my "new life." A mass of silver and blue to my left caught my attention. Pom-poms. Cheerleaders' pom-poms in a tree. "Very funny," I murmured. John had marked the path, but it wasn't cryptic at all, it was a taunt. After turning left, I ran into a cheer skirt, shoes, socks, and then bows, all marking the path that led me back to the cabin.

Lunch was laid out on the counter with a note next to it. It was from John.

You must've made it back or you wouldn't be reading this. I'm surprised you didn't miss the clues. You're definitely not average.

My breathing was hard and my face grew hot reading the note. It continued,

Stretch and then eat lunch while you watch and learn from some video footage.

Where was he? I still wanted to scratch his eyes out. He loved taunting me. That's when I realized I hadn't been in agony for a while. I was so concentrated on showing John up, that I hadn't noticed my sore muscles since taking my earphones out.

I stretched and ate my lunch standing, watching high school cheer videos, while I moved about, hoping to prevent the acid in my muscles from settling again. At the end of the video, I headed to the kitchen to look for John. I was ready to set him straight about the average cheerleader thing. Like he could read my mind, he walked into the room.

"All right," he said. "It's time to— "

"Okay. Enough is enough. You know as well as I do that being an average cheerleader is not going to work for me. I can't cheer, and I certainly can't be average." I couldn't help but lean toward him as I spoke, daring him to challenge me.

In a calm, steady voice, devoid of emotion, he said, "I have provided you with a new identity. You can choose to embrace it and survive or choose to roll the dice and be whoever your little heart desires."

I hated it when he trapped me. I didn't have the time or the resources to change my identity by myself. It wasn't like I was changing who I was on the inside. I would only be acting the part, right? I could do that. I could act just like I did in a debate when I didn't agree with the side I was told to argue for. I wouldn't be like the shallow cheerleaders I knew, who didn't care about anyone but themselves. I would be a new breed of caring cheerleader. Maybe I could get the other girls to follow me. I could lead for a change. Could that be possible? John made me believe anything was possible. I would let him see it was possible, just with my own twist. I would have to complete his impossible challenge.

Luckily, my teachers showed mercy on me that day, avoiding jumps and focusing on stretching and smooth movements. The day dragged on and on. John quizzed me at dinner on what I liked to call "snob" etiquette, forcing me to remain quite still, allowing the lactic acid to take advantage and settle in my muscles again.

Tumbling was a disaster. I couldn't keep my promise from yesterday. Coach didn't care about any pain I might have felt. He wanted results. My muscles were squashed, pinched, and stabbed with each move he forced me to make. Of course, I was only a beginner, so the danger factor was low that day.

The classical music that John put on for the ride home made me want to sleep, but I forced myself to move around as much as possible to keep from getting sore again.

I stared at my bed after getting home, debating whether or not I could stay awake and read from the stack of books on my nightstand. Deciding against it, I climbed in and fell asleep straight away.

By the end of the first week, with the soreness from my mega-workouts gone and me actually feeling good with the routine schedule, even a bit powerful, I started mastering the little things in all my lessons.

The only break in the monotony was Saturdays, when we met up with a driver's ed. teacher and then did service projects somewhere in the area with different groups of teens. The first Saturday, John listened in on my conversations as I worked alongside a hundred or so teens fixing a well-used hiking trail. He quickly discovered the depth of my nerdiness and immediately started me on some "cool training" everyday. He wanted me to attract others, not send them running away by talking about the stupidest stuff on the planet, like the names of all the different types of rocks in gravel. By the time that first service project ended, I had a six foot barrier between me and anyone else. I'd successfully alienated every youth there.

I could never hide my excitement about driver's ed. every Saturday. I couldn't believe I'd have my license in five short weeks! Sure, the classes were a big bore, but I could drive!
For that first class, my instructor had me look over the driver's handbook, which I couldn't help but quickly memorize and after a very simple test, I had my driver's permit. Now, John would have to let me drive everywhere so that I could have enough practice hours to get my license.

Walking out to the car to drive for the first time, looking at the driver's permit with my "fake" birthday printed on it, I realized that I had missed my birthday. In fact, it had been two days ago. I hadn't paid much attention to dates since getting to the cabin and hadn't even realized I'd missed it. My real sixteenth birthday. The birthday I'd been waiting for my whole life and I'd missed it. How was that possible? I looked at my driver's permit. Michele Mattingly. January fifth glared up at me as my date of birth. I was already seventeen, almost eighteen according to the plastic card. I really had skipped over my sixteenth birthday.

Chapter Twelve

A hole seemed to open in my chest and I found it hard to breathe thinking about missing my real sixteenth birthday. I leaned on the car door, trying to catch my breath and stop this alternate world from spinning. I no longer knew who I was and what I was doing. The world went silent and the next thing I knew, I was in the back seat of John's car, with John patting my cheeks saying, "Michele. Michele."

"Huu?" I said, trying to sit up, but finding my head hurt when I moved, I stayed put.

"Just stay still," John said, pulling out supplies from a first aid kit. "What happened to you out there?"

"Uh," I had to think. What had happened? The memory was strange, like a slow motion movie. "My birthday was Thursday and I'm sixteen now, but really I'm almost eighteen and…and I'll never be sixteen and never have a sweet sixteen birthday party or get to go on a first date or be sweet-sixteen-and-never-been-kissed again or…"

"What are you talking about?" John interrupted. He dabbed at my forehead, and it suddenly donned on me I was hurt! I reached up to feel my forehead, but he pushed my hand away. "Cut it out. I'm cleaning that. What's this about sweet-sixteen-and-never-been-kissed?" He eyed me with a look that said that was impossible anyway. "You kissed my son before you were sixteen."

He was right, of course, but it was still a huge letdown to never celebrate turning sixteen the way I'd imagined I would for so many years.

"I don't know, I guess I just..."

"You just what?" he asked, as he put a band-aid over the scrape. "Remember, you are Michele. That other person you think just had a birthday, doesn't exist."

I do too!

I wanted to yell it, but knew it would be a waste of my time. He wouldn't understand. He had told me to forget Christy Hadden and I almost had. It shocked me. Should I really forget that I was ever Christy? Was it possible to truly forget?

Forgetting, at least superficially, became easier as I poured myself into my training. I noticed how my muscles were already harder, tighter, and it had only been a few weeks. It seemed John's favorite form of torture was running. We ran for hours. He always had me listen to something while running— more indoctrination and training. I never had any peace, until one Sunday about three weeks into my training.

After changing into my workout clothes and meeting John at our starting point, I waited expectantly for whatever programming he would be delivering me that day. But John just took off running, leaving me with my thoughts.

At first, I focused on my surroundings, how beautiful they were, how different they were from home. Contrasting home with Florida had me quickly reminiscing. I pictured each detail of my house, my parents, my brothers and sisters, even school. Amazed at how clear everything appeared to be, I pushed my thoughts further— to less familiar parts of Helena, Montana.

I was with Alex at the lake all over again. I kept repeating each moment I'd spent with him, over and over in my mind. It was like I was on auto-pilot, running through the trees, my memories overlaying themselves on my present path without blocking it out. Before I knew it, John had stopped. We stood at the top of a small hill, which had an amazing overlook of the area where we lived.

"So, what did you think about while we ran?" he asked.

"I don't know."

"Yes, you do."

I looked away, afraid he really could read my mind.

"Tell me," he persisted.

I was silent, afraid he knew I had been breaking the rules and thinking of home.

"No, no," he cried. "Why? Why would you think of a past that is gone?" Frustration lined his voice.

I swear he could read my mind. "Why do you think I was thinking about my past?"

"Your silence tells me everything." He looked angry.

"Look. I can't forget sixteen years of my life just like that. I need *some* time."

"Yes, you can. And you must," he said, his voice stern and unyielding. "You are in control of your mind. You and you alone decide what plays on its stage."

"That may be true in theory, but in the real world—"

"No, it's not only true in theory. You have the power to control your thoughts. The thoughts you allow to stay in your mind create you. What do I have to do to convince you of that fact?"

He really believed what he'd said, but I wasn't sure if I did. You are what you think? Interesting concept.

"If you give it a chance, you'll see that what I say is true." He huffed and stared me down. "You *need* to be able to control your thoughts. On the run back to the cabin, I want you to block out any thoughts from your past. If one pops into your mind, banish it. Think of something else. Exercise this skill all the way home. See if you can block each errant thought."

After talking with him, my chest burned as I pondered the idea of directing my thoughts, and I suddenly didn't have any doubt that I'd be able to direct them. That is, until I tried it. Something inside me wanted me to remember—wanted me never to forget. Painful things as well as joyful things jeered at me, daring me to try to forget them as I ran to the cabin.

John beat me back to the cabin, of course, and had lunch set out on the table when I walked into the kitchen. I leaned on the counter, stretching my calves as John started to talk.

"Hopefully, that little exercise showed you that you can control your thoughts if you try. I need you to see thoughts can be powerful and recognize exactly what makes them powerful. Emotion fixes thoughts, but you can trick your emotions."

"I think I might be getting it, but it's hard."

"It is until you learn how your brain works. You can train your mind to attach a different emotion to an event from what was truly there. For example, fear is a powerful emotion. It keeps people from doing many things, but you can still change your response. Take the fear of spiders. It can make some people so afraid that they become catatonic. But, if those same people learned how to deal with that fear, their thoughts surrounding spiders can become so altered, they are no longer fearful. They've now *controlled* the emotion. That can only happen if they manipulate the emotion attached to the object. People do it all the time, really."

He had a point. "But what if I don't want to lose a memory?" I said.

"Deep rooted emotion mixed with memory is hard to delete, but possible," he said. "It all comes down to desire, doesn't it?"

He had me spend the rest of the evening on the computer, studying mind and thought control. It felt good to do research again.

The next day, I found a nice outfit lying at the foot of my bed when I woke up. It was still weird to have someone come in while I slept, but I trusted Marian even though I'd only known her for a short time. No workout clothes. It felt nice to put real clothes on to start the day. John was waiting for me in the kitchen as usual, but he had normal clothes on, too. What were we going to do today?

We drove into the city and parked in front of an elegant looking business called Mercury. Music played softly in the background of the immaculate lobby. The air smelled fresh and clean and the lights were low. Big leather couches and sleek chairs begged me to sit on them.

"Michele?" A lady with an extreme hairstyle and the wildest clothes I'd ever seen looked me up and down from behind a counter.

"Yes," I said.

"I'll see you later," John said to me. "You're in excellent hands."

"Come right this way," the wild receptionist said, in a smoky, soothing voice. We walked into a large room where I met Egor.

His name wasn't the only thing about him out of the ordinary. He must have been six feet tall, with hair blacker than anything I'd ever seen, the last half inch of which was tipped in bright red. His clothes were tight on his extremely thin body, and perfectly pressed. His shoes gleamed.

"Oh my, oh my, oh my," he squealed. "A blank canvas indeed. He wasn't kidding was he?" he asked the receptionist.

"I think not."

"Well, we'd better get started immediately if we're going to pull this off in the time he's given us." He had me follow him into another room and then directed me to a chair, snapped a cape around me and said, "Yes, Yes, we'll have to do that and possibly that, hmm."

I had to look around to make sure we were alone. I wasn't sure who he was talking to, or thought he was talking to. He walked backwards away from me, having a conversation with himself until he disappeared around a corner.

The whole experience since walking through the door to this business had been so surreal, that it only then occurred to me it was a salon. But, who was this guy and what was he going to do to me? It all seemed so serious. This could be bad. Would I walk out of here with some wild look?

He came back after about ten minutes with two ladies and carrying some bowls. They were talking about colors, and a bunch of stuff I didn't understand. Egor stood behind me and tugged and pulled at my hair. One of the ladies worked on my fingernails and the other my toenails. It didn't feel good. I couldn't wait for them to finish. After my hair was colored, Egor washed it and cut it. That's when the real fun began. Another guy, called Manis, came in and helped Egor put extensions in my hair. It hurt, but in the end, I had a full, thick head of light brown hair with shiny, yellow-blonde highlights that draped to my mid-back. I had to admit it looked amazing.

During two of the five hours it took to weave in the extensions, a lady named Marissa gave me lessons on skin tones and structure as well as how to apply make-up for varying activities. She did my make-up for me and then took it off, put it back on me and took it off again. Then she told me to give it a try. She taught me three different ways to do it to accomplish three totally different looks. She was patient and persistent. And I learned a ton.

When they were done, everyone who'd worked on me met John in the reception area to see his response. It was impossible for him to hide his pleasure. "Remarkable," he said in amazement. I felt like I was on a make-over reality show.

Egor actually cried. John complimented all of them profusely, and then we left with huge bags of hair-products, make-up, and written instructions. John must've been feeling good, because he let me drive to our next destination. Lunch. I could feel his eyes on me the whole time. After lunch, we drove home and it was work as usual in the afternoon.

The next morning, I again found regular clothes at the foot of my bed. After breakfast, John had me drive back to the same town as yesterday, and I spent three hours learning all about color wheels, bone structure, body shapes, skin tones, and how to dress to kill with what God had given me.

My instructor, Priscilla, took me window shopping for a few more hours to show me examples of what worked with my body and what didn't. The next day she took me shopping for real and tested me. She had me shopping in stores where nothing had price tags. Talk about stressful. When the cashier rang up the bill, all I could think about was how big a waste it was to spend that much money when I could get similar things at Wal-Mart and save a ton. It did, somehow, make me feel more important walking around in those clothes. In a way, I hated that fact. Why did clothes play such a huge roll in how I felt about myself? Did clothes have this same effect on everyone?

I awoke to workout clothes at the foot of my bed that Friday, a month into my training. A bit disappointed, I trudged into the kitchen for my drink of water. John and I were back to the regular routine—that is until after lunch.

"You up for some research?" John asked.

"Always," I said, feeling my lips curve into a big smile.

"Great," he said, handing me a stack of DVDs. Glancing at their titles, I realized he was having me watch the silliest pop culture movies and he expected me to treat them as serious study? He told me to try to understand the humor and memorize some of the sayings in them. Apparently they were movies that anyone who was anyone had seen and could talk about. I found them rude, disrespectful and often disgusting, not to mention, my parents would have freaked if they'd known. But, I didn't exist to those parents anymore, so they couldn't care. I cared, but that didn't matter, since I wasn't me.

I tried to put these types of thoughts out of my head, willing myself to do as John had said and exercise power over my own mind. I tried to imagine myself as Michele—the popular, athletic cheerleader I was becoming. She would enjoy these movies. She'd laugh and probably talk about them with all her friends. All her friends. This encouraging thought helped me pop yet another DVD into the player and settle in to take notes. I watched for about an hour, concentrating hard and trying to laugh at the appropriate parts. This was hurting my brain. I sighed and leaned forward to grab another handful of popcorn. At least I was allowed that little concession. Noticing my thoughts straying to the ratio of butter to salt, I willed my brain to concentrate on the film.

Suddenly, with a nearly silent whoosh of air, a cloth bag came down over my head. I screamed and reached out with my hands. Someone grabbed them, forcing them behind me and tying them together. My legs suffered the same fate. I bent my legs at the knees and kicked out as someone hard and muscular, who had to be male, hefted me over his shoulder, held my legs close to his chest and carried me away. The man laid me somewhat gently onto the floor of something. My insides raced, and I kicked out before hearing doors click shut. I screamed and thrashed about; but had a strange feeling that no one was there to witness it, so I rolled onto my side and curled up into a ball. Then I heard and felt three car doors shut and then the car I had apparently been stuffed into drove away—with me in it.

This didn't feel anything like my abduction in Montana. These people were too gentle—too devoid of anger. It had to be different men this time. Iceman couldn't be involved. It must be one of those competing factions John talked about. Their gentleness set them apart.

How had they gotten past John? If John couldn't protect me in his own safe-house, no one could. This was the end, then. It was strange, but an odd peace settled over me as I thought about dying. Maybe it wouldn't be so bad. I didn't have a family to miss me anymore, no Alex, no home. All I'd learned about the after-life was beautiful and good. What tied me to this life anyway? I would never be safe again and didn't want to live constantly on guard.

But what if these people intended to use me to become more powerful, like John had said? *That* I definitely couldn't allow. I had to escape or find a way to get them to dispose of me. I started to scream.

The car came to a stop after a few minutes. Great. I'd gotten their attention. My whole body shook. I didn't know how much longer my voice would hold out anyway. I made myself ready to strike, to find a way to escape. The door opened and I kicked in the direction of the sound, over and over, never meeting anything solid. Someone grabbed my legs and then a familiar voice sounded in my ears, "Calm down. You're safe."

It was John's voice.

"Sit."

I felt him sawing at the ropes on my legs while he talked to another man.

"Nothing? Absolutely nothing?"

"It was the easiest abduction ever. Really," a different male voice answered.

John sighed loud and long as he cut my hands free and lifted the hood off me. I closed my eyes tight against the bright sunlight. Blinking away dark spots, I finally saw John standing before me.

"Let's go." He acted bored; he turned and walked away.

Let's go? That was it? Someone had taken me under his supposedly watchful eye and he gave me no—I'm-sorry-I-didn't-protect-you or How-did-it-happen? No questions at all. Only "Let's go."

"Wait! What just happened here?" I held onto the side of the van and saw John headed for his car. My gut ached. "I thought—"

"Just get in the car," he yelled back.

I headed for the driver's side. It had become a habit. He was talking to some men who climbed into the van and drove away.

"No, no, no. I'm driving." And he climbed into the car.

John must've sighed twenty times before he spoke. His words rushed out like a flood. "You barely even struggled? *You had no idea they were there*?"

I just stared, not sure what he wanted from me.

"They stood behind you for five minutes, Michele, moving about, just to test you, and you didn't even sense them."

This was a test? A lousy test?

"Look, John," I said. "I was watching that stupid movie, concentrating, trying to understand why it was considered funny and trying to memorize the 'especially funny' lines. I had to concentrate. You should've warned me this could happen."

"Don't be so dramatic, Michele. You—"

"Dramatic?" I could hardly keep my voice low. "I thought one of those competing factions you told me about had kidnapped me. I wasn't about to let them use me to get the power they wanted. I was planning my death. So, don't lecture me about being dramatic. What do I have to live for anyway?"

Chapter Thirteen

The rest of the day, while going through my regular routine, I thought about why I hadn't sensed the abductors' presence. John had thought I should have felt something when they snuck in. Was there something wrong with me? Almost every day he had me look for "places of safety" or places I could find that were in plain sight where it would be hard for others to find me. I needed to learn how to escape and then hide without blowing my cover. He'd also taught me codes to use to identify myself with people in the Witness Protection Program, but he'd never taught me about feeling things going on around me. It wasn't until after tumbling practice that John sat me down, with chips and salsa—a gesture of peace maybe— in the living room to talk.

We talked about meditating and how and why it was done and how it would help me sense what was going on around me and anticipate what was to come. After the chips and salsa were gone, he had me practice going inward and feeling only myself—not letting anything distract me. Not easy.

After that, he wanted me to practice every chance I got. He assured me that I could learn to "sense" others around me. He took me to parks, malls, neighborhoods as well as other public places to practice. Some were busy, some not. My most memorable experience was when he put me in an old, spooky cemetery, with huge, crumbling gravestones and tall, towering trees, and expected me, without looking, to identify all the sounds that I heard, being as specific as possible. A deer walking on grass, a squirrel burrowing in a nest, a bird—to be more specific, a blue jay—calling out a song, a person wiping his hands on jeans, a backhoe digging a hole for its newest guest.

My schedule during the week remained annoyingly the same for another two weeks. Wake at five, stretch, run, lift, dance, eat, watch silly movies or read silly books, (which were actually starting to grow on me), martial arts, dance, eat at some fancy place, practice proper eating technique at meals and how and what to say in specific situations, and then tumble like crazy on mats.

At least Saturdays and Sundays had some variation. At the end of five weeks, I'd earned my driver's license and since I didn't have that class anymore, he added meditation to the Saturday rotation. I had to be able to sense abductions.

Afterwards, I continued to participate in different service projects. I met all kinds of kids my age, and John had me practice my "social skills" with them. Though I never saw any one group of kids more than once, I was growing more confident that I could at least hold a conversation with my peers without sounding like a dork or having them move away from me at the first chance they got.

Finally, after spending hours and hours with John on Sundays, and facing raid after raid day and night, I started to get it. The turning point seemed to be the day I almost got abducted on a run. John had me listening to recordings of different birds, their sounds, habits and appearance. When John ran far ahead, I didn't think anything of it. He often did that, trying to tempt me into over-doing it. I'd discovered that a chill seemed to settle at the base of my neck right before an attack.

Not one attack had come while I conditioned with John. I'd decided he didn't want me to miss one moment of that kind of torture. That's why I was shocked when I felt the chill. I immediately pulled an ear bud out of one of my ears, but was careful not to change my course at first. An unfamiliar sound hit my ears, a buzzing, a swish, or a scratch that didn't fit the sounds of the natural space or what I was used to hearing while here. I took off and then hid on the other side of some dense bushes by a large tree. After that, I was successful in avoiding three of the next five abduction attempts.

About my sixth week, John introduced me to a backpack, one he said was similar to one he would have tailored to me when I finished my training. It had all kinds of outdoor equipment as well as small, handy things like safety pins, tape, pencils, a pad of paper, a pen, and a compass in it. He said It would be fun to see what specific things would be in mine about a month from now.

I sat for six excruciatingly long hours meditating with John in the July heat once. I learned a tiny bit of patience and concentration. I thought I had good concentration before that. Martial arts had not only helped me be successful with that, but also with so many other things, including how to disable and kill an abductor. The disabling part had help me get away from my abductors a few times, but I hoped I'd never have to use the killing part.

I enjoyed learning everything I was taught. It was all so incredible. I watched a six-pack develop on my belly. It was awesome.

John seemed to be pleased with my "cool-training" and liked what he heard from my Saturday outings with other teens. Kids even started approaching me.

Gymnastics didn't come as easy. It required more than my mind to conquer the skills. It took me the full first two weeks after I arrived at the cabin to get my back-handsprings down. I had pressed my body against the wall, using my hands and bending backwards, I went into one backbend after the other, over and over, planting my heels closer and closer each day until I couldn't possibly get any nearer the wall.

After that, I did walk-overs on the mat until I could do them, one after the other, the entire length of the mat—at least one hundred feet. Then, Chris, my tumbling coach, had me springing back on the springiest mat, his forearm behind my lower back and his other hand on my leg to get my back handspring. He slowly let go of my leg and I was flipping over on my own. Two days later, I had it by myself. Once I mastered three in a row on that mat, I could do them endlessly.

We moved onto harder skills like the tuck. Coach Chris couldn't believe it when I hit it time after time after only one week of practicing it daily.

"Your progress is really remarkable, Michele. You learn so quickly. I'm going to have to attribute it to your high level of fitness. It has definitely made your learning curve small."

I gave him a high five.

"I've worked out a tumbling pass for you," Coach said. "I choreographed this to play to your strengths and really make you stand out at try-outs. It is difficult. But, I believe in you."

It was almost impossible not to believe in myself with Coach Chris around. My jumps looked good, my tricks were getting more and more solid, and after almost two months of daily gymnastic training, I could actually say I loved it—and was good at it. I wasn't naturally good. I had to fight for each trick, jump, tumble and dance move.

Coach pulled me to the side just as I arrived at the gym one day and said, "I think you're ready to learn about judging. You've accomplished a lot in the last two months. I've set up a mock try-out for you during the first thirty minutes of class. The judges should be getting here any minute."

My stomach lurched in a way I'd never felt before, like a lion was caught in there and just hit into the side, trying to escape. "But, I'm not ready." I tugged on my too-tight leo.

"That's what we're about to see. Now, go warm up."

Three women sat as judges at a table just off the mat. The red head at the end did all the talking and handed me a paper number and a safety pin.

"We'd like to see your cheer first, your dance second, your tumbling pass third, and your jumps last."

"Okay," I said, pinning the number on my leo and walking to the middle of the floor and wishing they'd wanted the jumps first. It was where I was weakest. Pausing for a moment, my back to the judges, I took a deep breath, then turned and focused, trying to tell myself they weren't there. They didn't matter. But they did. I missed my mark twice in the dance, fell six times during my tumbling pass, barely got off the ground with my jumps and forgot a whole section of my cheer. Disaster. Coach and John didn't even look at my score cards. The cards flew into the trash and coach was relentless for the rest of class.

The next day, once again, three judges showed up. Different ones this time. Great. Coach pulled me aside after I'd pinned on my number and told me it was just my nerves, that I had to calm down. I wondered if I'd ever be able to control them. Still nervous, I did make mistakes but not nearly as many as the day before. By the end of that week, I was used to being judged and had a bit of fun with it.

The next week at tumbling practice, a woman came and taught me a dance and cheer routine in just a few hours. Coach had told me that at the real tryouts I would learn a dance and a cheer that I'd have to perform right away. I practiced with my coach for another hour, and again, new judges appeared. I had to perform the new dance and cheer for them. I wasn't up to the task. How could I learn everything so quickly? That whole week, including Saturday and Sunday, I had to learn a cheer and dance and then be judged. I figured it out by the end of the week and scored quite high. The judges didn't even bother me anymore.

"You've still got room for improvement," coach said after I earned my highest scores yet.

"I can't imagine being any better. I hit everything as best I could," I said

"Well, if you tell yourself that, then it's true. So, don't."

I shook my head and went back to work.

I kept telling myself that the judges who came to critique me every day always loved my signature tumbling pass and that would set me apart like coach had said it would. I trusted him. But would I be good enough to make the team?

When I walked into the kitchen the following Monday morning, I knew something was up. Marian stood in the foyer with a man I'd never seen before, surrounded by a stack of luggage. I drank my water and looked around for John. He wasn't there. I checked out the workout clothes I had on. My cross-trainers had blue and silver shoelaces, I wore bumkins—tight underwear used in cheer—under my shorts that said, "I Love Cheer!" and a top with a stick figure jumping in the air holding pom poms. Somehow, it was classy, not cheesy.

The man, who had been standing with Marian, stood only feet from me.

"Tryouts start today," he said.

"What?" I asked.

"Tryouts are today."

"Who are you?" I asked, not wanting to sound rude, but failing miserably.

"Seriously, Michele," he said in his unfamiliar voice. "It's me, John."

I took a closer look. I never would have known. "Wow."

"Let's go."

I watched him head out the front door, still amazed at his transformation. After our trip to Florida and watching him change into several different disguises, and disguising me, I shouldn't have been so awed, but I couldn't help it. He was so good at it.

Once in the car I said, "Thanks for the heads-up."

"Would you have done anything different the last few days—besides worry—had you known?"

He had a point, but I wanted to be difficult, so I said, "Maybe."

He snorted, dismissing my poor attempt to deceive him. "You're ready. Your two and a half months of effort are about to pay off.

The back of the Jeep was filled with luggage, which I assumed contained everything I needed.

"Yes," John said, seeming to read my thoughts. "Marian put together everything you'll need for the next three days."

"Three days? Try-outs last three days?" I asked, stunned.

"Basically, yes. One day to learn the cheer and dance. One day to actually try-out, and one day for the new squad sleepover."

When he said the last part about the new squad sleep-over, it hit me—he thought I would make the team. I got butterflies thinking about it.

"So, you think I'll make the team?"

"I know you'll make the team—that is, unless you totally screw up. Which you won't."

I wanted to goad him a bit about my progress; but I could feel how painful it was for him to tell me I'd make it, so I held my tongue.

"After all," John said. "I designed a fool-proof training program for this. You'll be fine."

My fists balled at my sides and my whole body shook, wanting to go at him. A sickness hit my gut, like I'd been out to sea too long. How could he be so arrogant? He had to see his "design" succeed. I didn't want to be his design. I turned away and stuck my tongue out at the window, mocking him. The idea of him thinking he owned me made me feel all jittery. The only consolation I had was that he was torn with my success. I tried to focus on that and how proud Alex would be of me. I knew he wanted me to be great. He was the one that had gotten his mom to make his dad train me. I held on to the hope that Alex was cheering for me. Besides, I was the one doing all the work. I had created myself.

For the two hour drive west to Niceville, Florida, we listened and discussed a CD about why it was important for people to remember me in certain circumstances and what to do to be remembered. We'd done this with similar CDs before, but John hit it hard today because he expected me to make a splash at tryouts.

"You have to make them remember you the first time they meet you," he'd lectured. "You have to stand out—be memorable."

I thought I was ready, but walking into the Niceville High School gym, where fifty girls waited on the bleachers for the try-outs to start, I felt my nerves kick in and wondered if I could do it. It was easy to pick out the important players—who I needed to talk to—but could I? The last thing I wanted to do was to work the room and be remembered. What if I was an utter failure? It had all been theory up until this moment.

Then I remembered the debates and academic competitions I'd been in. I had worked the room then without even knowing that's what I was doing. I just sensed it was the right thing to do. I even did it naturally with teachers every day. No one had to tell me to do it.

More and more girls and parents filed past me. John, still in disguise, looked at me, bobbing his head toward the coach and the other girls who were obviously the captain and co-captain from last year. I smoothed the paper number I'd just pinned to my shirt, took a deep breath, and introduced myself to the coach, shaking her hand. With the first contact down, now I had to walk away and then come back, with an, "Oh, I forgot to ask…" question to be memorable. Surprisingly, it wasn't that hard. I just told myself I was an actor, playing a part. I joined John, taking a mental note that about one-hundred girls were competing for about thirty spots. This would be more difficult than I'd expected.

"Welcome to cheer try-outs," last year's captain yelled out. The room fell silent. "I'm Lillian and I'm going to give you a run-down of today's schedule."

We started with warm-ups. I felt silly. Me—a cheerleader? This was crazy. These girls were amazing. What if I didn't make it? I stole a glance at John. He smiled at me. I had to make it. He'd never let me live it down if I didn't.

Actor. Actor. You're an actor. I told myself.

I got in a great practice tumbling pass before we split into four groups to learn the assigned dance and cheer, which raised my confidence. The last two weeks I'd done this very thing every day. It seemed easy. My body had been trained to learn quickly. "Practice makes perfect" holds true with our bodies and minds. My body knew how to do this.

I thanked the coach and cheer captain, again, hoping to be remembered, before leaving for a nice lunch at Merlin's Pizzeria in Destin.. An hour later, after lunch, John drove me to a gym, where Coach Chris waited, with tapes of the girls, the dance, and the cheer. How had he gotten them? Did John somehow tape the whole thing while he sat there? We discussed everything. I showed him what I remembered of the dance and cheer and then we went to work. For four hours we went over every detail until I could do it perfectly. After dinner, nothing was more inviting to me than my hotel bed.

After a few hours of going through the routine at the gym the next morning, we drove back to Niceville High. We were an hour early. Fifteen minutes later, the captain and co-captain showed up, tried the door, discovered it was locked and sat down on the steps to chat.

"Go work it, now," John said, eyes wide.

I climbed out with my bag, unsure what I would say to these girls. I came from behind them and overheard them talking about a popular cheer movie John had made me watch. A ridiculous, silly, cheer movie, filled with teammates sabotaging each other and gratuitous sex. But, I knew the movie and I knew the scene they were talking about, so, taking a few steps around them, I said, "Yeah, well if cheerleading was easy, they'd call it football." They both laughed and they were laughing with me, not at me. I couldn't believe it! Cheerleaders were laughing *with* me, not *at* me. All that coaching from John and spending so many hours on Saturdays and Sundays with kids my age had really helped. We laughed about a few other scenes, and then the coach walked up.

"You're here early," she said. "You're the girl with the unique tumbling pass."

I'd done it. She'd remembered me. Now, I couldn't mess it up.

"Michele," I said. "Yeah, I was hoping to work off some of my nerves by getting here early."

"Good idea. Maybe you can help Lillian and Beth get the mats out."

"Sure," they both said at the same time.

I couldn't help grinning. While I practiced, they even played the music for the dance a couple of times, cheering me on. I kept a strict eye on the clock. I didn't want any of the other girls to see me getting preferential treatment. I didn't want anyone to know I'd been brown-nosing. At twenty to ten, I went to the table and got my number, acting as if I'd just arrived, and sat in the bleachers. Several girls came only moments later.

I had no idea how nerve-racking it would be to watch all the girls trying out. There was a lot of talent in the room. I was in the fourth group, number three. My tumbling pass stood out without a doubt. The signature move Coach had given me rocked. I heard mumbles from the audience about how I did it. My jumps were impeccable. It was like I was set on autopilot for the cheer and dance. I walked away confident.

But, watching the last six groups compete was agonizing. John had been right. I did need to be good at everything. If he hadn't manipulated me into working hard, I never would have made it. I kept hearing whispers about the coach and wondered what it all meant. "I never knew Mrs. Sill was a cheerleader when she was our age." "Crazy." "She's the hardest English teacher in the school. I bet she'll be the same on the floor." "She better not cut any returners." "I so miss Coach Higgins." I figured Mrs. Sill must be a new coach and she must also be a teacher at the school. I wondered why the other coach quit.

Everyone had to leave the school for two hours so the coach could tally the scores and put the team together. I couldn't eat anything at the restaurant John took me to. My stomach was in knots. With cheer, there may have been a standard, but when everyone makes or exceeds it, the coach is comparing you to each other. How many cheerleaders my size and skill level would they need? When compared to girls just like me, where did I stand? Did I have the right look, attitude, and abilities? There were too many variables to be sure of my success.

I wanted to wait for a while, and go look at the list of girls that had made the team later than everyone else. I was so afraid of being humiliated. But, John wouldn't hear of it. We arrived just as the captain taped the list to the door.

"Go. Now's the time for the truth," John said.

As slowly as possible, I got out of the car. There was already a sizeable crowd, many jumping up and down celebrating, while others sobbed. I cut my way through, in no hurry. Once on the top step, I closed my eyes. Lillian shook me, "Congrats Michele! You made it!" she said, wrapping her arms around me into a big hug. "And varsity at that. We'll be together."

I opened my eyes and saw my name in big letters under varsity. I'd done it!

"The varsity sleep-over's at my house," Lillian continued. "I'll text you the info. We get measured for our cheer outfits and everything." Then she disappeared into the crowd. Opening the door to the car, I pretended to be sad, a last attempt at getting back, if only for a moment, at John.

"Don't tell me you didn't make it," John said, as I made a feeble attempt to bring on the tears.

I couldn't look at him. My cover would be blown, because instead of crying, I couldn't help but smile.

"No," I said.

"Are you kidding me?" He yanked at the lever to open the car door, mumbling, "You were perfect. I made sure of it. There's no way…" He took one quick look at me because the smile I had plastered on my face told him the truth.

"Hrrr," he snarled, but a hint of a grin surrounded the sound. As he sat back in the car, relief and joy flashed across his face. And I was pretty sure this was John, the real John—not one of his characters. "It had to have been enough."

Had he been sure? Much of my confidence had come from his. He had manipulated me once again. Layer upon layer of his trickery had fallen on my shoulders. I shouldn't care, but without him, I never would have made it, and it ached to know I was weak and needed him.

After getting my stuff from the hotel, and driving to Lillian's house, I made a deal with myself. I wasn't going to let

John be my strength anymore. I wanted my own life, and if I had to be Michele through and through in order to achieve it, I would. I tucked Alex, Rick, Marybeth, and my family into the far recesses of my mind. It hurt to do it, but I said my goodbyes.

I had no idea sleeping at a friend's house with the fourteen varsity girls could be so much fun. I'd never laughed so hard in my whole life or felt as connected. I'd found my place and I loved it. Being Michele turned out to be rewarding in such a cosmically different way than being Christy. Unbelievable, but true.

The girls never stopped talking, even when a movie was on. I heard all kinds of stuff about boys, school, and something very interesting about our cheer coach.

"What do you think of our new coach?" a redheaded cheerleader asked the rest of us. We were making bows to use in our hair throughout the season.

"The verdict is still out," a blonde said, "but with the practices she's scheduled for us, I bet she's a beast."

"Yeah," the first one said, "I think you're right."

"I'm scared," another blonde said.

"She's new?" I asked.

"Oh, yeah," Beth, the co-captain, said. "Michele's new, so she doesn't know the story."

A rumble of thirteen excited voices began telling me the story all at once.

"Whoa, girls!" Lillian said. "She can't understand all of you at once. I'm the captain, I'll fill her in."

We all turned to Lillian and remained dead silent through the whole story.

"Coach Higgins was the best coach in the world," she told me. "Everyone loved her. She'd coached for fifteen years. She worked us, but also let us play—ya know? Anyway, try-outs were the last week of May and after everyone left the school to wait for her to choose the team, she disappeared with all the paperwork and stuff. Poof, just like that, she was gone."

Tears welled up in her eyes. I looked away, trying to hide the horrible idea that brewed in my mind. My heart hammered against my chest.

"Everyone in the county turned out to look for her, but she was nowhere. No one wanted to get a new coach until we knew for sure what had happened to her. After two months of searching, the cops still couldn't find her. So we had to hire another coach or we'd be without a squad for the whole year. That's why we had such late try-outs."

I tried to look sympathetic, fighting the horror welling up inside me. Was it just a coincidence that the old coach disappeared right when John was looking for a team for me to join? My head started to pound at the thought of it.

The conversation ended when five women showed up at the house to measure us for uniforms. Our coach had had to hire a local business that promised to have all the uniforms made by Tuesday for cheer camp. It seemed like an impossible feat to me.

All the girls just stripped down to their underwear and bras in front of each other, trying on the sample uniforms like it was nothing. I had a hard time exposing myself and moved into the background to change.

Since we didn't get to sleep until three-o-clock in the morning, five-thirty came too soon. We practiced every day from six to ten, even the day after the sleepover. I couldn't wait for a nap. Coach was demanding, but John had prepared me. I couldn't say as much for the other girls. Many felt she was the devil, but I liked her. She didn't coddle or show favorites to anyone—an equal playing field for everyone.

Chapter Fourteen

When practice was through, John dashed my hopes for a nap and I was exhausted. We didn't get on the freeway to head for the cabin after practice. Instead, we stayed in town. I had intended to ask him about Coach Higgins after a nap. I wasn't prepared now.

"We're not going back to the cabin?" I asked.

"Nope," he answered. "You won't be going back there again. We've got too much to do."

"Really? But Marian only packed enough for three days." I missed the cabin already. It may have been a source of grief at times, but it had become my home.

"All your stuff is at your new house. Marian brought it all."

"Just curious, but who's been footing the bill for all my private lessons and use of that safe-house and everything."

"There are quite a lot of perks working for a black-ops division of the government. The funds don't seem to ever run out." He smirked. "Monday is my last day with you and we have a lot to go over before then."

Only four more days and I would be free. I did want to be free, didn't I?

"But, school doesn't start for a few more weeks." My words betrayed me.

"You think I want to stick around forever?" The irritation in his voice bit at me.

"No," I blurted, feeling stupid. "I'm just surprised you're going so soon."

"So soon? Have you forgotten the last two and half months?"

"That's not what I meant. I just meant…" No words came to me. What had I meant? It seemed like we'd had a break-through after try-outs. I thought he really cared about me. Instead, he just wanted to get rid of me as soon as possible.

"That's what I thought. All you ever think about is yourself. You don't think about me being separated from my family and work all this time. I hope you abandon some of that selfishness soon. It could get you killed."

Daggers of betrayal stabbed at me. Invisible hands drove them deeper and deeper with each thrust.

He had put me in my place—once again.

I looked away, my face hot with embarrassment.

"Enough of that. We've got stuff to do. As I drive, I need you to find places of safety while you attempt to memorize the area. Niceville, as you know, is a small place, so we'll also be studying Fort Walton and Destin, before I go. You need to know where everything is. What buses run and when, how to get a taxi, the fastest ways out of town, the best places of safety."

I stared at him, wondering if I could find them in a real life situation.

"What are places of safety again?" John asked.

"They are places," I answered, "that people see every day and therefore ignore, or places that naturally give shelter that normal people wouldn't think to look behind, around, or through."

"There's a notebook and pen in the glove compartment," he said. "Use it to take notes."

I pushed the button on the compartment and pulled out the items. I didn't take many notes on our three-hour-drive. I didn't need to. I could tell it irritated John. I didn't care. I did make a little tally for every safe place I found, though.

Niceville didn't feel like the military town it was. Maybe because it sat right on Florida's panhandle by the Boggy Bayou and boasted a mere thirty thousand residents, who liked to run around in normal clothes. I knew from the statistics that John made me read that these people were quite average for the most part, but to me it looked like we'd stepped back in time.

Just five minutes west of the high school, past the large Catholic church, commercial development threatened to erase some of the town's old-town feeling. A few minutes further down the road, near the Rocky Bayou, we found several gated communities. My new house stood in one—the gated community at Bluewater Bay. All average-ness ended at the gate.

After passing the outer security gate (manned guard shack included), a nervous shock raced through me when I saw the second guard and gate at the entrance to the drive of the house that John told me was to be my home. So much security.

"This is it," he said, "Don't salivate too hard."

We didn't pass through the second security check, nor did John slow down in front of the home. He drove at his normal speed right on past, teasing me. It was a mansion—elegant and stately. It stood at least a hundred yards back from the street, with a sprawling green lawn, rows and rows of trees and colorful flower gardens sprinkled about. The white brick exterior of the home shone in the sun. That, coupled with the dark green plantings around the house, made it appear to float above the ground. I craned my neck back just in time to count seven white pillars that held up the enormous red tiled roof, before the house disappeared behind us.

My heart thundered as I thought about living in such a place. It took me a few minutes to regain my composure and pay attention to my surroundings again. I wanted to ask John questions about the home, but I didn't want to sound selfish and besides, he started talking first.

"We'll be making a big loop around the area from Niceville to Destin, from Destin to Ft. Walton Beach and from Fort Walton Beach back to Niceville. Pay close attention. Notice the things that others miss. How many landlords take care of their properties? How many people are just hanging around? What cars are parked in the area? How does the area make you feel? Are there a lot of places of safety?"

The two ways to get to Ft. Walton and Destin from Niceville began on the John Sims Parkway, snaking its way along the Boggy Bayou. The circuitous route took about an hour to drive.

We drove through the back roads, though. The slow winding of the streets gave me the chance to commit the area to memory. After making the round trip once, John headed back to Destin, over the toll bridge once again, quizzing me on what I saw, those places of safety, and miscellaneous trivia. My stomach growled just as John pulled into Merlin's again to eat. No one made a better pizza in my opinion.

Before walking into the restaurant, John threw me a backpack from the trunk and grabbed some folders. Was this my infamous backpack John had talked about the last few weeks? We sat in a corner, near the kitchen and bathrooms, away from prying eyes. Before ordering, he pulled out a map of the U.S. He folded it so that only the southeast states stared up at me. "Study these maps, focusing on the main routes out of Niceville and into other states."

Memorizing the map only took a quick glance. Looking for viable alternate routes posed me a bit of trouble, however.

"John, from what I can see, we have only a handful of viable exit routes." Eglin Air Force Base surrounded Niceville to the north-northwest, limiting my options. Not only was Eglin Air Force Base's footprint on Florida large, but only three roadways cut north through it, and one of these required an hour's drive east to even reach it. Further south and a bit northwest of Niceville lay the Boggy Bayou—huge and uninviting. All small roads in the area led to the few main roads. It would be difficult to leave the state by car unnoticed. The forests and waterways complicated matters even further. Niceville seemed an island, trapped by hills, forests, and bayous. It not only made it hard to get into, but it also made it hard to get out of.

"That actually works to your advantage if you come up with several different unique ways to get out of here. You must become familiar with everything, and come up with ways out that no one else will see, especially those not familiar with the area."

"But, we're so isolated."

"Yep. Trust me. It is an advantage. You'll see."

By the time we ordered lunch, I had found only two roundabout ways to get into Georgia. Alabama proved to be more challenging. With only four main roads leading away from Niceville, my options were limited. At least I was aware of the problem now and could continue to discover new ways to escape Niceville, if needed, as time went on.

John finally had me pull out the backpack and empty its contents on the table. A light jacket, wig, shirt, pants, sunglasses, phone, safety pins, make-up, energy bars, bottled water, as well as tons of other tiny things like paper clips, rubber bands, pushpins, tacks, and even a very mini calculator tumbled out.

"Shake it again," he said.

I did and a notepad fell out.

"Shake it again," he repeated.

I shook it and shook it, but nothing else came out.

"Does it feel empty?" John asked.

I shook it again. No, it didn't feel empty. One side of the bag was heavier than the other. I reached inside, feeling for a zipper or snap or something. Nothing, but I did feel something like a notebook inside the fabric of the pack. I turned it inside out and, feeling around for a false pocket, discovered it. "Ahh!" I looked at John as I reached in to pull out the goods. A couple of passports with my pictures, but the names weren't Michele Mattingly. Escape passports. Cool.

I also found two sheets of paper in the pocket. I pulled them out and one looked like jibberish while the other looked like a code.

"Memorize that code," John said.

I glanced at the code and then looked at John.

"Done?" He shook his head and then sighed, leaning back on the booth seatback. "How did you do that so fast?"

"I only need to glance at something to memorize it."

He held out his hand and I placed the paper in it and picked up the one that had looked like jibberish. Using the code I'd just seen, I was able to decode it without much effort at all.

"As you can see, those are the codes you need to know if you have to contact me. It will tell me it's you and what type of danger you're in."

The backpack didn't appear to be full when he had carried it in. Everything except the clothes were in miniature. Very clever. Even some bills, rolled into a tiny tube, lay in front of me. It appeared John had thought of everything. He went through each item, filling me in on various ways to use it to my advantage. After discussing each item, he carefully placed it inside the pack. It seemed really important, so I paid close attention.

Our pizza arrived, hot and steamy. Yum. I ate a huge slice of the meaty pan pizza while John finished talking about the items in the pack. When he'd finished, he dumped it out again, grabbed a slice of pizza for himself and said, "Now, you tell me what the objects are for and put them back in the pack in exactly the same order I did."

When I'd gotten through all the items without a single misstep, John stared at me and shook his head, taking a deep breath. A sweet happiness filled me. I loved to show him up. Now filled with everything and zipped shut, I set it on the floor next to me. Considering how much had gone into that pack, it felt light.

Determined to get the upper-hand, he quizzed me about places of safety I was supposed to have found. "How many did you write down?"

"Fifty-seven."

"Only fifty-seven? That means you only missed about 100."

He always had the upper-hand when it came to places of safety, and he loved to use it to make me feel stupid. He quizzed me about various sites we'd seen throughout the day and then he handed me a list of numbers and addresses for different types of transportation like buses, taxis, and limos as well as schedules for mass transit. I'd almost memorized all the pages by the time I realized the pizza was gone.

John asked the waitress to bring us salads so we could have an excuse to stay there longer. I had committed all the addresses and schedules to memory by the time they arrived. I ate as bus schedules, flight schedules, taxi company numbers from each city filled my brain. He also taught me other code words to use for extraction. I had to be able to escape Niceville if the terrorists happened to show up.

He handed me a detailed map of Niceville and started to point things out, when a slight chill sat at the base of my neck—my warning that something was wrong. Then, something out of the ordinary struck me. A sound and then a smell. I looked at John. He didn't even pause. He just kept on talking, pointing to things on the map in front of us.

"John," I said, thinking he was probably trying to make me stop paying attention to that feeling that told me to bolt out of there. "I'll be right back. I've got to go to the bathroom."

"'Kay," he said, leaning back into his chair, lifting the map up, studying it.

I grabbed the handy backpack John had given me earlier, hoping he didn't see it because of the map he held and slipped into the bathroom, wishing there was a window inside. Sure enough, there was. With effort, I finally opened the old, stubborn thing and fell through it, scratching my chin and drawing blood. I immediately crouched beside a car in the alley to check out the scene around me. Three places of safety were right in my view, but they were too close. I scampered beyond the trash bin, children's center, and the doctors' offices—the first three places of safety I'd noticed. Running up to the fourth, a stone library with an entrance to an outer bathroom facility, I decided to pass it up to hopefully find a less obvious one. I settled on the eighth place of safety I came to, hoping to give John a run for his money. I pushed in the numbers on the phone John had in the pack and gave him the code words. After John gave me his password, he said, "Well done, I'll be there to pick you up in about ten."

Well done! Wow! I'd earned a well done. I wondered when he'd realized I had felt the ambush coming and wouldn't be back. I heard footsteps outside my hiding place behind a tall trash bin and almost moved out into the open. But then I remembered I'd only spoken to John moments before and he couldn't have already arrived. I held my breath and waited for the footsteps to move away from me. I dared a peek around the corner and saw a man cross the road and go into an internet café. I took a deep breath and pressed my back against the building's brick wall. A few minutes later, I heard loud voices and peeked out again.

That same man walked out of the building and, laughing with a man from the business, said, "Yea, I knew she wasn't telling the truth. What would she be doing coming here? I'm sure she's at her boyfriend's, but just in case, remember, she's blonde and about this tall." He motioned with his hands. "Just call the number on that card if you see her. Thanks, man." As he started to turn around, I pressed my back against the wall again and looked for a way out. He was looking for me. I knew it. That description was mine! I thought this was just a drill…Could it be real?

My heart pounded hard in my ears and I couldn't hear a thing. I turned to meditation, another of John's tricks, and was able to clear the beating in only a minute or so by breathing deep and long and repeating over and over again in my mind, "I am calm and in control." With my heart calm, I was able to really listen to the things around me." My skin pricked and I heard the man's heavy breathing. A rock skittered across the pavement. I peeked out just in time to see a flash of color. It was all I needed to be sure he would find me if I stayed where I was.

I looked down the alleyway, away from the street. A tall fence—chain link, climbable, but way too noisy, blocked the path at the end of the alley. I noticed two doors near the fence. One went into the building on my left and the other on the right. I'd only have one chance. Which door should I choose? I couldn't recall which business the building I was leaning on housed. Or even if it was open. I hadn't been paying attention. I was such an idiot. It would be pure luck to find either of the doors unlocked, even if the businesses were open right now—unless one was a restaurant or café of some sort. I decided to look in the trash container I hid behind. The garbage could help me decide which to choose.

I'd have to be careful so he wouldn't see me. I dared a peek out to the street using a mirror from my backpack. No one showed up in the mirror, but I couldn't see around the corner. I decided to chance it. I grabbed the edges of the container and did a pull up to look inside. Food scraps dominated the far right side of the container while papers littered the left. Based on that, and another peek with my mirror to the street, with the faintest of footfalls, I ducked into the doorway of the business on the right and was pleased to smell the aromas and hear the sounds of cooking food.

I crouched in the door frame while I checked out the room inside the door. Metal pans clanged. One fell with a bang, like a gunshot. The head sous-chef came dangerously close as he yelled at one of his workers. *Please don't let them find me. Not yet, anyway.* Waiters hollered for this dish or that, and I wondered how long I could just stay where I was before someone would notice me. I left the door cracked just in case I needed to make a quick get-away.

After my butt went numb, I pulled out my phone. I'd been there a full hour already. Out of nowhere, a guy in a white chef's uniform told me to scram. My legs and rear ached as I stood.

It was five in the evening, but the sun blazed hot outside. There must be a problem or John would have come for me already. I pulled out a hat and sunglasses from my bag and put them on before leaving the alley. Should I find my way back to our hotel or should I head for my new house? How would I get into my house? Did the guards know who I was? Too afraid to risk it, I headed for the hotel.

The heat beat down on me like a sauna as I crossed the island that connected Destin to Fort Walton Beach. Except for the two bridges I had to cross, I walked the sandy beaches near the water. My clothes were drenched with sweat by the time I got to our hotel. The receptionist was more than happy to give me a key to our room, probably to keep my sweaty, stinky self out of sight of the other patrons, who'd lined up behind me. I stopped at the vending room and grabbed some ice before going into our room. I reached down into the tub to fill my cup but I didn't want to bring it out. I filled my mouth with it and crunched down. It not only took away the heat, it also woke me up.

I opened the door. My heart dropped. John wasn't here—which made my pulse race. Was I on my own? He had drilled it into my head to only use the phone once so he could get a lock on me, but shouldn't I try it again in this instance? Then again, what if someone else traced it? I decided to follow his advice. I dropped the backpack and went to the phone to see if I had any messages. The message light blinked. Should I push it? Would it somehow alert the bad guys? I snuck a sly look out the window, paced the room and finally giving up, I pushed the flashing button. The message said to call the front desk and ask to be connected to room 11B.

"Password, please." Was all I heard from the other end of the line when the front desk patched me through to room 11B. Immediately, the list of passwords came to mind.

"Sweet honey," I said with conviction.

Then the person in 11B said, "The lodge is a nice place to sleep."

"'Kay." I said and hung up. John had taught me all kinds of codes he liked to use when hiding. The one the person in 11B read to me meant to stay put. I sighed, fell into a chair next to the phone and let out a deep breath, a smile of relief on my face. I suddenly noticed how badly I smelled and rushed to the shower to be ready for whatever might happen next.

The cool shower felt heavenly and cleared my brain. I didn't dare stay in it long, afraid I'd miss something important. After dressing, I turned on the computer and searched all the facts I could find about Florida and where I would be living to take my mind off John and the danger that lurked behind every corner.

Several hours later, I heard the card key click in the lock, but the door didn't budge, so I clicked off the computer. Then just as I was about to climb into the nearest closet, I heard the key take and the handle depress. I pushed into the back corner of the closet, wishing to disappear.

I heard someone enter the room and move quietly about. Seconds later, the closet door flew open and a gun pointed at me, I screamed. John reached in and put a hand over my mouth and lowered the gun.

Chapter Fifteen

"Calm down. I had to make sure you were alone," he said.

I nodded and he removed his hand. I breathed hard.

"Get out here," he said, stepping back. "I'm glad you're safe."

"What are you talking about? What happened? I waited and ..."

"I know. We had a problem with one of our team members. He says he was only trying to up his game, testing you to see if you survive a double ambush, but I don't like the way it looks—or feels."

"That guy was after me?"

"Yes."

"How did he know where I was?"

"He tracked your signal when you called me, but he wasn't able to pinpoint your exact location as quickly as I did. He was closer to you than I was, though. When I saw him poking around the area your signal came from, I moved in on him and took him in to be questioned."

"You just left me there?" The hot hours of walking nagged at me.

"I knew you'd find your way back if you needed to. I had to take care of the security breach first, just in case he'd turned and had friends around. I couldn't risk giving you away. He says he was trying to make a good impression on me. Rookies can be dumb sometimes. He wanted to test you one more level and see if you'd discover him following you. You did. He wanted to show me he could help train you in a more thorough way. Such insubordination must be squashed." John looked ragged, worn out. It kind of freaked me out.

"I've got some things I need to do." He headed for his room. I heard the shower and then stopped listening when I decided to turn on the TV. I needed a distraction. I hadn't watched real TV since leaving Helena with John. I zoned out.

"What are you doing?" he said, heading for the TV and turning it off.

"Watching TV," I said, raising my eyebrows.

"You're not supposed to watch regular TV."

"Uh, my training's up in just a few days. Did you intend for me to never watch TV again?"

"Yea, right. Never mind."

I'd never seen John anywhere but at the top of his game. He didn't miss things and he'd just missed something. He worked the rest of the night on his computer, without saying a word to me. After walking so far to the hotel in the heat, I needed to zone out anyway, so I watched more TV and eventually fell asleep. John woke me at midnight and sent me to my room.

In the morning, after an uneventful cheer practice, John picked me up and said, "Time to get acquainted with your new home and family."

My body stiffened. This was it.

"I'll take you through the house," he continued. "Only Mangus and Katy will be there. The rest of the crew hasn't arrived yet. As you already know, your 'parents' are simply stand-ins. They won't be around a lot. The people you'll be leaning on are the butler, Mangus, and your nanny, Katy. Mangus and Katy are U.S. Marshalls, but your new parents are Special Agents and are doing me a favor acting as your parents. It's a secondary job for them."

I wondered what John held over their heads in order to get them to do double duty, especially such a dangerous one.

"You are Katy and Mangus' only assignment, however. Keep them in the loop."

I guessed my need for protection wasn't over yet. Would I like them? Would they be like John?

We drove through the gate into my new neighborhood, passing inspection at the first guard shack and then after driving through the neighborhood, we pulled up to the second guard shack in front of the mansion that was to be my new home. We stopped at the guard shack, where the man on duty studied me before letting us drive by. He pulled lightly on my hair and rubbed the skin on my face. I was glad I wasn't in disguise. My breathing sped up and my heart fluttered as we drove up the long driveway. Seven white pillars did in fact hold up the enormous roof above a large elegant front porch, and the towering windows lining the front of the house gleamed in the sun as we pulled up in front of them. I held my breath when John opened the front door, still afraid it was all just a dream.

"Your tour begins in this grand foyer," he said, speaking with a French accent. "Warning. This house is larger than it appears." We continued into a large room with six or seven seating areas and an enormous fireplace at the opposite end. Elegant draperies hung from floor to ceiling and chandeliers sent light dancing through the room, making it appear alive somehow. The intricate woodwork on the walls and high ceilings only added to the spectacle.

We veered right, through a large opening and into another gathering area with more open space and two fireplaces. The government owned this? We walked through room after enormous room, taking our time, absorbing the elegance and beauty of each. My favorite was the library, and after slipping through the kitchen and the stunning dining area, we ended up right where we'd started, in the first seating area next to the grand foyer. We'd made a complete circle. I'd counted thirty rooms. I couldn't wrap my head around the idea that the government had such an opulent safe-house.

The first floor of the house made me think this was not a home to be lived in, only to be looked at. Then we went upstairs and walked into my bedroom. While bigger than the first floor of my house in Helena, it felt homey and inviting. Marian had done a great job putting it all together. She'd left a little note on the pillow saying goodbye.

The king-size canopy bed, with its draping white and black linens, drew me in, but the sitting area with couch, chairs and TV created a surge of excitement inside of me. A large closet and bathroom hung off to the side like at the cabin. Ten racks for shoes and a center dressing table, brought me in one door from the bedroom and out another into the bathroom. The wood floors, mostly hidden by plush rugs or furniture, warmed my feet, and the smell of cinnamon cheered me. My heart pounded at the thought this was all mine. Never in my wildest dreams would I have thought I would live in a place like this. Then again, I was no longer me. I was Michele.

After leaving my room and wandering through the rest of the bedrooms upstairs, we headed back down to the sitting area, where I met the butler, Mangus. A short, almost bald man with a stern face and pointy nose did not fit the image of an FBI Special Agent and it felt right, somehow, that he worked for the U.S. Marshalls instead. I hoped his formal, stand-offish manner was only a part of his cover and not his true self.

"I will be accessible," Mangus said, his English accent thick, "either here in the house or on the grounds at all times, except on rare occasions and I will give you ample notice when it comes to those occasions. I am speed dial number two on your phone. Don't be afraid to use it. At the bottom of each light switch is a tiny button you can also push to call me. Try to use those only if you feel unsafe. Use your phone for all other cases."

I looked around the room for a switch and walked over to the first one I saw, carefully feeling for the tiny button. I pushed it and a beep sounded in Mangus' pocket.

"I dare say, you've found it," Mangus said, his face an unreadable mask.

"Thanks, Mangus," I said, following John out of the room.

"The pleasure is all mine," he said. I wondered if his words were sarcastic. Only time would tell.

John led me back to the immense library, where I couldn't help fingering the plethora of books lining its walls.

"This room is the one "safe-room" in the house," John said.

"Safe-room? I thought the whole place was a safe-house."

"This is not a government safe-house. Natalie and Mason bought this place and had it modified for them and you. It's more like a fortress, better than any government safe-house I've ever seen. Its walls are riddled with secret passageways and hideouts. It has more electronic protection than the White House." He grinned, so I knew that wasn't exactly true. "Katy will help you learn all the ins and outs of this house over the next few weeks. This room is a bit different. It's like a big vault. If you come in here and pull this book off the shelf and type in the code "465" on the spine, it puts the room into lock-down." He pulled the book out and pressed its spine. The thick doors slammed shut and I heard clicking noises. "The doors and walls look like wood, but they are solid steel. Also, it is impossible to bug this room. You don't need to put it into lockdown mode to protect what you say in here, however. Just shut the doors and voila! Complete privacy. This is where you can come to pass information safely."

I glanced around the room, quickly feeling a bit claustrophobic, sort of wishing my favorite room wasn't the "safe-room."

John looked at his watch. "Ah, your parents should be arriving shortly." He put the book back, after punching the spine with his fingers, and I heard the clicking noises again. I guessed the doors were unlocked now.

I looked at the big clock on the wall—the ticking suddenly loud in my ears—twelve-o-clock. We'd been roaming this house for a full hour. Amazing. Then it hit me and my nerves kicked into high-gear the more I thought about meeting my new parents. My foot tapped the ground and all the titles of the books blurred, my mind refusing to concentrate on anything. I moved to a soft, cushiony arm chair, hoping it would relax me. It didn't. My stomach gave a deep mournful growl as the door opened and two of the most perfect people I'd ever seen walked in.

Watching them shut the heavy door behind them and come straight at me, sent a surreal tingle through my body. My new family stood only feet from me, and I had no idea what to do or say. I stood up in one big jerk, thrusting my hand out to them.

The woman, presumably my mom, quickly side-stepped my hand and pulled me into a hug. Her warmth enveloped me, her soft scent pacifying me.

"Michele, we are so excited to welcome you into our family," she said to my hair, holding me several seconds longer than felt natural. Only as she pulled away did I notice I hadn't hugged her back. My arms hung limp at my sides, useless.

The next assault came a mere second later. The man, tall, with sparkling blue eyes and brown hair, grabbed hold of me and swung me around in a big circle like a rag doll. When he finally set me back on the ground, I stepped back. Not one, but two steps. Didn't he know that was weird to do to a teenager? Especially one you didn't know? With my eyes the size of oranges, I stared at them.

The first time I'd met Alex's parents, their beauty and perfection had shocked me. They hadn't seemed like parents at all, but movie stars. Now, standing before me, were two others just like them with perfect clothes, perfect faces, perfect voices. They looked to be in their late thirties, but I could have been way off. How could I be their daughter? I stared and they stared. Awkward. Finally, John had us all take a seat. My new parents sat, hand in hand, on a stylish sofa, and I retreated to one of the overstuffed chairs, three feet from them.

"This all must be a bit shocking to you," the woman said.

They weren't stupid either.

I guess I expected people like my real parents, comfortable and average, to be sitting in front of me. I regretted not having spent any time thinking about what these people would be like, or pumping John for information on them.

When I didn't respond, John eyed me.

I tried to pull myself together and realized my mouth hung ajar. I snapped it shut and made a feeble attempt at smiling—I might have grimaced instead.

"Are you okay?" the woman said, shifting in her seat so that she sat on the edge of the couch, like she wanted to get closer to me. She wanted me to like her. I could tell. Should I like her?

I wanted to say something witty or at least intelligent, but all that came out was, "Uh…. yeah." I quickly regrouped and blurted, "Nice house." A noise escaped my lips, a horrible grunt, and I let my head drop, sighing audibly. How ridiculous!

Quiet chuckles came from the direction of the sofa and before I knew it, the woman had her soft hands on my chin, raising it up so that our eyes could meet.

"Let me tell you something, Michele," she said, her quiet voice dripping with sympathy and her eyes soft, giving and kind. "We are so excited to have you be a part of our life. We know we will never supplant your real parents—."

Of course they would. I wondered if this is what it felt like to be adopted.

"But we'd like to give you the support you need after having lost them. We are merely substitutes," she continued, "for the time you need us. We can be as involved as you want us to be when we're here. Of course, we do have to fulfill our responsibilities with work, and will be gone a lot. But we can smother you with attention when we're here if you want. But from what John tells us, you wouldn't want that anyway."

Comfort emanated from her eyes and I rallied, nodding my understanding. Her hand slid away from my chin. What had John told them? Whatever it was, the stink eye he gave me made me feel I wasn't living up to it. I wiped my hands on my jeans.

"I'm Natalie, your mom, of course, and this," she said, pointing back at the man on the couch, "is Mason, your dad. We'd prefer you called us Mom and Dad, if that's okay with you. It makes it more real for all of us—if you know what I mean."

They were movie stars, acting their part.

I found myself smiling, acting my part, too. "Yeah. I know what you mean."

She moved back to the couch and Mason spoke up.

"Our jobs as CEOs of our companies take us away from home a lot." He winked. "Katy, your nanny," as if on cue, a spry woman of about fifty, I guessed, pushed the door open and bounded into the room, a bundle of energy, "has taken care of you since you were born."

"Hey cutie!" she said, storming over and gently pushing me to the side of the large chair so she could sit beside me.

John stood and shut the door.

I pushed hard into the side of the chair and grasped the arm rest with one hand, leaving my other where it was as if I didn't have a care in the world.

"Katy can sign your papers," Natalie said, "and do all the parenty things we're unable to do when we're away. We don't want to mislead you; we *are* gone about two-hundred and fifty days a year. Katy will be more like the real parent to you. We do expect calls from you at least every other day so that we know what's happening with you when we come back so we can talk intelligibly with your friends and teachers. Nothing long, five minutes tops."

"Katy will take the place of Marian and me," John interrupted. "She will make sure you stay on top of everything and, of course, help keep you safe."

She smiled at me. "We are going to be best buds." She rocked her body playfully into mine. She seemed like one of those rare adults that just fit with teenagers, but her stylish short hair and dress intimidated me a bit. Marian had never done that. I gripped my knees.

"So, I've got to know," I said, finally finding my voice. "Why did you decide to buy this house and why did you decide to take me in?" I looked at John, letting one of my eyebrows raise.

"John warned us you would want to know that."

I narrowed my eyes at John.

"He contacted us a few months ago about taking you in," Mason said, without skipping a beat. He'd obviously memorized this. "We'd just finished a lot of the renovations on this house. We've always loved Florida, with all its beaches and water, and even though we're not home a lot, we wanted a place that we could call home and that was worry-free, not only when we were here, but when we were away. Not an easy thing in our line of work. When we found this place, we had to have it."

How did two government workers afford a place like this?" It is pretty amazing," I said, not daring to ask that question out loud.

"As far as deciding to take you in," he said, a bit too clearly and concisely. "It did take a bit of persuasion, but it won't hurt anything to have someone here all the time. In fact, it's probably better. We'll come home to a lived-in home, a happy place, rather than a quiet, lonely one."

"Hmm," I said, wondering what had really persuaded them. I glanced at John. He gave nothing away.

"I want you to know," Natalie broke in, her face shining, "that we really are excited to have you here. As you can imagine, in our line of work, raising a family is next to impossible, and to have the chance to have a daughter, even on a limited basis, is an intoxicating proposition and—"

"Did we answer your question?" Mason interrupted, turning to look at Natalie, who had leaned back hard into the couch.

"I guess," I said, taking note to remind myself to broach this subject again when I had Natalie by herself.

We discussed what my schedule would be like for the next three weeks until school started and how John still needed to work with me for a few days until I went to cheer camp. Basically, I would be in classes or workshops for most of the time, with little or no time for myself. I found myself feeling excited for my ocean water classes.

"We're leaving this afternoon." Mason said, "But will be back next Sunday when you come home from cheer camp, to make sure everything is in order before school to starts."

I nodded, with a pressed smile on my face. They were leaving already?

"Do you have any other questions for us?" Natalie asked.

I could think of a few, but they could wait. "No." I clasped my hands together and smiled. A bead of sweat ran down my spine making me sit up straight.

"Then let's get some lunch," Natalie said. "Our cook is supposed to be amazing. He came highly recommended. We hope you like him."

"As long as fish or seafood stay away from my plate, I'll be just great." I wrinkled my nose.

"You do realize we live right on the ocean, don't you?" Mason said, forcing a smile.

"It doesn't mean I have to eat from it." I stood in a rush, leaving Katy sitting on the chair.

"No, it doesn't," Natalie said, putting her arm around my shoulders as we walked into the dining room. I liked her arm there.

"Just remember," John whispered into my ear, after sidling next to me and pulling a chair out at the table. "Act like you're their daughter. The cook and other household members do not know your story." He sat next to me.

Plates, silverware and glasses sat arranged at one end of the sleek, long table I'd seen earlier on the tour. More than twenty people could have joined us for lunch with elbow room to spare. The creamy goodness of the chicken alfredo proved their chef's capability. I wanted to lick the plate, but decided against it. Instead, I dragged my last bite of breadstick through the sparse white remains and, happily popped it into my mouth.

We retreated to the library again. Once the door was shut, Katy spoke up. "This house is full of secret passageways as well as great hiding places. I will show you all of them tomorrow." Mason nodded in affirmation.

The idea of secret passageways sent a quick thrill through me.

"We need you to remember," Katy continued, "how important it is for you to always act your part while in this house. The only room you are allowed to talk about your previous life is this one—and only if the door is sealed shut. If you need to discuss anything to do with your placement here, bring Natalie, Mason, Mangus, or myself in here to do it. Outside of this room, you must be Michele in every way."

I nodded.

"Really, Michele, it's so important."

"I understand." I hoped this lecture wouldn't last long, because I wanted to have that chat with Natalie before she left.

"Good. Now, Natalie and Mason need to be going and you have some training with John this afternoon and evening. I probably won't see you tonight. So, until tomorrow…" She grabbed me into a hug that actually wasn't too awkward and headed for the door.

"You're leaving already?" I asked, turning to Natalie, hating the idea of having to wait a whole week before talking to her in private. "Yeah," Natalie said, putting her arm around me. "But we'll be back before you know it." Her voice even *sounded* motherly. She gave me a tight squeeze and turned me over to Mason. After a stiff embrace, he said goodbye.

"What was all that weirdness about when Natalie and Mason first came into the library?" John asked.

"I don't know," I said, even though I really did. The same feeling of intimidation seized me. "I just lost it for a minute."

He scrunched up his face and said, "Ya think?"

"Sorry." What could I say? I certainly didn't want him to know they intimidated me. He'd love that too much. I'm sure he was upset that I had somehow made him feel stupid in front of his co-workers, and he didn't like to look or feel stupid.

John drove me around and quizzed me about all kinds of things to do with Niceville, Destin, and Fort Walton. He drilled and drilled me.

"How many houses are on Devonshire way?" "If I had to get from Madison Ave. to Franklin Street, what are my options and why would I take each one?" "Name the top four parts of town to avoid and why." Etc. Etc.

After a few hours of non-stop driving, he pulled up to a souvenir shop on the main drag in Destin and let me out with my trusty backpack. When he didn't join me, I leaned in the passenger side window, my hands gripping the door.

"Find a way to get to Tradewinds Restaurant within two hours while being seen by the fewest number of people possible."

"Huh?"

He repeated the instructions, said, "Good luck," eyeing my hands as they gripped the door, and then drove away the second my arms fell to my sides.

It would seem I'd have had a lot of options, but in truth, there were only a few. Walking the whole way to Niceville to get to the restaurant didn't appeal to me and I realized I didn't know if the bridges I'd needed to get over allowed foot traffic anyway. I looked in my money pouch in the backpack and found five dollars. John had really sprung on this one. A taxi was out. The bus schedule shuffled through my mind. A bargain at a buck twenty-five. But did it satisfy the requirement to be seen by the fewest people possible? Probably not. I could always pilfer from the roll of bills in the only-use-in-extreme-emergencies-container, but John would find out and would make me pay later for that somehow.

I turned around and looked at the store, hoping for some inspiration. I could beg a ride off someone in the store. No cars parked in the lot. Only a bright blue bike leaned up against the brick wall. I looked through the windows to find its owner and couldn't see anyone inside. Did the bike belong to an employee or had it been abandoned?

I touched the handlebar. With no lock, it was practically asking to be taken. Grabbing the bar and lifting my leg to hop on, I had second thoughts. I couldn't steal this bike. That was wrong. My foot came back to the ground. I could always make John drive me back later, and I could put the bike back. I could probably have it back before the owner's shift was over. No harm done. Right?

I climbed onto the bike in a flash, before I could change my mind, and pedaled away. I wanted to look back something fierce, but knew I shouldn't. Once I felt I had enough distance between me and the store, I veered into an alley and stopped. Taking deep breaths, I pulled out a shirt from the backpack, slipped it over the shirt I already wore and put on a wig. The short wig made my head itch almost immediately. It must have been ninety degrees outside. I pedaled away, hoping to make it to the restaurant and back, to return the bike, within the allotted time. I pedaled faster and faster, ignoring the incessant pull on my lungs and trying to quell the uprising of guilt in my conscience.

I brushed the unforgiving sweat from my eyes with the small capped sleeve of my shirt, knowing, but not caring that mascara was sure to have streaked across both it and my face. When I finally arrived at the restaurant, with fifty minutes gone, I realized John hadn't arrived yet. What did he do with his time when he sent me on these little missions? I pulled out my phone, standing in a lobby area and scrolled down to his name. I almost pushed the call button, not caring that he had told me only to call in an emergency. John sauntered in to the lobby and I slid the phone shut, running to greet him.

"Hey John," I said, trying to remain calm, but having to wipe away the sweat that beaded on my forehead.

"Hey. I see you took the bike. I wasn't sure if you'd have the guts or the sleight of conscience."

"Yeah, uh…" Was the bike a plant?

"You look terrible." His eyes focused on my face.

The mascara, the sweat. It all brought attention to me.

"The little details are just as important as the big ones, Michele."

"Sorry," I said. "I was a bit distracted."

As always, he read my mind. "The bike?"

"Yeah, I mean, can we run it back real quick? I've still have almost an hour on the clock and maybe they don't yet know it's gone."

He put his arm around my shoulders. It always creeped me out when he did that—and it usually meant I wouldn't be getting my way. "Why don't you go get cleaned up, and then we'll talk about it?"

My heart raced. "But…"

He gave me the look that said, *You know I'll win the battle, so just do what I ask.*

I flew like the wind into the bathroom just off the waiting area and cleaned up, cursing myself for thinking John would want to get the bike back as much as I would. I knew if I raged at him, he'd find a way to make me suffer even more, so I took a deep breath, composing myself before walking back out to him. I even managed a tight smile despite the war going on in my stomach.

"That's better," he said, smirking and standing up from the chair in the waiting area in the lobby. "Now, let's go eat some dinner." He headed out of the lobby and up to the hostess podium, leaving me standing there. "Come on," he said, after telling the hostess we needed a table for two.

I forced my feet to follow him, gathering courage with each step.

"Could I borrow your keys, John?" I asked through my teeth.

"Sure."

I stretched out my hand, palm up, but before I could congratulate myself, he added, "After we eat."

I grunted in frustration and sat.

The waiter asked what we'd like and John ordered for me—as always. I wanted to order for myself and blurted, "Actually, could you bring me a nice thick cheeseburger with all the trimmings, please. And a chocolate shake."

Both were things this Italian restaurant was sure not to carry.

"Uh," the waiter stammered.

"Just bring her what I ordered her. She'll be fine."

The waiter walked away in a hurry.

"Really Michele, what was that all about?" His calm, even voice irritated me all the more.

I huffed. I knew it was an irrational time to explode. I'd had no freedom for three months, but he'd made me do something completely against what I believed in and was standing in the way of making it right.

"One of the keys to being unnoticed is owning up to your decisions. How many people do you think might see us drive up with our car and return the bike, and in broad daylight, no less?"

When I said nothing, he continued.

"You can't feel guilty about each move you make to insure your freedom. Remember the cabin near Helena? You think the agents enjoyed killing and tearing up that guard to look like he'd been attacked by some wild animal? When it's your life or theirs, you have to make some terrible decisions. You must be willing to do what is needed to survive. Otherwise, you're just dead."

Those FBI agents who saved us from the terrorists in Montana tore up the guard outside the cabin? No wonder he was nowhere to be found. My body stiffened. "Yeah, but I took the bike even though I wasn't in danger."

"This time. And it took you too much time to override your conscience. You could have been here five minutes earlier had you made your decision and stuck with it immediately. Five minutes can mean life or death. You need to survive."

He had been watching me. He always watched me, and the sucky thing was that he was right. He was always right—and it made me so mad.

Could I have killed that guard at the cabin if I'd needed to? Or any of the bad guys for that matter? Did I have it in me? If it was me or him, could I do it? I slouched, not wanting to think about it. I lifted my sweaty palms from the table, noticing I'd left wet marks.

"Often, seconds are the only thing separating you from death. You need to grab those seconds and use them to your advantage. No more conscience checking. When your intuition tells you to act, do it."

We did take the bike back, but we left it in an alley two businesses down from where I'd stolen it. I took a piece of paper from the pad in the glove box and wrote, Thanks on it, secretly setting it on the bike before I left it. I didn't feel good about it. What if someone else stole it from there and the owner never got it back?

I didn't sleep well once we got back to my house. As I climbed between the silky sheets, my thoughts were a tangled mess of justifications for going against what I knew to be right. Could I be forgiven for those things under the right circumstances? Would my justifications be synonymous with the repentance process I'd learned about in my youth group back home? Were there truly any circumstances that warranted these actions? Who was I becoming?

Chapter Sixteen

During the night, I think I murdered about ten different attackers and woke up trashed. Cheer practice didn't stand a chance today. I couldn't do anything right. Coach pulled me aside at the end of the disastrous four hours and asked me if she could help.

"No, no, it's nothing," I lied. "It won't happen again."

"Okay, but if you need to talk, Michele, I'm here."

"Thanks Coach," I said, slipping through the open gym doors and into the parking lot, walking up to John's waiting car and wondering what he had in store for me today.

We ate an early lunch and went shopping in Destin.

Of course, it couldn't be a peaceful time trying on clothes and shoes. After only twenty minutes, I felt the tell-tale signs of an ambush. My skin prickled at a discordant hum and a few light shuffles, along with hesitant, uneven steps, still far away, but close enough, caught my attention. Small clothing stores rarely had bathrooms, but back doors were common.

Bursting out into the bright sunlight, I had to stop and let my eyes adjust before steamrolling my way down the alley. Once at the edge of the building, I used my trusty mirror to check around the corner to see if anyone waited for me.

Several people milled about, and I watched as a tall, well-built man entered the store. The hair on my neck stood straight up and the familiar chill settled on the back of my neck. I spotted the large black SUV, whose hum had first alerted me to his presence. I quickly checked the cash in my backpack and found thirty dollars. John must have felt generous today. I cruised across the street, angling my way to avoid detection by the man sitting in the driver's seat in the SUV, and ran into a hotel. Going out a back entrance, I pulled up the map of the area in my mind and went through a couple other buildings, pausing only to call a taxi. I told him to meet me outside the building I intended to be in front of in ten minutes.

When I got there, I looked out the window of the store and noticed my cab hadn't arrived. I browsed through the shop, looking out the window every few seconds. Fifteen minutes had passed. Too long. Where was it? Just when I was about to head back to the house another way, a yellow taxi drove up. I dashed outside and jumped in.

I gave the driver an address about one mile from my house and sat back to enjoy the ride. Ten minutes later, we stopped in front of that house, and I realized I'd never alerted John to my position. I pulled the phone out, punching the button for John. After the last fiasco, John had given me a new emergency phone, and I only had to push the button to alert him. I paid the driver and walked in the direction of my house, looking for places to hide if I needed to.

About ten minutes later, out of nowhere, a large white van pulled up beside me and screeched to a stop. Instinctively, I ran to the door of the house nearest me, jumping over a few small bushes and past a huge, weeping tree. I grabbed the door handle, willing it to be unlocked, but it wasn't. It was chained from inside. Someone must be inside. I heard loud footfalls behind me and out of sheer panic, I shoved my body into the door, breaking the chain and stumbling in. I slammed it shut behind me, hoping I didn't run into the owner before escaping out the back door. I ran through the family room, knocking over a side table and sliding into the kitchen, my fingers only grazing the back door knob as powerful hands brought me to my knees. I gasped as I fell to the floor, my knees screaming out.

I looked wildly behind me as my head pushed hard into the linoleum. I reached out with both hands, letting go of my trusty backpack, grasping for anything I could use to hurt this person—to get him off of me. My hand brushed against something cool, slick and hard in the corner by the door. I tried to get a hold of it, but the person who pushed me to the floor turned me over, pressing my shoulders down.

"Give up!" he said, his voice deeper than his looks allowed. His extremely short, blonde hair and young face gave him the look of a teenager. "Just give up."

I reached behind me, sweeping my hand across the floor and grabbing the thing I'd felt before. A small fire-extinguisher? With every ounce of strength I had, I slammed it down on his head, hearing a crack as he toppled over, his legs draped across mine. I scrambled to my feet, pushing his legs off me with one big shove. I scurried out the back door, glancing down at the man, seeing a large gash on his forehead seeping blood, pausing only to watch his chest rise. Just once. It didn't.

Crashing footfalls sounded somewhere in the house and a voice yelled, "Who's there?" I ran flat out through back yards of people I didn't know and side-streets I'd never been down, sticking to the shadows as I darted from house to house. Everything looked strange and distorted somehow, like I was looking through crazy, magnified Halloween glasses. I stumbled over roots and whipped over small fences until I reached the first guard shack to my subdivision.

Out of breath, I poked my head inside the shack so that the guard would let me go through without any delays.

I told him my name, giving him no explanation why I breathed like a tiger charging her prey. After pulling my picture up on the monitor, he gave me leave. He had no reason to detain me.

I slipped into the trees lining the street, ducking in and out, running until I made it back to the house. I knew the only way in was through the guard shack, but I still scanned the tall wrought iron fence wishing a hidden entrance would appear. I charged the gate, the guard at the foot of our driveway grabbing me before I could run past him. "Are you okay, Miss Mattingly?"

"Of course," I said, pulling out an excuse from nowhere. "I guess Martin hasn't tried to get past you yet, huh?" I kept my head down, just in case I had any bruises from my head hitting the floor.

"Martin?"

"Yeah. We're in a race and it looks like I'm winning." I laughed, running down the drive and then yelling, "And don't you dare let him sneak by you."

"No worries, Miss. Mattingly," he yelled after me.

"Thanks." I knew nothing would get past him now.

I ran into the house and bumped right into John.

"Whoa!" he said, grabbing onto me. "Slow down already." He pulled me into the library and shut the door behind him.

"A guy," I started, but had to take a few deep breaths before continuing, letting the backpack fall to the floor, "tried to grab me. But I hit him and I think I might have killed—"

"Devan?" John interrupted, chuckling and taking a step back while letting go of me. "You got the jump on Devan?

"What are you talking about?"

"I sent Devan after you, a kind of second wave thing. I guess he found you."

"Crap. He's a good guy? Crap. Crap. Crap."

"What?"

"I might have killed him."

"What are you talking about?"

"I hit…I hit," I stuttered.

"Spit it out."

"I hit him really hard with a fire extinguisher and he was just lying there. And—"

"How long ago was this?"

I pulled out my phone and looked at it. "About twenty minutes?

John pulled out his phone, turned around and said something I didn't hear. He waited on the line, pacing around the room for a minute or so and then turned to me, shutting his phone and putting it in his pocket.

"Devan's on his way to the hospital," he said, knitting his eyebrows together and staring me down. "What exactly happened?"

"I didn't know who he was. I-I-I was just trying to protect myself like you said to do yesterday." A hot rock of anxiety sat in my stomach. Sweat pooled at the base of my neck and under my armpits, but not from the heat. This room was downright cold.

"Hmm," John said. "I didn't think you had it in you."

"Had what in me?"

"The ability to do what it takes. No matter what." He grinned.

I felt sick. I had really hurt someone—a good someone. I sat down on the sofa, closing my eyes and cradling my head in my hands.

John pushed my shoulders back to make me sit up. He got down on his knees and looked me directly in the eye and said, "Good job. You did the right thing. Devan will be all right. He's got a nice goose egg and will need stitches, but he will live. If it happens again, though, feel free to kill any bastard that tries to take you."

A shiver spread slowly through my body when I saw the glint in John's eye. Had he made me into a killer?

Katy walked into the library and John said, "We had a really successful go today. She's stepped up her game."

And he left me with Katy.

The realization that I would have killed the man who chased me if I had to made my head drop again. John had made me into his novice-self, and he loved it. I felt numb.

Katy sat next to me, asking me about my day, a true look of concern creasing her brow.

"Could we talk about it tomorrow?" I asked.

"Sure Michele, sure," she said, leaning back and letting me get up and head to my room.

I totally loved that she let me have my space. We were going to get along famously. I opened the door to my room and stood there, unable to walk in. My heart ached as I looked at the luxury that was to be mine forever more. A haunting symbol of my true desire. What if I didn't walk into the room? Would I be Christy again? A girl with problems, but problems that seemed like nothing compared to what I faced in this new life? Could I turn back time and never again pray for a different life? Would I ever feel comfortable in my own skin again? Was God showing me that my old life hadn't been so bad after all? Was he punishing me for not being grateful for what he'd given me? Or was it all a part of His plan for me? Was there a light shining brightly at the end of the tunnel? If so, why couldn't I see the light? My eyes burned with tears and I let them rain down, unrestrained. Could I be strong and still feel overwhelmed sometimes?

I don't know how long I stood there before Katy pried my hands from the door casings, led me to my bed and tucked me in. I didn't dream, because I didn't sleep.

At eleven-o-clock, a horrible alarm sounded. I pushed up against my headboard, pulling my knees up tight to my chest. John had told me this house was more protected than Fort Knox, so why would the alarm be sounding in the middle of the night? It had to be one of his stupid drills. Well, I refused to play his game this time. I slid back down in the covers and pulled my pillow over my head.

Minutes later, Katy burst through the door. I pulled the pillow off my head and watched her run straight at me.

"Why are you still here?" she yelled, barreling toward me. "Get moving."

"No. This is one of John's stunts again. I won't play," I said, my eyes fixed on a spot on the wall behind her.

"We don't know that," she said in a breathy yell right at my face. "It could be anyone."

My heart charged.

"Now get moving." She pushed me to the opposite side of the bed and bounded over it. She reached for the dresser and when she touched it, it moved forward, revealing a hideaway behind it. "I should have given you the tour of the hidden passages and hideouts already," she mumbled. "It's too late for that now. Get in there. And hurry up about it, we've taken too long."

My backpack.

"Wait! I need my backpack." Then it struck me. I'd left it downstairs, but Katy was already on it. She ran and grabbed it from beside my bed, pushing me further into the little space. She pulled down on a little lever and the door, made of brick, slid closed behind us.

"But I left the backpack downstairs," I said, pushing myself into the deep nook behind me, expecting her to follow, but she didn't. It was inky black.

"I brought it up after you left the library," she whispered. "I couldn't believe you'd forgotten it, and I knew John would give you crap for it."

She wanted to protect me from John? I thought she was on John's side. A warm rush filled me. "But I've been awake this whole time and don't remember you coming in."

"You were pretty much in a zone…shh. No matter what, stay where you are. I'm closing you in behind a second secret door."

I felt a panel shut in front of me, separating me from Katy, and held my breath, reaching out to feel it. The smooth surface went from wall to wall and as high as I could reach to the floor. Where was Katy? My heart beat against my ribs without mercy, my ears focusing on what was happening outside our little safe-haven. Minutes passed with nothing, and I remembered the flashlight in my backpack. I unzipped it and reached in when I heard pounding. The pounding seemed to get closer and closer. They were pounding and then tapping on the walls. The booming and tapping got closer and closer and I pulled myself into the smallest ball possible.

The sounds continued past me, and I finally dared breathe. Without warning, Katy screamed and then I heard what sounded like a big scuffle. I cupped a hand over my mouth. Moments later, I heard a swishing noise on the panel that had separated me from Katy, like a hand brushed across and around it, feeling for any sign of a false door. I shrunk into the corner of my hiding place. The noises behind the panel stopped and I leaned against the wall behind me.

Something was in my hand. It was hard and sharp. I'd cut myself. I held back a cry of pain. Had I unconsciously grabbed the knife out of my backpack instead of the flashlight? I would have had to click it open. It was a switchblade. I didn't remember doing that. I laid it next to me, and while sucking on my bleeding finger, I felt around in my backpack with my other hand for the tiny flashlight I knew was inside. I clicked it on, checking my finger out. It was still bleeding. I used the flashlight to find a band-aid. The white pad on the band-aid filled with blood immediately when I put it on. I then used the beam of light to look around my hideout.

That's when I heard a shrill cry and a few loud thumps. A freaky silence remained and I couldn't move for several moments. I couldn't just sit there any longer. I had to see what had happened to Katy. On the wall to my right was a button that had a label next to it, open/shut. I paused and listened hard for any movement in the room outside my safe spot and when I heard nothing, I pushed the button. The panel slid to the side, and for a moment, I thought I saw a person there in the shadows, but it was only that, a shadow.

Before me sat the empty space where Katy had been only moments before. I moved forward and peeked out the opening, pulling back when something clattered to the floor. I shone the light back in the space. My knife. It lay on the floor by my feet. I grabbed it and held it up, ready to strike if anyone came for me, but looking out of the hideout, the room appeared empty.

Time ticked on. I stood paralyzed for what seemed an eternity until a terrible thought struck me. The attackers could come back. I tried not to make a sound as I slipped the flashlight back into the backpack and stepped into the room, knife in one hand, and the backpack in the other.

Where was Katy and why had they taken her and not me? I looked back into the secret spot. Katy had saved me. I had to find her. Help her. I had just started around the bed when I heard the unmistakable sound of footsteps outside my room. I dropped down and slid under the bed, my back raking the bedrails as I scooted under. I kept my breathing shallow.

The footfalls went straight for the hiding place in the wall. A man called out, in some foreign language I'd never heard before. Maybe telling them it was empty? Then I remembered. I'd left the panel open. They'd know I'd escaped. I turned my head to see where the man's accomplice was and instead, saw Katy, lying still on the floor next to the bed, her blank stare looking at me. I gasped, turning my head back to the other side of the bed only to see black shoes peeking under the ruffle. Just then, someone at the foot of the bed grabbed hold of my feet and pulled me out. I screamed, holding tight to the knife and backpack. My back scraped the bedrail the whole way out, the back of my head banging into it as I emerged.

The man flipped me over the second I was clear of it. Automatically, I sat up and with one crazy swing, jabbed at him with the knife right where I hoped his heart would be. His eyes flew wide open and he fell to the side. Horror moved over me but all I could think about was getting out of there.

Blood already pooled next to him by the time the other man with the black shoes made it to the end of the bed. When he saw the stabbed man, he came for me. With no time to think, I crawled, with some difficulty, because I still held onto the bloody knife and backpack. I tried to get to my feet but his strong hands grabbed me by the waist and hoisted me up over his shoulder, holding my legs to his chest. My head bobbed into his back as he ran to the door of the room. With all the strength I could muster, I pulled myself up at the waist and struck with the knife over and over into his lower back. Blood oozed out, the knife crimson. He fell forward, flipping me into the hall wall. The knife and backpack flew out of my hands on impact. His head pressed hard into my stomach and forced all the air out of me.

It took me a minute to be able to breathe, enough that I could push him off of me, my clothes and hands dripping with blood. I reached for the backpack, almost leaving the knife, but thought better of it. I ran down the hall to the back stairway, stumbling down them, through a narrow, creaking hallway and passing a blur of rooms before reaching the kitchen. I looked around the room for Mangus, my fake butler. No luck. I should go to the library-the safe-room, but it was still so far. I pushed the button under the nearest light switch and stood there for a second. I heard noises above me. I couldn't wait.

I spied keys hanging by a back door. I grabbed them and ran blindly to the garage. I had to get away. Shocked to find the side door open, I ran inside and stood next to the first car in the row, a Lexus SUV. I shuffled through the keys—three carried the Lexus logo. I pushed all three until the Lexus chirped. I jumped into the car and started it. The large garage door opened at the same time. I jammed the car into reverse and pressed hard on the gas. That's when I noticed John standing next to the car. I slammed on the brakes and laid my head on the steering wheel, taking deep breaths as he tapped on the window. I opened the door for him and he pulled me out.

"Katy's dead and two other men are dying up in my room," I sputtered.

"Is that all?" he said, raising his eyebrows.

A blast of cold air seemed to slap me in the face. "Don't tell me this was a freaking drill!" I yelled.

"Okay," he said, a smile dominating his face.

"I should kill you right here, right now for that." I clutched the knife in my right hand, squeezing it for all I was worth, only inches from his body.

"Whatever you do, don't use the knife. I don't have a knife suit on."

I let the knife roll out of my hand, my palms slick with blood, and it landed with a clatter on the floor. I stared at my blood-soaked hands. "Knife suit?" I squeaked. My world tilted.

"Those men you so callously stabbed were wearing knife suits, filled with blood to make it all seem real. It did seem real… didn't it?" It was more of a statement than a question.

John held his hand out to me, "Come on."

I swatted it away, grabbing the backpack out of the car, and then plopping it onto the cement floor. I walked toward the driveway and he put his hand on my back, pushing me forward. I squirmed away from him, speeding up the pace. A fire burned inside me, making me want to scream and cry at the same time.

Katy and two men from the attack stood only yards away from me on the front porch. How could I trust Katy ever again? All I could manage was a loud 'uggh'. Without my consent, a few tears dripped down my cheek.

I looked at Katy, but spoke to John, "How could you do this to me? It's all just a big game to all of you, but this is my life you're toying with."

"Exactly," he said. I refused to turn and look at him. "You have a life and will continue to have a life because of this training." He walked around me and joined the three people whom I had thought were dead only minutes earlier. They all looked at me.

"Why do you want me to save my life but take others' lives?" I called out, fight still bubbling out of me.

"It was important to force you to act in a deadly way again. after your reaction to slamming Devan on the head, I wasn't sure you'd be able to do it. I couldn't have you turning gun-shy."

I scowled. "I'd rather die than kill anybody."

"You proved that isn't true now."

Moments passed in silence. "I thought I was going to die. And they'd killed Katy." I whispered. A nasty sob rose up in me. I was capable of killing someone to stay alive.

"That, my dear, is what I needed to see. I'd figured you'd decided your life wasn't worth sparing. I had to show you it was."

"That makes no sense at all."

"I had to show you that you can have an impact on good and evil in this world, and I knew I'd have to give you a pretty big trigger. Enter Katy. You need to understand that the men looking for you want you to be alive. They want to flaunt you, use you for information and power. If they get their hands on you, you'd wish you'd died instead."

"I wish that already."

“Stop it. You’re acting like a baby. You have everything.”

“But nothing of value.”

“Now you’re being ridiculous.”

Katy stepped in. “Look, Michele, I realize this situation isn’t ideal, but once John leaves for good tomorrow, you’ll have a pretty normal life and under much better circumstances than you found yourself in Montana. Your life is what it is. You have an opportunity to make a difference. Don’t squander this chance.”

For a mere second I wanted to tear into her, let her know I’d never trust her again, but then tears streamed down my face and I readily accepted a tight hug.

“You are going to live a long, fruitful life. You’ll see.”

I really did want to live. I needed Katy. At some point she took me to my room. I dreamt of conquering the world

Chapter Seventeen

The next morning, I sat in the car, my body aching and wishing I could just sleep, waiting for Katy to take me to cheer practice. After she hopped in and started the car, she gave me a once over and pulled my face to the side to inspect the make-up-hide-job on my bruised cheek. She'd come in to my room after I'd showered and described how to cover a bruise.

"Good job," she said, nodding her head and driving onto the street. "People will mistake it for a shadow."

"I hope so," I said, knowing the cheerleaders wouldn't miss it.

And a few of them did comment on it, but I gave them some excuse about running into a pole while texting. We didn't have time to practice because the people from the uniform company were there and handed out our uniforms and shoes. Several girls threw fits when their orders had problems like the skirt's hem hanging too low or high or their names spelled incorrectly on some part of the outfit. The uniform reps either fixed them on the spot or promised to have them done by morning when we left for cheer camp.

Mine was perfect. I felt like a real cheerleader in that uniform and couldn't help jump up and down and scream with the girls whose uniforms fit perfectly. By the time we'd gone over the schedule and what we could expect to happen at camp, it was time to go. I couldn't help thinking cheer camp sounded like one big party. It would be so different from reality. On the one hand, I was being trained to kill people and I had to hide that fact. On the other, I had to be a sweet cheerleader that everyone trusted and followed. Creepy.

I ran out to the car, bouncing with every step. I couldn't wait to pack. I'd have to run to the store and get stocked up on treats.

I expected to see Katy in the driver's seat, but John was there instead coming to pick me up. After I climbed into the car, he said, "We have a few things to do today, but I think you'll like them all." No smile crossed his lips.

I doubted it.

He surprised me when he took me home. He pulled into the garage and I remembered about packing for camp.

He pulled into the garage and I gathered my things and climbed out of the car while saying, "Cool, now I can pack for camp."

"Katy will take care of that," he said, "We have more important things to do."

I knew it. I would not like today. "But I need to get my things together and I want to get a bunch of stuff from the store." I stood, holding my cheer bag and water bottle, throwing darts with my eyes at him. He had his back to me. I followed, down the long row of cars, passing three, when he stopped. I set my things down with a loud thump and sighed as loudly as possible, while I waited for his instructions. He turned, raising his eyebrows at me. We stood behind a little yellow convertible bug. He kept his eyebrows raised and I knew he expected me to go to him. I took a few steps standing right next to him, staring him down.

"This, my dear," he said, "is your car." He made a grand sweep with his arm.

I squished my eyebrows together. Had I heard him right? I turned, looking at the furiously bright car, trying hard to reconcile my feelings. I'd always dreamt about getting my own car, and yet I had no desire to have this particular one. I forced a weak, "Wow."

He chuckled.

Oh, this was just a joke. I was supposed to blend in. This car stood out—way out.

"You jerk!" I said, with as much venom as possible, suddenly sad it wouldn't be mine. At least it was a car. Not what I'd choose, but a car, nonetheless

"What? I hand select a car for you and you call me a jerk?"

I didn't know what to think. Why would he give me such a conspicuous car?

"When I pulled up the computer page to the dealership and saw this yellow bug, I thought it screamed Michele Mattingly." His words dripped with sarcasm as he emphasized the word yellow.

I finally got it. This car was one more way for him to stick it to me. He knew I wouldn't want something so bright, so gaudy.

"Don't you think it fits your bubbly cheerleader personality? This car will remind you everyday who you are."

He knew I'd need a car and he didn't want me to have any control over it at all. I retreated back into character as Michele as fast as I could and said, "You're kidding, right?" I tried desperately to remove all sarcasm to force him to take my words at face value. "A car?" I gushed. "I thought you were just teasing me. Is it really mine?"

He turned to me, looking me square in the eye. I put all my effort into erasing all the hateful feelings I had about that car. I didn't want to give him the satisfaction. Whether he saw through it or not, I'd never know. He handed me the keys and a rush of exhilaration spread through my veins. I ran to the driver's side door and hopped inside. As I pushed the key into the ignition, John opened the passenger side door and climbed in.

I felt the excitement drain from me.

"Can't I at least take the maiden voyage by myself ?"

"Don't worry about it. I'll be gone tomorrow, and besides, I need to make sure you can drive this little beauty."

He was determined to take all the joy out of everything.

After backing out of the massive garage, I drove down the driveway, out the gate and immediately back through it, up the drive and into the garage, just to irritate him.

"Very funny, Michele," he said, "Let's try that again."

"Why don't we take a different car?" I said, not wanting to give him what he wanted. "I just don't feel like driving."

"Too bad. I've already loaded the trunk with the supplies we need. Now, go!"

I turned the key again and started the car, knowing I had no choice. I drove out of the subdivision. He told me to drive to Destin Beach as fast as possible. Once there, he had me help carry bags, towels and snacks to the beach. We ate lunch, and while he sat on a beach chair under an umbrella, I played in the water for several hours. The water, lukewarm, gave no relief from the burning sun, but I couldn't resist paddling out and just lying on my back, letting the water lap over me. Of course, I couldn't completely relax and waited for the unavoidable ambush.

I had swum out, past the breaking waves, secluding myself as much as possible. I kept an eye out for anyone coming too close. When I finally made my way back to the shore, John pulled out a snack for us and he talked about the ocean and how it could be used to my advantage if I learned how to harness its power. We cleaned up and walked over to a dock where we jumped onto a wave runner. After about a half-hour of training, John took me back to the dock to try it on my own. We stayed out another hour. The waves increased in intensity for some reason and my body ached and my thumb throbbed from holding in the accelerator. I didn't particularly like driving the wave runner, but I could see how it could help me escape from the beach. The unavoidable ambush never came. At least I got a chance to think about what I'd do in this situation if someone did attack.

As we climbed into the car at sunset, John said, "Now, there are a few things that you need to work on. One big one is getting more familiar with the ocean. It will give you another exit from Niceville."

I started the car and pulled onto the highway, listening to him.

"A couple of times a week you'll be coming here, to Destin, to learn with a water-sports expert. You only have a month or so before the weather turns, so give it your full attention. Also, you'll continue working on tumbling, two types of martial arts, and I'm adding kick-boxing."

"Is that all?" I said, rolling my eyes.

"Katy has your schedule," he said, ignoring me. "Stay close to her. She'll be a great asset to you."

The car was silent and it was never quiet in a car with John. He always had me doing something or at least listening to something educational. He reached over and turned the radio on. The whole way home, I stayed on high alert, still waiting for an attack of some sort.

It never came.

Once we pulled into the driveway, he turned the radio down and said, "Katy will give you the in-depth tour of the house." Then he went on reminding me about staying true to my new self and not standing out in ways that would betray who I used to be. He warned me about having a Facebook account, and ending up on TV or in the spotlight. I was to remain average or less within my small sphere of a hot-popular-cheerleader.

Talk about confusing!

Once inside the house, after parking the car, John had me sit down in the first sitting area and said, "By the way, keep your spidey senses on. You never know when you'll need them."

"What?" I protested. "You mean I have to live in fear every day? Even after all we've done the last three months?"

"Just expect an ambush about once a month. I can't have you going soft on me and getting caught, now can I? Besides, I think you'll find it will become second nature to you to be on your guard at all times." It only took him a second to continue. "My time with you is over. I've given you everything you need to stay safe. By the way, it's time for you to apply to colleges. Pick only large, state-run universities. Your transcripts won't get you into exclusive ones. Your future is yours, but stay on the path I've set out for you and you'll remain safe. Remain Michele and you'll live."

"Okay," I said, both hating and loving the new me, while fighting a strange urge to hug him.

I thought about Alex for a split second. But the thought was gone as fast as it had come. I knew I couldn't see him again.

He turned to leave, but looking back he said, "Remember, Alex is off limits." Then he was gone.

How had he known I'd thought of Alex? He was so aggravating. To think I'd wanted to hug him. "Self-serving egotistical maniac," I said to the closed door before running upstairs and flopping onto my bed, taking a deep breath. I was free. Of John, at least.

I ran to Katy to see if we could go get some treats at the store. "I've already taken care of that."

"Really?" I said. She must've seen the sadness on my face and finished with "No worries, I stuffed your suitcase with licorice, M&M's, popcorn and other awesome snacks. You won't want for anything."

A smile sprung up on my face and I hugged her. "Thanks, Katy!"

"No problem. We're going to do something even more fun." We explored the house and she showed me all the "finer aspects" of it: the hidden passageways, the secret hideaways, the secret exits, and all the extreme safety measures they'd put in place. Mason and Natalie must either be completely paranoid or have pissed off a ton of bad guys as black-ops agents. I lived in a freaking fortress. Our tour ended in the library.

"Here's your credit card," she said. "Just know that you only have 1000 dollars to spend each month."

My jaw hit the floor.

"That should be enough to cover your hair and nail appointments, clothes, make-up, gas, food and fun."

"A thousand dollars?"

"If for some reason you need more, let me know."

"Katy," I said. "You've got to fill me in on this money thing." I tapped the credit card and then flung my arms to my sides and looked about the room. "Where does all this money come from?"

"Oh, inheritances, businesses, things like that," she said, trying to hedge. It was obvious she was skirting the truth.

"Come on, Katy. I'm not stupid."

"Let's just say agents get a cut of the money they retrieve when bringing down the bad guys."

"Are you serious?"

"How do you think black ops divisions get financed? The government can't give us the money we need to be successful, and it's nice to get paid what we're worth."

I nodded my head slowly, thinking this over. Was it right to use the money this way? It was good that they took the money from the bad guys, but shouldn't they somehow get it back to the people who the bad guys took it from?

"I know what you're thinking, Michele. There is no way to return the money to the rightful owners. This money is laundered so many times there's just no way to do it."

Cheer camp started early the next day and was all that it promised to be. I even became BFFs with my roommate,

Wendy. At least that's what she called me. I did like her, but I still had to get used to her incessant talking about nothing. At least she seemed to believe in a lot of the same things I did. I fell asleep to her chatter every night. She extolled my virtues to everyone that would listen and stayed with me twenty-four/seven except when Lillian and Beth pulled me into their planning sessions. I seemed to mesh with them all.

Lillian and Beth were masters at making everyone like each other and stick together. I'd never had so many friends and it was a bit overwhelming keeping all the gossip and nonsense straight when I didn't care about it.

It wasn't all a party. We did work really hard in all the classes. In the end, we won the first place spirit and tumbling awards as well as the most inspiring team award.

Natalie acted thrilled each day when I called and reported. I liked reporting to her. It made it seem like she really was my mom, only more attentive. For a moment, a tiny moment that third night, I let myself long for my real mom, but pushed the longing back in its corner to suppress the grief that threatened to overtake me.

Once home on Sunday evening, I hit the pillow and slept until the next morning. The sun, the hard work and the chatter had worn me out. Katy actually had to wake me. I drove my car to school for cheer practice. It's hard to describe the feeling of freedom it gave me. I drove with the top down, music blaring, even though it was only six in the morning. Despite the freedom I felt, I couldn't let go of constantly surveying my surroundings. It would be just like John to send an ambush team my first morning alone.

We worked hard at cheer practice, and it didn't end soon enough. I couldn't wait to drive again. I'd told Wendy at cheer camp that I could give her a ride home from practices now that I had a car, and I couldn't wait to fulfill that promise. I checked my phone on the way to the car. I had a message from my "parents", wondering why I hadn't checked in yesterday—and one from Katy reminding me to turn on the GPS when I got in the car.

Even though the ride to Wendy's house was only five minutes, we made the best of it, running through a drive-up and getting a shake before dropping her off. I pushed the GPS on and found directions to my water training. The route the GPS gave would take twenty-eight minutes. I wanted to beat that time. I took some back roads and arrived in twenty-five flat. Shaving three minutes off wasn't bad, but I bet I could do better.

The lesson lasted two hours, but my instructor warned me that most days for the next week until school started, we'd be together three hours. After that, I'd only go on Saturday mornings for a few hours until the weather turned.

I looked at the schedule Katy had put into my phone. Mondays and Wednesdays I had training in two types of martial arts, and Tuesdays I had an hour of kick-boxing. My first martial arts instructor focused on using my instincts and wits while the second worked on my power.

Most games would be on Fridays for varsity sports, but some fell on other days. When there was a conflict with my classes, Katy would change them to fit my schedule. I would never just miss them.

I wasn't home a lot, but when I was, Katy made it fun and I quickly felt at ease. After a few weeks it no longer felt weird to be alone at the house with Katy and Mangus and the chef. Occasionally, I'd see another staff member who worked on something like the yard or cleaning, but it was a pretty solitary existence and it drove me crazy. I was used to a house full of kids and noise. The enormous house didn't help any. I didn't know what to do with myself when Katy was gone. I'd been with John or somebody else every moment the last three months and it felt odd being alone.

When the next Sunday rolled around, I couldn't help thinking about church and how much I missed attending, feeling the peace I always felt there. But it was more than that, I'd felt like I belonged. It surprised me how much I longed for that feeling again. I hopped down to the library and hopped onto the computer there. John told me it was safe to search anything I wanted on it, but to do it sparingly. He had forbidden me from attending the same religious denomination that I had at home, saying they could track me that way, but I needed to go to a church that was familiar. I looked up churches outside the boundaries for my school and its rival school. I printed out a list of ten different ones I could attend.

After pulling on a nice dress and heels, doing my make-up and putting on a wig, I called Katy and left her a message that I was going for a drive. I pulled up into a church parking lot an hour later, just a little late for the eleven-o-clock session. I sat on a pew near the back and let the speakers' words fill me with comfort. I had intended to leave before the end, but found myself bowing my head as the closing prayer was spoken. As I made my way out, several people asked me if I'd just moved in. I let them know I was just visiting but wished I could return. I should have left before the closing prayer but a big part of me was glad to have met the people I did—glad they had wanted to make me feel welcome. That began my weekly clandestine visits to churches on Sundays.

I spent all my free time the last week before school with the cheerleaders, goofing off and falling into my new life as deeply as possible. I even started getting used to all the mindless chatter. I found that if I spent an hour here or there researching something intelligent, I could handle it. I became Michele through and through.

Chapter Eighteen

I woke on the first day of my senior year to the sun glittering through my window and wondered if I could handle going back to school. I wouldn't be able to go straight to college, but at least I only had one year of high school left. The last six months of high school in Montana had been horrible. Would I revert back to the shy, smart, overly helpful girl I used to be just because I was walking into a high school? Christy snuck out of the woodwork, jeering at me.

Once out of the shower and ready for the day, I looked at myself in the mirror, my long light brown, blond streaked, luscious hair streaming down my back, my face, flawless, and the cheer uniform completing the package. Christy retreated. I was not Christy anymore. I felt powerful. I could do this. I had it all—everything I'd never had before. This must be God's gift to me for losing the most important parts of my life. It would all work out. I would do more than survive. My new life was awesome.

Katy met me for breakfast, like always, and went over my schedule with me, reminding me I needed to call my parents by five or it'd be too late where they were.

I'd spent the summer in the gym of the school, and now finally got to see the whole building. I felt like a queen walking into the plain, sprawled out, one level brick high school. It reminded me of my elementary school. People stared, but in a worshipy way. The cheerleader outfit automatically drew people's eyes to me. Would they still look tomorrow when I didn't have to wear it? I had to constantly fight the urge to sit front and center in each of my classes, though, the perfect student wanting to take root in my life again. But, I pushed myself to the back of the room, played on my phone, searching the internet and playing games throughout all my classes.

Lunch that first day reinforced my feelings of invincibility when the cheerleaders grabbed me in the hall and brought me to a bunch of guys sitting on some steps in the hall.

I leaned over to Lillian as we approached and whispered, "They're all so hot."

"Aren't they, though," she whispered back and then giggled, the kind of infectious giggle that you had to join in on. "Watch this."

"Hey guys," she said to everyone. "Let me introduce a true newbie to our group, Michele Mattingly. Not only is she our newest varsity member, but she's new to Niceville." She moved a few steps away from me and motioned her hands toward me, like I was a prize they could all win.

All kinds of appreciative noises came from the guys as they looked me over. Two guys scrambled to their feet and muscled their way in front of each other to talk to me first. Mack was the bigger of the two and won out.

"How about we head to the beach Saturday and I'll teach you to surf." He smiled his best smile.

I looked to Lillian. She grinned at me and nodded her head.

"Sure," I said, my insides about to burst with excitement. Not only was this going to be my first real date, I would be learning to surf. So cool.

He roared like a gorilla, flexing his muscles, as he turned back to the group of guys.

I shook my head and noticed Wendy's golf ball size eyes before the second guy asked me out for my second date. She was one of the few cheerleaders I thought held values close to mine. What was she worried about?

Most of the cheerleaders cozied up next to their boyfriends and picked at their food while the boys inhaled theirs. About five of the girls and ten of the boys weren't attached to any special and sat clumped together just to the left of those who were paired up.

"What was that look all about?" I asked Wendy, sitting next to her.

"Just be careful with these guys," she whispered. "I gave up on dating guys in this group a long time ago."

"What? Why?" I asked.

A boy, taller than a tree and as skinny as a twig, most likely a basketball player, fell at my feet, kneeling, pretending to beg.

"Please. Please, Michele," he said. "Go out with me on Tuesday night to a soccer game. I will shower you with…well, myself."

I laughed and nodded, forgetting my discussion with Wendy.

Lillian pulled me into a conversation she was having with another cheerleader about the hot math teacher at the school. I didn't see it.

At first I liked the way the guys looked at me, but then the ogling made me uncomfortable, especially when the ogler had a girlfriend.

The rest of the week all I could think about were my upcoming dates. I loved being Michele.

Mack picked me up at six-thirty Saturday morning to go surfing. The thought of finally learning to surf sent a big, slow smile rolling across my face as the music blared and we drove to the beach.

"You are going to love this," he said, parking the car and jumping out. I knew it would be fruitless to wait for him to open my door because when he'd picked me up, he'd texted me to come out. He didn't even bother to meet me at the door. Instead, he peered out the driver's side window and waved at me when I opened the front door. Dork. This wasn't how I'd imagined my first date to pick me up. We hadn't said much more than "hi" before he blared the music and took off down the driveway.

Once on the beach with our boards, he started "teaching" me to surf. First, he showed me how to lie on the board and jump up into a standing position. I pretended to have a bit of trouble the first few times, thinking this would be so girl-like. It was a mistake.

"Here, I'll help you," he said, coming to my aid. He wrapped his arms around my waist, supposedly to help me get up. Instead, after lifting me to my feet, he pulled me to the side of the board and we rolled into the sand. I lay there, his large body on top of mine and he proceeded to kiss me, all wet and animalistic. Turning my head to the side proved fruitless, he just followed my lead. I took my hands and I placed them on his cheeks and pushed his head, back. Hard.

"Get off me," I said with a breathy yell.

He just stared down at me, his large body unmoving. I squirmed and kicked my legs and pushed at his shoulders until I was free. My jujitsu training came in handy. I sat on the beach, breathing hard from the effort. He gave me a dirty look, grabbed his board and ran into the water. I thought about waiting for him. That was the polite thing to do, wasn't it? But then I remembered the feel of his body on top of mine and I quickly called Katy to come get me. I don't know when he discovered I was gone.

The next two dates that weekend were practically an exact replay of my "date" with Mack. The boys seemed to think I owed them something for going out with them. After that, I thought the answer would be to only go on group dates.

Following the game the next Friday, I went with Nickolas and two other couples to the beach. We were meeting a big group of kids there for a bon fire. After roasting hot dogs and marshmallows on sticks, the six of us headed for a walk on the beach to cool off.

Nickolas wrapped a blanket around his neck and grabbed my hand as we walked. I liked this guy. He was a gentleman, not only getting doors for me, but making sure I was taken care of before he took care of himself. I figured I'd found a winner. The waves lapped with a little slapping noise against the sand, and the moon shone down with meager light. Already this had been much better than my individual dates. Nickolas told some super funny stories and asked me a ton a questions about myself. When he stopped and threw the blanket down, I jumped on it and laughed until I noticed one of the other two couples was gone and the third kept walking past us. He plopped down next to me and made his move. All arms and lips and legs. I found myself in yet another compromising situation. The only thing that made this better than the individual dates was that he actually acted a bit ashamed when I protested and then offered to take me home.

I wasn't going to give up after one group date, but I should have. The next two group dates, which were really just a group of us hanging out together, quickly regressed into make-out sessions all around me, and I had to get creative not to fall victim to the boys' charm and their trickery. I now understood why Wendy never went out on dates with these guys. After telling her about my botched date with Mack, she had said the same types of things had happened to her too many times. She had sworn off dating the guys from school unless it was a dance when she had to go.

I should have listened to her, but dating was supposed to be fun. I wanted to experience that rite of passage. After the third group date left me with no hope of not being mauled, I realized

I didn't want to date anymore. I made up all kinds of excuses, which didn't go over very well with my new cheerleading friends, and wished I had a way to let them all know to bug off. They persisted. I guessed I was the new meat and every guy in the cheerleader clique wanted a taste. I couldn't take it and no one outside this popular group dared ask me out. I was an untouchable to them. I was sure good guys were out there, but they, I guessed, felt they couldn't get to me.

I'd gone a week dodging dates when I discovered all cheerleaders were *strongly* encouraged to go to set an example and go to the homecoming dance. Lillian informed me that the varsity cheerleaders always went to every dance together. I didn't want to go, but said yes to the boy I thought posed the least risk. Even Wendy thought he was safe. But, least risk didn't equate to no risk. My first dance and it turned out to be a bust. By the end of the evening, I left my date, who'd started drinking before the dance and then became loud and obnoxious once the alcohol took effect. I found my own way home. Thank heaven for Katy.

That night, I hatched a plan with her. I'd find a nice guy like my old-self, shy, smart and somewhat clueless, to call my own.

Looking around in the classes John had enrolled me in, I realized the guy I was looking for wasn't there, but thought I knew where to find him—in AP or college classes. Classes I wasn't supposed to take. I couldn't think of an easier way to find the right boy, nerdy and insecure. Sure there were some of those in the classes I was already in, but I craved intelligent conversation. I knew John would be mad, but he wasn't here to stop me, so I went to the counseling center and talked with my counselor about getting into a few AP classes. I'd follow all John's other rules. What could he do anyway?

The counselor discouraged me.

"Let's face it, Michele," she said. "You don't have the background you need to be successful in those classes. Besides, you'd be way too far behind. We're five weeks into school already."

I didn't let her deter me. That night, I wrote a paper, an almost perfect one, full of reasoning and logic and took it to a few of the AP teachers explaining that I'd just moved here and needed a challenge. Could they accept me? AP European History and college Psychology took the bait and wrote a note to the counselor to admit me. I'd have a lot of catch-up to do, they'd warned me, but with writing abilities like I had, they'd take a chance on me.

The first few days in these classes, I found a few guys that interested me, and I chatted with them, to see if they would fit my requirements for a boyfriend. I really focused on one boy in AP Euro, Kaleb—tall, tan, and brilliant, with completely average looks. He seemed the best choice, but at lunch he was always surrounded with a group of kids, more girls than boys, and although I never saw him with one particular girl, I could tell several in the group adored him.

In casual conversation with a couple of my cheerleader friends, I asked about him.

"Do you like him?" Wendy asked, eyebrows lifted.

"He's tall and all, but come on, you're way out of his league," Lillian said.

Exactly what I wanted.

"Yeah, put him out of your mind," Beth said. "You can have anyone you want. Tons of guys are always asking us about you."

"Yeah, we'll set you up," Lillian offered, helpfully.

"No you guys, really, I was just wondering."

They gave me the craziest looks after that and continued to badger me to let them have so-and-so ask me out.

Asking around the intellectual crowd gave me more information on Kaleb. He appeared to be above reproach. I had to go for it. I made sure I sat by him the whole next week and chatted with him. Most of the cheerleaders had already asked guys out for the girls' choice Halloween dance, but it was only two weeks away. I didn't want to seem too eager, but I couldn't risk someone else asking Kaleb.

I bit the bullet and tried something to set me apart. I knew here in Niceville, kids simply called or walked up to someone to ask him or her to go to a dance, but I wanted it to be more fun. I ordered fifty helium filled balloons to be delivered to his house. I talked to his mom on the phone and scheduled the time to come. Every balloon in one of the three school colors had a roll of paper in it with a letter on each. He had to pop the balloons to get the letters in order to figure out the message they contained.

One color spelled *Halloween Dance.*

The next spelled *with Michele*.

And the last spelled *Mattingly.*

I hoped he knew my name.

The note on his door said, *We'd have a popping good time together if you say yes.*

His mom and dad and Katy helped me get all the balloons inside his room and shut the door. They laughed and laughed.

I still hadn't heard from Kaleb on Friday. The dance was a week away. Had I made it too difficult? I didn't think so. Kaleb was pretty darn smart. I'd say he was in the top one percent of our class. Besides, his parents knew who I was. I'd look toward his big group of friends at lunch only to receive dirty looks. I wondered if he'd told them and they were mad at me.

In desperation, I asked Lillian about him again.

"Kaleb? Oh, Kaleb. He's cute, but I don't know if he dances. I think his religion forbids it or something."

"Hmm," I said. Why would his parents let me ask him if his religion forbids it? It didn't seem logical. As luck would have it, leaving school late that day, I saw him standing near the road, waiting for something. I had to know.

"Hey, Kaleb," I said, steeling my nerves, walking up to him.

"Hey, Michele," he said, looking at his shoes. He did know my name.

"Look, I didn't know you weren't allowed to dance or anything, so, I…"

He laughed out loud just as a car with several of his friends in it drove up next to him and stopped. "I'm *allowed* to dance," he said, laughter creasing his brow as he climbed in with his friends.

Sure he was laughing about what I'd said with his friends, my heart raced. He was no dummy and knew what I was getting at. Had people been wrong about him? He was avoiding me, but why?

I sat in my car thinking about Kaleb and the dance and decided there was only one thing I could do. I started the car and drove over to his house to get some answers. His mom came to the door.

"Hi, Michele," she said, smiling brightly.

"Is Kaleb here?" I asked.

"No, not yet." She looked at her watch and then said, "but, he should be here any minute. You want to come in and wait for him?"

I almost said no, my nerves suddenly catching up with me, but decided to brave it out. "Sure."

She led me into the kitchen filled with the smell of fresh baked cookies.

"I just made some cookies. Would you like some?"

Hoping I didn't sound too eager, I said, "Sure."

"Have a seat."

I sat at the large table as she brought me warm chocolate chip cookies and a tall glass of cold milk. I ate one gooey cookie, washing the remains down with several gulps of milk. I liked the feeling in this house.

"These are great," I said.

"Thanks, I..." she said as Kaleb came through the kitchen door yelling, "Mom, there's a car..."

I jumped up, thinking about running and chickening out, but I couldn't see a door that led outside. I glanced back in the direction the yelling had come from. My eyes met Kaleb's. Now, I couldn't escape. He couldn't escape. He'd stopped short, a panicked expression on his face. I'm sure mine matched his. I grabbed hold of the chair I'd so hastily jumped out of, just in time to see the flicker of a dagger look Kaleb gave his mom as he took a few steps further into the room. Not knowing how to explain what I'd just done, I took my seat again.

"Michele got here a few minutes ago. She came to see you."

There was an awkward pause as the dagger look deepened.

"Well, I've got laundry to do," she said and left the room.

He turned to me, his eyes the size of silver dollars, then he followed his mom out, "Mom!" he said, his voice a loud whisper in my ears.

"You will go with that cute girl to the dance and you will have fun. Go tell her right now."

"But Mom, we're all going to go as a group—like every other dance and..."

"I realize that, but not one of those girls thought to ask you. This nice girl did."

"You've always told me to date wisely, mom. I'm trying to here. She's a cheerleader, and Zack said she doesn't go to church."

"Again, facts I already know. It will not hurt you to broaden your circle of friends. This is one date, not marriage. Now, go in there and treat this girl like the princess she is."

"Mom—"

"End of discussion, now go."

He was horrified. I was horrified. How could I make him go with me? I needed a back-out plan and fast. He came through the door and stood, arms crossed, staying as far away from me as possible, like I was a leper.

"Listen…" I said at the same moment he said my name.

"You go first," he said.

"No, you," I said.

He was silent, so I decided to make it easy on him. The truth seemed the easiest way out.

"I heard what you said to your mom. I don't want to cause any problems. I'm new here and don't know all the right ways to do things. This is my first year being a cheerleader and it's been pretty overwhelming in that crowd. It's not me. I like a bit more peace and quiet. I asked you because I thought you were a good guy. One that maybe even had the same values as I do. I just wanted to have a fun time without having to worry about what my date might want from me. I understand what might happen to your reputation if you go with a cheerleader to a dance, so I take back my invitation. Go with your group and have fun. No hard feelings."

"No, wait," he said. "It's not that…"

I gave him a look that said, "Yes it is."

"Well, part of it is," he continued speaking so quickly I had to concentrate to understand. "But there's this group I hang out with and we kinda do everything together and I don't date outside my religion."

"No worries," I said. Sad, but honest. I knew how he felt from being Christy. I'd felt the same way and had the same ideals growing up, but when push came to shove, I'd let some of those ideals disappear with Christy. I'd given in on a lot and I couldn't see letting him do the same. I couldn't ask him to compromise his beliefs. "I really understand. No hard feelings."

"Thank…"

Just then, his mom walked in and addressed me, "Michele, Kaleb would be happy to escort you to the dance." She gave him a stern, motherly look. "Michele, would you mind going with his group?" she continued. "Everyone needs more friends. I'm sure they'd be happy to have you. Don't you think, Kaleb?"

The pause was deadly and when he didn't answer, she turned to me.

"I think that's a good compromise, don't you, Michele?"

I turned to Kaleb, who looked dark red now, "Maybe I could just be included in your group, and we wouldn't go as a date." He would never be my fake boyfriend, but at least I'd be safe for the dance. I never dreamt someone with perfect values would be difficult to catch. Wasn't I that person? I'd always been that person.

"Okay, as long as it's not a date," Kaleb said, wringing his hands.

Relief washed over me and my heart finally regained its normal rhythm.

His mom shook her head and sighed. "Then it's settled."

I left, wishing I'd had time to eat another cookie and wondering if Kaleb would hate me forever, but feeling like it was worth it not to have to fend off any guys at the dance.

Tuesday I still hadn't heard from Kaleb and wondered if I'd have to ask someone else at the last minute. Maybe he'd agreed to include me in his group date just to placate his mom, when in reality he had no intentions of doing so. I stared at him all during college psych, wishing I could read his mind. I watched him leave when class was over and thought about confronting him, but chickened out. I headed for lunch, my mind focused on reasons why I hadn't heard from Kaleb. Someone grabbed my arm. Instinctively, I threw the person to the ground and almost shoved my heel into his throat, when I realized I wasn't being attacked, it was just Kaleb.

"Oh, sorry," I blurted, offering him my hand to help him up.

His eyes were once again the size of silver dollars, but at least he took my hand.

"I'm really sorry. Really," I said, helping him up, feeling my face burn.

"That was weird," he said, suspicion filling his eyes. "Where'd you learn that?" Just as I was about to speak, he added, "Why would you learn that?"

I said the first thing that came to my mind, "Oh, I think my kick-boxing classes are getting the better of me."

"Kick-boxing, huh?" It looked as if interest supplanted his suspicion.

"Yeah, it kicks my butt every Thursday."

He actually chuckled. "Well, we're meeting at my house to make plans for the dance tonight. Can you come?"

"Sure, what time?"

"Seven."

"Crap! I can't—there's that special JV game tonight. Just make the plans and let me know what you decide."

"I thought you'd want a say in the costumes," he said, giving me a soft, slug punch in the arm. "Would you be done at nine?"

"We totally should be."

"I'll move the meeting, then. Just leave your kick-boxing skills at the door. We don't want to scare all the girls away." As he disappeared around the corner he called out, "Or the guys, for that matter."

He had joked with me. I drew in a deep breath, knowing I'd dodged a bullet and wishing I could turn off my spidey senses.

"Michele."

I turned to see Lillian coming my way. "Wasn't that Kaleb?"

"Yeah," I said.

"What was that about?" she asked, looking in the direction he had gone.

"We're going to the dance together."

"Shut up!" She shrieked. "You are not!"

“Am, too,” I said, turning to open the lunch room doors.

She grabbed my arm. “Traditionally, all the cheerleaders go to all the dances together, Michele. You know that. You can’t bring him. Let me find you another date. I know so many—”

“Lillian,” I said, shrugging my arm out of her grip. “I’m going with Kaleb. Deal with it.”

She stepped back, gave me a menacing glare, and pushed past me into the lunch room.

I took a deep breath, relaxing my fisted hands and turning away from the lunch room, knowing I wouldn’t be welcome at my usual spot. Later that day, while walking to English, someone slapped me on the butt. I turned around, ready to break someone’s arm. It was Manny, a big jerky football jock. He towered over me and said, “Rawr” and grabbed my arm.

“Let go Manny or I’ll—”

“Or you’ll what?” he said, pulling me into him, grinning. “I just want one little kiss is all. Just one.”

“Get back!” I said and stomped my three inch heel into his foot.

He yelped, grabbing his foot. “Crap, Michele, I was just kidding. I just wanted to ask you to the dance. Lillian said you needed a date.”

“Well, I don’t, Manny,” I said, moving away from him down the hall. “And don’t touch me again.”

I turned around and noticed Kaleb watching me. He gave me the tiniest of smiles and stared at me as I walked away. Ugh.

After school, I high tailed it to my car, not wanting to talk to anyone.

“Michele. Michele.”

I heard my name and quickly pulled the door open to climb in.

“Michele.” Kaleb reached my car just as I was closing the door for a quick escape. He grabbed the door and opened it wide.

"Hey," he said, a strange look on his face. "I-I wanted to apologize for how I've treated you."

I stared at him incredulously. "Huh?"

He lowered his voice as students swarmed the parking lot. "I misjudged you. I'm sorry."

The car next to us honked, wanting me to close my door. "Get in," I said, curious why the change of heart.

"Sorry," he said as he climbed in. "Did you need to be somewhere? You seemed like you were in a hurry."

I looked at him. He looked different somehow, no longer wary and untrusting. Should I tell him? His eyes were insistent. "No. I just had to get away from the zoo."

He laughed, looking back at the school. "It can be pretty overwhelming."

"So, why the change of heart?" I asked, turning to look out the window.

"I don't know. I saw you with that guy in the hall, and I realized you aren't like most of the cheerleaders."

I wanted to say, *duh.* But instead, said, "Thanks. Can I take you home?" Our eyes met.

"Sure."

I pulled out.

"Haven't you told your friends you're going with me?" Kaleb asked.

"It's complicated."

"Well, I'm a pretty smart guy."

I chuckled and shook my head. Should I be honest with him? Why not? "Traditionally," I took on the same annoying air Lillian used when she lectured me, "the cheerleaders go as a group to all the dances." I paused and saw him shaking his head out of my periphery vision. "I'm in a bit of hot water for breaking the tradition."

"What are they going to do? Shun you?" He laughed.

I didn't.

"I was just kidding. But they would, wouldn't they?"

"Yeeeeep!" I said popping the "P" sound with great exaggeration.

"Oh man. I'm sorry."

"Don't be. They need to grow up. I should be able to go with whomever I want."

He chuckled.

"What?" I said as we pulled into his driveway.

"You said *whomever*."

I gave him a look. Not in the mood to joke around. How could I mend fences with the cheerleaders and still go with Kaleb?

"Whatever smarty-pants. Thanks for the ride. I'm really sorry about your friends."

"They'll get over it," I said, hoping it was true, but not completely believing it.

Katy and I plopped onto the couch in my room trying to figure a way to work it out before I had to go to the game to cheer. We ended up laughing more than plotting, however. At the game, I learned just how fast Lillian could work her terror. All the cheerleaders gave me the cold shoulder. I sought out Wendy or Sandy, but they were never alone for me to get the scoop. I was glad I was a base for all the pyramids. I shivered to think of them purposefully dropping me or something.

I saw Wendy run off the field toward the bathrooms and quickly headed after her. When she went to the sink to wash her hands, I approached her, looking around the bathroom to see who might be listening.

"Wendy," I whispered.

She jumped slightly, looked at me, eyes round and then looked down at her hands full of bubbles.

"Come on Wendy," I said.

She reached for a paper towel after rinsing and dried her hands as she walked out the door, looking anywhere but at me.

I was shocked. Truly. This was Wendy. Wendy, who I could always count on. I snagged her arm as we turned the corner to head back onto the field. I had the advantage. I was stronger than she was. I pulled her to the side of the building. "What's going on? Why the deep freeze?"

Other students milled about, but I couldn't concern myself with them. I had to know what Lillian told everyone. Wendy looked around and then whispered, "Lillian has forbidden communication with you until you wise up and come with us to the dance."

I sighed, letting go of her arm. "That's ridiculous."

"I know, right. But, really, did you think you could cross her? Just tell Kaleb you can't go anymore and come with us." She looked around, staring in one particular spot.

Great. Was Lillian behind me? Had I just gotten Wendy in big trouble? I turned to look. Kaleb stood there, lips pressed and his eyebrows pulled together. By the time I looked back toward Wendy, she was gone.

"I thought my group was tough." His wry expression surprised me. Had he overheard? He moved closer to me. "Listen. Would it help if we went with your group?"

Was he serious? Would he actually go with the cheerleaders? "What about your group? You always go with them. Remember?"

"I might be able to make an exception just this once."

"No. I can't ask you to do that. They need to deal with it."

"It doesn't sound like they will. It'll be okay. I'll let my group know. Heck! They'll understand. This will just reinforce what they already think about the cheerleaders. No biggie. They'll get it."

The time clock buzzed. Half-time.

"Gotta go." I said, moving backwards toward the field. "If you think I'm in hot water now, just think what would happen if I didn't show up for the half-time dance."

I got there just in time to march out with the team. I was able to do the dance without effort and thought about Kaleb's proposition. He had given me the out I needed. Could I take it? The pros and cons tumbled through my mind for the rest of the game. It wasn't right to give in, but if I didn't, I would definitely be breaking my cover.

I had no choice. I had to give in. Peace settled over me. Instead of driving home after the game, I went to Lillian's. The party was at her house this week. The house was locked when I got there. I rang the bell. I heard someone come to the door and then run away. I pulled out my phone and called Lillian. She wouldn't pick up. I texted her.

I'M GOING WITH YOU GUYS. OKAY?

After a few minutes, the front door opened. I hated groveling. Lillian stood there, hip pushed out, holding onto the door. "Then you'll go with Manny?"

"No, Lillian. I said I'd go with the cheerleaders, but I'm bringing Kaleb."

She started to shut the door. I jammed my foot in it and pushed with my hands, easily overpowering Lillian. "Look. Let's compromise. I'm going with you, but I'm going with Kaleb. It's girl's choice after all, isn't it?"

She stared at me, obviously considering.

"Fine," she finally said. "But I don't get it. I really don't get it." She shook her head back and forth and let me in.

They'd already decided to be pirates for the dance and I wondered if I'd be able to find a costume so late in the game. I ended up having to buy both Kaleb's and my costumes at a professional shop. They were so expensive at this shop, but it was the only place not cleaned out and they were totally awesome.

Katy took a thousand pictures before we headed for the dance, saying my parents wouldn't want to miss a second of it. It was so fun. My first real dance with a *gentleman*. At the start of the dance, after we'd taken the group pictures, all the cheerleaders and their dates danced together in one large blob. On the slow songs, Kaleb kept me to himself. I truly felt like a princess instead of a pirate. For a large portion of the night, we joined his group for many of the fast songs. At Kaleb's suggestion, we headed back to the group of cheerleaders, but I was so thirsty, I had to grab us drinks. That's when I bumped into Lillian.

"What's up, Michele?" she asked a tipsy smirk on her face.

"Nothing. You?"

"I don't get the allure," she said, "Why 'r you slummin' it?" She tossed her head in the direction of Kaleb's group.

"I'm not slummin' it, Lillian. They're fun," I said. "Don't hate."

"I don' get it. You coulda gone with aaanyonnne."

If Lillian didn't understand Kaleb and me, none of the cheerleaders would. They were an important part of my cover, and I needed them to understand. Going with someone outside the *approved* group looked really bad. It made it seem like I thought I was better than them. I was the only varsity cheerleader not hanging out with the varsity cheerleaders. I looked around. Most of the couples we'd come with were either dancing way too close or making-out with complete abandon on the chairs. Only Wendy and Jessica sat apart from the rest, laughing and chatting with their dates. A few others sat dazed around the tables we'd claimed when we'd first arrived.

"Kaleb's just a friend. Someone I can feel comfortable with and not have to worry about what he wants at the end of the night."

She noticed I was watching the other cheerleaders attack and be attacked and looked at them, too.

"Wouldn't you love to go out with a guy who wanted nothing more than to be with you?"

"No one… like thaat exists, Michele, and yor naivvve if you think any guy is realllly like thaaat." She bobbed into me, her finger pointing into my chest. "You'll see, he'll come for it… sooner or laaater." She staggered away to be with her date who had just come out of the bathroom.

I wondered if she'd even remember this conversation in the morning.

At eleven, the dance was over and I left on a high. While there was no real attraction between us, I knew this was the beginning of a new friendship. Kaleb hugged me on the doorstep.

"I had the best time ever, Michele. We should definitely hang out."

"For sure," I said, grinning broadly.

He bounded down the steps and drove away.

When I walked in, Katy accosted me.

"Tell me everything," she said, grabbing my hands and leading me into the library. "Oh wait, I told your mom I'd call her when you got in. She didn't care that we would be waking her. She's so excited to hear about it. You can fill us both in at the same time." It took a good hour to fill them in. They were definitely living vicariously through me. The daughter neither one would ever have. While glad I had someone to tell the truth, it felt good to get into bed.

The following Monday, I had a mission. I had to find a boyfriend. I scoured my classes for someone "good, but not perfect." I decided he needed to be more of a loner than Kaleb, good looking in his own way, and a hard worker who practiced Christian values. While it turned out there were a lot of choices, by Friday, I thought I'd found the perfect guy for me.

Chapter Nineteen

Matthew Parker, skinny and about six inches taller than me, had chocolate brown hair. I loved chocolate. He also had a permanent seat front and center in both the advanced classes I had with him. He was the male form of Christy minus the photographic memory. While he didn't dress like a total nerd, fashion obviously wasn't a priority. His pants were pulled up just a touch too high, he never wore a t-shirt and the button-downs he did wear were always tucked in. And his dark socks always peeked out from the bottom of his pants.

How was I going to get this smart kid to like me when he thought I was a snotty cheerleader? While hoping someone would ask me out, I knew that if a jock had approached me back home in Helena, warning sirens would rage. I would've known it was a joke. I needed advice. I went straight to Kaleb.

"Do you think he could ever like me?" I said, propping my feet up on the coffee table in Kaleb's family room.

"Are you kidding?" Kaleb said. "Of course, he could. But, he'll probably pee his pants when you talk to him."

"He will not," I insisted. In truth, if it'd been me in Helena, I probably would have.

"You'll probably just need to be forceful, that's all. You'll have to show him you mean business or he'll never believe you aren't trying to make a fool of him." Kaleb ran his fingers through his hair. "You don't really want a boyfriend do you?"

"I don't know. It might be fun. It would definitely keep all the gorilla boys from manhandling me every day."

He chuckled, "I think you may be over estimating Matthew's powers."

I glanced at my phone, vibrating in my hand. It was time for Tai Chi. I'd actually been doing some fun stuff in class and was excited to go tonight. My instructor had been tying me to various objects and I had to free myself. Recently, I'd been working on freeing myself from a pole when both my hands and my feet were tied to it. I'd already conquered escapes while seated.

"See ya," I said, standing up. "Time to become a karate master." I put my hands together as if in prayer and bowed to him.

He stood and bowed, too. "Good luck!" he called after me.

"I'll need it, Sensei Mau is a slave driver," I said.

"I mean with Matthew."

"Ah! Thanks!" I yelled as I ran to the front door.

Today was the day. I was going to ask Matthew out. I didn't dally like I had with Kaleb. I didn't have the time. As soon as all the guys saw that Kaleb and I weren't an item, the cheerleader groupies came knocking, again. I was tired of making up excuses why I couldn't go out with them and really tired of the in-hall-groping. After A.P. Euro, I bit the bullet, making it up as I went.

"Matthew," I said, stepping in his path just outside class. "I'm Michele and I was wondering if you wanted to go see *Macbeth* at the college with me on Saturday." It spilled out in a rush.

His eyes got big and round and he looked a bit green. Kaleb had warned me about this. He then glanced behind him and pointed to himself and said, "Are you talking to me?"

I looked past him too and said, "Of course." My palms were like Niagra Falls and I scrubbed them on my pants. "Who else would I be talking to?" I had to remind myself I was an actor. Keep acting.

"Is this a joke?" He looked all around.

I knew how to handle this. I had thought about it all night.

"No," I said. "But if you don't want to go..."

He was silent, so I took courage, determined to get to *Macbeth* with him. I was certain I knew him and could persuade him.

"Uh, Matthew, this is where you say, of course I want to go." My insides were quaking, but I held firm.

Silence.

"Don't you want to see the person they cast as Lady Macbeth? I heard she is chilling in the 'out, out' scene."

He stared at me, his eyes quizzical. "Uh, I guess so," he croaked, his face red as a beet.

"Great. I'll pick you up at four."

"Four?"

He still looked shocked.

"Four. Now, what's your number?"

I fully expected him to give me his home number. Guys like Matthew (and girls like Christy) didn't own cells, but he pulled out his cell and rattled his off then asked me what mine was.

Matthew had a cell. This was going to work even better than I'd anticipated.

I invited Wendy to come with us. She brought her brother and met us there. Matthew didn't say one word the whole afternoon, but at least he'd gone with me. I made more of a connection with Wendy and her brother than Matthew. They were easy to talk to and liked to laugh.

I thought I might get more traction with Matthew if I invited him to one of Kaleb's game nights. No pressure. That proved a correct assumption.

We played Mad Gab first. Boys against girls.

It shocked me when Matthew yelled out to our team, "Be prepared to weep, girls."

One girl shot back with, "You'll be the ones weeping." And sounds of assent rose up from the girls as the guys yelled out refutations. He didn't hold back the whole night and often grabbed the guys into a huddle to discuss their next move in this game or that. Then, when the girls won, he was a gracious loser, congratulating everyone. Who was this guy? I thought he was shy and awkward when in reality, that only held true in threatening environments, like school.

Next, I took him to my house to play the Wii with Wendy and a boy she was friends with. When I invited her, her excitement showed in her eyes.

"I just love doing stuff with you, Michele. I know I'll have a good time. No pressure, no stress." She laughed. "I'll bring my neighbor with me. He's always up for a good game night." From that night on, we became dating buddies. By the end of the date, Matthew sat within two feet of me on the floor. He still looked totally uncomfortable, but it was a step in the right direction.

It took longer than I'd expected, but after I'd asked Matthew out about five times over the following few weeks, he finally understood that I liked him and wasn't going away. He started initiating conversations and everything. He no longer sat front and center in his classes, he sat in the back with me. I wasn't sure that was a good thing. He even asked me on a real date. His shyness at school melted the more attention I gave him, and he also began dressing better, no more wearing pants up to his armpits or cinching his belt too tight. His pants even covered his socks.

While I could tell he liked the attention he got from everyone now, one thing was for sure, he would be fiercely loyal. One day, a month into our relationship, Manny came up to me in the hall and smacked my butt.

"Keep your hands to yourself, ape," Matthew said, giving him the fiercest of glares.

I moved into position to make it look like I got in a lucky shot, when I knocked meaty off his feet, but he walked away.

"No harm, no foul, big man," Manny said, strutting past, laughing.

"I hate that guy. If he touches you again—"

"You'll give him a piece of your mind and move on." I interrupted. "No fighting." I couldn't have him getting in a fight he would for sure lose. I was surprised the meat head hadn't laid him out. That's when I noticed the football coach standing in his doorway looking at us.

Where ever we went, Matthew made sure I was taken care of before anyone else. He waited until I had all my food out of my lunch sack to even start pulling his out. At dinner when I ate at his house or he mine, he would wait for me to take the first bite and would always clear away my dishes.

The cheerleaders couldn't help but stare at us each day we sat together in the "cool" zone in the hall. Everyone looked to Lillian for direction, though she didn't do anything right away. But, when Lillian called an emergency cheer sleep over, I knew there would be an intervention.

It came right after the pizza arrived and before we painted our nails.

"Michele," Lillian said as all the girls circled around me. "We called this emergency sleep over to save you."

"Save me?" I tried to act dumb.

"Yes." She got this scolding librarian look on her face and then continued. "We need to talk about that, umm, that umm, boy."

She said "boy" like it was a question.

She continued, "that you've been bringing to *our* lunch area the past while." She paused for emphasis. "It's got to stop."

I had to speak in terms she would understand. I had worked it out with Katy before coming over. "I just get off on nerdy-good guys. There's nothing like training 'em just how I like 'em. All the jocks in the group are all so, so, un-trainable. I like being in charge, if you know what I mean."

There was a very silent pause while they all digested what I'd said.

"OHHH!" Lillian finally said, leaning into me. "You're just using him. I get it."

"Yep," I said, feeling a bit sad. "Just using him." Maybe, I wasn't using him for what she thought, but I was using him, all the same.

"But do you have to bring him to our spot at lunch?"

I gave her a what-the-heck look and huffed. "Come on, don't tell me that every one of you wouldn't love to have a guy that treated you right—all the time—sitting next to you at lunch. I shouldn't be punished because I've got guts."

They all gawked, even Lillian. Then as suddenly as the silence descended, she spoke. "I vote to let Michele *train* whoever she wants. Who knows, maybe I'll be training someone soon."

The girls laughed and the intervention was over. Matthew was in. Whew!

Another month passed, and Matthew and I spent all our free time together, coming and going from school, going on dates, and hanging out together. We became best friends. I loved being with him. It was so nice just to be together. Sometimes we wouldn't even do anything, not even talk, just sit or lie next to each other, listening to each other breathe. Most often, he would take my hand in his. I came to expect the comfort his presence always brought me. He didn't make my pulse race, but I really liked him.

I ate at his house a few times a week and enjoyed talking with his parents and playing with his little sister, Annie, who was the happiest most caring fifteen-year-old-girl ever. While she was only two years younger than Matthew, her Downs made her seem only five.

We also spent a lot of time at my house studying. He liked all the easy access to technology I had. Of course, I still had all my extra-curricular activities and cheer that kept me pretty busy, but I made time for him. Everything was too perfect and I knew something had to give. It did in early January.

We were lounging in my room studying and Matthew said, "We need to talk."

"We do?" I said, deciding to be coy. "We always talk. Don't we always talk?"

"Yes, but get over here." He patted the couch next to where he sat.

My heart slammed into my chest as I sat next to him. This was something big. I could feel it.

"Why are you with me?" he asked.

"What do you mean? I'm with you 'cause I like you."

"There's something that's just not right."

"What isn't right?"

"Well, we've been dating now for two months, and we still haven't kissed."

I sat still, hoping the conversation would just disappear. I wrung my hands and looked at my knees.

"Every time I go to make a move, you stop me or avoid me in some way."

"No, I—"

"Yes, you do."

My slamming heart pounded on my ribs. I thought he could see or hear it for sure.

"I guess I'm just not ready for that," I squeaked out.

"Not ready? Are you not attracted to me? Drawn to me?"

"Of course," I blurted, too quickly.

"I love you, Michele," he said, his eyes all puppy-doggie. "Really love you and I want to kiss you. What do you think?"

"It's not that I don't have feelings for you—"

"You could've had any guy at school and you chose me. Why?"

"Because I think you're amazing."

"That's not going to cut it…Couples at school always hold hands, kiss and are together as much as possible. But not us. Why? Why don't you look at me with the same starry-eyed look they have?"

"We don't need to do all that stuff all the time," I hedged. "We're best friends. We have a real relationship. One that will last. That has lasted."

"But we're not just best buddies. You call me your boyfriend. I'm nervous you're using me as an excuse for things."

My heart throbbed as I tried to figure out what to say. I was using him, and for that express purpose. Our relationship, however, had changed. I loved him, just not in the *let's get physical* way.

"I guess I'm just scared."

"Me, too," he said, "I've never kissed anyone. It's awful being seventeen and never been kissed."

Did he think I was virgin-lips? Should I clue him in?

"It's not that," I said. "I have kissed a couple guys, but I'm afraid of what happens after that."

"Huh?"

"I'm no longer with either of those guys…"

"You're afraid if we kiss it will end? I thought you were worried about sex."

"Yeah, and obviously I don't want to have sex, but I also don't want things to change."

"That's just madness. I adore you. It would take something major to scare me away."

I pressed my lips together and looked at him.

He took my hands in his. "I can't imagine being with anyone else. And, as you know, everything changes."

I knew he spoke the truth.

"I can't imagine life without you either." Memories of both Alex and Rick reared their handsome heads. "I feel closer to you than anyone in my life. It's not that I haven't thought about kissing you. It's just, after the first kiss there's always more and more and I don't want our relationship to be only physical."

"That's why you picked me, isn't it? I saw you when you first arrived at Niceville High. You weren't just watching me, I was also watching you. You dated all those guys, those jocks, and I guarantee you they didn't ask for a kiss, they just took it."

"Hold on there," I said, "I didn't kiss them. They tried, of course, but it's not my thing." I pushed my side against his. "I'm sorry I made you feel like I don't care about you. I love you. It kills me to have you question it. I know it's a lot to ask, but please, can't we wait?"

He shook his head and inched away from me.

"I can't imagine life without you," I said, reaching out to touch his arm.

"Then prove it. Kiss me." He looked me straight in the eye, firm and resolute. He was nothing like those jocks, who tried to force themselves on me. There was nothing disgusting about his request.

I looked back, trying to look firm and resolute, too.

"Kissing won't prove a thing."

"I want to kiss you."

I shook my head, ever so slightly.

"Say it then," he said, shaking his hands out in front of him and turning his whole body to face me. "Just tell me you don't want to kiss me because I disgust you and you've just been using me all this time for…for…I don't know what…"

"I just…"

He leaned toward me. I could feel his hot breath. "Kiss me. Kiss me, now."

I drew a deep breath, knowing that I had strung him along too long. I did love him. He was a dear friend. I could always count on him. Maybe I could learn to love him in a different way, to have a physical connection like people in arranged marriages often did. I had to act now or I'd lose him for sure.

I met him half-way. His lips touched mine, sweet, gentle, warm and brief. Different, but beautiful really—like he was gifting me a part of his soul—and yet, no tingles, not even a whisper of one. I pulled away feeling kinda like I'd kissed my brother or something. I tried to hide the *yuck* that I suddenly felt. His eyes remained closed for several more seconds.

"You're trembling," he said, looking down at my hands cupped in his.

"I'm sorry." I pulled my hands away and clamped them together in my lap.

He reached out and grabbed them back, sandwiching them between his own. "No, I like it." He smiled with that sheepish, I-love-you-grin boys and girls get.

"We are really part of each other, now," he said. He kissed me again. "No one can take you from me, now."

I wish I desired him like he desired me. I just didn't. But, I owed him. It was twisted and wrong, but true. I never had to work at kissing Alex and Rick—emotion was on overload with them.

He finally pulled away. "Awesome."

I smiled and hugged him, my mind a total tangle of thoughts and emotions. Could I learn to love kissing him? Was all this worth it to try to find out? Could I live with myself if my feelings never changed? Any way I looked at it, I knew his feelings were going to be hurt.

After a few more hours of studying—at least *he* studied—he kissed me long, hard and wet before he left.

Great, I had this to look forward to every time we were together from now on? I should have refused that first kiss. I should have found a way. Things would be complicated from now on. Truth be told, I bet he would have stuck with me even if I never kissed him. I felt a stab in my heart. No peace. It wasn't right.

I went to bed, tears streaming, wondering where all this would lead. I didn't want to have to find someone else to hide behind. Matt and I were so comfortable together. I didn't want to be alone even though I felt I could deal with guys asking me out now, the realization of which made me feel empowered somehow. I'd have to limit my time with Matthew from now on.

The next day at school was even worse. At my locker, Matt met me. He laid a big, fat kiss on me. I must have gone a bright shade of pomegranate and my face burned. I pulled away from him.

"What's going on?" Matt looked around. "Are you embarrassed to kiss me at school? It's not like people don't know we're together."

I pulled him aside, around a corner and said, "I would never be embarrassed of you, but I don't like P.D.A. Kissing is private. Private things need to stay private."

"Everyone kisses in school…all your friends—"

"I don't."

"Come on!"

The bell rang.

"Look!" I said, with all the force I could muster. "I listened to you yesterday and gave you what you needed. I need you to listen to me now, and hopefully give me what I need."

He hung his head to the side.

"It makes me uncomfortable when I see others kiss in front of me, and I have no intention of doing it in front of them." I gently touched his arm. "I need you to understand me."

"I want it, though. I want people to know you kiss me."

"Is that what this is all about? How others see us? I couldn't care less." I huffed and turned my back on him. The part of him that was using me came to the surface.

He grabbed my shoulder, turning me around. "I'm sorry. I didn't realize we had such different definitions of affection." Playful fingers touched mine. He was afraid of losing me, losing his new status.

"We had to kiss, didn't we?" I said, not wanting to lose him either. I totally didn't want to start over with a new guy. "I told you it would change everything."

"Don't. Please don't."

"Matt, I show you affection every day at school. I do hold your hand sometimes, we look at each other with that *look,* we sit by each other. You wait for me and give me that amazing smile. We are always together. That affection is okay. People who throw themselves on each other at school have no control."

"You think a quick kiss at your locker shows no control?"

"Please, Matt, please. Honor this one thing. Let's only kiss in private. School is too public." I thought of Alex kissing me in front of those girls at Helena High and how that had felt. I knew Matt wanted the same thing. I just couldn't give it to him. "I can't stand the idea of others watching something so intimate."

He bowed his head and sighed.

"It doesn't change how I feel about you," I said. "I love you and want to be with you. No one but you."

"You keep saying it. I just wish I felt it inside. I feel like there is someone else you want to be with and—"

"There's no one else I want to be with." Lie. I tried to say it with conviction, but it fell a little flat. Why did he have to be so intuitive? "I guess I need to work on showing you how I feel about you. I don't know how, but there must be some way to do it. There has to be, because I adore you and want you to feel that when we're together and apart."

"Okay," he said at last. "No P.D.A."

"Thank you."

"But that doesn't include your house and mine. Even when friends are around."

I suddenly saw Matthew for the first time, it seemed. He was sort of using me. He liked that people noticed him more since being with me. He liked the attention. I was a means to an end for him, just like he was to me.

Things weren't perfect after that, but it bought me time. I spent more time at my house and had Katy bind up my schedule so that I wasn't with Matt as much anymore.

I really liked spending time with Katy. She was just a big kid. My favorite was singing karaoke with her. Neither one of us could sing worth a darn.

Natalie and Mason were almost never home, but when they were, Natalie made a point of spending a lot of time with me. She wanted to be my mom so bad, it was easy to love her. It was also easy to call them mom and dad. It felt like they were.

I wished they'd have been home at Christmas, but they weren't, so I had no excuse not to go with Matt and his family on vacation. It was only to Miami and only for three days, but still. At least his parents didn't like PDA either.

That vacation is where I discovered just how dependent on them for a quasi-family they'd become. Sure, Katy came down to Miami, too, to watch out for me, but still. I loved his family despite their idea that I was godless.

They believed they'd remedied that by taking me to church with them as often as possible. While I didn't believe all that this new religion taught, I did like to worship regularly and still snuck away to attend the church I used to go to whenever I got the chance.

I didn't want to disappoint his parents and did my best not to taint him with too many cheerleader activities unless completely necessary. I wanted Matt to change, but on my terms. I wanted him to stay safe and he tended to change a bit in ways his parent's wouldn't approve of when around the cheer team.

We spent hours upon hours with his sister, Annie. She brightened my world. One day while watching Matthew push her on a swing, all bundled up and laughing loudly, I had this great idea. The cheerleaders were in charge of the Valentine's Day dance every year. What if, instead, we did a big fundraiser for the whole community? We could do dinner and dancing. Cheerleaders and athletes could serve the food and even set up. I bet we could get all the food, supplies and advertising donated. The fundraiser could help Down syndrome research and in effect help Annie.

Her Downs was pretty severe and his family had huge medical bills from taking care of her. They also had her attending a pretty pricey school, too. I passed the idea onto my coach who was all for it. I made sure she understood that I was too busy to head it up. I definitely couldn't be in the spotlight. She suggested I ask Clarissa to head it up, because she had a cousin with Down syndrome. It didn't take much effort to convince Matthew to Emcee the event. He thought being the center of attention on a stage would be a blast.

Chapter Twenty

Time sped up once the decision was made to hold the community Valentine's ball fundraiser. So that we had enough time to get everything ready, we decided to hold the dance at the end of the month. Odd for Valentines, but it worked in a weird sort of way. It was almost the third week of January already.

Behind the scenes preparations consumed most of my limited free time, and before I knew it, the day had arrived. We received overwhelming support from the community. So overwhelming, in fact, that the state media picked up on it. Our school was all over the news as we counted up the donations each week.

A huge, drawn thermometer gauged our progress with each $25 donation adding a centimeter of red to the gauge. Once we reached a hundred thousand dollars, even the A.P. picked up the story. We were the goodwill story of the month. I hid anytime a reporter was around, just to keep my word to John. Hiding became more and more difficult as time went on. Katy helped me escape more times than I could count. She kept abreast of the news coverage for me. I was too busy scrounging up and keeping track of donations as well as everything else I had to do. Sure, Katy was mad at me for starting this fundraiser without discussing it with her, but she also understood my need to help Annie and was willing to work overtime to help me make it a success.

Who could have predicted that Clarissa would get sick the day of the dance, when all the national reporters would be there? I tried to get Lillian to take over her responsibilities, but she wouldn't, saying I deserved the glory. It was my idea after all. I even tried to get our coach to take over for Clarissa, but she insisted I do it. At first I was petrified, but looking at myself in a mirror, I convinced myself that I shouldn't be. No one would ever recognize me. I didn't even resemble Christy. My hair was a different color, full, and beautiful, I wore make-up and most importantly, I had completely rocking clothes on. I wouldn't be on stage a lot, only announcing new donations and winners of the silent auctions each half hour. Matt was more than willing to do everything else.

Dinner went without a hitch. One cheerleader's dad worked in food service delivery, one owned several restaurants, and yet another ran a catering business. We got all the goods and services free of charge. Of course, the cheerleaders and all the sports teams helped set up and serve. Local and national businesses donated all sorts of stuff for the silent auction.

Cameras rolled the whole time, and when I announced we'd hit the 250 thousand dollar mark, the stage was overrun with reporters. Feeling a bit overwhelmed and concerned about all the exposure, I tossed the mic over to Coach and snuck out for some air. I slipped out the side stage door and leaned against the outside wall, drawing deep breaths of the crisp, inviting air.

"John is going to kill me," I said into the night. "What if he sees coverage of this? Am I really unrecognizable? I better be."

After calming myself, I tried the door, it was locked. Great. I'd have to walk around to the front door and, more likely than not, run into some reporter out front taking a smoke break. I stayed close to the wall and made my way to the front. Peering around the corner, only one person waited outside the doors with his back to me. He didn't have a camera that I could see, or a cigarette, for that matter. I decided I would hurry around him and run through the door. He'd be none the wiser. He really posed no threat. As I braced myself and took off for the door, he turned and leaned his back against the wall. I stopped short.

No way! It couldn't be. I stared, my mouth wide open, unable to believe what my eyes saw. This wasn't happening. And yet, he was real and walking toward me. A smile spread across his perfect face as panic gripped my heart. I looked from side to side, hoping I was the only one to see him. Alex.

My promise to his dad hung in the air. I had to send him away. The better part of me wanted to stop his advance but I couldn't, my mind simply wouldn't command my arm to stop him. I wanted him in my arms. He kept coming, closer and closer.

With his face only inches from mine, Alex said, "Finally." And kissed me senseless.

It was both shocking and thrilling at the same time. The moment slipped away too quickly. His warm, firm arms wrapped around me and it felt as if I'd come home at last. I no longer cared that his dad would kill me. I was sure his sixth sense had already told him Alex had come. To die after that kiss would be okay. I could wait in heaven for Alex to join me. This kiss would last until then. He held me tighter than he'd ever held me before. He sighed and then said, "We have a visitor."

Had his dad already made it? I changed my mind. I didn't want to die yet. I needed more time to feel his touch, his warm lips. He lessened his grip on me, staring behind me. I had to look, ever so slowly. I turned to see Matthew, at the bottom of the steps, looking up at us. I involuntarily jumped at the sight of him.

"So, that's what it would be like if I were the one," he said.

"I…" My words choked out in my throat.

"You're on." Matthew said, his words hard as steel.

"I'm on?" I said, stupidly.

"Yes, you're on."

"Right, right," I said, realizing I had one more appearance on stage before I was done. "Alex, I'll be right back. Don't go anywhere." I stroked his face, his five-o-clock shadow felt like sandpaper, but I longed to keep my hand there.

He brushed his lips across mine before I could walk away, and I took one long look at him before entering the school. Matthew grabbed my hand right inside the door and asked, "Is he the one?"

"The one?" I asked, not giving him the chance to slow us.

"The one you dream about. The one that holds you back from loving me the way I love you?"

We had almost reached the stage door. What could I say? Callously, I chose to say nothing, grabbing the door and going in. We'd have this talk later. He followed me on and held himself with exactness, as if he hadn't just seen me kiss someone other than him, with no anger or frustration in his voice as he continued to Emcee.

I had almost made it all the way down the steps from the stage, when Matt grabbed my hand and stopped me. He towered above me and must've felt uncomfortable, because he stepped down to the bottom of the steps, still holding my hand, tight. His eyes held the look of one betrayed, but longing lined them.

"Tell me who he is. You at least owe me that," he said.

"No, Matthew, I owe you a lot more than that." My lip quivered looking into his sad eyes.

He relaxed, letting his grip lessen, his eyes softening.

"Is it possible for me to ask you to wait, just a little longer to explain it all to you? It's a complicated story and I don't want to leave anything unsaid."

"Just tell me this. Have you been seeing him behind my back, all this time?"

"No," I said, glad I could be honest. "I haven't seen him in almost a year."

"Okay. When can we talk?"

"Is tomorrow soon enough?"

He sighed and looked down at the ground. "Michele, you have been nothing but honest with me our whole relationship, but this is just crazy." His intense stare seemed to go right through me. "I don't know."

"Please. I'll tell you every last detail, just not right now."

"Okay, but let's talk over breakfast. Nine-o-clock."

"Okay," I said, taking a step down. "Tomorrow I'll tell you everything, and could you please cover for me for the rest of the night?" I knew I was asking a lot, but couldn't stop myself. I think it was easier than I expected simply because I knew he was using me, too. At least to some degree. Breakfast would tell me more exactly.

He had never been impulsive, but at that moment he pulled me into his arms and kissed me, softer and more gently than he ever had before. Then he said, "Just so that you don't forget me."

He let go of my hand. I had to call on every ounce of restraint I had not to run all the way back outside to Alex. I felt Matthew watching me and I didn't want to hurt him anymore than I had. The hall seemed to lengthen with each step I took toward the door. My mind raced, and I was Christy once again. One night. We only had one night. I'd end it after that. I'd cry insanity to John when he found out. Maybe he'd let me live.

Opening the door to the humid, cool, February night air, I saw him, exactly where I'd left him. Losing every ounce of restraint I had, I ran to Alex, jumping into his waiting arms, wrapping my legs around his waist and kissing him. I meant to give him only a brief kiss, but once I felt his soft, tender lips, I couldn't hold back like I'd planned. My world ceased to exist. There was only Alex's magical touch.

He was the one who had to pull back. "Let's get out of here," he said, his lips still touching mine.

"Okay," I managed to squeak out, releasing my legs and standing next to him. He took my hand and led me to his car.

Chapter Twenty-One

Fire. A hot fire that burns your skin in a good way on a cold night. That was how it felt to be with Alex again. I couldn't stop smiling as we drove to grab some food and took it back to Alex's hotel suite in Destin. We sat on the balcony. The moon gave off enough light to see the waves in the ocean, and the sound of them lapping on the shore soothed me. While we ate some perfectly moist red velvet cupcakes from Ambrosia! Exquisite wedding cakes, the best cake bakery in the world, we laughed and laughed, talking about everything I'd been through since parting.

"You are so beautiful," he interrupted me. "I want to kill all those stupid guys who tried to take advantage of you."

My face burned. I reached across the small table and took his hand in mine, his grip firm and strong.

"I missed you so much," he said. "I'm so glad I found you."

"I think your dad would feel otherwise."

"Don't bring him into this."

"He has a point, you know. I do put you in danger, and together, we double that danger."

He got up and came around to me, pulling me up into a hug. He whispered softly in my ear, "Who said danger was bad? Danger brings excitement."

"Or it can bring death," I whispered back.

"Uh, uh," he said, pulling back and looking me in the eye. "We are at the end of that conversation. I have to leave tomorrow, and I want our time together to be perfect."

He started dancing with me. I could feel his heart beat against my chest and hear his shallow breathing in my ear. We danced our way back into the suite's living room area and he paused, to turn on the music player. I blushed, feeling his body, firm against mine.

How had I lived these last nine months? How had I let myself forget? He called me Christy, not Michele, and it made my insides buzz hearing it. All my good memories jumped out of their box, leaving the bad ones behind.

We enjoyed each touch, sigh, and movement. When he pressed his lips against mine, a fire burned out of control throughout my body. My hands rediscovered his arms, chest, and back. Somehow, we danced into the bedroom and right up to the bed, toppling onto it. I laughed at first, but as his touch became more aggressive, more insistent, fear welled up inside me. I pushed against him. He knew how I felt about this. After restraining myself for several minutes and after telling him to stop quite a few times, I pushed him off me without much effort. He lay on his back next to me, breathing hard and fast.

We didn't speak for several minutes. I waited for him to catch his breath so that he could apologize. As the minutes ticked away, I realized he wasn't going to. So, I did.

"Sorry, Alex," I said, hoping he would return the gesture.

"Sorry for what exactly?" His tone was sharp. "Leading me on?"

"What?" I sat up. Mad, now. "You know where I stand on this. Did you think it had changed in the past year?"

"It's not like you're fifteen anymore. You're almost seventeen. What are you waiting for?"

"Marriage."

"You've got to be kidding." He sighed loudly. His mocking tone irritated me even more. "No one waits for marriage anymore."

"So what…last year you were just placating me. You didn't really mean it when you said you would wait for me?" Anger sizzled on my tongue.

"No. At least not at that point. But you're not under your parents' thumbs anymore. You can choose for yourself, now. Don't you love me?" He sat up and grabbed my hand. At that moment I didn't want his hand in mine and I jerked it away, standing.

"I wasn't choosing to save myself for marriage for my parents. It's for me. Not only does it feel right to wait, there's tons of research that backs up my decision. Just think. If everyone waited, there'd be no STDs, no unplanned pregnancies, no heartache and pain. At least for teens. I shouldn't have to tick off the research to you. You know it. You just let your physical feelings take over your brain. My body may want you, but I won't give into it. It doesn't rule me."

"I'm gonna take a cold shower," he said, getting up and leaving me there to stew.

Memories I'd buried deep were roused, and I went through the saga between Alex versus Rick all over again. How could it be wrong to be with Alex, when my body told me it was right? Could he ever be happy with me, if I wouldn't give him what he wanted? Was I strong enough to continue to resist him? Did I even want him anymore? His intentions had been clear. He wanted to take what he could get and then disappear, leaving me to deal with the consequence. Rick would never have put me in this position. My choice at the airport when I was leaving DC had been the right one. Rick fit me so much better. Not that I'd have the chance to explore them. I'd never see Rick again. Another casualty of DC. I'd let my feelings get in the way just like Alex had. The difference lies in his moral integrity.

Alex walked out of the bathroom with only a towel on. His well defined body held me captive until he turned, opened a drawer, pulled out some skivvies and dropped his towel. My eyes flew wide open as I looked away, my heart pounding fast. I'd never seen a boy's derriere before. At least not a teenage boy's. My face flushed and I got hot all over, so I left the room. Actually, I ran into the living area. I bent over, put my hands on my knees and breathed deeply.

He laughed loudly. "You can always change your mind, you know," he called out to me. "I won't think badly of you."

I looked up. He stood in the bedroom doorway, leaning against the door frame with nothing on but boxers. I looked away and said, "Please get dressed."

"If you insist," he said, chuckling. He was an insufferable tease.

I moved to the couch, clicked on the TV and searched the channels—my mind elsewhere. Once dressed in jeans and a T-shirt, Alex pounced onto the couch, pressing against me.

"Sorry," he said, with a ridiculous grin on his face. "It's just…I was so …worked up, and it's hard to stop once I get that way."

It hit me at that moment what was meant by those words. He'd been there before. "So, exactly how many times have you not stopped once you were so worked up?" I hoped he felt the bite in my question.

"Never," slid out before he was able to think it through. I saw regret, or rather, *Uh, oh, I shouldn't have said that*, cross his eyes.

"So," I pushed him away. "Just how many times have you given in?" I was so stupid. Why had I thought he would wait for me? I refused to take my eyes off his, hoping he'd say they were all before he met me, but his eyes betrayed him.

"A few. Let's just leave it at that."

"A few? More than 3…5…7?"

"Stop it. You're not helping things."

"I naively thought you'd be true to your word and wait for me. I thought maybe you'd been with girls before meeting me, but I thought you saw me as special and wanted to save yourself for me. I thought I knew you. I thought I could trust you."

"It has nothing to do with trust. I just wasn't sure I'd really ever be able to find you. I couldn't stop living. You sure didn't."

I snorted. "Matthew? Are you referring to Matthew? There's a big difference between having a boyfriend who honors, respects, and protects me from all the other sex crazed boys at that school, than sleeping with every nice pair of legs that walks past."

"You've got it all wrong. The *boyfriend* part is the disturbing part. At least none of mine meant anything."

"First off, Matthew is my best friend—"

"Exactly," he interrupted under his breath.

"And." I emphasized the "and." "I don't love him in any other way. I could never marry him. There's no spark."

"Does he know that or are you just leading him on?"

"Don't change the subject," I said, pulling the knife of betrayal out of my heart. I took a mental note that I should not kiss Matthew any more. It wasn't right.

"What is the subject exactly?" His eyebrows raised and he pressed his lips together.

"Oh yeah," I said. "Wasn't it something like all the reasons you and I aren't meant for each other?"

Our eyes bored into one another's.

"Christy, please don't say that. You've consumed my every waking moment. Don't give up on us because of my stupid mistakes. Please, you'll see, I won't even look at any other girls ever again if you say you'll be mine."

I wished it weren't true, but I knew deep down the pulsing fire between us would never die down, but at the same time it burned a gorge between us. We were too far apart. Even knowing that, a part of me still wanted to tell him it would all work out, but a pain deep in my belly told me otherwise.

I'm sure he was like me and could feel the fire between us, only he couldn't comprehend the gorge that separated us.

"Just give me another chance. Now that I know where you are, I will control myself. You're worth it to me. You are."

It was like he was trying to convince himself of it. "Please." He grabbed by my hands and looked so sincere.

"Arghhh. I don't know." I did know, but couldn't bring myself to tell him when he looked at me that way.

He sighed and then let out a "Yahoo!" as if I'd consented. "You'll see, it'll be great. You and I are meant to be together. When I saw you in that picture with all those cheerleaders on that news report a few days back, I called the airport and bought a ticket so I could be here for this. All the tickets were sold out except for the one I bought, and it got me here thirty minutes after the fundraiser started. I can't believe you're a cheer—"

"Crap!" I said, pulling back from him, reality washing over me. "You had no problem identifying me?" My heart beat hard and slow, dread pressing on me.

"Of course not."

"Don't you know what that means?" I cried. "If you could recognize me so easily, so could others. Especially after tonight. My face will be all over the place."

His face paled slightly. "No, I mean, you do look different, even more beautiful. I recognized you because I know you better than anyone and I've been looking for you. No one else could possibly…" He stopped, apparently deep in thought.

Rick flashed across my brain. A deep, calming warmth spread through me and I knew this would be the last time I'd be with Alex. I should have stuck with the decision to forget about

Alex that I made so long ago in DC. I'd tell him in the morning, I was too tired now.

He put his arm around me, and I leaned into him, resting my head on his hard chest, settling in to watch the movie. I breathed in deeply, feeling a bit intoxicated by his spicy smell. Tomorrow. I'd tell him how I felt tomorrow, right before he went home. The next thing I knew, it was morning. I was stretched out on the couch, covered with a blanket. Alex was gone.

Chapter Twenty-Two

There was something in the air. I couldn't put my finger on it. It was a tinniness of some sort. I called out to Alex. No one answered. I looked for a note but couldn't find one. His bag lay on the floor by the bed, his shoes sitting next to it. Had he gone to pick up some breakfast without his shoes?

Breakfast! My meeting with Matthew at nine! A quick glance at the clock on the nightstand told me I was already late. 9:02. I jumped to my feet. The strange feeling about Alex's absence disappeared as my worry about Matthew took over.

I tried his cell. No answer. I called a cab and frantically tried to fix my ratted hair. My wrinkled skirt and top stared back at me as I glanced in the mirror. I looked around, realizing I'd left my backpack at the school. I hadn't even noticed. Alex was so distracting. Without a backpack, I had no clothes to change into. Not only was I a wrinkled mess, I was way over-dressed. Maybe Matthew wouldn't notice. I wrote Alex a note before running down to meet the cab. It was twenty past. Please wait, Matthew. Please wait. The twenty minutes it took to get to the café seemed like hours. I kept texting him, but he never answered.

I mulled over what I should tell him. He'd know if I tried to lie, and I'd lose him. I needed him. He was more than my cover now. He was my best friend. My only choice was to give him a version of the truth that would satisfy him. Just enough. After paying the driver with some cash I had in my pocket, I rushed into the café.

Seeing him sitting alone at our regular table, I took a deep breath and I hurried over. "Sorry I'm late, it was a long night." I couldn't help but notice my backpack sitting on the chair next to him. I smiled. He never ceased to amaze me.

"I can see that." He looked me up and down, obviously not missing the fact that my clothes hadn't changed. "You never made it home?" I was foolish to think he wouldn't notice. He saw everything.

My smile faded as I sat across from him. "I fell asleep at Alex's watching a movie." It was the first time I'd seen doubt in his eyes about something I'd said. I desperately wanted him to believe me. "Really Matthew, nothing happened between us. I slept on the couch. I promise."

Some of the doubt in his eyes faded. It was what lingered that worried me.

"You're my best friend. I wouldn't lie to you," I said. *Unless it was totally necessary.*

"No, but you'd leave out the fact that you could never love me because you were already in love with someone else?"

"I do love you."

"But not like you love him." His voice was firm and resigned, but lacked anger. "That kiss in front of the school was something else."

"I'm sorry you had to see that." I buried my face in my hands, feeling horrible.

"Me, too. But I did. So, spill it." The betrayal in his eyes sat hard on my chest.

The waitress brought my favorite breakfast: bacon, eggs, and hash browns. Matthew just had coffee.

"Thank you," I said, breathing in the rich aroma of his coffee and moving to Matthew's side of the table. I looked him straight in the eye. "I'm sorry. I wish I could explain."

"Why don't you start with this?" He set my backpack on the table.

"My backpack?" I said, stupidly. I couldn't believe I'd forgotten it. It had been with me almost every second since I'd arrived in Niceville. Alex had messed everything up. Seriously, he was so distracting.

"It is yours, right?"

I reached for it, but he pulled it close to him and began unzipping the zipper.

I took a sharp intake of air. His eyes traveled to mine. They showed total determination. He would open the pack despite my horror. It took everything I had not to reach out and snatch the pack away from him. But, I knew he'd already looked inside and what good would it do? He knew what was inside.

"It looked so out of place behind the stage," he said. "And I immediately thought it was yours. Same color, brand, size as yours. I was just going to take it and bring it to you, but then I thought it really could be anyone's. There were so many people at the school that night. I had to verify it was yours. A simple thing. So, I unzipped it. Nope. Not yours. All kinds of crazy stuff was in it. It couldn't be yours. Why would you need those things? I started to zip it back up, but then saw a passport and figured I might as well take a look and get it to the right person."

He pulled the passport out and opened it, flinging it across the table at me. It jumped twice before landing only inches from my chest. "Who are you anyway? Michele? Christy? Addy?"

Addy was the name on my emergency passport. I had been sloppy yesterday morning when I'd refreshed the pack because Matthew had surprised me before school and had brought me breakfast. I had to hurry and shove everything into the pack before he saw it. I hadn't had time to put it all back in its proper place before the fundraiser. What could I say? No words found purchase on my tongue and I sat there silent, hoping for a miracle.

"You better come clean with me or I'll tell the police. I don't like being tricked. You're crazy if you think you're going to steal all the money we earned for Down's research."

He thought I was a thief? I had to make a quick decision. Should I confide in him? I already knew I could trust him, but why had he brought up the police? A bit of nausea seeped into my gut thinking about the possible repercussions if he told anyone.

"You can't tell a soul what I'm about to say."

"Of course," he said, a deep sarcasm swirled about his words and I knew he was calculating my demise if he felt a hint of deception. I had to make sure he understood.

"No, really Matthew," I said, looking around the room for signs of danger and then letting my eyes rest on his. I had to concentrate, let my senses help me do the right thing. "This conversation can never leave the spot we're in right now. A lot of people would be in danger if you ever said anything."

"Okay, okay. My lips are sealed." Anger and expectancy danced in his dark eyes.

I paused, hoping the silence would emphasize the importance of his promise, which unfortunately gave me a chance to doubt my decision again. "On second thought, maybe I shouldn't tell you. I would be putting you in danger, too."

"I don't care. Tell me." His eyes almost looked black now.

Some irrational fear of him gripped me at that moment and I whispered, "I'm in witness protection."

I felt my eyes widen and I covered my mouth with my hand at the same moment his eyes showed belief. With my mouth still covered, I looked around us, hoping no one had heard.

His look said it all. The blackness in his eyes disappeared as he seemed to be considering what I'd just spat at him. I wanted him to believe. I needed him to believe, but at the same time, I knew I'd broken the cardinal rule—never, under any circumstances was I to blow my cover. John would be furious. Good thing he wasn't around anymore. But, really, I hadn't done it. Matt had discovered the pieces that would eventually lead him to that conclusion anyway. At least now he wouldn't have to rule out anything more sinister.

After giving him time to digest the information and giving me time to convince myself I'd done the right thing, I continued. "Please. You've got to keep this between us. No one else knows. No one but the people at my house, that is. This backpack has everything I need in case my cover is blown."

"You're serious aren't you?"

"Yes."

"So, your real name is Christy?"

"Yes, but how did you know that? This pack doesn't have anything with my real name on it."

"*He* called you that before he kissed you."

Oh, right. Alex had given away much too much with his visit. I didn't know what to say.

"Why are you in witness protection?" He continued to whisper. "I mean, what did you witness?"

"That, I can't tell you. Just know that I did not do anything wrong. Someone else did."

He looked at me, almost like he was trying to look inside my brain and pull out the information he wanted. "Where does Alex fit in all this?"

"He doesn't. Not anymore. He's just a guy who once told me he loved me and then disappeared. I didn't think I'd ever see him again and then he just showed up last night. We are just too different. He's like all those jocks at school I try to avoid. "

He said nothing.

I poked at my cold, hard, rubbery food. Matt must have noticed and called the waitress to ask for a new plate.

We sat in silence for several more minutes as he seemed to absorb it all.

"That's a pretty far-fetched tale…" he said, his eyes locked on mine. "But I believe you."

I sighed, relief washing over me. "Remember Matthew, never tell. Even if I disappear."

"If you disappear?" His eyebrows knit together.

"If my cover gets blown, I'd be relocated without warning."

His eyes looked worried and sad as he said, "I don't know how I would live without you. You've changed my life so dramatically."

"I feel the same and Alex leaves today and he won't be back." I felt a flutter of loss saying it out loud.

"The way you looked at him. I want that. You can't give that to me, can you?"

Why was he forcing me to say the words? I looked at the ceiling, debating quickly what I should do. I needed to be honest with him. I owed him that. He deserved someone to look at him that way.

"I do love you, Matt, just not with the same intensity that you love me. I wish I did. We are so perfect together. I guess it's just the spark that's missing for me. I've been so afraid of losing you. I played a part that wasn't mine to play, just to keep you close to me. You're my best friend and I need you. I've been so selfish. I'm sorry. Will you ever forgive me?"

His look caused a deep pain in my chest and he said, "I don't know. I need some time."

I was losing him even though I hated to admit it and it was the right thing. He deserved to be loved by someone who was wild about him. Trying not to show the panic I felt, I said, "You've been the only thing that got me through this. I love you, and I'm sorry."

Out of the corner of my eye, I saw a car drive up and that familiar, tingly, deep feeling that I should run, filled me. Really? A drill right now?

"I'll be right back," I said, giving a head nod toward the restroom. I grabbed the backpack from the table and slid the passport inside as I walked to the restroom.

"'Kay," he said.

When Matthew looked away to take my new plate of food from the waitress, I slipped out the side door, wishing John had chosen a different time for this month's drill and hoping I wouldn't lose Matthew forever after having to ditch him now."

Chapter Twenty-Three

I walked into the business next door, browsing briefly through the clothes on the racks and leaving through the front doors. I headed in the opposite direction of the café, passing a couple of safe places that would have been perfect for an extraction. Instead of stopping, I found myself brooding over the fact John had interrupted such an important conversation with Matthew. He had such bad timing. I could lose Matthew forever. On a whim, I decided to have a bit of fun with my attackers and extractors and let them feel some of my pain. I passed another ten spots of safety before putting on a nutty-brown wig, slipping on a light black jacket and hopping onto a bus to head back to Alex's hotel.

Sitting on the bench, I couldn't help but smirk when I thought about making John's cronies wait for me to push the extraction button. Either the abductors John had chosen for the latest kidnapping attempts were very much amateurs or my Tai Chi instructors were making headway, because the abductors hadn't gotten close in months. I got off at the stop before the hotel and hummed a song while looking through the windows of the shops I passed on my way to the entrance. The air smelled heavily of the ocean, like the early heat of the day held it to the earth, compressing it, making it more pungent than usual.

Before even hitting the lobby, I knew something was wrong. It wasn't an off-sound, how something looked, or even an odd energy in the air that made me turn back the way I'd come. It was a deep, horrible heat that gripped my heart. I snuck around to the back of the hotel and looked through the glass door and down the empty hallway lined with hotel rooms. I tried the door. It was open, so I went in. A deep ringing raged in my head the whole time I walked down the narrow hallway. I peeked around the corner into the lobby, hiding myself behind a large green plant. Other than a man in a suit sitting near the lobby entrance, reading a newspaper, and a woman, leaning against a wall near the elevator and stairwell, the lobby was empty. Something about how the man sat and how the woman looked around told me without a doubt that they were bad news. At that moment, I knew this was no drill. I thought of Alex. Surely he'd already come back.

The picture of Alex's shoes sitting next to his bag in his room filled my mind. Ice crept into my soul, and I thought my heart would seize. I took a look at the people in the lobby again. Neither looked like they came from the Middle East. Their skin was the wrong color. They were not the terrorists I'd come in contact with before.

John had warned me that if I didn't send Alex packing if he came for me that he would kill me. Had he sent these goons to do the job? I took a deep breath, the dust from the plant tickling my nose. I couldn't sneeze. I had to get out of there. I tried to get rid of it by looking at the lights and holding the bridge of my nose, but it was coming all the same. I took off down the hall and out the door just as the sneeze exploded. I looked behind me. The door hadn't shut yet. Had they heard? My heart brimming with fear, I raced around the building to the sidewalk and stepped in front of a group of people walking away from the hotel, hoping I looked like I fit in with them. I knew I couldn't look back, but was dying to. I wanted to know if either of John's men had even heard the sneeze. If they were following me, wouldn't it be better to know so that I could get away? My Tai chi instructor, popped into my mind.

"You do not need to see, to know," he had said.

I closed my eyes and breathed in, hoping to tap into the abilities he had taught me. Digging deep, I separated myself from what was happening around me and projected out, feeling for the energy of others. I felt eyes, searching the group, but they looked away.

I kept walking with that group until the next crosswalk, then I left them, hurrying to catch a bus I knew left in about one minute on the next block. It's a good thing busses tended to run a bit late. I got to the stop just as it arrived. It smelled like dirty feet. I dropped coins into the slot. Sitting on the bus, I thought about John. Would he really kill me for seeing Alex? It seemed absurd. I pulled out my phone. Alex had texted me. I pushed the button to display it, my heart thudding hard.

Dad found me. Sorry. I love you. He can't keep us apart forever.

Then my phone flashed that I had a message from an unknown number. I dialed my voice mail.

It was John. "If you're listening to this, you somehow escaped. Guess I taught you too well. Reneging on your promise, however, will have consequences.

"I'm sure you're thinking I sent those people after you. Be assured that if I wanted you dead, you would be. Even the completely clueless terrorists could find you now. While this particular terrorist faction that's tracking you as we speak might be smart enough to find you before anyone else and use people who do not look like they are Middle Eastern, they are too sloppy to be effective. I smelled them from a mile away and was able to get Alex out of that love nest of yours long before they arrived. You were dead asleep. How did you manage to escape?

"If it were up to me, I'd let you rot, but I've gotten word that they need you for something, so, I won't prevent your extraction this time. Get somewhere safe and alert your extractor. Trust the man who comes for you. He is good at what he does. Don't make me look like a fool by getting yourself killed.

"By the way, this is the last contact we'll have. My number will no longer work for you. Your decisions have determined mine. Oh, and Alex sends his love." He chuckled.

I listened to the message a good four times before getting off at the Whataburger restaurant on Highway 93. I walked the two blocks to the Niceville library and went inside, stopping to take a long drink at the water fountain before going into the main section of the library. The smell of well-used paper invited me to pick a few books before sitting at my favorite desk in the far corner of the library. I'd found this spot at the beginning of the year when I was trying to avoid all the octopus-handed guys at school. Even when I invited them to join me, they'd get a conflicted look on their faces and find an excuse as to why they couldn't. It was the perfect place to ditch them and get some peace. This particular spot was ideal, because I could see out all four sides of the building by just shifting a little in my seat and using the mirrors that were so aptly placed to catch people who were up to no good.

I placed the backpack on the desk and pulled out the tracking phone. I looked hard at it. If I pushed the button, would help come or would it just lead John's goons straight to me? I listened to his message one last time and still wasn't sure. I looked at the clock. It was already eleven-thirty. Since it was Saturday, the library closed in only a half an hour. I stared at the tracking button on the phone. Should I trust John? Still not sure, but feeling like I had no choice, I pushed it. I decided I liked my chances here in the library. John had warned me some extractions took hours. I hoped this wasn't one of those. I had twenty-five minutes, forty-five tops, if the librarians let me drag my feet. I focused inward while lightly reading one of the books I'd picked up, hoping I'd sense the bad guys if they even thought of coming near the library.

Feeling a tremor up my spine, I looked behind me. A rough-looking man with long greasy hair and a several-day-old beard, wearing baggy, dirty clothes and carrying several large volumes of books, ambled in my direction. I snorted, thinking my spidey senses were feeling a bit conflicted. The worst this man could do to me was try to rob me. That wouldn't be bad, all things considered. I could handle him. I resisted the urge to slide my chair away from him when he set his books on the desk next to me. I looked up and gave him a pressed smile, hoping he was just some homeless dude and not a criminal. He smiled back, his rotted teeth staring back at me, and sat down.

I gulped and tore my eyes away, trying to concentrate on the book in front of me, while fighting the urge to stare at the odd man. Out of the corner of my eye, I saw him lift one of the books. He tapped it and said, "It's never been my thing. I'm more into Captain Hook."

I looked up, unable to stop my eyes from bulging. The title of the book he held was *Peter Pan.* He had just given me the code words. My contact sat beside me. A bum. His crystal blue eyes sparkled while he waited for my response.

"Uh, yeah," I stuttered. "But Peter Pan saves the day." I had wondered how those code words could ever make sense in a conversation. Now I knew.

He chuckled. "Good thing this joint closes in ten minutes. I have to get that beauty," he pointed at a rusty, spray painted beater car parked near the entrance of the library, "to the shop a couple blocks east of here in the next twenty minutes before they close. I'd like to just stay here and read all day. A library and a garage that both close at noon on a Saturday? That's just madness." He winked at me and left.

I looked at my phone to mark the time. I was to meet him in twenty minutes two blocks east of here, and he'd pick me up in that super nice car. I flipped through my book aimlessly for the next ten minutes until I heard the announcement that the library was now closed. I stood up, leaving the books I'd picked up on the return rack before heading out the door.

I hurried down the side street, walking two blocks east. I stood in front of a small veteran park. A yellow bow was tied around each tree. I couldn't see any sign of the beater car, so I looked for a place to sit. A gigantic boulder only a few feet from the sidewalk called my name. I walked over the soft grass and leaned up against it. I let my backpack slip from my fingers. My eyes closed for a short few seconds. I couldn't detect anything dangerous. The rumble of a car coming down the road made my eyes open. The beater car, in all its beauty, pulled up to the curb beside me. I grabbed the backpack and climbed in.

The car's stained seats had tears that exposed the padding beneath and it smelled of cigarettes and old, rotten food. The seatbelt held no tension as I pulled it across me. It sat useless on my lap. The bum snorted and smiled while putting his index finger to his lips, indicating I should remain silent. Then, he gave me a toothy grin. His yellow and black teeth made me run my tongue across my own, checking for any food particles or rotten teeth I hadn't noticed. His eyes still sparkled, hiding their secrets.

I couldn't help but think sending this guy for me was John's idea of partial payback for letting Alex stay when he showed up instead of sending him away.

We clunked along the road, the radio cutting in and out as we went. I hoped the ban on speaking would end soon, so that I could get some answers. I fiddled with a Harry Potter lanyard hanging from the glove box. We stopped at a run-down gas station, the fluorescent lights over the two pumps flickering on and off. The bum went inside and when he came back out, he carried a plunger with a key attached to it. Setting the plunger next to the pump, he started to fill the tank and then motioned for me to get out of the car. We walked around to the side of the building. One bare light illuminated a door that read: "Toilet." Not "Women" or "Men," just "Toilet."

He used a key attached to the plunger to open the door and directed me to go in. I hesitated, wondering if this bum was one of John's lackeys and I was about to be disposed of. He nudged me in. I breathed hard and fast until the smell of urine and B.O. assaulted me. I made a conscious effort to breathe in and out of my mouth. He followed me in, flipping on the light as he did. He locked the door and before I could let my imagination run away with me, he pulled out a familiar pen shaped object. A bug detector—just like the one Chris had used at the airport in DC Maybe he didn't intend to kill me tonight, after all.

He held his finger up to his lips one more time before running the detector over my whole body. He moved slowly, going over sections of my pant's hem and inseam several times. At last he smiled, I guessed satisfied that I was bug free. He pushed a button on the detector and stuffed it back into his shirt pocket. He held out his hand to me and said, "Hi, I'm Cort." I took his hand with some reservation.

He shook it with a strength that didn't seem congruent with his appearance, and that deep, sexy voice couldn't have come out of that rotten mouth.

I stared, jaw on the floor.

He raised his way too bushy eyebrows and I squeaked, "I-I-I'm Michele."

"Nice to finally meet you," he said, letting his hand drop. "I can't tell you how glad I am that you are clean. It makes my life a lot easier. Now, let's get out of here."

I followed him out the door. While he put the nozzle back on the pump, I climbed into the car, my feet hitting my backpack. When he got in, I held my fingers to my lips and pointed to the backpack. I couldn't bear to get caught with another tracker in my stuff after what had happened at the airport in DC .

He smiled and I hefted the pack onto my lap. After checking all the contents and the bag itself and finding them clean, we drove away.

Chapter Twenty-Four

We chatted aimlessly about the library, the car, and the gas station. It all seemed very funny now, and we laughed out loud. There were moments of awkward silence, but Cort seemed to end up telling some joke or saying something to make me smile. As long as I avoided looking at him, I felt relaxed and even soothed by his voice.

After about half an hour, we turned right, off the main road, on to a narrow dirt one marked only by a large, beat up gray mailbox. We pulled up to a little wooden cabin. The exterior walls had obviously once been white, but time and the elements had stripped them of most of the paint leaving a graying wood behind. It didn't look very sturdy. We pulled up to a twin garage that doubled the size of the house. Trees hovered all around and wild brush encroached on every side.

Cort got out and inserted a key into a silver handle on the garage door and then lifted it. He climbed back into the car and pulled it in. When he climbed out, he left the car running, so I stayed put. He shut the garage by hand and locked it. Once back in the car, he pulled out a white remote from the console between us, and said, "Watch this."

The floor in front of the car went down. Goosebumps covered my arms. It created a ramp that went deep into the earth. He grinned and then drove the car down the ramp and into a huge underground garage. Several cool looking dune-buggies, a jeep, three motorcycles and a Hummer filled the space. After we got out of the car, he pushed another button on the remote, and I watched as the ramp rose up and clanged into place, looking like a ceiling above us. He then opened a panel on the left wall of the room and punched in a code. The wall slid to the side, revealing an entryway into what looked like a small kitchen. He motioned for me to enter, so I did.

The kitchen opened up to an average-sized family room with furniture covered with white sheets.

"Welcome home!" he said with exuberance, turning on a light switch which also turned on six monitors that hung on a far wall, showing the outside of the house and the area around it.

I watched him as he walked to the kitchen table and sat in front of a familiar, large mirror on the table. John had had one exactly like it. Next to the mirror sat the same type of make-up kit John had used to make me over on our way to Florida from Helena.

I stared at the bum. He couldn't be John, could he? I took a deep breath and held it as I walked over to study him. He must have sensed it and looked up at me while tugging on one of his wild eyebrows, revealing a tidy dark brown one underneath. He did the same to the other eyebrow and then yanked at the greasy hair on his head to remove it. He ran his hand roughly over his almost bald head, only a hint of dark hair gracing a two inch path around his head just above his ears. Sighing loudly, he moved his head in large circles, eyes closed. He definitely wasn't John. Whew!

"You'll have to excuse me," he said, opening his eyes. "It always feels so good to get out of a disguise."

I kept staring, speechless, as he removed a set of fake teeth. He walked over to the sink and rubbed his face with some kind of cream before washing it vigorously. He brushed his teeth and then grabbed two water bottles from the fridge and walked back over to the table, handing me one.

I couldn't take my eyes off him. This couldn't be the same man I'd met just an hour ago. His five-o-clock shadow accentuated his strong jaw and his physique screamed Alpha-male. I snapped my mouth shut when he spoke, showing a perfect set of brilliant white teeth.

"Just give me a minute to change."

"Uh," I said, still amazed at the transformation that had just taken place before my eyes. Despite the ratty clothes he still wore, Cort was handsome. He couldn't have been more than thirty-five. His blue eyes twinkled at me, and his tan skin was wrinkle free. He got up and walked through a door on the opposite side of the living room.

"Then I'll fill you in on what has been going on when I'm done," he said, shutting the door behind him.

I gulped the water, wondering how many people I'd met in my life who were just playing a part. It seemed forever before he came back and sat across the table from me again. He wore jeans and a vintage purple T-shirt that only accentuated his muscular body beneath it. He took a swig of his water and then looked straight at me.

"When I saw your picture on the news two days ago, I had to anticipate the worst. I headed to this safe-house and started setting it—"

"You saw it, too?"

"It was on national news. You and your cute little cheer team."

My insides burned.

"Yep," he said. "I figured if I'd spotted you, there was a good chance others would, too. John did a great job at making you disappear in plain sight, but that assumed nobody would be looking for you. Ever since your school started showing up in the news, I've been watching, waiting for you to screw up. But, you surprised me. John trained you well. He has a knack for that. I thought you were going to make it through without any exposure, then bam! Your team's picture ends up on national news and not only on one station, but every last one. Don't you watch the news?"

"Not recently," I said. "I've been too busy with the fundraiser."

"Well, all that good you did with that fundraiser just about got you killed."

"Katy told me the team had been on the news a lot, but I thought I'd been careful not to be in any of the pictures. I had no idea they'd put the team picture up."

"And you almost made it. But, I'm glad I came down here and started to get it all set up. Otherwise we'd have had no fresh food for the next two weeks." He raised his eyebrows at me.

I felt a bit numb but managed a "Thanks."

"I just don't get what the trigger was to get them here. There's no way the terrorists saw you on the news. They bought the idea that you'd burned in that car explosion, lock, stock and barrel. It only took two days for the chatter about you to completely stop. They wouldn't have even been looking for you."

"Really? I wondered if they'd truly bought it."

"How could they deny it? They knew they'd set the bombs and they'd worked, just as they'd planned, except that it had been you they'd killed. They probably hoped to knock out an FBI agent or two. On top of the chatter stopping, Azeez, Iceman, as you call him, all but disappeared off the grid. We thought we'd seen the last of him. But the night of that Valentine's fundraiser, for whatever reason, the chatter of his group exploded. Sure, your picture with all the cheerleaders had been on TV, but you hadn't shown up on the news in all your glory on the stage at the Valentine's dance, yet. What were you thinking letting them film you at the fundraiser anyway?"

"I couldn't get out of it. I tried." I wondered what had tipped them off, too. Something tickled the back of my mind, as I searched for answers.

"You could have just left. There's always a way out."

"Well, I figured I looked so different, no one would recognize me." Was there another leak in the FBI?

"It's not like you had plastic surgery or anything. Your face looks as it always has. And your voice is still your voice. Anyone really looking for you could've found you… Anyway, I knew I'd be getting a call, so I stocked up on things here and followed you around. I saw you leave with John's kid. What was that all about?"

"Long story, but it's over, now."

"I like long stories."

"You wouldn't like this one."

"Well, what took you so long to push the extraction button? I thought for sure you'd been caught at Alex's hotel and I'd end up having to rescue you."

I took a deep breath. "I thought it was one of John's drills and I wanted to bug him a bit. Give his cronies a run for their money."

"Spunky. I like that."

"It was stupid. I seem to be a pro at stupid."

"Don't be ridiculous. John called you incredible. And he doesn't do that."

I sat, dumfounded. Had he really said that?

"I can understand you not liking him. He tends to rub people the wrong way, but he is the best."

I gave Cort a distasteful look, remembering the voicemail John had left me, and shook my head.

"He knows what he's doing. He's never botched a mission or lost a protection detail. The guy's a legend whether you like him or not. If you do as he says, you'll stay safe."

My face fell and I tried to hide it by blurting out, "Look are we just gonna talk about John all night or can I go get some rest? I'm bushed."

He chuckled. "Fine, I'll leave John out of it from now on, but it's only three and I'm guessing you're not really looking to sleep. I bet you're freaking curious to find out what happens next."

I snorted. He had me pegged.

"Great! Here comes the thick and thin of it. We'll be here a couple of weeks or so. I still don't know what's going to happen after that. We're waiting on your placement details. As soon as they come, I'll prepare you for your new life."

I felt a deep ache in my stomach.

"While we're holed up here, waiting for the bad guys to clear out, we won't be able to leave. I didn't get enough fresh stuff to last that long, but we've got enough canned goods for a good month. We won't starve, for sure."

"Two weeks?" It hardly seemed long enough.

"Don't worry," he said, misinterpreting my question. "I'll keep you busy, starting with making this place livable."

We freed all the furniture from the dusty sheets and loaded them into the washer. We dusted and vacuumed and then he had me clean up my bedroom and the main bathroom while he made dinner. He had already cleaned his room because he'd slept here the past few days.

My room was small but cozy. A chair sat in the corner with a lamp and a bookshelf full of books next to it, most of which I'd already read but was willing to read again. I figured I'd spend a lot of my time there. Everything seemed to be in miniature in comparison to my home in Niceville. Things had been perfect there, why had I let myself be exposed?

The toilet in the main bathroom had a permanent hard water ring. Try as I might, I couldn't remove it. After finishing cleaning, I sat on the couch and flipped on the TV. The smell of something yummy made my stomach growl, and I stood up and headed for Cort and the food.

Cort had made us chicken and rice with fresh greens and pears, but wouldn't let me eat until he'd turned off the TV and lectured me that while TV had its uses, we didn't need it while here. The food tasted great. Cort let me know that I'd be cooking tomorrow.

After dinner, we watched a movie and went to our rooms. Wanting to get my mind off starting a new life, I picked up *Pride and Prejudice* and fell asleep reading it.

Cort woke me with a knock on my door. Looking at the clock, I discovered it was only five-thirty. Why were we getting up so early? After getting dressed in some clothes I found in the dresser, I saw Cort sitting on the floor in the family room, obviously meditating. I had spent the last five months learning all about meditation and so I sat in my own space and zoned out. After that we did a lot of sit-ups and push-ups and some basic cardio, then had a simple breakfast of bagels, eggs and strawberries. That over with, he pulled several big boxes out of his room and asked me to take a look.

Inside were bags, all labeled with words like: clown, old man, old woman, fat woman, fat man, CEO, biker, pop star, groom, etc.

He grabbed a cowboy costume, went to his room and came out acting just like a bonafide cowboy. He even twirled a rope around. I laughed out loud at his perfect accent.

He threw me a bag and told me to get into character as the captain of a ship. I felt stupid walking out of my room all dressed up.

Noticing my discomfort, I guessed, he said, "A disguise is only as believable as the person in it. But you know that already, don't you Michele?" When he said Michele, something gave in his voice and he raised one eyebrow. I raised both of mine and he said, "Just curious why you said your name was Michele and not Christy."

"I don't know," I said, thinking about it for the first time. "I guess that's who I am now."

His thin smile looked concerned. "Never forget who you are at your center, Christy. You'll lose yourself for sure if you do. Bend yourself to your character. Don't lose yourself."

I thought I was supposed to lose myself. It was a struggle even to remember who Christy was, especially now as I was trying to also be a ship's captain, with nothing to go off of but memories of movies like *The Titanic*. I had to modify my thoughts and allowed myself to remember only the characteristics I liked about Christy, and even then, Michele called to me.

After practicing becoming a bunch of different personas for the rest of the morning, we made sandwiches, and Cort put on a video he'd compiled. The title was *Who Do I Want To Be Today?* He let the first scene play while we ate.

Clips of different U.S. Presidents eating, walking, talking and hanging with their families graced the screen. He paused it when the title "Secret Service Agents" popped up.

"So, you just watched presidents doing various things. Can you be a president, now?"

I shrugged.

"Give it a try," he said. "Think about what you saw and pretend you are the President of the United States eating breakfast with a senior advisor. What do you say and how do you act? Concentrate on mannerisms."

I straightened in my seat and opened a napkin onto my lap. I took a sip of water and asked, "What's on the agenda this morning, Henry? Please tell me I have a light schedule. I'm dying to spend some time outside under that hot sun."

"Sorry Sir," Cort said. "Your day is packed to the brim. You'll have to be on your toes most of the day and into the evening. You're meeting in …"

We spent a good fifteen minutes pretending and then we discussed what we'd done. He skipped to various parts of the video and we watched them again, Cort pointing out things I'd missed.

We spent the rest of the day studying various categories of people on his DVD, continuing through dinner. At about seven, he called it quits, and we watched a movie called, *Bad Bikers Gone Good*.

Every day for five days straight, we followed the same pattern and it fascinated me. Just like John, Cort had mastered the art of disguise, and he was teaching me to master it, too. After the fifth day, he started teaching me how to use makeup to enhance a disguise. He had me visualize something, draw a picture and then try to re-create it on my own or his face. Talk about difficult. By the tenth day, I could create several easy looks. I had a lot of work to do to make scars look real, though. I found myself drawing a picture of Christy later that day.

"I know that girl," he said.

I looked up at him. "She's dead," I said.

"No she isn't."

"Yes, she is." I insisted. "She died in a car explosion—or at least that's what they tell me."

"Christy, have you seen footage of the explosion?"

"No."

"Would you like to?"

"John said it would only cause me pain."

"Do you believe that?"

"Not really, but maybe."

"How about we watch it together?" He smiled at me and nudged me in the arm.

After a few moments of hesitation, I said, "Yeah. I mean, yes. Let's watch it."

It was like watching a movie. It didn't seem real. I saw the car explode, the ambulances, the police. Then I saw the "bodies" taken by the coroners. The funeral was huge. Every kid in school must have come. They even cried. I didn't understand that at all. As the camera panned the crowds, I spotted Rick.

"Pause it there. Can you pause it there?"

Cort paused it, and I stared at the screen. Rick had come to my funeral.

"Okay, let it run," I said, getting my fill.

Then I saw Rick weep, on an older woman's shoulder. His mother maybe?

It was surreal to see the scene, hear the words spoken. It tore at my heart to see my mother and my father's tear streaked faces. My brother's and sister's stoney and sad expressions. Once it was over, Cort offered me a hug and I gladly accepted. The curious thing was, that while I felt torn up inside, I couldn't find any tears.

As engrossed in my lessons with Cort as I was, I started getting stir-crazy, needing to see and feel the sun. I found myself spending more and more time watching the monitors that showed outside the cabin. I hated not having real windows to look out.

Feeling a bit claustrophobic one day, I lifted the blinds in the living room to peek out. The wall looked back out at me. I wanted to cry. I needed fresh air. It was a good thing Cort kept me so busy or I might have gone mad.

When the twelfth day came around, the anticipation of being able to go outside in about two days boosted my spirits. Cort had said we'd have to stay two weeks and at the end of two more days, those two weeks would have passed. The closest we ever got to outside was going into the big garage and practicing getting in and out of different types of cars, depending on who we were pretending to be at the moment. We even practiced getting on and off the Harleys. It was harder than it looked. I went to bed excited to get up the next day.

I woke to the sound of voices very early in the morning and crept to my door and peeked out. A man in dark clothes and a hood stood talking to Cort in the kitchen.

"…ASAP and it better be good. You've got your hands full with this one. Be careful."

"I will be. Thanks for the supplies."

The man in black left through the only exit, the kitchen door. I tried to ease my way back into my room before Cort noticed me.

"Christy, just come on out," he called, a disgusted look on his face.

Feeling guilty for sneaking, I slowly opened the door and joined Cort in the kitchen. He stared at me and I blurted, "Sorry."

"What did you hear?"

"Not much," I hedged. My cheeks burned. "Only something about your hands being full with this one."

"It appears they are." He stared at me, a dark look flickering in the back of his eyes.

It scared me.

"We need to get ready to move. There have been some…developments, aah, ahh, ahh, ahh," He said, faking a sinister laugh and drawing out the word "developments" so it sounded like, "Deevelopmeentss", the edge to his fake, evil voice, gave me the chills.

I felt my eyes go wide. "What developments?"

"Your boyfriend blew your cover, well, sort of."

"My boyfriend?" My stomach filled with butterflies as Alex filled my mind, a connection coming to the surface. The fact that the terrorists seemed to show up right after Alex arrived in Helena and how they just showed up once again after he came to Destin hit me hard. Had he led them there? How?

"Go turn up the TV. I'm sure you'll find it enlightening," he said, rifling through some bags and boxes that now sat by the table.

The TV was on, but the sound was way down. The display read 5:00 and *Breaking News* flashed at the top of the screen. I reached for the remote and turned up the sound.

"It has been confirmed. Michele Mattingly, the young woman behind the hugely successful Down's syndrome research fundraiser at Niceville High, is missing. We have the wildly successful political investigative reporter, Tavien Adair, who broke the story late last night, to fill us in on the details." The screen changed to show a man sitting in a chair at some other location being conferenced in. "Welcome Tavien," the reporter said.

"Thanks for having me."

"Just how did you come across this story?"

"TLC hired my good friend, Heather, to film a documentary about the amazing community fundraiser Niceville High just held. Several of the students mentioned the original idea came from a cheerleader named Michele who mysteriously disappeared the day after the event. Heather couldn't make the facts line up and called me, giving me the beat on the missing girl. I was intrigued, came on down, and started asking around about her. Her long time boyfriend, Matthew, told officers he had had breakfast with her and then she had left on vacation with her family to France. It appeared to be true on the surface, but a bit of digging revealed some major problems."

I leaned into the TV and said, "What?" to the screen.

"I tried to telephone her for an interview, but she wasn't anywhere to be found. I mean, the story Matthew was selling me, what the other kids said, and the trail I found, which I think had been fabricated, by the way, didn't add up. I alerted the police and they picked Matthew up after discovering he had fought with Michele the morning she disappeared."

I turned and gave an exasperated look to Cort, who shrugged his shoulders and raised his eyebrows. "He's good."

"The curious thing," Tavien continued, "is that after ten hours of interrogation, they released the boy and seem to have dropped the case altogether. They have yet to explain that to me. It all smacks of a cover-up, and I intend to get to the bottom of it. In the meantime, Michele is missing. The question is, is she on the run or did someone take her? I think we owe this girl and her family some answers." A fiery glint shone in Tavien Adair's eyes.

"How was he able to get all this information?" I spoke out to the TV. "How? Katy would never be so sloppy."

"Sometimes it doesn't have to do with being sloppy," Cort said. "Sometimes it has to do with having the right connections."

"Who do you think had the power to stop the investigation?" the reporter asked.

"This whole thing stinks of a government cover-up. I have some leads, and I don't like where they're taking me. The government doesn't have the right to turn people's lives upside down just to get what they want. We need to find this girl and keep her safe."

A picture of me flashed on the screen with a number underneath it.

"If anyone sees Michele," the reporter said. "Please call the number on your screen. You could be saving her life." It went to commercial.

My heart raced a million miles a minute.

"I had planned a nice, easy water exit, out of Destin," Cort said. "But it turns out that the ocean is being watched, too."

"Being watched, too?" I walked over to Cort in a fog, wondering what I'd done to poor Matthew and why he'd said I'd gone on vacation.

"Yep. Sneaky buggers. They're using those advertising planes companies use every day here, but these ones are flying all day and late into the night, three men with binoculars in each plane. Just a bit obvious, don't ya think?"

I nodded, trying to grasp what he was saying. "What about the four roads out of here?"

"All watched."

"Let's just stay here longer then." Even as I said it, I wondered if I could handle being in the ground much longer.

He motioned for me to sit next to him.

"We have our orders and need to get you out of here. You're heading back to Washington, DC, to tell what you saw."

It felt like someone stomped on me, leaving a throbbing ache behind. "I already told them."

"Apparently, they need it again."

"What did you tell Matthew anyway?" Cort asked.

"Nothing, really," I said, wishing it were true.

"It wasn't nothing. It eliminated him from being a suspect."

"I mean I did tell him stuff, but he'd already guessed it. He found my backpack and heard Alex call me Christy."

"I know John taught you the number one rule is to never, EVER break cover."

My breathing sped up. He'd only covered that point almost every day for two months.

"I know, but Matt looked in my backpack and saw my passport and everything. What could I have said?"

"Anything but the truth. You lie until it all fits together."

My eyes stung with tears. "I'm sorry."

He sighed. "You are so young. Most kids are allowed a mistake here and there, but not you. You are not most kids. Never forget. Never compromise your identity. Never. At least your boyfriend did his best to keep you safe. He lasted ten hours before he broke. That's pretty good for a teenager."

"Broke? What do you mean, Broke?"

"Before he spilled his guts to the cops. Before he told them you are in witness protection."

I took a deep breath. "Well, he's not your typical teenager," I said, my back aching from the tension that had settled there. What had he gone through?

"I imagine not," Cort said. "Especially if he was *your* boyfriend. Really, it's not his fault Ahmed came out of obscurity. It's not even his fault the world knows about you."

"How do you know what he said?"

"You still don't get it, do you? We are the FBI. We are everywhere. It wasn't hard to get the info. Even Tavien scored some of it. After Matthew told the police you were in witness protection, they made some calls and dropped it. They were happy to be rid of the whole thing. If you believe what you see on TV, you'd think the cops and the FBI fight over cases. Police departments are so over-worked, they're happy to give us whatever we'll take. The good thing is that they followed protocol and once Matthew said you were in W.P., they came straight to us and didn't ask Matthew any questions that would reveal your true identity. Otherwise, Tavien would probably have it all. They told Matthew to keep his mouth shut and put a protection detail on him. And, like I said, Iceman and his band arrived just before the fundraiser dinner, before your mug on the stage showed up. Any ideas about what might have triggered that? The chances of them seeing you on TV were slim to none."

Alex's too perfect face flashed through my mind, but I answered, "No… But I don't get it. If you know they are here, why not just get 'em. Arrest them." Why did danger always seem to follow Alex?

"Good question. My boss obviously has some plan in action or he wouldn't have everyone tracking all the freaks so closely without picking them up. I just wish they'd clue me in on the whole thing…No idea at all what or who might have triggered Iceman's resurfacing?"

"No." I'm not sure why I lied. Maybe I was letting my feelings for Alex influence me. I just couldn't imagine him having anything to do with the bad guys. Maybe I just didn't want to deal with his dad ever again.

"Hmm. The good news is that they've moved your family and they are safe."

"Natalie and Mason?" Did they need protection now, too? I thought they could take care of themselves.

"Hello! Are you in there? Your real parents and family."

A hot rock seemed to be searing my heart. I reached out and grabbed his wrists. "Are you sure they're safe?"

"All I know is what Special Agent Flitton told me. Your family is in custody and they are rounding up your friends from DC and their families. The heat is on again."

Not them, too. I was such an idiot.

"I'm assuming you'll all be relocated—at least for a while. Hopefully this investigative reporter stops his nosing around before he blows the whole operation. This area, however, is getting too hot, with Iceman resurfacing and all. We do have an opportunity to get you out of here tomorrow, but, I've got to get you ready. This isn't going to be pleasant. We have to go hard core. A complete transformation."

"Am I going to get to see my family?" The thought both horrified and electrified me. They were a part of a past I'd left behind. A past I did not want back, and yet, I knew seeing my family and being able to talk to them would give me comfort.

"I doubt that, but you never know. I guess if they got every last filthy-rotten terrorist, they might let you go back. But, we need to get you ready. Don't think about any of that. Just think about now."

"Why is Ahmed still after me?"

"I don't know everything, but from what Special Agent Flitton says, Ahmed is desperate to save face. He thought you were dead. He knows he's been played the fool. He has to prove himself as the leader all over again. And other terrorist groups want to take over. He has shown weakness and other terrorists want to capitalize on it. If Ahmed, the leader of the most venerated terrorist group, wants you, all the others do, too. If they can get to you first, they can take Ahmed out. Think of the power."

"This will never be over."

"We have a chance to end it by getting you to DC. Let's do it, okay?"

"Ok. What's my cover going to be?"

He stood and moved behind me saying, "Not a chance. I want to surprise you. I don't want to freak you out just yet. But, your new name is Ari. I'm Lenny, your dad."

My thoughts focused on the people I'd put in danger until I heard the snip, snip, snip of scissors. Long strands of the hair I'd loved so much fell softly to the ground, mingling with my tears. In an odd way, I was okay with him cutting my precious hair. In some way, I wanted to be punished.

I imagined the terrorists cutting Marybeth's beautiful waist length hair and wondered how she was able to keep it together. It was hard enough having someone who cared for me do it. Cort put black dye on my hair and eyebrows. After rinsing out the dye, he started cutting again. I tried to focus on something else, but couldn't find anything that didn't make me want to break out sobbing. My hair was so short! He used some sculpting gel to put spikes all over my head. He then rubbed some cream over one of my eyebrows, on my nose, lip and ears.

It tingled for a minute and then seemed to go numb. My lip felt fat.

"You shouldn't be able to feel this, but let me know if you do." He took out a long silver needle-like object. He pinched my eyebrow and I jerked away.

"Wait a minute," I said. "What is that?" I eyed the huge curved needle and leaned even further away from it.

"It's a piercing needle. I said this wouldn't be pleasant."

"I thought you were talking about my hair." I stared longingly at the hair piled on the floor. "Why not just use those magnetic-fake ones?" I stared at the needle again.

He motioned for me to sit upright again. "You've got to look like the real thing. Nothing can give you away. You can remove them in a couple of weeks. No worries."

After sitting back up, he pinched my eyebrow and pushed the needle through my skin. I felt a quick prick. My first piercing. He set the needle down and inspected his work. He did the same thing to one of my nostrils, and my bottom lip. He then used a piercing gun to load my ears with studs and rings. He had me paint my nails black while he clicked away several times up my left ear. It wasn't the best paint job ever. But, it was okay. I tried to reconcile with the fact that I would be a freak when he was done. Beauty, turned into a beast. Next, he put fake, press-on tattoos on both my arms, my neck, and the small of my back. He pulled out some black make-up and lined my eyes and lips with it. I couldn't help thinking I was going to be afraid of myself when Cort, no—Lenny, was done.

"How come these can be fake and the piercings can't?" I asked pointing at the tats.

"They can't get knocked off or fall off. These will, however, wear off in about two weeks. You ready to see yourself?"

I shook my head.

He chuckled. "How about you put these clothes on and then you'll get to see the full effect. Take a look in the bathroom mirror once you're dressed." He handed me a bag.

"Okay," I said, resigned to be whoever he'd created. It took me a while to figure out how all the pieces to the outfit went together. I had to lay them out on the bed and by elimination, decide how to put it all on. I pulled on the two tank tops and then slipped a short, shredded shirt over it. I yanked on some very short, very tight shorts, slipped into leather pants and laced up some tall boots before and sliding a big tutu like skirt over it. The finishing touch was a Harley jacket. I slid five silver and black rings on three different fingers and hung the six different skull and cross bone necklaces and crosses around my neck. Why people put them together, I'd never know. I shook my head and stood next to the bed, thinking I looked ridiculous and not wanting Lenny to see me.

"What's the hold up, Michele?" he called, knocking on the door.

I grunted and opened it.

"Excellent," he said, taking a step back. "A true goth biker girl."

I huffed. "I look ridiculous."

"How do you know? You haven't even looked." He motioned for me to go to the bathroom.

I took my time walking there, feeling my insides quake. I had liked being Michele and I'd blown it. Now, I had to be some extreme girl for the rest of my life. I wanted to turn back time and be better to Matthew and reject Alex when he came. Maybe everything would be different if I had. But, I couldn't go back, and now my family and friends were in danger again. I had to make the best out of the circumstances I now found myself in. When I looked into the mirror, I gasped. I did look like a goth-biker girl—at least what I'd imagined when he said it. I couldn't help but move right up to the mirror and gently touch the piercings, one by one. I could feel a slight ache in my eyebrow and lip. I ran my fingers over the tattoos and then took a step back to see the whole look again.

"Pretty great, huh?" Lenny said, appearing behind me in the mirror.

I nodded. "Wow. You are good."

"Thank you," he said. "But you really ought to thank the special agent you eavesdropped on earlier today. He did a bang up job picking this stuff out. Tomorrow I'll be adding a scar right here," he said, running his index finger across my cheek. "You'll also be wearing dark brown contacts."

I nodded, trying to imagine it.

"How are your piercings? Throbbing yet?"

"Actually, my lip has its own heartbeat now," I said, moving close to the mirror again to inspect it.

"I've got something for that," he said, walking back to the table and reaching into a box. I followed him. He handed me some pills and two tubes of ointment. "Put this on tonight." He held up one of the tubes. "It's an antiseptic that also prevents swelling and reddening. This," he continued, "will numb the area you put it on for up to one hour. Use it sparingly. And these pills will take the edge off." He dropped two pills into my hand. I walked over to the sink and chased them down with a glass of water.

"Now, you need to learn about being a biker chick." He continued. "As you know, I'm already a fabulous biker-dude, so I'll guide you."

"Ha, ha, ha," I scoffed.

He went to his room and came back with a DVD that he stuffed into the player. "We are motorcycle enthusiasts—not to be confused with being a part of a motorcycle gang." We watched half an hour of biker enthusiast footage before he took me out to the garage to practice getting onto the Harley.

He got on first and then I climbed on. We did it like a zillion times and my legs ached afterward. My muscles already felt the effects of not getting a good workout the past two weeks. He gave me tips on how to look more natural around the bike as we practiced.

We watched more footage on the DVD and then discussed it. If I were to be a goth-biker, he explained, I had to be serious and only give short, one-word answers whenever possible and never say anything positive. Scowling was my new favorite pastime. I had to really work against my naturally positive disposition. I discovered I normally talked a lot and had to work hard to hold my tongue through most of our conversations.

He gave me the manual for the bike so that I could learn all its parts and then pulled out ten biker magazines for me to study before bed. I read everything, even the ads, filing the information away in one of those folders in my brain. I noticed that the biker chicks in magazines had long, luscious hair and wore almost nothing. I didn't look anything like them. Would I fit in or stick out like a sore thumb?

The next morning he taught me how to tie a head scarf. He made me do it over and over until I could do it without any effort. He also had me practice putting on and taking off my helmet. To make it appear as fluid as he wanted, I had to numb the piercings because they all got bumped each time. By the end of it, they all throbbed. We practiced getting on and off the bike again. My legs hurt even worse, but I managed it.

"Why can't we be a part of a motorcycle gang?" I laughed and tried to pout. "It would be so much more exciting."

He chuckled. "Yeah right. Really exciting. We could knock some heads in for being in our territory. Nope we're just a couple of motorcycle ennthuuusiastsss from Austin, Texas joining the fun of the biker friendly Panama City Beach—Thunder Beach 13th Annual Spring Rally." He took a deep breath and I had to grin.

"Boy, that was a mouthful."

"Ya think?" he said, continuing like he was reading an advertisement. "It's where we'll find music, art, babes, pageants and bands—all on the beach. Oh, and don't forget about the constant partying we can join. Marijuana and alcohol will saturate every nook and cranny of the beach. We just can't wait. But, while we're there to party, we're most interested in the 100-mile Poker Run to Tallahassee and back to raise money for families of law enforcement officers killed in the line of duty, *The Ride for the Fallen*. Ya see, it just so happens that your uncle is one of those that fell." He held up a T-shirt with the name and picture of my supposed uncle who was killed in the line of duty and tossed it to me.

I read the name printed on it out loud, "Barry Wall. Officer Barry Wall? Funny." I draped the shirt over my shoulder and said, "Aren't there any police there to control the mayhem?"

"Oh, there will be a lot of police there, but they tend to turn a blind eye to all the illegal stuff unless it causes a problem. Seems their ability to smell marijuana disappears during this event. All they smell is money. It's a huge money maker for them and the area, and they want people to come back next year to do it all over again. It's what they call controlled chaos.

"It's the motorcycle gangs that you so desperately want to be affiliated with that tend to cause the problems. Last year, some Hell's Angels came down and beat the crap out of a T-shirt vendor for selling in what they considered their territory. The police arrested the lot of them. There are actually a lot of arrests for disorderly conduct, but it has to be really bad. Thousands of people are in Panama City for this. They've recruited help from all the surrounding police agencies to handle the crowds, but there are never enough eyes."

"Why are we going into crowds of people? I thought we didn't want to be seen."

"Today is the last day of the four-day festival. Most of the bikers will be too drunk, stoned, or hung over to even take notice of anything and all the cops are over-worked and tired by now. With any luck, the terrorists will stay far away from this police infested event."

"Hmm. Weird event to honor cops."

"Warped isn't it? Anyway, we're going to hop on the bike, head on down to Panama City and register for the ride, giving our donations to the families who've lost loved ones. Then we'll join the riders as they head out for Tallahassee. We, of course, will continue to ride through Tallahassee, up to Georgia, then through South and North Carolina as well as Virginia, and right to Washington DC. The ride starts at noon, so we need to get out of here."

I felt hot all of a sudden. "We're going to DC today?"

"No. In two days. We're heading for a hoity-toity country club up there. The FBI wants to cover their butts in case Tavien, that reporter from the news this morning, who never covers up a juicy story, no matter how hard my bosses go down on him, breaks the real story. They are having your whole group go and get your testimonies on video. I don't know all the details, but we have to get you there safely first."

My heart raced and I felt an ache in my lower back. The stress of it all was getting to me.

"Looks like you're going back to the scene of the crime," he said, suddenly staring hard at me. "You going to be okay with that?" His look turned to concern.

"I think so," I said, trying to ignore the sick feeling overtaking me. I wondered if I'd see any of the seven from my mini-tour group. What would I say? "I don't get what happened. John told me he thought Ahmed's terrorist cell would forget about me once I was dead."

"Once you were thought dead, Ahmed was treated like a hero. He had avenged his brother's death and everyone wanted to be a part of the organization that stuck it to the U.S. However, once you resurfaced, it became a whole new ball of wax. Ahmed realized he'd been tricked by the U.S. This showed a major weakness on his part. Now, a lot of terrorist groups want to show him up. Do what he couldn't. If any of the other groups get to you before he does, he loses everything. No one will respect his power. He's having to act fast; his people are starting to desert him. He's furious and he's never been more dangerous."

I shook my head and shivered in fear. He had been pretty darn dangerous at the cabin in Montana. I couldn't imagine what he'd be like now.

Lenny had me load up the bike with food and supplies while he put on his disguise and packed his bags. I spent the extra time thinking about Kira and Summer. I could run into them at the country club. Summer hated me with a passion and didn't try to hide it. Would she feel any differently now? Kira just about gave me whiplash as she changed from my friend to my enemy depending on which would give her the most purchase with any good looking guy that happened to be around. I still wasn't sure if she was my friend or my enemy. Did I want to see either one of them?

Lenny walked out of his room twenty minutes later, looking like many of the bikers I'd seen in the magazines and footage. He had long and stringy hair, big glasses, a few strategically placed tats and scars, and leather from head to toe. Even his head scarf was leather. He had a few piercings in his ears and nose.

I laughed. He laughed, too.

"You look great," I said.

"Thank you very much," he said with a bow. "So, daughter of mine, let's roll."

With that, we left Cort and Michele behind in that windowless safehouse.

Chapter Twenty-Five

After securing the door that led into the safe-house from the large garage, Lenny drove the bike up the ramp of the hidden garage below and into the garage above. I walked ahead of him and opened the garage door to let him outside while the ramp clicked back into place and acted like a floor once again. I pulled the garage door shut and locked it after he rode out. I took a moment to breathe in the fresh air and look at the trees and sky, reveling in being free of our underground home. The exhilaration I felt filled every part of my being. I raised my hands up above my head and twirled in a circle, yelling a loud *yahoo* to the birds flying overhead. Lenny revved the engine and I jumped on, ignoring the pain that crashed up my leg as I lifted it over the seat.

Climbing onto the bike felt a bit weird when it had nothing to do with training. I suddenly wasn't sure where to put my hands. Lenny, I guess noticing my hesitation, said, "Just like we practiced it. Either put your arms around me or hold onto the seatback. I suggest you hold onto me for the first little while."

I was surprised at how scary it was the first few times we took a curve. My instinct was to lean away from the turn, but I quickly remembered Lenny had told me I'd have to lean into the turns. Watching everything fly past me made my heart leap, and leaning into the sharp curves took my breath away.

I spent some time creating the new me in my mind, but mostly I worried about what I would say to Marybeth and Rick if I ran into them at the country club. Did Marybeth hate me now? I had made her watch the scene in the ballroom, and then they'd caught her and they'd shaved her bald and tortured her—the very men I'd told her to watch. Would she want to tell me what happened or would she never mention it? I wanted to hear the story from her. Alex didn't know all the details of her abduction. He only knew what the FBI had told him, and I knew how reliable that information could be. Could I face Rick, knowing I'd betrayed him? Had he betrayed me? Had he called me just like Alex had and I'd never gotten the message?

We arrived in Panama City just before eleven. Even at the end of March, the sun beat down on us and sweat tickled my back once we dropped to city street speeds.

Within two miles of the beach, the enormity of the event jumped out at me. People were everywhere. It was one big party. It took us a good twenty minutes to find a place to park and another twenty to weave through the crowds and sign up for the ride. Vendors selling everything under the sun lined the walkways and dotted the beach. The steady thrum of drum beats played in the background while laughter and loud talking filled the air along with the unmistakable scent of marijuana.

Lenny discovered the terrorists before I did. They stood about ten feet in back of the registration table, and while they tried to look casual, their eyes never left the line of newly registered bikers. A smart place to find us, but apparently our disguises were clever enough to fool them. They didn't bat an eye at us. I figured we'd have no trouble leaving them behind when we rode off toward Tallahassee.

Then, I heard Lenny make a phone call and say, "I just registered and realized I left two bills behind the table that have to be paid in the next ten. Could you take care of it, please?"

I was sure that call alerted the FBI to the two terrorists behind the registration table. Guess we wouldn't have to worry about them. It felt good to know they'd be taken care of.

We had ten minutes before the ride to Tallahassee began, so we grabbed some tacos from a nearby vendor and sat on the sand, looking out toward the ocean. On the rare occasion when there was a break in the mass of people walking by, I got a peek of the blue water. No one paid us any attention, but I looked on in awe as I ate, taking it all in. I saw a pack of goth-looking-biker-girls, ushered by what must have been their fathers, walk about twenty feet away from us. One girl, towering above the others, looked my way, staring a bit too long for my comfort.

"Time to go," Lenny said as he stood, disrupting her gaze. Once I got up, I looked for the girl, but she had been swallowed up in the mass of people migrating to the parked bikes.

We walked the short distance to our bike and joined the crowd waiting to start their engines once the cannon boomed to signal the commencement of the ride. I wondered if I'd be able to hear it over the rumble of the motorcycles. The riders kept revving their engines in anticipation, inching forward, staring each other down. Even after the cannon blasted, there were so many people, it took Lenny and me a good thirty minutes to get on the road. I choked on exhaust. Thousands of bikers forced their way to the street. Lenny had been right, this was the perfect place to get lost.

It surprised us to meet up with a bike check at a park that served as the first pit stop for the ride. Apparently some bikers, near the front of the pack, had caused some trouble. We watched as most bikes were waved past. Only a few were signaled to pull off to a second row where the bikers were required to show ID and remove their helmets. Others pulled off to a third row and were given what looked like sobriety checks. We, of course, got singled out to go to the second line. As I removed my helmet, butterflies filled my stomach. Lenny had never given me an ID! He had taken my picture at the house, but had never given me the ID. I repeated over and over again to myself that my name was Ari. I was seventeen and my birthday was on September fifteenth. I held my breath as the officer approached and asked for them. I let it out as Lenny handed him two driver's licenses. The officer looked him over, and then moved on to me. I had to remind myself not to smile and say hi. Ari was not friendly.

"Is this your daughter?" he asked, staring hard at me. I snorted.

"Yep," Lenny said.

"Well, as I'm sure you know, Florida law doesn't require wearing a helmet, but she really needs to wear hers at all times. And be careful, folks. Please." He nodded at us and took a step back to let us pass.

A man to my right was trying to walk a straight line for one of the officers in that third row. I chuckled as he stumbled.

Lenny found a spot to park at one end of the park and pulled out our lunches and a blanket. We sat in the shade of a tree surrounded by most of the others from the ride doing the same thing. It was too hot to sit in direct sunlight. I felt a bit self-conscious; sure people were staring at me because of my outrageous looks. It made me blush from head to toe. Lenny must have noticed my discomfort because he gave me a quizzical look. I shrugged and dug deep to find the ability to act the part again. I told my brain to like who I was and convinced it that I was cool and not a freak. As I took a deep, cleansing breath, I heard a voice behind me. "Hey, you wanna hang?"

I looked behind me and saw a group of seven girls led by the tall, anemic-looking goth girl I'd seen earlier. Dressed in black from head to toe—even her eyes were an endless black—she peered down at me like a crow looking for a succulent treat. I worked hard not to shrink in her shadow.

I turned to Lenny and said, "I'm going," glad that my voice didn't crack with discomfort.

"I don't think so. We're leaving soon and you haven't eaten yet."

Wishing I could agree with him, but knowing it would not be in character to do so, I said, "Whatever, Dad! You just don't want me to have any fun."

I heard chuckles from the group of goth kids.

"We have been having fun," he said in an even, stinging tone.

"You tell me to make more friends and then don't let me meet anyone new!"

"Go!" he said. "But get your butt back here in half an hour."

Shocked he allowed it, I felt my mouth drop open and my eyes turn to silver dollars. Has he just given me permission? Crap! In truth, this girl had scared me since the first time I'd seen her, and I didn't want to go with her and her friends.

He raised his eyebrows and a mocking look spread across his face. I forced myself to stand, taking note of the time on my phone as I picked it up and put it in my pocket. I had to truly concentrate, to force myself not to smile, my defense against all uncomfortable, scary circumstances, as I turned to join the pack.

The tall, thin girl said, "I'm Teleah," as I walked toward them.

"Ari," I answered, joining them.

"Nice maneuver man." She nodded at me. "Most dads are such a drag. Mine excluded, of course." She introduced me to the other six girls as we walked a crooked path through the blankets.

"This your first time to ride in this poker run?" a girl named Max asked.

"Yep," I said, starting to fall back into character.

"It's my tenth year. My dad's a die hard. Most of us," she said, gesturing to the other girls, "have been together at least the last five years."

I nodded.

We ended up sitting at Teleah's "compound." She wasn't kidding when she said her dad was a die hard. He had set up chairs, a table and even a small shelter and was busy grilling burgers and steaks.

"How'd you get all this stuff up here on your bike?"

"We didn't. My aunt lives in Tallahassee and sets this up for us each year. That's her in the little tent thing."

I glanced at her. She sat at a table with another woman, playing cards.

"My mom's in there with her. She's the one with the bright red hair."

Another man stood with her dad at the grill, smoking cigarettes and gawking at passersby. We plopped onto some chairs, and the girls started drilling me with questions. Was I going to come next year? Yes. Where did I live? In Texas. Did I have a boyfriend? Yes. It went on and on. What was my latest tattoo? I showed them one on my arm and made up why I'd gotten it. They weren't shy in the least and showed me tats in places I'd rather not see. I noticed the belly rings all of them sported and silently thanked Lenny for not making me get a navel ring.

I discovered I liked being able to play Ari. Being surrounded by others who looked just like me gave me courage to be who I had needed to be. Or maybe I'd discovered that these goth-girls weren't that different from other girls. They wanted acceptance. Just like me. They wanted boys to notice them and like them. They wanted friends and to feel like they belonged. Best of all, they wanted food. It didn't even feel strange anymore, being dressed like a freak and being able to let go and just be the character I was becoming. It was fun being the center of attention again. I started asking the girls about their boyfriends and what they did for fun. All of them had boyfriends but were actively looking for new and better ones.

One girl, Max, even bragged that she would have a new boyfriend before leaving the rally. “That molten lava cake that came by earlier will be back, you’ll see,” she said.

Teleah’s dad brought us all plates of food, and we pigged out while we talked some more. When we were finished, Teleah pulled out a joint, lit it and passed it to me. Why did I have to be sitting next to her right then? I took it and contemplated playing the fake-drinking card again only with marijuana this time. But, I knew I couldn’t. I’d decided against such idiocy after the Alex fiasco. Without missing a beat, I passed it to the girl next to me, turned to Teleah and said, “That crap turns me into a violent jerk.”

“No way!”

“Put me into a locked room with that crap of a boyfriend who burned you and a hit of that stuff and you won’t be sorry.”

She laughed.

“Hey,” Max said. “Look who’s back.” She gestured with her head in the direction of the walkway. We all looked. At first, I didn’t know who she was referring to, then Pyra said, “There are two more of them. Grrr. I want one.”

“The one in the dark blue is mine. Hands off,” Lei said.

My eyes fell on the four dark-skinned men across the walkway, standing in front of their own little shelter. An undeniable chill swept over me, and nothing, including the ninety degree heat, could warm me.

“They’re just a bunch of horny girls,” Taleah said, gesturing to her clan. I turned to check out the guys again while she talked.“They can have those guys. I don’t want them. Something’s just not right about them. Who goes around asking people if they’ve seen his friend, a sixteen-year-old blond cheerleader, when he’s obviously too close to the grave to be friends with a sixteen-year-old.” She snorted. “I mean, do we look like we’d be the type to hang with a blond haired, blue-eyed cheerleader? Come on.”

I almost choked on that one, but I couldn't take my eyes off them. I felt sicker by the second.

"Not you, too," Teleah said to me.

I turned to her just as I caught a glimpse of a very familiar and scary face, coming out of their tent. Iceman's.

For a split second, my blood stopped pumping. I ducked my head and said, "I'm not into old geezers."

My mind reeled, trying to figure out a way to escape. I glanced at my phone. I still had five minutes before I had to get back to Lenny. I couldn't wait, and yet I couldn't bring attention to myself by leaving in a rush. I watched the group of men until they disappeared into the shelter.

"I've gotta go in a minute, so give me your numbers so we can hook back up at Thunder Beach."

"Just ditch your dad. We'll get ya back to Thunderbeach."

"Nah," I said, like it was the most natural thing in the world. "I'd rather not sport a black eye my last day here."

I expected shocked looks. Instead, several girls nodded their agreement. Yikes. After programming their numbers in my phone and having them program mine in, (at least what they thought was mine), I stood and hit my knuckles to each of theirs, and said goodbye as I walked away, making sure I left through the back side of the compound.

I hurried back to Lenny, who was already sitting on the bike, waiting. I put my helmet on and climbed on my seat. As soon as we were away from the park, away from listening ears, I said into the helmet com, "Guess who I saw at the park." My stomach clenched.

"Who?"

"Iceman."

"He was there, too?"

"What do you mean, 'too'?"

"I spotted at least six terrorists and sent word to the FBI."

A white hot anger boiled up in my chest. "Why didn't you come get me when you discovered them?"

"Why would I do that?"

"Uh, I thought we were trying to stay away from them."

"Obviously they didn't recognize you."

At that moment, I understood how confident Lenny was with his abilities, but it didn't lessen my disgust. "Didn't recognize me?" I hissed. "I could have been taken. I was right across the path from them. What if Iceman had recognized my voice?"

"He didn't." His voice had a calm finality.

I huffed.

"Look. Ari is a good character for you," he said. "You are believable as Ari. I knew no one would see anyone but Ari if they looked at you or listened to you. Those girls approached you and you rocked the conversation. Did you talk boys?"

"Don't change the subject." Even though my anger was softening, a ball of anger and fear remained in my chest.

"Were you trained by John or not?"

"I was."

"I wanted to give you a chance to use your skills again."

"Huh?"

"I wanted to make sure you still had it."

I squished my eyebrows together. "Still had it?"

"You haven't been able to practice for a few weeks and I thought I'd give you the chance. Did you see them or feel them?"

"I saw them," I said, expelling a breath of air loudly, feeling as ridiculous and disappointed in myself as I had been angry.

"Then it's a good thing we did this little exercise, isn't it? Just remember, you can never relax. No matter what's happening around you, you can't let anything overshadow your senses. You must let them play in the background at all times, like computer virus protection,"

"Uggh! I'm never going to get it!"

"Yes you will. It's a skill. You have to practice every day or you lose it."

I shook my head.

"I knew they'd never spot you. Not the way you look. I figured this was a relatively safe way for you to practice. Especially after I'd reported them to the FBI."

"You have way too much faith in me," I said, resigned. "The terrorists were so far from my consciousness, I almost didn't discover them. I only knew they were there because I saw Iceman. Sure, I felt a chill, but I didn't recognize what it meant."

"Don't worry. I was ready for anything. I'm here to protect you. Trust me. Trust yourself."

I allowed myself to stew in my own self-pity for a good five minutes and then slipped into my Ari persona once again. No self-pity allowed. Several bikers drove the same road we were driving. We slowed, allowing them to pass us. When we were alone, we took a quick detour off the main road, starting our trek to Georgia. By the time we pulled into a safe-house near the border of Georgia and South Carolina, I couldn't feel my butt any longer. It had ached earlier, and just when I thought I would have to make Lenny stop at a motel instead of making it all the way to the safe-house, it had gone numb. Grabbing onto Lenny and leaning into him, I slid off the bike, hoping my legs weren't the rubber I'd feared they'd turned into it. I was wrong and my butt hit the ground with one big plop. Grinning at me, he set the kickstand and hopped off to help me up.

"Let me guess. Your butt went numb, right?"

"Yep," I said. I dusted off my rear and walked, bow-legged, into the house, my insides feeling like they were still being jiggled by the bike. We ate some sandwiches and apples I'd packed that morning, and then I sacked out on a too-soft-mattress in the little room Lenny assigned me.

In the morning, with achy legs, I showered. Lenny had me apply my own make-up, and I was excited that I only needed a little direction. My piercings stung and I still had to use both the antiseptic and numbing ointment every day. Breakfast was a bagel, an orange, and some beef jerky. Bracing myself for the long ride, I slipped into my place on the bike's seat. I wondered if I'd last. Thankfully, Lenny stopped every two hours and had me walk around and stretch. It made for a long day, but at least my butt and legs didn't fall asleep.

We finally made it to Virginia and stopped for the night in a stately white two-story house with pillars and an expertly manicured lawn.

Lenny put me up in a room with a queen poster bed and rich cherry woodwork. I even had a private bath. I filled the tub with blistering hot water and, with care, slid in with a book I'd pulled off a shelf next to the bed. I rolled a towel up and put it behind my neck and read until the water was ice-cold. I opened the drain and pulled my legs up to my chest and continued to read until all the water disappeared down the drain. Reluctantly, but shivering, I laid the book on the floor, pulled the shower curtain around the tub, turned the warm water on full blast and showered.

Climbing out of the tub, a wrinkled prune, I wrapped up in an amazingly soft towel and, after quickly getting into a tank top and shorts, I jumped into bed and read until I fell asleep.

When I woke, the sun was peeking through the curtains. I had to take a look outside. Some white puffy clouds dotted the brilliant blue sky but it looked chilly.

I made my way to the kitchen and could hear Lenny talking on his phone. He walked into the room and gave me a nod before saying, "I'll have to get back to you," to the person on the other line. He put his phone in his pocket and said, "Slept well?"

"Yeah. What time is it, anyway?"

"Eight."

"Wow. I not only slept well, I slept long."

He chuckled.

"When'd you get up?"

"Around five."

"What've you been doing?"

"Same ole', same ole'".

Something in his voice made me not believe him.

"Anything else?" I ventured, turning to open the fridge and acting like I didn't care, but straining to hear every word.

"I did talk to my boss. That's always fun."

"Did he have anything interesting to say?" I asked, pulling out some eggs and milk.

"I wouldn't say interesting. Maybe irritating. But definitely not interesting."

I broke the eggs in a bowl and heated a pan. "So, when do we take off today?" The thought of being on the bike for several more hours made my legs ache. I poured the eggs into the pan and scrambled them, waiting for an answer.

"Not sure yet. It depends on how long it takes the others to tell what they know."

My stomach lurched, and I wondered if eating eggs was the best choice to make. I had a good chance of meeting up with the whole gang today. Could I handle it? Could I handle seeing Alex and Rick in the same space again? Could I handle telling the story from beginning to end, once again? A ripple of fear tore through me.

"You're tentatively scheduled for two," Lenny continued. "But it may not happen until tomorrow. They're working out some security problems at the country club."

The way he said security sounded wrong. The tone was flat.

"Let me guess. You don't like the place they chose. You don't think it's safe." I put the eggs on a plate and walked over to the table and sat down to eat, not knowing if I'd be able to eat with a lump in my throat.

He snorted and shook his head. "Let's just say there are better places and better plans," he said, walking out of the room.

I couldn't finish the eggs and opted for a big glass of water instead. Then I went looking for Lenny. I had a few questions for him. I found him in a formal office area, standing over a large desk looking at some blueprints, dressed like Cort again. I walked over and took a peek, my mind capturing each line and word and recording it, never to be forgotten. Noticing me, he pulled one side of the blueprint over the other in one swift, but somehow natural manner, folding it in half to hide the information from me. Little did he know that the information already sat in my brain, waiting for me to call on it. I'd have to do some research, though. I'd never read a blueprint before and had no clue what all the symbols meant. I'd let him think I hadn't seen it.

"Whatcha doing?" I asked, looking back down at the closed print.

"Just some research."

"I love research. Can I help?"

"Naw. You wanna go outside for a bit?"

I knew he was putting me off, but I figured I'd get it out of him one way or the other. "Sure," I said. "It looked a bit cold earlier, though."

"By now it should be warm enough," he said, walking out of the study. I followed. We walked around the grounds for a good thirty minutes, chatting about nothing in particular. I could tell he was preoccupied. I wondered if it had something to do with that blueprint.

"Can I get on the internet?" I asked as we walked back into the house.

"Uh sure," he said, sounding a bit hesitant. "There's a computer in the study, but—"

"I know, I know." I said, rolling my eyes at him. "No Facebook, Twitter, email, etcetera, etcetera."

He took me back to the office, to the computer that sat on a desk next to the folded plans. He logged me on and then grabbed the plans and said, "I'll be in the kitchen if you need me."

I nodded and set to work, researching blueprints.

A couple of hours later, he came in and said, "We'll be taking off in about an hour. You should probably get yourself ready."

"Okay," I said, pushing the shutdown button before I had a chance to think about what I was doing. I couldn't turn it back on now and delete the history. If he checked, he'd know something was up. I took a last look at the blank screen and crossed my fingers, hoping he wouldn't have the time to boot up the computer and check on me.

When I'd finished getting ready, I bounded down the steps and found Lenny once again looking at those plans, but at the kitchen table this time. He made no effort to hide the plans from me. Uh oh.

He turned to look at me as I entered the room.

"So," he said. "Why didn't you just ask me?"

"Ask you what?" I said, stopping in my tracks, knowing full well what he was about to say.

"How to read a blueprint?"

My face burned and my heart thundered. "I, uh, I—"

"Look. If you have questions about something you discover, you should ask me. What did you think I'd do? Didn't we go over the trust thing just yesterday?"

"Yes, but I knew by your reaction that I wasn't supposed to have seen those plans, and my mind doesn't let go of things once they're in there. I didn't mean anything by it. I just needed to make sense of what I'd seen."

"It was my fault you saw the blueprints. Not yours. But you've got to be straight with me. Don't keep things from me."

"But it's okay for you to keep things from me?" The words had escaped my lips before I could stop them.

"That's different," he said. "I'm your handler. I'm supposed to keep things from you. You have no excuse."

"My handler?"

"Your teacher, trainer, protector. I am here to keep you safe whether that be by teaching you skills to keep yourself safe or by using my own skills to do it."

"Sorry," I said, deciding he really did have my best interest in mind.

"It's over and forgotten. But next time you sneak around on a computer, remember to delete the history before abandoning it."

I nodded, and said, "It won't happen again."

"That's a rookie mistake, and you're no rookie." He winked at me.

I nodded, wanting to tell him John had never taught me anything about computers.

"I think you'll recognize the blueprints soon enough. We're heading to that country club right now."

"Why that country club?"

"You tell me. You just studied it."

"Well, it has a ton of secret passageways. But how do they intend to protect them all?" I couldn't help but think of the secret passageway at the safe-house in DC—how I'd almost gotten killed and Jeremy had been paralyzed because the passageway hadn't been protected. And that was only one passageway. This country club had nine.

"It isn't just any country club, it's The Linden. Senators, congressmen, the President, and heads of state go there all the time. Even though it has been historically very safe, it seems an odd place to record your testimonies. I want to be prepared if the unexpected happens."

"It seems to me that if so many important people go there, the plans would be well known by a ton of security people."

"Actually, you saw the top secret plans. Only the President's security team is privy to them. The plans most security details see include only four secret exits."

"How'd you get them, then?"

"I have my sources."

"And so do others," I said, still re-living the pain of the DC safe-house.

"That's why I've spent so much time studying these." He gestured to the blueprints on the table. "It could be powerful information in the wrong hands. However, no one has ever tried to use these four exits." He touched the four different exits with his index finger. These four haven't been used in the last fifty years. Believe me. I've checked. Unlike you, however, I have to work on memorizing the prints and deciding on an escape route."

"Did you find one?"

"Yep. And I'll teach it to you on our little drive up there."

"'Kay," I said, turning to go.

"Wait." Lenny's look was serious. "I don't like this at all. You heard me call the FBI about our friends at the beach. I also called them and told them to get the guys at the park right after you went to play with your friends. No one got them, even though I spotted several Special Agents around the park. I don't know what game they're playing, but it doesn't feel right. Keep your spidey senses turned on and pay close attention to everything around you."

"Okay. I'll be ultra-aware." I turned to go into the garage.

"I'll be right there," he said. "I need to get rid of these."

I looked back to see him lighting the blueprints on fire at the stove and dropping them into the sink. The fire blazed only a few short seconds and was gone. He turned the water on and used the disposal before joining me.

Chapter Twenty-Six

After he went over the plans to escape the Linden, Lenny had music playing over our helmet coms. I tuned it out, thinking of my mini-tour group from DC. What would they all say to me? Worse, what would I say to them? I felt more and more queasy the longer we drove.

I didn't know exactly what to expect at the Linden Country Club, but not what I got. When we arrived at the white wrought iron gate with a large "L" in the middle, only a lowly rent-a-cop hopped out of his little shelter to investigate. Once Lenny gave him a card identifying him as a member, the no older than eighteen boy hurried back to the hut. He must have pushed a button inside, because the gate swung open, the "L" breaking in two, allowing us entry. No lines of men with big weapons waited for us. I couldn't even see the country club from the gate. Only the open green expanses of a golf course dotted with all colors of bushes and trees every so often.

No one appeared to be around. It looked deserted. Not a soul played golf. A hard rock formed in my throat, making it hard to swallow. Driving over a rise, the Linden Country Club sprawled in front of us. The blueprints didn't do it justice. I felt some satisfaction hopping off the bike when we parked it right in front of the country club, thinking my long rides on motorcycles were over. I admit I was tired of it. We parked next to a row of painfully expensive cars, most of which had either a professional driver inside, sleeping or sitting outside chatting with other drivers.

The white brick along with the painted white trim and oversized wooden wrap-around porch made me feel quite insignificant. Red flowers flowed from the plethora of planters set about. Hanging on the wall outside the large French door entryway, an elegant sign read: The Linden.

I made sure my spidey senses were on high alert as we entered the ostentatious building. The inside boasted even more shades of white than the outside. Glass from the chandeliers and sconces reflected a rainbow of colors on the walls in the foyer. A large, white settee sat near the left wall, and two white-washed arm chairs graced the right.

Lenny went straight up to the reception desk and gave his name to the much too beautiful woman standing behind it. She had the right features that allowed a woman to cut her hair that dramatically short and still stun every pair of eyes that lit on her. Her large eyes and lips begged others to adore her.

She asked us to take a seat, and told us someone would be with us shortly. I noticed several patrons enjoying some drinks through an archway to the left. Some were enjoying a late lunch even though it was three in the afternoon.

A tall, obviously muscular woman walked through one of the large, arched doorways that led to the right. "Follow me," she said, turning and leading us back the way she had come. I could see several full and partially filled tables through another archway on the same side.

We passed a large room with both round and square tables completely set, just waiting for people to sit at them and be served what I supposed would be an amazing meal. Various shades of white surrounded me, sparkling with silver and glass accents.

Remembering the blueprints, I realized the main area of the country club consisted of three dining areas. The first one we had seen as we entered. We walked down a hall to the meeting and gathering rooms patrons could rent for their special occasions that abutted the back wall of the third dining area. I peeked in the empty dining area as we passed by, trying to see the powder rooms. Oddly enough, they were placed smack dab in the middle of all three dining areas, helping to section them off from each other. Our planned escape tunnel hid beneath some tiles in the men's room. It felt good to know the layout of this place. I was glad I'd seen the prints.

We entered one of the meeting rooms, which had been turned into a green room of sorts. A long table, exactly like the one in the FBI interrogation room in DC, stood in the center, along with the same kind of chairs. People stood on the periphery behind cameras and a few were clumped together around a big screen that appeared to be some kind of Smartboard computer screen. The woman who led us here, gestured to me to sit at the table and then talked to Lenny before he left the room, winking at me as he went.

She sat down beside me. "Does this look familiar to you?"

"Yeah. It looks like the room in the FBI building in DC, where Jeremy took me to question me."

"Good. So you remember that day?"

How could I forget? "Of course."

"Well, we need to recreate that day. We will be adding a few things here and there. Just go with it. We will also shoot a separate interview. It will be a complete fabrication. We will pretend that we flew you back out to DC to answer a few questions we had neglected to ask the first time."

I was on a movie set. "'Kay," I said, wondering what was up. "But why?"

She ignored my question. "That means we need to make you over so that you look like you did back then."

"Really? Can't you just edit it somehow? Paste my old face over my new one?"

"I wish we could, but it would be too easy for someone to tell we'd fabricated the video. I'll get Special Agent Adams in here to turn you back to your DC-self."

"Whatever," I said, suddenly realizing that would mean my group from DC would have no problem recognizing me.

Agent Adams, a make-up artist, took off all my make-up, removed my piercings and then had me change into some different clothes in an adjacent room. After that, he put a wig on me that made me look just like I had in Washington, DC.

I spotted a man who looked remarkably like Special Agent Durrant standing at the back of the room. A scream started in the pit of my stomach and started to slide up my esophagus, but I couldn't get it out. The rational side of me told me it couldn't be him, but my emotions were getting the better of me, trying to convince me otherwise. Durrant was the mole who had led the terrorists to our safe-house last year, and Jeremy had told me he was in a government prison.

My eyes lit on a door at the back of the room and then rounded in surprise. All my fear associated with Agent Durrant instantly dissipated as Jeremy sauntered into the room! He was walking!

I couldn't contain myself and jumped up, much to my make-up artist's chagrin, and barreled over to him. His eyes lit up when he saw me, and he swept me up into a great big bear hug. He smelled fresh, clean and musky. We were laughing as we stood, holding each other. I didn't want to let go but eventually did.

"You look like yourself," I said, grinning from ear to ear.

"So do you," he said, looking me over.

I wondered what he would have said about one hour ago when I looked like Ari.

"You're walking!" I said, looking at his legs. I hadn't been able to write Jeremy since becoming Michele, and he still hadn't been walking then. But now, he was standing right here in front of me, and I was so glad the doctors in DC had gotten it right. The paralysis from the bullet the terrorists had put into him while he'd protected me seemed to have left no lingering side-effects.

"Of course. I told you I would be."

"So, you're back to work?" I asked, giving him a once over to see if I missed something.

"Yep," he said, his blue eyes never leaving my face and my heart finding the smooth, even rhythm that usually accompanied his presence. "But I'm at a desk until I can pass all my tests again. I'm having a little trouble with all the fine-motor skills in my left hand still. But, it won't be long now."

"Well, I can't—"

"We don't have all day, people," a man's voice shouted over us. "Come take your seats."

I assumed he meant for me to go back to the seat I had been in and did so. Agent Adams did a once over on my make-up and left. Jeremy and the man who looked like Special Agent Durrant, sat opposite me—just like when they'd questioned me so long ago. An awful sense of foreboding settled in my chest. I tried to focus on Jeremy so I'd feel more peaceful. Someone came and read Jeremy, Nathan, and Agent Durrant's notes about the case aloud, like a review for a test. The camera men moved the cameras around while we chatted, until someone said to stop, and then all but one camera man left the room. Other people moved different props around until they were told to leave, too.

Our guide left us and I took the opportunity to talk to Jeremy. "What's up? Why are they having us recreate this? She wouldn't answer me."

He moved a chair next to me and talked in a low voice. "I don't know exactly, but I can guess."

I leaned in with interest.

"That reporter, Tavien, is really good at finding dirt about the government and blowing the whistle. He won't listen to reason. Important people are running scared. The whole idea of the government carrying out vigilante justice with Azeez, if it got out, would cause a huge hullabaloo in Washington. Powerful people would have a lot of explaining to do. All kinds of people would be in the hot seat and many would lose their jobs. Can you imagine what the general populace would do if they heard there is a whole section of the government that isn't on the *books*, people that summarily torture suspects for information and then execute them? Remember all the media frenzy over water boarding? What Tavien could uncover is astounding. So, the FBI is basically covering their butts. They're even training someone to be Azeez, just in case."

"Places, please," the man said in a loud voice, and Jeremy slid back to his side of the table. The inquisition had begun. Jeremy and the fake Agent Durrant had apparently already been briefed and had memorized the questions to ask and how to ask them. Someone rolled the big computer screen, behind me. It displayed a check off list to remind Jeremy and Agent Durrant what questions to ask. It felt like I was starring in a movie but it felt wrong. Sure I was telling the truth, but the whole set-up was a lie. I had to remind myself not to talk about what had happened with Ahmed after I got home from DC. I had to pretend that he hadn't kidnapped me and that I hadn't been in witness protection all this time. It was hard, and I had to focus and think before I answered each question. It felt good to have it over with when the director called out, "Cut!"

Unfortunately, we had to do it all over again in an adjacent room with new props. The room had office furniture in it, and another Smartboard sat behind me. It reminded me of the lawyers' offices on TV shows. They even had me change clothes and say it was a different date—two weeks after the beheading. Jeremy and fake Special Agent Durrant were gone and a judge and a couple lawyers introduced themselves to me. I had to re-tell the whole thing.

Four hours later, with a my brain fried and my nerves frazzled, I was relieved to have the people in the background clap. It was over. I turned around and looked at the board. Everything had been checked off. They had had a lot to cover. I sighed loudly and Jeremy appeared out of nowhere. My heart warmed and I knew everything would be okay. We chatted again until we were once again interrupted by the manly woman who'd brought me to this room when I'd arrived.

"It's time to get you back to Lenny, young lady. Hungry?" With that, she took hold of my upper arm and guided me through a side door. I yelled goodbye to Jeremy and promised to write him. He gave me one of his winning smiles, and I told myself to remember him this way forever.

Lenny wasn't in the first room we entered. Two or three special agents sat in the room whispering. They stared at me as the strong woman led me past them and through another door. Lenny stood in the middle of the room, arguing with the very make-up artist who had returned me to my former DC self. "You will get me what I need, and I mean now!" Lenny said.

The make-up artist, Agent Adams, huffed and turned on his heels, leaving the room through yet another door. I remembered this section of The Linden from the blueprints. A maze of rooms made up the west wing.

I smiled at Lenny just as the woman let go of my arm. She didn't say another word before going back the way we had come. He did not look happy and neither did she.

He shook his head at me. "This is not good. I knew it."

"What?" I said.

He gestured for me to have a seat and then sat next to me. "The government is playing a very dangerous game."

"I don't understand," I said, feeling a hot rock drop in my gut. The look on Lenny's face making the rock burn even hotter.

"I shouldn't have brought you here."

"Tell me what's going on."

"It seems you kids are the bait to catch some big fish tonight."

"Bait?"

"I spent some time with some of the agents who are in charge of protecting your friends."

"Are they all here?"

"Yes. Now listen up," he said, a bit impatiently. "We don't have a lot of time. The government leaked the fact that all you kids were going to be here giving your testimonies."

I felt my eyes get big. I now understood.

"The FBI is counting on the idea that all these power-hungry terrorists will come here in hopes of taking you out so that they can grab Ahmed's power. They have this grand idea that they can force all the terrorists to come out into the open, here at this country club. That way, they can get them all in one big raid. That's why they didn't go after the terrorists at the beach and the park. The FBI didn't want to give away the fact that they knew the bad guys were out and about again. Can you believe that they wanted you to go out there and eat dinner looking like you do now? Just like you did in DC? I had to put my foot down. Agent Adams, your makeup artist, is bringing your clothes and stuff back as we speak. I won't make it easy for the terrorists to get you."

"But we have our escape plan, right? Can't we just leave?"

The look on his face said it all. He thought their plan had a chance. He wanted to take it! I blurted, "Okay, so we stay and..." I petered out at the end because I didn't know what I thought I was going to say.

"Look Ari. I know this is scary, but I think their plan will work simply because I now know a lot of the men we'll be working with. I do have my doubts, but I think we've got to give it a shot. You deserve a normal life and this just might be the ticket. The FBI is telling me they have it all worked out and the terrorists won't get near you. They have men on the perimeter, just waiting, and much of the staff tonight are undercover agents. The guys protecting your friends truly are the best. I'd be shocked if any of you got hurt. But I know how it works. The head honchos of the FBI will wait until the big fish terrorists arrive here to move on the rest, and that could be too late. But, I believe the men protecting your friends will do the right thing at the right time and you can be sure that I certainly will.

"The FBI has you to thank for saving the security of the nation because you witnessed what you did and acted. If not, no one would have ever known and we would have been brought to our knees—being stripped of our own natural resources. It seems absurd, but it is totally real and possible. The plan is amazingly intricate and while we don't know every last detail. Not immediately anyway, but about twenty years down the road. If the stakes weren't so high with these terrorists, the FBI wouldn't be giving this top priority.

"This reporter could really screw things up. They have to not only protect themselves from what has happened in the past with this case, but they also have to protect their future by getting any remaining terrorists. When he breaks the story, which he will, then the FBI will have everything cleaned up and it will appear as if they saved the day, not you."

I was bait. My friends were bait. My friends—in danger again because of me. Trying to be braver than I felt, I said, "So, what's the plan?" I knew it was the right decision to try to end this. No more fear, no more pretending. But I was still really scared for them and myself.

"We'll make sure we get seated as close to our escape route as possible. Then, we'll eat and wait…wait for the right moment to disappear." His unfocused gaze turned to one with renewed intensity.

"Wait, then disappear," I said, nodding, unable to make sense of it all.

"Look, Ari, you don't need to be freaked out. I've got you covered. You are my responsibility. John's not the only one with a perfect record around here."

I did feel safe, but my nerves got the better of me. "What about my friends?"

"The FBI strung your friends' agents along, too. The agents had no idea until they got here that they were also a part of the bait. Like I said, the agents protecting your friends are some of the best protectors around. I have to give that to the government at least. While acting like idiots, putting you guys in this dangerous position, they did try to make it less likely that you could be harmed." Between the lines, I could see he was proud of the FBI. "They have clever escape routes prepared for you guys, too."

Agent Adams returned with my belongings and a make-up kit. Lenny quickly transformed me into Ari again, telling me it would be faster if he just did it. "I can't have you so completely vulnerable to the terrorists. At least this disguise will hide you—hopefully long enough for us to escape."

"Are you sure they're coming?"

"Oh yeah. There's crazy chatter over this. The various terrorist groups think they're sneaking up on us. And maybe they are. I don't like it at all. But, we've got to make the best of a bad situation. The FBI has a truly great exit plan for you kids and they've assured me the country club grounds are protected."

I didn't like it either, but I knew saying it out loud would make my anxiety worse. Instead, I tapped into active meditation, controlling my speeding heart, and kept my mouth shut. Besides, I trusted Lenny. With his jaw set and his eyes resolute, he looked infallible.

"Ouch!" I screamed as he jammed the earrings back into holes that had already started to crust over. I couldn't hold back the tears. It really hurt.

"Sorry about that. I didn't think they'd be changing your appearance for this. I left the numbing solution on the bike. I can get you some later."

Each piercing seemed to burn worse than the previous one. After forcing all the rings and studs back into their respective holes on my face and ears, he looked me over. Then, after fixing the last spike in my hair he said, "Perfect. Now, I'm going to wait for you in the dining hall while you get dressed. Oh, and a couple of 'family friends', the Brown's, are going to join us for dinner."

"'Kay," I said, dreading changing clothes with the piercings throbbing they way they were. I glanced at the clock. It was already eight.

Chapter Twenty-Seven

After slipping back into my goth-biker-girl clothes—the ballerina skirt and all—I went out the same door Lenny had exited. I stood inside a big dining area, Lenny just a few feet away. He walked over, took my arm, handed me four pills that I hoped were pain killers, and led me to one of the round, beautifully decorated tables, fresh white and yellow lilies scenting the air, where another couple sat. I quickly spotted Summer, who couldn't help but stand out wherever she went. At our table sat "the Browns." Lenny pulled out a chair for me and he greeted them as if they were long lost friends. I scowled. The man's forehead shone in the light like a piece of the polished silver on the table, and the woman's short, bushy, platinum blonde hair matched the shade of the table cloth perfectly. Her gorgeous, dazzling blue evening gown seemed to make her eyes pop off of her face. She did not have a traditional beauty. It was all her own.

A waiter slid over to our table like a dancer, moving in a smooth, silky way across the floor. His nose crinkled when he saw me. I'm sure it was an unconscious reaction, but enough to remind me I didn't fit in here.

Focus, Ari. Focus. I tried to keep my eyes from darting around the room, searching for disapproving stares. Until becoming Ari, I'd welcomed staring eyes because they'd been about admiration, not disgust or curiosity. I hated the way his look made me feel.

"Ari?" Lenny's voice brought me back. He looked at the waiter and then back to me. My eyes widened, hoping Lenny would save me. I had no idea what had been said. "You did want the filet, right?"

"Uh, yeah," I said, sitting up straighter. Then I saw Lenny's eyes widen, a silent warning that I had left my character behind. I slumped once again. "Yeah, and I only want a line of red in the center. None of that uncooked crap. Oh, and extra butter on the baked potato. I don't get why you guys can't just chop it and fry it up for me. I thought a French chef would know how to make *French* fries." I emphasized the French, just for fun.

"Ignore her," Lenny said to the waiter and then whispered to me, just loud enough for all to hear if they strained, "You better behave yourself or we'll find ourselves eating here every evening for the next week." Without missing a beat, he said to the waiter, "I apologize. We're still trying to table train her." The waiter gave Lenny an understanding nod and flicked a condescending glance my way before gliding away. Lenny didn't look much different than I did, although he did sport a blazer over his biker duds, but he'd said and done enough to earn the waiter's respect.

While we waited for our food, after a bit of chit-chat with our new friends, Lenny started in on a story. It was about a couple who, while remodeling their house, were being chased by burglars. They ended up having to slide down a garbage chute the construction workers had set up in their kitchen to get rid of remodeling waste. I didn't like the serious look he had on his face while he told the story.

I suddenly realized how badly I needed to go to the ladies' room and stood up to leave. I thought it might be nice to check out our escape route anyway. Lenny put his hand on my arm. "It's rude to leave in the middle of someone's story."

"It's not like I don't hear your stories all the time, Dad," I said, giving him a mean look and sitting, trying hard to hold it.

"You haven't heard this one." The way he looked at me told me I should pay attention.

I huffed and crossed my arms, pretending not to listen, but paying close attention.

He continued, "Once they landed in the garbage dumpster, they leapt out and climbed down through a cellar door they'd found earlier that day. It was hidden by some bushes and provided another exit through a tunnel to the other side of the property."

"Did the burglars follow them into the cellar?" Mrs. Brown asked.

"Nope. They were quiet enough and fast enough that they weren't discovered."

"That's the story?" I scoffed. "Pretty lame if you ask me." What did it have to do with me?

The waiter came offering to refill our drinks and appetizers, interrupting any further comment on the story. After eating canned and fast foods over the last week, the ultra-fresh salad and bread he placed in front of me captured all my attention. Delicious. Right as I finished eating it, I was about to go the restroom, but he returned. The amazingly pure and simple meal he placed before me looked like heaven and I decided I could wait just a little bit longer to go to the bathroom. The steak sizzled, butter pooled in the center of the baked potato, and steam drifted away from the deep green broccoli, almost too amazing to eat. My grumbling stomach called to me, and with no regret, I dug into the potato.

Lenny struck up a completely boring conversation with the Browns, and while chewing my steak, I looked around for more of my friends from DC. No one but Summer, the girl who hated anyone different from herself, looked familiar. I looked harder, wondering if any of them were in disguise like I was. I checked out each face at each table and none of them were my friends from DC.

A hostess brought another couple to the table nearest the entrance to the restroom. The three dining areas in the Linden spoked out from the bathroom. The word *odd* didn't do it justice. I'd wondered about that when I'd looked at the blueprints, too. Maybe I could peek into the other dining halls. Maybe I'd see Rick. My heart jumped. I took several quick bites of my steak and finished off my broccoli before asking if I could go.

"I need to pee," I said, pushing back my chair and standing up. I did need to pee, but I also wanted to find Rick.

"Excuse me," Lenny said.

"You're excused," I said, snorting as I turned to go.

"Ari, I expect an apology before you go," Lenny said. "Our guests deserve better."

"Oh," I said, turning to our fake friends. "Mind if I take a pee in the *lavatory*?" I stared them down.

The platinum haired lady, Texie, said, "Well, I never."

"I can tell," I said, quickly walking away.

I felt Lenny gaining on me and I picked up speed, hoping to have a chance to speak privately. I just wanted to reach the wall that separated the restroom area from the dining areas. As I whipped around it, Lenny grabbed my arm. The look of sheer anger on his face made me wonder if I'd over done it.

"I-I-I'm sorry, Lenny. I guess I just got carried—".

A smile spread across his face and the goose bumps littering my arms disappeared as he said, "You are incredible. Well done, well done." He let go of me.

My heart all but burst at his praise. "Really?"

"Really. Now, hurry up. I don't like having you out of my sight. Do not leave this *lavatory* area." His eyes held mine and he grinned. Then he added, "And remember the story."

"No worries there. It was captivating." I sighed deeply as he rounded the corner that led back to our friends at our table and disappeared. Turning, I grabbed the ornate door knob and pulled the door open with gusto, feeling great. However, I only barely missed hitting someone with it as it swung out. "So sorry," I blurted.

I heard, "No problem." The voice fell on me like a soft pillow and I turned to look.

Rick! For a mere second, my heart stopped beating. I was looking at Rick. I almost couldn't breathe. His soft blue eyes blazed as he turned and walked into the men's room. I stood, holding onto the open door, unable to get my wits about me enough to let go. He looked right at me and hadn't stopped. Oh my gosh. He hates me, I thought. He's mad at me. My thoughts raced. I didn't like the possibilities. He hadn't even given me a second glance. Did he know about Alex. Did he think I gave up on him and in turn, he gave up on me.

My mind kept searching for an explanation until a girl, leaving the ladies' room, dressed in a short, pink dress with silver high heels, gave me a look of disgust. I let go of the door, reached up and ran my hand over my spiked, black hair and pierced ears. He didn't recognize me. He just hadn't recognized me. Maybe I didn't want him to recognize me. I sighed, ready to finally go inside the restroom, but Rick exited the bathroom and for some stupid, unexplainable reason, I just stood there. My eyes desperate to look at him.

He stared back.

"Do I know you?" he asked, as the door shut behind him. He took a mini step forward.

"Uh," I stuttered. "Uh." I wasn't sure I wanted him to know it was me. Would he care how I looked? My eyes met his and my insides both writhed in pain and sang for joy. My face burned with shame. I had betrayed him with Alex. Even when I knew Alex wasn't good for me. I could feel that my mouth hung open, and I knew I looked ridiculous. No words would come out of my mouth yet I ached to speak.

He moved closer, his eyes quizzical. "I feel like I know you."

All I could do was give a tiny nod in agreement and say, "It's me." His imperfect perfectness pulled at me, caused a tiny ache in my gut to blossom and grow.

Realization must have struck him, because his eyes suddenly grew to the size of apricots and his head began to swing from side to side as his mouth said, "No. No. It can't be," almost too silently for me to hear. At the same moment, he reached for me, pulling me into a hug I desperately wanted, but felt I didn't deserve. I breathed in his musky scent, a wave of pure bliss washing over me. It felt right to be in his arms. He pulled away, taking my face in his hands. Our eyes locked.

"No," he suddenly repeated. "It can't be. You're dead. I saw you dead on those cell phone pictures on the internet." Bitterness laced his words and he pushed me an arm's length away and then let his arms fall to his sides.

Stupid camera phones. I don't know if the shock had worn off, if I'd given up on anonymity or if I simply couldn't stand to remain silent any longer, but my mouth began to work.

"No," I said. "No. That was just for show to get me into witness protection. I'm alive." I reached out to him, but he took a few steps back, away from me. I let my hand fall.

"You died…with Alex."

The bitterness of the betrayal lacing his words smacked me in the face. My heart slammed into my ribcage.

"I buried you. You are not real." There was an anger I'd never heard in his voice before.

He had been at my funeral. I'd seen the footage. I knew he meant he'd buried me figuratively, but he had to understand. "I'm real," I said, my lip quivering, wondering how this had gotten so out of control. Why he moved back, away from me. My eyes filled with tears.

He reached up and absently fingered something that hung on a chain around his neck. "No. You're gone." Something wild shone in his eyes.

"I'm not. It's me, Christy." For the first time, it felt good to use that name to describe me. It was okay to be Christy with Rick. With Rick, Christy was safe.

His eyes began at my black Converse shoes, traveled up my tanned, long legs to my fluffy ballerina skirt, over the metallic belts and the tight, black, grommet filled shirt and finally over my pierced and fake-scarred face, to the very tips of my spiky hair and then back down to my eyes.

"No," he concluded. "You are not Christy. Not my Christy."

A deep part of me leapt at the words, *my Christy*, while a greater part felt the resolution forged in the word, *not.* His pale, withdrawn face lacked an ounce of trust.

"This is just a disguise," I pleaded. "It's all just a disguise. Make-up."

Moments hung in the air, unwilling to go forward and refusing to go back.

"Please, Rick," I heard myself beg. "Please."

"No. The Christy I know would have contacted me." He was obviously wary, untrusting.

"I couldn't. I was in witness protection." I moved toward him and he stepped back once again.

"Before that." Emotion flowed from his eyes. "And you were with Alex."

The almost imperceptible catch in his voice caused an ache in my heart. "We don't have long distance at my house." I whispered. Panic gathered in my stomach.

"You could have found a way."

The pain in his words crushed my chest. "Please, hear me out."

"I can't. I just can't." He stepped to the side, fingering the thing at his neck. "I've already said goodbye. I refuse to do it again." He walked back the way he had come, without a backward glance.

I stood there shaking, feeling the echo of pain in his words as my stomach clenched. I watched him go—until my bladder forced me into the bathroom. Rick's objections ate at me.

After I finished washing my hands, I couldn't help myself and looked in on the dining hall where Rick had disappeared. Was I a masochist? Did I need to have him reject me again? Eugene sat two tables away from where I stood, quietly eating his dinner in his very own precise way. No disguise. I searched the room and found Marybeth. She looked different, but she wasn't in disguise. It was hard for me to recognize her without her yards of beautiful auburn hair—now only shoulder-length—thanks to the terrorists having shaved her head in DC. I admired her, and wanted to save her more pain. Why wasn't she in disguise? Was I the only one who wouldn't be in danger when the terrorists came? Worry settled at the bottom of my stomach. This wasn't right.

My eyes flicked to Rick in the back corner of the room. My luck had run out with Rick. I don't know how long I stood and stared, unable to go to him, but when his agent gave me a nasty look, I headed back down the hallway to the second dining hall, where the others had to be. Josh was the first one I spotted. It was hard to miss the huge freight-train-of-a-guy. Then Kira caught my eye. She looked my way and I stepped behind the wall, not wanting her to recognize me. Then I stepped back, thinking about Rick not being able to recognize me. I scanned the room one more time, looking for that someone that I hoped wasn't there—Alex.

I checked each face but didn't see his. I headed back to my dining hall, realizing that if something bad did happen tonight, it would be the first time Alex hadn't been there with our group from DC. I was glad he wasn't here. I wasn't sure if I could resist him. I brushed him out of my mind and walked out. When

I turned the corner, Lenny stood and his eyes met mine. Even though we were only fifteen feet away from each other, the wild, nervous look that played in his eyes was unmistakable. I sensed fear.

A chill swept over me just before the club, without warning, fell into darkness. Every light in the club went out at once. Now past nine, without any lights, I couldn't see a thing, until the room lit up like a firecracker. Yellows, greens, blues and reds filled the room. With each explosion, a new burst of light gave me momentary sight. I watched as people fell to the ground during each flash. What were the bad guys up to? Were they just going to kill everyone? Did they see this as an opportunity to get rid of a lot of FBI agents as well as me000?

I instinctively leaned my body against the wall, hoping to melt into it, so that no one would notice me. I tried to adjust my eyes to the inky darkness, looking for any light from the windows. I was rewarded with only the sparks from gunfire. Total chaos reigned. An all inclusive gasp went up before screams echoed through the dining hall. *My friends. Marybeth. Rick. The others*. A rush of pops, bangs, and crashes filled the room. I took a sharp intake of air as I felt someone pass close to me, almost without a sound. I heard the men's bathroom door open and shut. I felt the innate warning at the base of my neck. Our escape route had been compromised. I pushed harder into the wall. After only minutes, muffled pops, instead of big explosions, filled the air.

I could barely make out the outline of each drapery-covered window in the room. Lenny and I hadn't discussed an alternate escape route. The blueprints shuffled through my mind. I blinked hard, trying to see something, wondering where Lenny was. What if he never came? I couldn't navigate my way to our table in this blackness. It would be suicide. Surely he was coming to me. On cue, someone grabbed my shoulder and then my hand and started dragging me to the restroom. I assumed it was Lenny and pulled on his arm to stop him. I whispered in his ear the code word, "Compromised."

He pulled me in close and whispered back, "Okay. The story. Remember the story." It was definitely Lenny's voice. He tugged me faster, away from our planned escape route.

The story. Duh! The story described our new escape route. We had to get to the kitchen. Why had he changed it? I cursed myself for not insisting that Lenny bring night-vision goggles for me too. I raced behind him, trying to be confident in his ability to lead me safely. I ended up stumbling several times. As shots rang out, screams echoed and bodies thudded to the floor. He had me crouch, to avoid detection. Then he urged me over lumps on the floor. People? We dashed around tables and chairs, zigzagging our way out of the dining area, the noise surrounding us threatening to deafen me. I wished I could cover my ears, but I needed my arms to keep my balance. Even with them, I fell often, having to scrabble back to my feet. Screams of pain, chaos, death, and fear filled the room.

In the confusion, I lost my bearings and had no idea where we were until I felt a smooth floor devoid of carpet and then smelled food. The kitchen. We'd made it. Now, we would go down some sort of chute. Without a sound and as fast as lightning, Lenny took both of my hands in his and stopped our flight. He pushed me forward and lifted me up. I felt an opening in the wall. The chute. He shoved my feet inside and pushed me. I gasped, but really wanted to scream.

Only seconds after beginning to slide, I found the chute disappearing beneath me and I sailed through the air for a few seconds before plopping into something slimy. A garbage chute. How nice. Shortly after my feet hit, my knees gave out. I wasn't expecting to land so quickly and I fell onto my hands and knees. I heard a whoosh behind me and figured I better move. I rolled to the left, knocking my head on the side of the bin. I felt and heard Lenny's feet hit the garbage. Unlike me, it sounded like he'd stayed upright. I could barely make out his body shape in the meager sliver of a moon that seemed to frown down on us.

He peeked over the edge of the trash container and pushed me down. I heard the quiet pit-pat of feet hitting the ground beneath us, then the slam of a door. Silence. He peeked again. I felt garbage in my hair and slimy goo all over my hands and legs. Lenny didn't give me a moment to wipe it away. Instead, he lifted me over the side and dropped me to the ground. I heard a soft thud as he landed beside me. I felt better being able to see the shape of him outside the building at least. He grabbed my hand tight and we walked a few feet. Lenny seemed to be looking for something. I had no idea what, but I strained to look for something, too.

He jerked me to the left and let go of my hand. I heard what sounded like heavy metal sliding against cement. I knew Lenny was strong, but could he lift and move a manhole cover by himself? Had Lenny been told about another underground tunnel that wasn't on the map? My mind switched to the kitchen area of the blueprints and hovered over the tiny bit of exterior on them. Something was marked on the map right where we stood, but I had never found out what the symbol stood for. Now I knew.

I felt a nudge and reached down, finding the edge of the manhole. Turning around, I let one foot fall into the hole, searching for a ladder of some sort to help me down. Once I found it, I hurried down and down and down and down. The ladder seemed to never end. I heard the echo of the manhole cover gently clanking into place above me and the blackest darkness fell over me. I couldn't even see my hand in front of my face. I stopped climbing down until I heard the soft thuds of Lenny's feet hitting the ladder rungs above me, getting closer. My feet found their way again. A sigh of relief escaped my lips when my foot hit solid ground. I moved only a step back from the ladder, not knowing where I was. The musty air stank of old feet and nastiness. I gagged. I heaved. Then I got control, being careful to only breathe through my mouth. The goo covering me had already begun to cake and harden. I scratched at some of it on my hand until Lenny grabbed it once again. Then we ran. It didn't take long for my breathing to become labored. Ugh. I should've trained harder the last two weeks. Thankfully, after a while, my breathing finally found its rhythm.

I sucked in hard when Lenny slowed, pausing for only a second. We turned right and ran some more. Fast and furious. I slipped and I often fell, always touching something slimy and gooey when I did. I wished I'd drunk all the water in my glass at dinner. My mouth was so dry. I thought my tongue might completely dry out, become brittle, and break into tiny pieces. The darkness began to cave in on me. Despite the pounding of my feet, my loud breathing, and the thudding of my heart, I could hear the pattering of Lenny's feet when on dry cement, the splashing of water when he couldn't avoid it, the light tinkling of water dripping around us, the scurrying feet of small animals, and the flap of what I assumed were bats. It freaked me out. I tried to picture bright, sunny things so that I wouldn't lose it.

We ran and ran, slowing only to branch off in a slightly different direction. Finally, we stopped and he whispered in my ear, "I'm going up. When you see light up there, start up. Don't talk."

I could barely hear him climb, the slight squeak of a shoe on a rung, the minute whisper of his foot hitting the metal rungs. I expected to hear the sliding metal again, but didn't. My mind raced. Truly scared, I wrapped my arms around my waist. Finally, seeing a round area of light surround the stairs, and without waiting one second, I climbed, even though my hands shook and my legs felt like rubber. Sweat dripped down my forehead and back. Once at the top, I climbed out and lay on my back on the cold, wet grass of the country club's golf course. I could see at least a trillion stars keeping the tiny sliver of a moon company. They seemed so far away. Clouds threatened to put out their light.

Lenny pulled on my arm to help me stand. We were completely exposed. Two trees standing together on a hill for all to see. So, we ran to what appeared to be the only clump of trees and bushes around. I heard the hoot of an owl and then an eerie silence filled my ears.

He whispered, "Stay here. I have to make sure the team the FBI put together to guard this place did their job. If I'm not back in ten minutes, I want you to run in the direction of that bright star right there. The one in the middle of those three less bright stars." He pointed east.

I looked to find the star, following his finger. "You mean the one that's kinda purple and pink?" I pointed.

He looked back at the star. "Yes. You can't see it, but there is a big garage that houses equipment over there. We need to get there as soon as possible. In ten minutes, if I'm not back, run there and go inside. Keep your eyes open and your senses on high alert."

As if they weren't already.

"Get under that wisteria bush." He pointed to a large, umbrella-looking bush to my left.

"Let's just go together," I said, hoping he wouldn't leave me here. "I can make it."

"Look. I just have to be sure it's safe before we run totally out in the open again."

I nodded and scampered under the wisteria and closed my eyes. It didn't seem as scary if I closed my eyes.

"Wait." I suddenly remembered. "I don't have a watch or phone on me to track the time."

"Count it out then," he said, as if I should have thought of that. "Ten minutes. No longer."

"Yeah. Right." I felt pretty dumb.

He slinked away and I started counting. I heard noises and tried to focus on the counting. *Only an animal. It's only an animal. It's the wind,* I kept telling myself. The damp leaves around me, chilled me. I had to focus. I got into the zone and pulled on the energy around me to feel for changes in the air that might signal someone's approach.

It reminded me of one of the times my parents left me at a gas station while we were on a trip. The memory hit me hard. I had stood, staring at the spot my family's van had been only minutes earlier. I'd wondered if I was that forgettable, that my family had just deserted me. I'd looked at the dirt-smeared windows of the building where dad had paid for his gas and shuddered at the thought of having to ask the old, scary looking man if I could wait inside. But, it was so hot. I'd found some bushes at the side of the building and sat behind them and waited. As the sun moved in the sky, I'd actually gotten some shade, but the heat remained. I'd fallen asleep. Someone had touched me and I'd jolted up. It was a creepy man and woman asking if I needed help. When I said no, the man grabbed me.

"Come with us," the man cooed.

I screamed.

The man inside the store came out to see what was up and the people backed away. I 'fessed up, deciding he must not be so bad if he'd come when he heard me scream. I sat behind his counter, cool and comfortable with the window air conditioning unit blowing right at me. It took my parents five and a half hours to come back for me.

The memory faded and I scrunched up into a ball, shaking it from my brain. Please don't let anyone try to grab me. Please let Lenny come back. Please. What if he got caught? At least here, Lenny had empowered me. I knew where to go to be safe and had the ability to get there. I'd been so caught up the scary childhood memory, I'd stopped counting. Crap!

I employed biofeedback to calm down, until I heard a faint voice and looked around, careful not to make any noise. I couldn't see anyone. Was my mind playing tricks on me? Surely I was just remembering the voices I'd heard while hiding behind the bushes at the gas station, waiting for my parents.

The next thing I knew, the voice was very close and it was real and coming toward me. My heart sped up as the voice continued to get closer. Like a scared rabbit, I was ready to scamper out at the least provocation. I needed air. The darkness pressed on me, suffocating me. I couldn't understand the language he was speaking, but knew it. It was Iceman's language. The closer the voice got, the quieter it was until he stopped talking all together. He walked like a cat, no sound to his steps, but I could barely make out his outline against the sky. He brushed his hands over the bushes only feet from me. He would check this bush. I was in trouble. He'd find me. I couldn't run; I would expose myself and for sure be a victim again. I couldn't get any smaller and I couldn't disappear.

Out of nowhere, my Tai Chi training took over, focusing me. I would not be afraid. I was powerful. I had to somehow use his strength against him. I would not be abducted again. I could take him.

Fear tried to weasel its way back into my mind. *This is real. Not a simulation. You're a little girl. He's a large, strong man.* But then again, I'd been taught well.

I pushed on the taunting thoughts and, determined, readied myself. I would overtake him. Somehow. He rifled through the bush next to me, and I smelled his sweat. He was nervous, too. It gave me courage. I was who I'd been taught to be. I crouched a bit lower, hoping he would overlook my hiding place but knowing it was too much to ask. My movements were slight. Slow. Not a sound. I had to be patient and not act too soon. I needed the right moment. I had to use his power against him. A drop of sweat dripped into my eye and I blinked it away. Patience! Prayer filled my mind, and I became more and more confident.

Pass by. Please pass by. He bent slightly, ready to jostle the bush. This was it. My moment to be who I'd trained to be. I took the heel of my hand and shoved it with all the strength I could summon, in an upward thrust to his nose. A sickening crunch filled the air and he fell over. Not a word from the man in black. Not even a sound.

I shuddered, adrenaline rushing through my body, unwilling to be satisfied. Had I killed him? My self-defense training had taught me a hit like that could kill a man. If I had, I needed to get out of there. Whoever was on the other end of his radio would be coming soon. If I hadn't, I needed to get out of there. He would be coming after me soon. I couldn't bring myself to run away without knowing for sure, though. It was all so painful, scary. Not daring to put my head close to the body, I used my foot to push on his leg, hoping it wouldn't rouse him if he was alive, but hoping to somehow feel if he was dead. The first time I pushed on his leg, I was too scared to do it hard and it ended up barely being a poke. No movement. I pushed harder this time, moving his spread eagled leg close to the other. No movement. My eyes drifted to his face. His open, blank eyes looked back at me. Horrified, I ran. I took off in the direction of the star as fast as I could, not knowing how long I'd waited for Lenny. Had it been five minutes? Ten? It no longer mattered. I had to get to the shed.

I tried to put a myriad of happy thoughts into my mind, but they always circled around to the crunch of the man's nose, the thud of his body hitting the ground. The blank stare. Had I killed him? No! I'm a little girl.

I felt more than heard someone behind me. Was it Lenny? I didn't dare look, knowing it would slow me down. If it were

Lenny, he would follow me all the way to the garage anyway. If it was a bad guy, I had to get to the garage and tell Lenny.

The sound of feet, smack, smack, smack, hit my ears and I pushed harder. Who was behind me and where was that garage? I came over a rise and it loomed before me, the sight of it seeming to give me more energy, more speed. Only a hundred more yards to safety. The sounds behind me changed. The smacks came quicker, no time between them. Did this person behind me have some sort of superpower? No one can run that quickly. It was faster than a sprint.

Fifty yards to safety and my strength was failing me, while the feet of my follower seemed to gain speed, I lost it. Tendrils of fire licked my throat and my legs seemed to grow weak. Please, please, just let me make it to the door, or let it be Lenny behind me. I knew, the second the prayer hit my mind that I wouldn't make it to the door and it wasn't Lenny behind me. Was it the guy I thought I'd killed? No way. He was dead.

I felt something brush my back and I arched it forward. Only ten feet.

A soft *pfut* sounded to my right and I saw a flash of some sort come from the side of the garage. The man right behind me gasped and fell, some part of him hitting my foot. I stumbled, but didn't fall for two more steps. I looked to my right and a body emerged from the side of the garage, a familiar shape in the darkness. My head hit the ground hard, my hands forgetting to catch me.

Moments later, I became aware of two sets of hands carrying me. The smell of stale mown grass and dirt filled my nose before a sour, awful smell replaced it. We passed two large, silver mowers before I was placed into a large SUV of some sort.

Chapter Twenty-Eight

"OHH! What is that smell?" Summer's voice was unmistakable. It seemed to echo from the back of the car.

"Be quiet Summer," an unfamiliar voice said, at the same time the doors to the SUV shut. I watched Lenny raise my legs and put them on top of him as he sat on the same bench I was on. He patted my legs and I felt something drip down the side of my head and into my ear.

"You made it. You made it," Lenny said, smiling at me.

I felt the car vibrate beneath me, and we pulled forward.

"We made what?" I asked, closing my eyes and reaching for my aching head. A sharp pain screamed out from the left side of my head. Then it came back to me, and I bolted up right. My head seemed to split into two, but I was able to sit.

"I thought I killed him," I sputtered. "The crunch. His eyes."

"Shhh," Lenny said. "Lay back down."

"No!" I shook my head slightly. "He was dead, but then he wasn't." My body shook.

"Okay, Okay," Lenny said, sliding over to me and dabbing the side of my head with his headscarf. "Slow down. Tell me what happened."

"I waited in the bushes, but then I heard a voice and it kept getting closer and closer and finally I could see a man, coming right for my hiding spot. I didn't want him to get me and I hit him hard, right in the nose like my Tai Chi instructor said: up and back with all my strength."

I moaned. "I heard and *felt* a crunch. He never told me there'd be a crunch." I looked wildly at Lenny. "Then he just fell." I tore at the clothes on my middle. "His eyes. Oh my gosh. His eyes. They just stared. They just stared out into the night." A sob pressed my body forward. "He was dead. Dead." Sobs over-took me, a violent barrage.

"It's okay, Ari. It was self-defense."

"No," I pressed through a sob. "That's just it. He wasn't dead. He came after me. He came after me."

"No, he didn't." I jerked my head around, ignoring the pain. Jeremy sat on the seat behind me. I tried to move to him, but Jeremy's hand held me to my spot. "The man who came after you wasn't the man you killed. It was his partner."

"What?"

"I was following someone's heat signature about thirty yards from where you killed that guy. I was about to take him out, when I heard him scream out into his headset and run like a bat out of hell in the direction of the garage."

No one dared interrupt.

"I followed him. He was too focused on your clump of trees to notice I was behind him, I guess. I didn't see you, only a guy on the ground. I watched him try to rouse his friend. When he couldn't, he looked around and must have seen you running and started after you. I should have taken him down when I first saw him, but I thought he might lead me to more like him. I'm sorry to have put you in danger, Christy."

I slid out of my seat, pushing past Lenny and grabbed Jeremy into a hug. He started coughing and I backed up.

"Sorry, Christy, but you reek."

I looked down at myself, covered in grime and grossness and returned to my seat.

Lenny handed me a piece of gum from his pocket.

"Thanks, Lenny. But if you were behind me, Jeremy, who shot that guy?"

Lenny smiled.

I moved to hug him, but he backed away. I looked him over instead. "I'm sure you don't smell any nicer than I do," I said and retreated back to my seat.

"You both need to get the heck out of this car!" Summer called. "I'm gonna get sick."

We chuckled. We'd made it to the expressway and the driver sped up.

"Ari," Lenny said. "I'm proud of you. If you hadn't done what you did, those two could have come after all of us. You saved us. You did what you were trained to do."

I knew he had to be exaggerating somewhat because if I hadn't killed that man, Jeremy would have.

"I know you're thinking Jeremy would have saved the day if you hadn't, but think about it. The man Jeremy was tailing never would have come running out if his partner hadn't been unresponsive."

I huffed.

"It's true," Jeremy said. "I would've stayed with that guy until he made a move."

I didn't know what to say. We drove for what seemed a lifetime and the adrenaline rush I had felt earlier ebbed along the way. Eugene and Marybeth sat together on the back row. Marybeth was asleep, leaning into Eugene with her mouth wide open, while Eugene's face was smashed against the window, muffling his snores. I didn't know how our reunion would go, but I'd never imagined it like this. I wished I could talk to Marybeth, but I couldn't get the sound of the crack of that man's nose out of my mind and had to retreat into nowhereville in order to keep my wits about me. The breathy sounds of the men's whispers filled the otherwise silent car.

At last, we pulled into the garage of an average looking home in an average looking neighborhood. We'd been driving for two solid hours. Our agents ushered us into the house attached to the garage and into a kitchen where everyone but me was to get a quick and yet somehow thorough make-over. I would be taking a thorough shower. Jeremy opened a fat manila envelope labeled "Top Secret" and disappeared into another room as Lenny went one way to shower and I went the other.

When I returned, Marybeth, Eugene, and Summer looked nothing like themselves. Marybeth wore a short black wig, Eugene had a longish red one on, and Summer wore a sleek, long brown one. Could every FBI Special Agent create identities on the fly?

Once clean, Lenny reappeared, smelling like soap.

"All right," Jeremy said, "Now that we're all here and no longer stinking up the place…" He looked pointedly at Lenny and me. "We'll go over what's next." He waved the envelope for emphasis. "I've just read through our orders. It appears that you are all going on a little trip to Europe, back home to your 'families.' You've been visiting relatives here in the States and your vacation is over."

"What are you talking about?" Summer said, her lips creased into a fine line. "Our families are in Europe? Where's Josh?"

"Welcome to witness protection," Jeremy said, seeming to ignore her, his eyes glowing. "You will all be getting a new life in Europe. It's essential that you do not break cover until you return from Europe. You will all have new identities. Marybeth is now Melanie, Summer, you are Sasha. Eugene is Elmer, and Christy is Ari. To help you remember each other's names, they all start with the same letter as your real name, except for Christy's, that is, who is Ari."

"Christy is always the exception somehow," Summer/Sasha murmured.

Lenny looked on with interest.

"Spend the next ten minutes memorizing the facts about the 'new you' with your agent, then we'll do some drills to help you become the character you are playing for the next little while. As for your parents? No, they aren't in Europe, but they are all safe. As for the rest of your friends? There were two extraction points. Hopefully, they're on their way." He handed manila envelopes to each agent except Lenny.

There wasn't going to be a "new" me after all. Jeremy gave me a quick smile before Summer/Sasha hit him with a barrage of questions.

Lenny led me into another room. "Good thing the only two who made you at the country club are dead, Christy. You get to play Ari for a little while longer. How are you doing?" He looked at the road rash on the side of my head.

I reached up and almost touched it. It brought me back to the disaster at the country club. I'd actually forgotten it for a short while. "Okay, I guess." Then I realized he called me Christy. "Christy? You called me Christy."

"You are Christy." He looked at me like I was crazy. "I wanted to remind you."

I guess I looked back at him in the same way, because he then added, "You left Michele behind in Niceville, and even though you are going to stay Ari for the next little while, you will always be Christy at your core, remember?"

John had told me to never return to Christy. Ever. Lenny, on the other hand, had told me it was important to remember my true identity.

"No matter what part you play, always remember who you really are. It will help you stay grounded."

I'd done as John hold told me, and I'd left Christy behind a little less than a year ago. I wasn't eager to be her again. I mean, there were good things about being Christy. Really. I'd just have to take those good things and create a me I liked. People change all the time, after all. If not, they'd just be stagnant and that was bad. I would not let the old Christy define me.

"Remember," Lenny said, "never lose sight of your true self or you will lose yourself for sure. You've got to hold on to what makes you, you."

"Wait! I don't get it. How will holding onto a person I will never be able to be again help me?"

"At your center, you are Christy. If you lose sight of that, you will be lost. I've seen it over and over with agents who end up going rogue or just plain crazy. You need a rock to fasten yourself to. Christy is your rock."

Something clicked in my mind. I finally understood what he meant. I had to be me at my core. That is what made it possible for me to play these other characters. My core would ground me—make me able to be anyone perfectly. I could always return to *me*. Just because I played a part for a day, week or a year, it didn't make me that person. John's advice to lose the old me and become, completely and totally, the new character, seemed like good advice at the time, but he'd missed the mark.

After the ten minutes, Jeremy asked all the kids indirect questions about who they were. Direct questions were too easy. He had to try to trick them. He helped each person know how to answer possible questions about themselves. We played a game to help us memorize each other's names. Ten more minutes had passed and still Kira, Josh, and Rick hadn't arrived. No Rick. That hurt the worst. The agents' three watches chimed again and they looked at each other before Jeremy spoke up. "Time to go. We'll talk more in the car."

An eerie quiet settled over us as we climbed into the car and it sent chills racing up my arms. Leaving the U.S. for the first time and having to abandon all that I knew was both scary and exciting. I would ask what no one else dared. "Are we leaving the others behind? I thought they needed to meet us at the house."

"We thought they would, too, but they must have had a change in plans. If they aren't at the airport, they'll have to catch up with you guys later." His tone was strange. Not hopeful.

Sasha/Summer glared at me and spit through her teeth, "You better hope they're at the airport."

Jeremy looked at Sasha and rolled his eyes, moving on. "Get as much sleep on the plane as you can. You'll arrive in the late morning. Stay awake that first day. Do not take a nap. It will help with jet-lag. Don't talk to each other like you know one another. You don't. It's okay to chit chat a little like you're strangers just sharing a flight. Be the character you were assigned today. This plane will have others on it going on assignment in various places. There could still be a mole somewhere, waiting to fulfill his "calling." We don't want anyone to know the real reason you're heading for Europe or what you really look like. It's still too dangerous. Besides, you really should all be sleeping, not talking."

"Where are we going exactly?" Elmer/Eugene asked.

"We don't have that information," Jeremy explained. "We only know it's somewhere in Europe. The less we know, the better."

"Could it be Paris?" Sasha suddenly perked up.

"It could be," her agent said. "We just don't know."

"I hope it's Paris," she said. "I just love Paris."

Elmer started drilling them with questions, but I tuned out, thinking about Rick, Kira, and Josh, hoping and praying they would be at the airport. Please God, please bring them to safety. I kept repeating various versions of the same prayer in my mind, pleading for their safe return.

"Ari. Earth to Ari." Lenny was staring at me. It kind of shocked me to have him call me Ari again, but I guessed he wanted to help me get back into character. "What's up? What's going on in that head of yours?" I glanced at Sasha and then said, “Just sending up a good word for the others to be safe and meet us at the airport.”

“Good idea, Ari. Good idea. Thinking of others always makes you think less of yourself.” He gave a pointed look at Sasha, and I had to suppress a laugh. Melanie/Marybeth lowered her head, and I immediately felt guilty for being happy about Lenny’s jibe at Sasha. We spent the rest of the ride in silence.

Chapter Twenty-Nine

We pulled right onto the tarmac after going through two separate security gates. Our "parents" were top officials in the Air Force and we were special.

Sasha was the first out of the car, and everyone followed but me. I grabbed Jeremy into a super tight hug and whispered in his ear, "Thank you. Thank you for being there for me." I kissed his cheek. He wiped a tear away from mine and smiled. I climbed out, shutting the door behind me. Everyone had spread out, like they really didn't know each other. I looked around, hoping to see our missing friends, but we were alone except for a few men dressed in army fatigues next to a large gray plane.

"Time to board," one of the army fatigue men said.

Sasha shot me a nasty look and headed up the stairs just as another large truck squealed to a halt next to our car. The side doors flew open and a woman agent stepped out, followed by none other than Kira, dressed up to look twice her age. I could only tell it was her by her mannerisms. I wondered what her name was now. Then another agent climbed out and helped the next person get out. Rick. Why was the agent helping him? Rick was limping, favoring his left leg.

I ran to him, barely feeling Lenny's finger brush my arm in a feeble attempt to stop me. When only a few feet from Rick, I remembered with vivid clarity how he'd recoiled from my touch only hours before. His eyes met mine and I kept on, not caring what Lenny thought, and grabbed him, helping him walk. I needed him to know I was there and cared and was willing to risk this for him. I wouldn't leave him hanging again.

"What happened, Rick?" I asked, pushing back the tears.

"I'm Reese, and I don't know you." He didn't recoil, but he didn't welcome me, either. He lifted his arm from my shoulders and my eyes immediately searched his. They were softer than in the country club and a grin slowly spread across his face. I exhaled loudly. I smiled as Lenny moved toward me, rolling his eyes.

"What happened?" I repeated, knowing my time with Rick, now Reese, was limited.

"I was shot."

"No!"

"Yes! Brad here," he motioned to his agent, "carved the bullet out and stitched me up. I'll be as good as new in a few days."

"Weeks," the agent said, nicely.

Watching Lenny move in for the kill, I quickly got up on my toes and whispered in Rick's ear, "I'm sorry. I'm so sorry." Those were the only words I had time for. Lenny took my arm and led me away.

After a long string of profanity, he said. "Ari, are you already blowing your cover?"

"No, I just—"

"No!" He spoke in a firm, commanding voice. "You do not know that guy. He is new to you. Do you understand? You are Ari and you darn well better not forget it."

"I won't. I'm sorry." My face burned.

"Don't be sorry. Just don't blow your cover. Letting your emotions give you away is dangerous—as you already should know. Now go get on that flight and sleep. And Ari, don't trust anyone. I mean anyone."

The last two sentences he said so quietly, I barely heard them. I looked him straight in the eye and nodded. Still, I looked back at Rick, or Reese, rather, and wished I could hold him and comfort him like he had me in DC's airport forever ago. I wanted him to know I was listening, I was there. I cared, and I was so horribly sorry. He had been so tender, so sweet. I wanted to return those kisses, those tender touches, but it would have to wait. The hundred things I wanted to say would have to wait until we reached our destination, wherever that was. I hugged Lenny, hard. I loved that man and hated parting from him.

I leaned on the window, both thrilled to be with Melanie and Reese again and horrified at the idea that something terrible had happened to Josh. Once again, I sat back on a plane, wondering what my future held, determined to make a new life for myself, a better life.

Acknowledgements

MANY THANKS

To my in-person critique group, Susan, Gary, Angela, Chris, Jenny and Gaynell, for plowing through my very rough drafts and finding the gems inside. You rock!

To my online critique group for locating those persistent problems. Kathleen, Karyn, Shelly and Nicole.

To my many beta readers who found the lingering rough spots in the story so I could smooth them out.

To my amazing second run betas, Liz , Jenny, Susan, and Charity for their final thoughts.

To Melody for her rush formatting fixes.

To my amazing editor, Charity West, for knowing how to make my characters and story the best they could be while making each line clean, crisp and beautifully edited.

And finally, to my family for picking up the slack and doing more than their share so that I could shine.

I love you all. A million thanks.

ABOUT THE AUTHOR

Cindy Hogan graduated in secondary education at BYU and enjoys spending time with unpredictable teenagers. More than anything, she loves the time she has with her own teenage daughters and wishes she could freeze them at this fun age. If she's not reading or writing, you'll find her snuggled up to the love of her life watching a great movie or planning their next party. To learn more about the author and sequels to this book, visit her at cindymhogan.blogspot.com.